SHANGHAI

Huangpu River

N
W   E
S

YANGPU
DISTRICT

— Financial District

artment

PUDONG
DISTRICT

Airport →

#2 SUBWAY LINE

0 Miles   1   2

0 Kilometers   2

THE
RISK
AGENT

Author's Note

Between 2003 and 2009, China investigated 240,000 cases of embezzlement, bribery, dereliction of duty and corruption. In 2009, 3,193 people were punished for criminal liability in offering bribes. From 2001 to 2009, state-owned land granted through bidding and auction increased from 7.3 percent to 85.3 percent.[1]

In 2009 the U.S. Justice Department's Public Integrity Section charged 36 people for corruption and related offenses.[2]

It is estimated that between 250 and 400 million U.S. dollars were paid out to international kidnappers in 2009–2010 at an average rate of 400 thousand dollars. There is no figure for the number of hostages recovered alive.[3]

1. White paper, *China's Efforts to Combat Corruption and Build a Clean Government.* Information Office of the State Council of the People's Republic of China, Beijing, December 29, 2010.
2. mainjustice.com.
3. Various sources.

THE
RISK
AGENT

RIDLEY PEARSON

G. P. PUTNAM'S SONS
New York

PUTNAM

G. P. PUTNAM'S SONS
Publishers Since 1838
Published by the Penguin Group
Penguin Group (USA) Inc., 375 Hudson Street, New York, New York 10014,
USA • Penguin Group (Canada), 90 Eglinton Avenue East, Suite 700,
Toronto, Ontario M4P 2Y3, Canada (a division of Pearson Penguin Canada
Inc.) • Penguin Books Ltd, 80 Strand, London WC2R 0RL, England • Penguin
Ireland, 25 St Stephen's Green, Dublin 2, Ireland (a division of Penguin
Books Ltd) • Penguin Group (Australia), 250 Camberwell Road, Camberwell,
Victoria 3124, Australia (a division of Pearson Australia Group Pty Ltd) •
Penguin Books India Pvt Ltd, 11 Community Centre, Panchsheel Park,
New Delhi–110 017, India • Penguin Group (NZ), 67 Apollo Drive,
Rosedale, North Shore 0632, New Zealand (a division of Pearson New
Zealand Ltd) • Penguin Books (South Africa) (Pty) Ltd, 24 Sturdee Avenue,
Rosebank, Johannesburg 2196, South Africa

Penguin Books Ltd, Registered Offices:
80 Strand, London WC2R 0RL, England

Library of Congress Cataloging-in-Publication Data
Pearson, Ridley.
    The risk agent / Ridley Pearson.
        p.   cm.
    ISBN 978-0-399-15883-4
1. Shanghai (China)—Fiction.   I. Title.
    PS3566.E234R57   2012   2012001184
    813'.54—dc23

Printed in the United States of America
1   3   5   7   9   10   8   6   4   2

BOOK DESIGN BY AMANDA DEWEY
ENDPAPER MAPS BY JEFFREY L. WARD

This is a work of fiction. Names, characters, places, and incidents either are the
product of the author's imagination or are used fictitiously, and any resemblance
to actual persons, living or dead, businesses, companies, events, or locales is entirely
coincidental.

While the author has made every effort to provide accurate telephone numbers
and Internet addresses at the time of publication, neither the publisher nor the
author assumes any responsibility for errors, or for changes that occur after
publication. Further, the publisher does not have any control over and does not
assume any responsibility for author or third-party websites or their content.

To the students of Fudan University,
who made my year in Shanghai possible

Acknowledgments

My family was given the chance to spend a year in Shanghai (2008–9) and live in a Chinese *lilong* among the Chinese people. We rode bicycles in the snarl of Shanghai traffic and survived a rainstorm that dumped three feet of water into the streets on the first day of school. This opportunity was, in part, arranged through Mary Gillespie and her connection to Dr. Joel Glassman and the University of Missouri, St. Louis. My expat friend, Patrick Cranley, provided many foot tours of Shanghai and helped me with the manuscript (any mistakes are all mine at this point!) and together with Tina, his wife and business partner, showed us not only a good time but things we could have never seen without their eyes. Spencer Doddington gave us some fine architectural tours as well.

Dr. Sun Jian of Fudan University employed, entertained, and informed me for the two semesters I taught creative writing in the College of International Language and Literature. My wife, Marcelle, and daughters, Paige and Storey, and I made many friends in that year, including Steve and Liz and Tucker, Michelle, Bruno, Shelley Lim and Eddie, Bianca Bao, Xue Ayi, Jojo, Shelley Tseng, Lawrence Lo—many of whom make (sometimes pseudonymous) cameo appearances in this novel. Thanks to everyone at the American Consulate, including the Consul General and the head of security, for opening their doors to me.

Fay, at Quintet, provided our visiting guests with cheer and me with a good deal of research.

On an editorial and helpful level, thanks to my editor at Putnam, Christine Pepe, along with Mih-Ho Cha in Publicity and Ivan Held at the helm; Amy Berkower and Dan Conaway at Writers House; Phoebe Jane McVey, Jenn Wood and Nancy Zastrow in my office; Ed Stackler and Genevieve Gagne-Hawes for their advice and guidance; Laurel and David Walters and Judi Smith for freelance copyediting; BigWideSky for social media; Robbie Freund at Creative Edge; Todd Ransom and his StoryMill software.

Writing a novel set in Shanghai has reminded me how much I value China's people, its culture, and the unforgettable year we spent there. It's my hope that a tiny bit of that appreciation rubs off on the reader along the way.

FRIDAY
September 17

Lu Hao, a slim, well-dressed man in his twenties, stood on the roof of a subcompact car the size of a toaster, peering over a ten-foot-high concrete-block wall and into the parking lot outside an aging tannery.

There was almost too much going on for the senses: the acrid smell of tar, the clamor of dump trucks and road rollers, the din of Chinese spoken in machine-gun staccato.

Lu Hao had been schooled from an early age about the role chance and fate played in one's life. If he hadn't driven past that particular fuel station at that exact time, he would have never recognized the foul Mongolian, a man he knew from his deliveries over in Shanghai; would have never followed him to the remote location. Would have never witnessed the meeting where three men went into a factory building, and only two came out. He had watched through a crack in the hanging doors as the smallest, youngest of the three argued with a portly Chinese man wearing

an expensive suit. With a nod from the businessman, the younger guy
was then bludgeoned by the Mongolian.

A moment later, back outside, the Mongolian shook the hand of the
businessman, who then walked over to a black Audi sedan and was driven
away. As the license plate flashed in the glare of a floodlight, Lu gasped:
the plate carried only the number 6, indicating a person of extreme
importance, a high-ranking official without question. Why here, of all
places?

Trembling now, Lu Hao clung to the wall. Refusing to move and risk
attracting attention. Terror rippled through him: opportunity, risk, re-
ward. Chance. Fate.

A part of him wished he could forget what he'd seen, wished he
could sneak off in the Chinese-made subcompact. He was about to do
just that when the Mongolian, inspecting the paving job, jerked his head
up quickly in the direction of the yard's far corner.

Lu Hao looked in the same direction.

Cao! he cursed silently. A glass lens winked from above the wall. It
belonged to a sizable video camera in the grip of a pair of white-skinned
hands. A *waiguoren*—a foreigner!

Lu Hao dropped from the wall like a stone, fumbled for his keys and
was into his car in a heartbeat. *No more!* He would determine how to
best use this information later, when he could be calm and reasonable.
He might appeal for help.

He might go to the temple and burn incense.

But for now, he'd get gone, return to Shanghai, and hope that he, too,
had not been seen.

THURSDAY
September 23

1

Lu Hao rode his lovingly restored CJ750 motorcycle, its sidecar seat covered by an oilcloth tarpaulin hiding a duffel bag that minutes earlier had contained cash. A good deal of cash. The kind of cash Lu Hao needed in order to repay his father for his own foolish mistake. But now the duffel was nearly empty—a few thousand *yuan* was all that remained. He returned his eyes to the street. To glance away from Shanghai traffic for more than a second could prove fatal.

13 . . . 12 . . . 11 . . .

The middle lens of a Shanghai traffic light was an LCD timer that counted down to the light change, giving motorists on both sides of the intersection time to at least consider the traffic laws. Not that anyone obeyed them. The traffic laws in Shanghai were offered more as suggestion than enforceable law.

Lu Hao revved the bike—a thing of beauty, a sound like that. He drew a few envious looks.

4 . . . 3 . . . 2 . . .

Hundreds of waiting vehicles crawled forward. A Darwinian exercise commenced in the wide bike lane to the right: motorcycles assumed the lead, followed by motor scooters, electric bikes and finally bicycles. Not a horn sounded. Not a curse was thrown. Everyone knew their place.

Lu Hao turned off Yan'an Road, a ten-lane arterial, and traffic immediately lessened. A few more turns, and he entered a time machine: Shanghai as it was a century before.

Laundry hung like colorful prayer flags from bamboo poles jutting from apartment windows. There were more pedestrians than vehicles on the street. He slowed, straddling the motorcycle's sonorous rumble. A delivery man had dumped a half-dozen fifteen-gallon water cooler bottles off his motor scooter, stopping traffic.

Lu Hao swung right again down a narrow street lined with stalls. Old, toothless men in white undershirts commandeered second-floor windows. The spirited laughter of a mahjong game echoed down the lane, mixing with an out of tune piano implausibly working through Gershwin.

He caught movement from his left: a man running toward him at top speed, head down. *An ambush*, forced upon him by the spilled water bottles. The lane was a choke point. He glanced to the sidecar and the hidden duffel.

His attacker led with his shoulder, connecting with Lu Hao and knocking him off the bike. Two more men appeared. They grabbed hold of him. He was dragged, facedown, barely conscious, and thrown into the back of a microvan, where yet another man slapped duct tape over his mouth and pulled a plastic tie around his wrists.

Then everyone started shouting at once.

Clete Danner wore the motorcycle helmet's mirrored visor down to hide his American face. He bent into the handlebars to disguise his size—there weren't many Chinese who were six-three and two-thirty. When the threat came from Lu Hao's left, Danner vaulted the bike and, in an infinitesimal misjudgment, caught the toe of his right shoe on the frame. He overcompensated, suddenly finding himself off-balance and thrown back on his heels only a few meters from the van.

A nunchaku came at him like an airplane propeller, its aluminum cylinder striking his raised right forearm. He felt a bone snap. He went light-headed and a deep purple overtook his vision.

He cocked his right leg and kicked. The nunchaku connected with his upper thigh, but the man holding it went airborne, slamming into the metal frame of the van and sliding down unconscious.

His assailant was hauled inside. There was much screaming in Mandarin.

The van's motor strained and coughed exhaust from the tailpipe. The van backed up, knocking Danner over. His helmeted head bounced off the asphalt. Everything went dark.

A second or two—*more?*—had passed, followed by pain. The broken arm. The bruised thigh. His concussed head.

He was dragged into the van, the smell of sweat, oil and blood overwhelming him. The van doors banged shut. A flurry of angry Mandarin as the van took off. His helmet was ripped off his head.

"Waiguoren!" he heard.

He knew he could not possibly be part of their plans. He'd had Lu Hao under surveillance for months. Where had these guys come from? His cover was now blown. The entire operation was blown.

The pain subsided, replaced by a deep and welcome silence.

FRIDAY
September 24

7 days until the ransom

2

11:00 A.M.
HONG KONG
SPECIAL ADMINISTRATIVE REGION, CHINA

The twenty-fourth-floor corner office overlooking the bustling Hong Kong harbor and, on the opposite shore, Kowloon, was spacious, its appointments comfortable. Three flat-panel screens surrounded a sitting area, one displaying a black-and-blue logo of mirror image Rs beneath which was written RUTHERFORD RISK, SECURITY MATTERS.

Brian Primer ran Rutherford Risk's Asian division. He wore a golf tan beneath a full head of hair, his face punctuated by gray, flinty eyes. Turning to his left, he addressed David Dulwich, one of his six key field operatives, picking up on Dulwich's reference to a take-away food container in a photograph.

It was but one of many photographs on the coffee table between them, along with a brown paper take-out food container with a wire handle.

"Jesus," said Allan Marquardt, the boyishly handsome forty-five-year-old CEO of construction industry giant The Berthold Group. Marquardt sported a tailored suit with a blue pocket square and matching tie. The corner of a China Air ticket envelope peeked out from his breast pocket. He was reacting not to the photo, but to the memory of opening the food container less than ten hours earlier and discovering its contents: a photograph of two men—a Chinese holding a newspaper and an American holding his broken arm—taken against the backdrop of a hung bedsheet; a carefully folded ransom note; two plastic bags, each containing a single Q-tip.

Dulwich said, "The one on the right. He's ours. Cletus Danner. He was keeping tabs on Mr. Lu. Must have walked into this. Both alive at the time of the photo. Confirmed POL."

"'Proof of life,' he means," Primer informed Marquardt. "You'll get up to speed on the acronyms quickly. Anything you don't understand, just ask."

"Like why somebody would do this?" Marquardt asked.

"It's a business. Don't personalize it. U.S. concerns paid out four hundred million dollars last year in ransom in Mexico alone."

"Come on."

At thirty-nine, Dulwich had a face lined with worry and consternation. A fleshy scar that looked like melted wax climbed out from beneath the T-shirt he wore under his open-necked Oxford button-down.

"The Q-tips are assumed to be DNA swabs," Dulwich said. "We're running them now. Another two days, minimum. But they'll come back Lu Hao and Cletus Danner. Used to be, you sent a severed finger for the sake of the print. We haven't seen swabs used before: our takers are young, educated and enterprising. Seems a stretch for a Triad—an organized gang—though not out of the question. Whatever the case, it's very clever and tells us these are not people to mess with. We want to get this handled and get both hostages home ASAP."

Brian Primer passed Dulwich the plastic evidence bag holding the ransom note.

"The brown paper's common enough in China," Dulwich explained, having already studied it. "Easily purchased. Simplified Chinese characters written in pencil—nothing terribly interesting about that. The lack of a political manifesto suggests it's all business. That's good for all of us."

"Our insurance will pay our half of the ransom," Marquardt said, "as I assume yours will as well."

Primer nodded.

Just like a CEO, thought Dulwich, *thinking about cash before lives.*

"They'll kill them once they're paid," said Dulwich.

"You can't know that," Marquardt said.

"Our man's dead for sure at that point," Dulwich said calmly, "if they don't do him before. Our one hope is that as an American he's worth more to them alive."

"Why kill him at all?" Marquardt asked.

"Because at some point he's too great a liability. A Chinese kidnapping a *waiguoren*. An American, at that? You don't want to get caught. Better to bury him."

"Jesus."

Mission accomplished. Dulwich had gotten the human cost to sink in. Marquardt had turned ghostly pale.

"The ransom demand names the first of the month, so we're already short on time," Dulwich continued.

"Our clients typically are given weeks or even months until the drop. This shortened schedule is disturbing," Primer said.

"The first is the start of the National Day holiday," Dulwich said, "which coincides with the Autumn Festival this year. It's an interesting choice." He set the ransom note on the coffee table.

"You make it all sound so . . . ordinary," Marquardt said.

"If only," Primer said. "The DNA samples. The hurried schedule. By no means 'ordinary.'"

Dulwich screwed up his courage and asked the question Primer wouldn't.

"What's more important to The Berthold Group, Mr. Marquardt? The recovery of Lu Hao's recordkeeping, or Lu himself?"

"That's a hell of a thing to ask," Marquardt said.

"That's not an answer," Dulwich said, to his boss's obvious discomfort.

"What Mr. Dulwich means is: it's important to clarify and prioritize your goals," Primer said.

"I won't lie to you," said Marquardt. "Lu Hao's records of the incentives could be extremely damaging to the company and to me personally."

"You're referring to the two Australians who just got twelve years in Chinese prison for similar 'incentivizing,'" Dulwich said.

"The case won our attention," Marquardt admitted.

It had stunned the entire expatriate community. Bribery, overpayment, "incentives," were part and parcel of Chinese deal-making. For nearly a decade the Chinese government had been working to ferret out corruption among its officials. But reaching into the private sector and imprisoning foreign businessmen had never seemed remotely possible.

"Remember, Allan," Primer said, "we're your representatives in this. We're not here to judge you. Only to get the job done. The job you want done. And that means prioritizing. If the documents are more important, then so be it. We lost one of our men in this. He's our priority, so don't think for a minute we're going to abandon extraction. But how we approach recovering Mr. Lu for The Berthold Group will be adjusted depending on your priorities and needs."

"We're talking about human lives," Marquardt said. "I never thought there'd be any question of priorities. We pay the ransom. We get them back."

"Like I said," Dulwich told him, "it isn't that simple. We wish. But if these people are professionals—and we have no reason to believe otherwise—then they'll have a half-dozen separate groups in play: the person overseeing the entire operation is called the intellectual; then there's the hostage-takers; the hostage-keepers; one or more surveillance teams; ransom retrieval, delivery and processing; hostage return."

"Jesus!"

"It's big business," Dulwich said. "Only the intellectual has the full picture, sees all the parts. And he's removed from the others. We never get to him. None of the groups knows of the others, which is what keeps it safe for the intellectual and makes it nearly impossible for us. So, yes, we work to help you stay calm and to negotiate the release of, or extract, the hostages. As you know, we have a rate of success in the mid-nineties. We know what we're doing. If this was Colombia, Bolivia or any of the 'stans,' it'd be simpler. But this is China. And our guy's an American, even if yours isn't. They kidnapped an American. That gives them two things: a rationale to make a high money demand; and a reason to kill the hostages."

Marquardt looked even paler, Dulwich noted. He seemed to miss the fact that four hundred thousand dollars was a paltry demand. That point had not escaped him and Primer. Ten million would have been a typical starting point. So why not?

"When a Chinese is kidnapped and safely returned, that's the end of it. An American? The kidnappers will be hunted down by police, caught and executed. Period. They know that. We know that. Whether they meant to take our man or not, it's too late now. That's why they've set a relatively short timetable for the ransom—to get this over quickly. Get out of Dodge. But make no mistake: once it's paid, they'll kill and bury at least our guy, maybe both hostages. It's the safest move."

"Mother of God," Marquardt whispered.

"But remember," Primer said, "they still want the ransom. To win it, they need to offer us at least one more proof-of-life. Maybe two. We have a week to locate and extract the hostages, maybe push back the demand, certainly negotiate the amount down because they'll expect that. It's doable. All right?"

Marquardt nodded.

"Back to the accounts," Dulwich said. "There's another aspect to it. Lu Hao's records of the bribes could be extremely important for us, as well as to you. You want to keep the incentives secret. Fine. We might be able to use the list of people receiving the bribes to find our men. Any one of the recipients of those incentives could be directly or indirectly responsible for the kidnappings. With so little to go on and so little time, that's one area we intend to explore."

"There are many other avenues we'll pursue," Primer hastened to add. "But Lu Hao's records are our best lead. Equally important, everything Rutherford Risk does in Shanghai has to be done virtually invisibly. So while we're searching for Mr. Lu's records, it can't look like we're involved. For one thing, it would put the hostages at added risk. The kidnappers' demand is for no police, and that includes us. For another, we can't legally operate in China. The Chinese authorities have not been notified of the kidnapping, as you know."

Marquardt nodded. "I understand and agree."

"What we need," said Primer, "is someone level-headed and preferably Chinese to act as our Berthold Group contact and lead this search." He paused.

"We have someone in mind," Dulwich said.

Marquardt looked anxiously between the two.

"This person," Primer said, "happens to be the one who recommended Mr. Lu Hao's services to your company in the first place. Which means she has a personal connection to Mr. Lu. You need to know that, to approve that, going in. It's not SOP for us, but China presents us with . . . unusual difficulties and restrictions."

"You're forbidden from doing business there. Yes. I'm well aware of that," Marquardt said.

"Of having any professional presence whatsoever within the PRC," Dulwich said. *People's Republic of China.*

"David will put together a freelance team—people not on any security company payrolls, including our own—to try to find Mr. Lu's accounts, and to perform the ransom drop and/or extraction. You need not know, and should not know, the details. It's imperative that you trust us and, more than anything, that you cooperate *fully* with us."

"Of course."

"With the help of your HR division, David is prepared to put our person in position today. You may communicate with her as you wish, but only where and when she determines it appropriate."

"I understand. Who is she?"

"Grace Chu. She's a Chinese national. Convenient for our purposes.

She took her undergraduate in Shanghai, a master's in economics at Berkeley and another in criminology at UC Irvine. She works here in Hong Kong as a forensic accountant. Technically, as far as the Chinese are concerned, she is a private contractor, not our employee, and untraceable to us. But she's one of the best forensic accountants we've worked with. You will meet her in a moment."

Primer gestured to Dulwich, who left the room. Little was done by telephone inside Rutherford Risk—interoffice communication was accomplished through runners.

"We have never officially signed an employment agreement with Ms. Chu," Primer continued, "nor has she ever been on our payroll. Ms. Chu can enter China as a recent hire of The Berthold Group with no one the wiser. She can lead the search for Mr. Lu's records, as well as aid your accounting department as necessary. She can also make adjustments to correct 'discrepancies' in your public accounts. She'll know what to do with Mr. Lu's books as well, when they're found."

"You sound so . . . confident," Marquardt said.

"David should have a second person on the ground in Shanghai by tomorrow. Ms. Chu will be in place by this evening. Noon tomorrow, at the latest."

"The sooner, the better," said Marquardt. "After all, we only have until—"

"The first of the month," came a woman's melodic voice.

Grace Chu entered the room with Dulwich, who closed the door. Her gray, tailored business suit complimented a figure that for most Westerners needed some help up top. Marquardt rose and the two shook hands. She took a chair immediately to Primer's left.

"Honestly," she said, "I would have thought the eighth. We Chinese believe in the power of numerology. Eight is good *yunqi*—good luck."

She had a wide face, peaceful and serene. Her shoulders were broad, the muscle tone in her arms taut and impressive. Her skin looked airbrushed. But it was her nearly unflinching eyes that unnerved Marquardt.

"You will forgive me, Mr. Marquardt," she said. "I have made a cursory examination of your company's general accounts for the past quarter. Lu

Hao's contract—the incentive money—is paid from your GA, your general accounts ledger. It averages one hundred seventy-two thousand U.S. dollars per month. I will need to see the rest of your accounts, the end-of-year, to know how to better conceal these expenditures, because right now you're open to questions. Questions your people may have difficulty answering. I have drafted some recommendations, at the request of Mr. Primer." She handed Marquardt a clear plastic file folder.

"Thank you, Grace," Primer said.

She took this as a dismissal and stood from her chair.

"Please . . ." Marquardt said, motioning for her to stay seated. "You knew Mr. Lu?"

"I *know* Mr. Lu," she corrected.

Grace checked with Primer, who nodded. She leaned forward.

"He is the younger brother of a close friend of mine. I helped in the selection process when you requested a person to pay out the incentives for you."

"Do you have any idea where we might find his recordkeeping? As I understand it, that's possibly key to his and Mr. Danner's survival," Marquardt said.

"Ideas? I follow money. Money that wants to be followed; money that doesn't want to be followed. I will start with the obvious, proceed to the likely and continue to the possible. It's a process of elimination."

Dulwich said, "You two will likely need to discuss this more thoroughly once you're back to Shanghai. We need to work out how to do that in a believable way. Grace? Ideas?"

"Correct me if I'm wrong, but a Chinese employee such as an accountant," Grace said, "would rarely if ever be in direct contact with the CEO. So we must find a believable way for us to come together without arousing suspicion. Pardon my impertinence, but do you take a mistress?"

"What?" Marquardt blushed.

"If your secretary or assistant is aware of such a companion, then it would make things easier for us. I could assume that role—platonic, of course."

"No. I'm married. Happily married." Marquardt rolled his wedding band. "As to our Chinese employees . . ."

"Below the level of vice president," Grace specified.

Marquardt stammered.

Dulwich said, "Face it: your Chinese employees are invisible, right? Grace's U.S. education helps us a little, but there's still no good excuse for the two of you being seen together. Unless you're jumping her, that is."

Nonplussed, Marquardt said, "It can't be this hard."

"More difficult than you can imagine," Dulwich said. "You are already likely being monitored by a variety of competing interests—the police, the kidnappers, your competitors, possibly even the press. There are eyes and ears within your company—we can count on that. This kidnapping is on the street."

"Good God, you can't be serious."

"Your every movement will be under constant surveillance for the next week. We have little doubt you were likely tracked to this building."

Marquardt looked clearly out of his depth as he glanced from face to face around him.

"Might I suggest," Grace said, awaiting a faint nod from Primer, "that I file a complaint with HR within hours of my taking my position? Nothing sexual, not harassment. But something of a financial origin. Breach of contract, perhaps? Dissatisfaction with whatever lodging has been arranged? Mr. Marquardt, anxious to keep me, could request an audience with me to settle the complaint. Following this initial meeting, he will then upgrade my housing, and we might have reason to follow up on occasion."

Primer checked with Dulwich, then Marquardt.

"I like a woman who can think on her feet," Marquardt said.

"Better on my feet than the alternative," Grace said.

For a moment it appeared Primer might reprimand her. Instead, he laughed.

"Grace did service with the PRC's army for two years. Was assigned to Intelligence for her final eleven months. She's trained in surveillance, hand-to-hand combat, small munitions and communications." He smiled at her. "In the workplace, you'll find her passive and demure. One-on-one, well, let's just say she's no shrinking violet."

"You're a welcome addition, Ms. Chu," Marquardt said.

"When next we meet," Grace said, "remember, it is for the first time. You may or may not be taken with my appearance, as you wish, but you will be in no mood to accommodate my accusations of breach of contract. It's best if I have to fight you at least somewhat for that victory."

"Understood."

She stood and they shook hands again. He held on to hers a little too long, but she made no attempt to separate. Instead, she hung her head slightly, suddenly a different woman. "Pleasure's mine."

She backed up a step, pivoted smartly—a hint of sandalwood and cinnamon—and waited for Dulwich to open the door for her before leaving.

3

Accompanied by a local guide and driver, a mosquito-bitten John Knox had been traveling for nine days through the jungles of Cambodia on a buying trip. He had packed the back of his Land Rover to the ceiling with tribal arts and crafts, primarily hand-carved stone boxes and some hammered bronze. He had spent the past two days in Virachey National Park, the most direct route to Ban Lung.

Knox checked his appearance in the Land Rover's rearview mirror before climbing out. He'd run out of soap three days earlier and his beard had grown in quickly, the dark stubble contrasting sharply with dark blue eyes that shone richly in the afternoon light. His hair was oily, his shirt sweat-stained and soiled. He ran his tongue over teeth, cleaning up some of the gorp that had sustained him over the last forty miles, and washed it down with a swig of warm water from a plastic bottle.

His driver spoke some Thai, the one language common between them. "Unpack car?"

"Find yourself a room," Knox said, handing him a considerable amount of cash, knowing the man would keep it and sleep in the car. "Unload everything into my hotel this evening. We'll ship it in the morning."

The village was a mix of aging concrete blocks and palm-frond-roofed huts on stilts. Knox refocused on the front porch of the small hotel and a line of chairs beneath water-stained sailcloth paddle fans turning lazily against the heat. He met eyes with the man occupying one of the chairs. A grin swept painfully across his chapped lips. He licked them.

David Dulwich lifted his sweating beer bottle and gestured to an unoccupied chair.

"Look what the cat dragged in," said Knox, mounting the steps.

"You look like shit." Dulwich, a former army sergeant, had as a civilian managed the trucking contractor that had hired a young John Knox as a driver to convoy supplies from Kuwait into Iraq. The runs paid eighty thousand dollars a month, hazard pay that Knox had banked to cover his brother's long-term medical expenses back home.

The two men shook hands and slapped each other on the back. Dulwich signaled a waiter for two beers.

Knox simply stared, waiting him out.

"What? I was in the neighborhood."

"Uh-huh. Sure you were, Sarge."

"I wanted first dibs on the teapots, or prayer wheels, or nose flutes, or whatever the hell it is you've stolen off the unsuspecting locals."

"Only Tommy knew I was coming to Ban Lung," Knox said. "You took unfair advantage."

Knox had lived his entire life protecting and defending Tommy, about whom many jokes had been cracked. "Not the sharpest knife in the drawer." "Room temperature IQ." Knox had heard them all; had broken a few faces over them.

His brother suffered from bouts of epilepsy—controllable by medication—migraines and moderate learning disabilities. With proper oversight, Tommy could function as Knox's business partner, but he also possessed a savant-like ability in math and computer sciences. He displayed remarkable processing speed and bandwidth, while often proving himself socially immature and inept despite his thirty-one years. Tommy was the one and only absolute in Knox's life. The two were joined at the hip, the wallet, by blood, and by telephone and Skype.

Dulwich shrugged. "Tommy sounded great. Told me he's running the online sales."

"Which he's good at, as it happens."

The beers arrived. Knox was tired and hungry. He cautioned himself about drinking the beer too quickly. He needed to remain on his toes given his present company. He pledged to sip, not gulp.

Now it was Dulwich's turn to stare. Cutting. Penetrating.

"I'm not interested," Knox said, the bottle finding its way to his lips a little too quickly. It didn't take a giant leap for Knox to understand what was at play. He'd turned down the offer of joining civilian convoys in Afghanistan more than once. He'd been lucky to get out of Kuwait intact—he realized that now. Others, including Dulwich, had injuries that had nearly taken their lives. Now he and Tommy had a business up and running. With their parents both gone—or as good as gone—it was important that Knox stay alive and the import/export business continue to succeed. But it was also paramount to keep Tommy supervised, something that required a constant stream of money. At present, things were decent. Not great, but decent. No doubt the man sitting across from him had run a credit check. Dulwich did due diligence. No doubt he knew of Knox's desire to set up a fund to cover his brother's medical costs. No doubt he knew he and Tommy were walking a knife's edge, that an infusion of capital was exactly what the doctor ordered. Shithead.

Dulwich showed him a photo and told him a long story about a kidnapping in China that had involved someone named Lu Hao. The story ended with, "I had a guy shadowing Lu. He got caught up in it. They took him hostage along with Lu. It's Danner." Dulwich unfolded a photocopy of the ransom demand and passed it across to Knox. "This was part of a lunchtime take-out order delivered by a Sherpa's guy to the construction company's CEO, a man named Marquardt. Runs a construction firm called Berthold."

Knox glanced at the note, then back at Dulwich. Sherpa was a popular food service delivery company that delivered from dozens of city restaurants.

"Not interested," he lied. In for a penny, in for a pound.

"DNA swab accompanied the ransom note, along with a photo. We need a comparison sample."

"Danny's DNA," Knox said.

"Yes."

"Try Peggy."

"We don't involve spouses until we have confirmation."

"Is that common? A DNA swab?"

"No. First time for us."

"Young."

"Yes," Dulwich said.

"You have a photo," Knox reminded.

"Ever heard of Photoshop? We need a DNA sample. This is Danner."

"Can't help you."

"It's Shanghai," said Dulwich by way of explanation. "You work out of Shanghai."

"Sometimes."

"Six trips there in the last fourteen months."

Knox eyed him for a moment. Dulwich's new gig gave him access to far too much information for Knox's comfort. "I like China."

Looking at Knox, people might have taken him for a nomad, but few would imagine the extent of it. When not living out of a tent in some trading outpost, he called hotels and rentals home. Tommy ran the online side of the company back in Detroit, unaware the guests at the house were paid home health aide supervisors, while Knox roamed all corners of Asia, from the Middle East to eastern China, parts of South America and Eastern Europe as their buyer.

With the death of their father three years earlier, Knox had assumed full responsibility for Tommy. He'd left the high-paying, high-risk work, forming the more manageable trading company and bringing Tommy in on it. So far, so good.

"What do you make of the ransom demand?" asked Dulwich.

Knox studied the photocopy.

"Left-handed. Under thirty."

"Because?" Dulwich leaned forward.

"Writing Mandarin in simplified characters began in the nineteen-twenties. It didn't take hold until the fifties and sixties. This character," Knox said, circling one with his finger, "was modified more recently than that, and began being taught in schools in the late eighties. That gives us the relative age of the writer. As to the calligraphy—the tails are from a lefty. I can't tell from the photocopy—was this written in ink or pencil?"

"Pencil."

"The continuity of the lines, the lead, suggests a mechanical pencil. Common enough there, but maybe he works as a draftsman or engineer, or he's a bean-counter. The date, the first of the month, is Western nota-tion, not Chinese. That's interesting. Why not Chinese notation?" Knox slid the document back across the table with his index finger. "But you know all this already."

"Some of it, not all. I need you, Knox. Danner needs you. We need a hair sample, an electric razor—anything with his DNA for verification."

When he was first getting to know Dulwich back in Kuwait, Knox had read him as a steak-and-potatoes guy. The kind of person who got his reading from the back of shampoo bottles while on the can. But over time, he'd revealed a deeper intelligence and far broader interests than Knox had initially suspected. Now Dulwich had the resources of a major security company—Rutherford Risk—at his disposal. Companies like Rutherford Risk operated like a private CIA or NSA. Knox knew better than to get sucked into one of their operations.

"I see two people."

"In his capacity as a consultant for The Berthold Group," Dulwich continued, "Lu's main job was incentivizing certain individuals and companies involved with the construction job."

"You mean he was paying out bribes."

"Yeah." Dulwich shrugged. "He's known to have kept a set of books of these confidential payments. One theory is that one of the individuals receiving the kickbacks realized how valuable a man like Lu Hao was to Berthold and snatched him up. Another—"

Knox cut in. "Listen, I feel horrible about Danny. I do. But I've got Tommy in a good place. I can't afford to step out on the business, even for a short time. I'm sorry."

"You're SERE trained. I paid for it in the first place."

Few civilians were allowed into the military's Survival Evasion Resistance Escape training program. A lifetime ago for Knox, Dulwich had arranged for him and six others to go through SERE training, as well as the FBI's Quantico course. It made Knox a uniquely qualified civilian.

"You know plenty of others with SERE training. Ex–Air Force. Hire one of them."

"They don't do regular business in Shanghai," Dulwich said. "This is Clete Danner we're talking about, man. Maybe I judged you wrong."

Knox sighed, looked away. "Maybe so."

"You ever seen the inside of a Chinese prison?" Dulwich asked.

"Give it a rest. That's beneath you."

"If PSB get Danner, that's where he's headed. For an eternity. You know the laws. He'll be considered a spy. We need to beat them to it, and we need to move quickly." The Public Security Bureau—the Shanghai police—was nothing to mess with.

"And if I slip up, it'll be the same thing for me. I've got Tommy. No go."

"We've put a woman into Shanghai. An accountant who knew the hostage personally. She'll pose as a new Berthold employee and go after the bookkeeping with you. She can interpret it once you've got it. The hope is, those docs will help lead us to the kidnappers in time. Meanwhile, we'll be preparing to negotiate the ransom and the drop."

"Dangerous to play both sides like that."

"Yeah, but what are you gonna do? If a Triad took Lu Hao and Danner, what do you think they'll do to the American once the ransom is paid?"

"Don't lay this on me."

"It's not about you. It's about Danner. He's facing prison or death. You know I wouldn't ask you otherwise."

Knox shook his head. "Bullshit you wouldn't."

"Look, you have a legitimate reason to be in Shanghai. Pretend like it's a business trip. Meet up with the woman we're putting in place. Support her. Help find Lu's accounts. We'll supply you with whatever we can on the sly. And if we find Danner, you bring him out."

"And what if I don't get out?" Knox snapped, realizing as he said it that his mouth had betrayed him. "What happens to Tommy then?"

"We'll pay your fee to him," Dulwich said, sensing his progress. "We'll double it. Deep pockets on this one."

"I don't like it," Knox said.

"Tommy says you're bored."

"Tommy talks too much. Enough with the cheap shots."

"You know what I think?" Dulwich said.

"I don't remember asking."

"You once said pulling me out of that truck changed everything. Remember that?"

"Yeah. That's about the same time I decided not to go to Afghanistan and to get out of the contracting business."

"Peggy is eight months pregnant with their second," Dulwich said of Danner's wife. "She went hysterical when I told her he'd gone missing. She's forbidden from flying. Stuck in Houston."

Shit. Knox should have known about the pregnancy. Should have stayed in better touch.

"I can't put any of our guys into China right now," Dulwich said. "We've had inquiries—formal inquiries asking if one of our employees is missing. They'll be watching Immigration. But since you do business there on a regular basis, you go in as you. Just another buying trip. You meet up with the woman and together you find the books, find Lu Hao and Danner."

"I don't babysit," Knox said.

"You won't have to. She's former Red Army, *very, very* smart, and a looker."

"Shit, shit and shit."

"We have to leave tonight," Dulwich said. Checking his wristwatch, he said, "Wheels up in ninety."

Knox drummed his fingers on the rattan tabletop. "And what if they do kill him?"

"Then we deliver the wrath of God upon them. You and me. Whatever it takes."

Slowly, Knox stood and stretched. "Do I have time for a shower?"

"God," Dulwich said with a smile, "I sure hope so."

4

The waiting area of the Guangdong Road PSB was a gray, tube-lit room with a poster warning of avian flu, hung thickly with cigarette smoke. The officer-of-the-month photo hadn't been changed since June. A black-light bug-killer sparked randomly above the door.

Into the station strode a wide-shouldered Chinese man, Shen Deshi. He had cropped hair, a crushed nose and thin lips. He wore a black leather jacket, a gold chain around his neck and tinted glasses that partially hid searching, distrustful eyes.

He proffered his credentials to the receptionist, who worked to disguise her alarm. The People's Armed Police was the most high-ranking, the most respected and feared in all of national law enforcement. An armored division of both military and police bureaus, PAP officers carried concealed weapons and were free to use them at their discretion. Officers of the elite corps were often referred to by the nickname "Iron Hand."

Shen Deshi leaned onto his forearms on the countertop. His fingers were blunt, wide, and bent awkwardly, each having been broken multiple times.

"May I help you?" she inquired in Shanghainese to test his origins.

"I am Shen Deshi," he said, also in Shanghainese. "I will speak with your most senior officer on duty. I do not wish to be kept waiting."

She glanced toward the phone, but then thought better of it. "One moment please."

Shen Deshi took a seat between two women waiting in chairs against the wall. He gave the younger of the two a slight smile as he appraised her from ankle to chest. Then he looked straight ahead, as if alone in the room.

The desk officer returned with a slight man in a captain's uniform. He was in his mid-fifties, with hollow cheeks and cheap eyeglasses.

"Officer Shen," the captain said, "this way, please."

In the captain's tiny office, Shen Deshi brushed off the chair, unnecessarily, before sitting.

"We are honored by your visit," the captain said.

The two men exchanged business cards, proffering them held at the edges by both hands and with a slight bow of the head.

"The honor is all mine, I assure you," Shen Deshi said flatly, wanting the formalities out of the way.

"May I offer you some tea?"

"I would be delighted but do not wish to trouble you or your staff."

"It is no trouble at all, I assure you." The captain worked the intercom and ordered some tea. There was no further conversation until the tea arrived some five minutes later.

Shen Deshi accepted the cup and immediately set it aside.

"Thank you," he said.

"It is my pleasure," the captain said behind clenched teeth.

"I need everything you have on the severed human hand that was fished from the Yangtze. You will withhold nothing." He sat back, eyed the steaming cup of tea one more time, but did not reach for it. "I'm waiting."

The captain worked the intercom to request the evidence and all documentation.

"An unusual case," the captain said.

Shen Deshi offered only a disapproving look.

"We followed procedure, of course."

"Then I am sure to write a glowing report."

The captain swallowed dryly.

"Such discoveries are to be reported quickly," said Shen Deshi.

"The skimmers—the trash skimmers at the mouth of the Yangtze—snag bodies on a regular basis," the captain reported. "Maritime accidents."

"Of course."

A Utopian society did not foster suicide.

"I did not know how to report this severed hand," the captain said carefully. "Its existence implied a violent crime or accident but one having taken place well upstream of Shanghai."

"A difficult situation," Shen Deshi said, though his face said otherwise.

"I checked the reports."

"Of course."

"Saw nothing that might connect."

"Of this, I am sure," Shen Deshi said. "The Ministry"—the Ministry of State Security, the Chinese intelligence agency—"is interested in this hand. A quick resolution to this investigation could benefit all concerned."

"It has my full attention."

"The movement of certain members of an American film crew are at the heart of it."

"Indeed?"

"Let us say they may have strayed from the parameters set forth in their visas. The Ministry is intent on knowing where they have been, and more importantly, *why*."

"To cancel the visas."

"Perhaps," Shen Deshi said. His eyes warned the captain not to get ahead of himself.

The minutes stretched out. The captain complimented his guest on the strength of his name: Shen, the family name, meant "don't yield." Deshi, "virtuous." The combination of the two was outstanding. It had obviously brought the man much *yunqi*—luck.

Shen Deshi avoided pointing out the captain's name was weak, his family name sounding too much like the number five, which was bad *yunqi*.

The captain reached for the phone as a knock sounded on his office door. A uniformed officer entered with a fogged plastic bag containing the human hand, along with an assortment of photographs and paperwork.

"We have kept it at a constant temperature of two degrees," the captain explained.

Shen Deshi looked it over through the plastic, handed it back to the messenger and told him to keep it frozen. He then studied the photographs, all properly scaled, and a sheet of partial fingerprints. He read the paperwork carefully.

"The ring?" he asked.

"Oklahoma State University," the captain replied.

Shen Deshi leveled a look on the man. "You see? Not so difficult. An American. It is a fortuitous start." Burned into his eyes was the fact that the captain had failed to notify anyone of the apparently dead foreigner.

The captain picked up on this and quickly defended his actions. "It was our intention to complete the preliminary investigation before troubling our superiors."

"Yes, of course."

"Third document. We have faxed a copy of the fingerprints to the Ministry and are awaiting a response."

"You covered yourself properly," Shen Deshi said, his voice grating, barely able to contain his temper. "The hand was cleaved cleanly at the wrist. There is either a one-handed American out there looking for his school ring, or a dead American butchered on Chinese soil, his body parts floating down the Yangtze—the rest of him long gone by now. The Americans must be notified."

"Right away."

"The evidence—*all of it*—must be shared with them."

"I will see to it. I will contact the embassy myself. Personally. I will do so immediately." The captain reached for the phone.

"Not the embassy," Shen Deshi said, finally venting. "Your idiocy is a pox on us all. You bring us great shame."

The captain recoiled. This was the gravest insult one could deliver. Great shame obliterated careers. Great shame could lead a man to the noose.

"Let me think a moment." Shen Deshi reached over and took up the teacup and sipped. "Nice tea," he said, suddenly pleasant. "I thank you for it."

"My pleasure." The captain was sweating.

"The better course is to deliver the evidence to the consulate here in Shanghai," Shen Deshi said. "You will notify the U.S. Consulate."

"Humbly begging your pardon, honorable Shen, but it would be faster to—"

"Faster, yes. But that's the point. It will take the consulate time to determine exactly what they have. I need that time to further my investigation and get ahead of them. I must be able to answer the obvious questions they will have. You will quietly make inquiries if any upstream districts are reporting any assaults, murders or disappearances involving foreigners."

"Right away."

"I will need duplicates of all of this."

"Immediately."

"We must not lose face with the Americans. Bad *yunqi* for us all."

"I will make the calls."

"Quietly."

"As a mouse. And I will deliver the information to a low-level bureaucrat I know at the consulate. And even then, not all the evidence. Not until they officially request it. That may factor in another day or two for you."

"This is very good thinking, captain. There's yet a chance that you can undo these mistakes that were no doubt made by your subordinates."

"You are gracious."

"Perhaps," said Shen Deshi, smiling grimly, "some discipline is in order to set the proper tone."

ey, there." Skype video challenged Knox, not for the technological issues but because his brother looked so normal. Boyishly handsome. A kind face. One would never suspect the problems that lurked behind the man's warm eyes.

"You haven't called me in a long time," Tommy said. The child-like singsong to his voice gave him away.

How long had it been? Knox wondered. Tommy was prone to exaggeration.

"I'm heading to China for a week or two."

"I thought you were in Cambodia?" Tommy didn't miss much—the doctors got that part wrong, time and time again.

"En route to Hong Kong. Then on to Shanghai."

"More pearls? I think our inventory is okay, Johnny."

"There's always something good in Shanghai." Like a paycheck that might begin to endow Tommy's future medical costs. Their partnership gave them a reason to work together. It was something Tommy not only could handle but was good at. It kept Knox traveling. It was never going to make them rich. "It could be good for us."

"I thought you were coming home?" Pouty.

Knox rarely went home. He made a million excuses to himself, all of them convincing, but the truth nibbled at the edges, stinging.

"I am, buddy. Just need to get this out of the way first."

"Business first," Tommy said, sounding like a mynah bird.

"You got it."

"I'll tell Eve."

Evelyn Ritter, their bookkeeper. Tommy had a crush the size of Texas.

"Good idea."

"What's wrong?" Tommy asked.

That was the thing about Tommy: what he lacked in academic intelligence he compensated with intuition. Maybe he'd learned to read Knox's expressions, though Knox was well practiced and tried not to send conflicting signals. Maybe he'd heard something in his voice. Or maybe it was far more subtle: Knox's timing; his choice of short sentences. Maybe his kid brother just got him like no one else.

"It's a side job, Tommy. Moonlighting." He wasn't going to lie. Talking down to Tommy resulted in regression, a lesson long since learned. "Something for Dave Dulwich."

"Mr. Dulwich?" Excitement. "The soldier you rescued?"

Dulwich had been a soldier once, but not when Knox had pulled him from that truck.

Knox said, "You know Mr. Dulwich."

"Can I speak to him?"

"I think you already did," Knox said, not meaning to.

Silence. He'd stung him with that. Tommy lived to please his older brother. Any sense he'd inflicted something on Knox would burrow down deep inside him and come out later as something far more vile.

"I wouldn't have gotten this offer," Knox said, "if it hadn't been for you."

"You think?"

"I know. Are you kidding? You're taking care of me. I thought it was supposed to be the other way around?"

Tommy's laughter coughed static across an otherwise surprisingly clear connection. Knox, at forty thousand feet in a private jet; Tommy on a smart phone in Detroit.

He leaned to get a good look out the window at the chunks of land and water so far below. From somewhere within came the urge to refuse Dulwich's offer. Or was it too late?

Knox laughed along with his brother as a cloud pulled the blinds and the space inside the plane grew mildly claustrophobic.

SATURDAY

September 25

6 days until the ransom

5

Knox arrived at Shanghai International's sprawling new terminal wearing a khaki-colored ScotteVest windbreaker with most of its fifteen concealed pockets occupied by his passport, cash, documents and electronic devices. He wore a pair of white earbuds, the wires from which disappeared into the jacket's collar and connected to an unseen white iPhone provided by Dulwich. The iPhone was apparently one of Rutherford Risk's newest toys. During calls, it switched cellular carriers every ten seconds, limiting any electronic eavesdropping to a few spoken words here and there.

Customs let out into an L-shaped gauntlet of web-strap retainers beyond which stood hundreds of Chinese holding signs or waving frantically. Loud and chaotic, just how Knox liked it.

He blended into the crowd heading for the Maglev train—a friction-less marvel, the envy of the engineering world. The thirty-kilometer train trip took only seven minutes, bypassing what would have been forty minutes of congested highway traffic. He determined he likely wasn't being followed, though video surveillance was another matter. China employed seven million closed-circuit surveillance cameras and the world's fastest computers for face recognition. Shanghai operated half a million of those cameras.

Knox boarded the Number 2 line and switched trains at People's Square, arriving at a busy corner on Huaihai Middle Road. The sidewalk was jammed, a light rain falling. The colorful umbrellas moved like a dragon dance beneath an awning of plane trees, a throwback to the French Concession's storied past when, in the mid-nineteenth century, an outlying part of the burgeoning city had been given to the French to keep the foul-smelling foreigners in their place.

A weary Knox reached the four-star Jin Jiang Hotel with wet hair and damp jeans. He paid a discounted price in cash, part of a long-standing deal with the manager. This was not the first time he'd created a double-blind to hide his place of residence; twice before, in the thick of difficult negotiations with black market traders, he'd feared for his safety and had created a false residence at the Jin Jiang which, like all hotels, registered their guests—foreign and domestic—with local police.

He entered his fifth-floor room—as a general precaution, he never stayed above the fifth floor of a hotel—and placed his bag on the desk, then tore back the bedding, ran the shower and dampened a bath towel to mimic a person's use of the room. He tore the housekeeper's V from the toilet paper roll, removed a bar of soap from its wrapping and passed it under the faucet. Poured some shampoo and conditioner from the complimentary bottles and flushed it down the toilet.

The mirror revealed a face now permanently tanned and ruddy from the elements, juxtaposed against unnerving royal-blue irises. It was his eyes that caught the attention of women and men alike, the eyes—more so than the asymmetrical eyebrows, or the scar by his left ear, or the cleft in his chin—that gave him an air of confident stillness some mistook for hardline arrogance. This stillness had the unnerving effect of concealing the machinations of his thought process. And while there was nothing in his affect that projected menace per se, neither was one ever in doubt about his capabilities. Instead, the doubt surrounding Knox had to do with what brutal efficiencies might, if pressed, emerge from beyond his mask of calm.

Back in the bedroom, he moved the television's remote to the bedside, and drew the blackout curtains. One last ruffling of the pillow and he admired his work as he awaited the knock on his door. He tipped the bellman for returning his passport and slipped it into one of the jacket's internal pockets.

He donned a tan Tigers baseball cap, checked the hallway through the door's peephole and left. If possible, he'd return to disturb the room for a second or third time, depending on his perception of risk.

Soon he was back on the street in the thick of pedestrians. It took him fifteen minutes to reach the alley entrance behind 808 Changle Road. He shook off the rain and entered the Quintet guesthouse and climbed a narrow staircase to the first landing. He pushed open the door with a light knock.

"John Knox!"

"*Ni hao ma?*" Knox said. *Hello. How are you?*

"*Hen hao,*" answered Fay, Quintet's owner and manager. She was in her late twenties, with a long, graceful neck and wide-set eyes. She wore a simple gray T-shirt and no jewelry. Knox stirred at the sight of her, pleasant memories rekindled.

"A blind for a week?" Knox said, speaking English now. "Officially, I'm registered at the Jin Jiang."

"What is it this time?" she asked.

"Jade," he lied, not feeling right about it.

She nodded. "You do get yourself in some binds."

She checked the computer. "I've got nothing tonight. After that, if you don't mind moving rooms a few times, I can take care of you." Her attention still on the screen, she pointed back at the couch. "You can sleep here, if you like."

"Yes. Perfect. Thank you, Fay."

"There's the toilet." She indicated a door. "No shower, I'm afraid, until we get you into a room."

"I'm grateful."

She spun in the chair. "It's good to see you."

"And you." He fished a stack of *yuan* from his coat—the largest Chinese bill was a hundred-RMB note, about fifteen U.S. dollars—and peeled back twice her rack rate. Fay accepted without counting and slipped it into the desk drawer.

"I would invite you to stay with me," she said, softly, "but I have a boyfriend."

"Good for you. Bad for me."

"My guy has converted a lane house into office space. Leases the ground floor to a coffee shop. Good salads, if you're interested. Cobb, isn't it?"

Fay didn't forget much. He made a mental note and nodded, smiling.

"I will tell my staff you are not here," she continued. "That they never saw you. But you will want to avoid our night watchman. I don't know him well enough yet. He just started. He smokes out in the front patio from midnight to dawn. You should be fine using your key on the back door."

"I don't have a key."

She tossed him a loaded key ring. "A man like you, you must be pretty used to back doors."

He switched to Mandarin and cursed.

She laughed and returned one worse. He prepared to continue the exchange of insults—good Chinese sport—but she was interrupted by a call.

When she turned around a moment later to speak, Knox was gone.

4:15 P.M.
PUDONG DISTRICT
SHANGHAI

The pressure of lost time beat down on Knox as steadily as the rain. The likelihood of Danner being found alive diminished with each passing hour. Some friendships carried debt—classmates, survivors of catastrophe among them. Danner was both: a fellow civilian classmate of Knox's during SERE training; his shotgun rider on the resupply convoys from Kuwait City into Iraq. They'd grown rich together, both avoiding serious injury and death, and had each other to thank for it.

But "Danny" was even more: Tommy's legal guardian should anything happen to Knox. A lifelong burden he'd readily accepted when asked. Now it was evidently Danny's life at risk and Knox knew that to turn his back was akin to Danny turning his back on his brother when pressed.

Knox rode a city bus across the Huangpu River into the Pudong district. Before attempting a search of Lu Hao's residence, where he hoped to locate Lu's bribery records, Knox first wanted to visit Danner's apartment. He knew the DNA was crucial. But he also knew Danner to be a thorough researcher. If he were minding Lu Hao for Rutherford and The Berthold Group, then he would have known all about Lu's "consulting" work. So there was at least a small chance he'd have made a copy of Lu's books, or created his own version, or perhaps even made notes about where Lu Hao kept his confidential documents. Likewise, if Danner had had any suspicions about Lu Hao's clientele, he might have noted it in advance of their abduction. Knox would gladly follow any leads that Danner had left behind.

Pudong had arisen from shipyards and rice paddies twenty years earlier and was now the Wall Street of Shanghai. Inventive office buildings and gorgeous apartment towers lined the wide streets. The security guards in Danner's river-view co-op were twenty-year-old boys in ill-fitting gray suits. Knox knew they wouldn't mess with a *waiguoren*—a foreigner. Their job was to put a face on the compound and to keep out potential thieves and robbers.

Knox introduced himself as a friend of Mr. Danner's and saw in their faces that they were aware of their resident's absence.

"He asked me to get a few of his things and send them to him," Knox said. Again, he monitored their response. What he detected surprised him. What were they expressing? It looked like fear—just below the surface. It took Knox a moment to make sense of it, but once he did his heart sank: someone had beaten him here. He had a fairly good idea who that might be.

"Entrance to Mr. Danner's apartment is not possible," said the most senior of the boys. "So very sorry. Must hear from Mr. Danner directly."

Knox switched to Shanghainese, a local dialect few Westerners could command. Politely, he berated the man for his insolence.

The guard flushed.

"You will join me," Knox said, still in Shanghainese. "Together we will take inventory. Anything I remove, I will sign for. No problem. Would you like to check with your manager?"

"I think this arrangement is good," the guard said, chastened and relieved.

"I am glad you thought of such a workable solution," Knox said. "I will make certain to let your manager know how promptly and efficiently you handled my request."

He withdrew two hundred *yuan* from the vest on their way to the elevator, making sure the guard saw him do so, balling the money in his left hand.

Knox kept the brim of the Tigers cap toward the floor for the sake of the hallway cameras.

Danner's contemporary Chinese luxury apartment was the perfect example of decorative contradiction: marble floors, faux-leather furniture, glass dining room table, all under the glow of low-voltage lighting—mixed together with red velvet curtains, polished brass "gold" plumbing fixtures and leaded crystal lighting sconces. Gaudy, pretentious and over-the-top.

Knox planted the man outside the door in the hallway, then, inside, conducted a thorough search of Danner's desk, closets, drawers and bathroom. He searched for hair samples to provide Dulwich his DNA sample. Maid service had scoured the place; he failed to find a brush or comb offering hairs. He located an electric toothbrush, but doubted its sample strength. He was about to give up when he spotted a clear plastic razor dispenser holding new and used razor blade cartridges. He studied the used blades more carefully—all were caked with thick black lines beneath the blades: whiskers. He pocketed the dispenser. He would overnight it.

He continued the search for evidence of a kidnapping. Danner was far too careful and clever to leave anything important where it might be easily discovered, so Knox also searched for hidden panels and loose floor tiles. He accessed and unscrewed four air vents, peering inside. The closet safe was locked, but if he was right about the man who'd preceded him, its contents were now gone.

Five minutes dragged into ten. Fifteen. Knox took it to the next level, patting down and searching his missing friend's clothing. An elliptical trainer faced a flat-panel TV, a neatly folded white towel draped over its handlebars. He checked in the slight inclined gap beneath it. Checked behind the flat panel. Checked the flat panel itself for a USB drive or memory card. Dug down into the soil of the potted plants. Searched the refrigerator and freezer. Pulled both away from the wall. Removed the stoppers from the sink and tub drains and looked for hidden wires or chains used to lower contents out of sight. Inspected the toilet tanks. Put his hand down the garbage disposal in the divided sink.

A framed bedside photograph of Peggy and a two-year-old boy won Knox's attention, stopping him. He studied it, then removed it from the frame, but found nothing. For show, he gathered a pair of pajamas and placed them in his backpack along with two paperback books. He would show these to the security man.

He took photos with his iPhone and disassembled the apartment's phone, looking for eavesdropping bugs. He collected a power supply from behind the desk, taking note of the absence of dust on the power strip where a grounded plug had been connected—Danner's laptop. Also plugged into the strip was a lonely charger cord, its power supply marked "Garmin." A GPS. He zipped it in his backpack as well.

He found the Garmin's owner's manual in a desk drawer, along with another for a Honda 220 motorcycle, and one for the elliptical trainer.

He called the security man inside and showed him the few items he was taking out of the apartment, but did not reveal the Garmin power cord. The man nodded, not asking for Knox to sign anything.

"The other man or men that came here," Knox said calmly. "Chinese or *waiguoren?*"

"I did not say other man come here."

"Same question."

The man didn't answer.

"It is up to you," Knox said. "The issue of the computer being removed will have to be addressed, of course."

"Waiguoren."

"Tall. Hair shaved close. U.S. Consulate credentials." It was the only person outside of a fellow Rutherford Risk employee whom Knox could imagine talking his way inside and leaving with something like Danner's laptop computer.

Still, the man said nothing.

"Did he sign for it? Is there an inventory of what else was taken?"

"No one here. No one take anything. No need to sign."

"I beg your indulgence," Knox said, keeping it polite, "but I believe you may be mistaken. You see, Mr. Danner asked me to collect his laptop computer for him. And yet it's not here. Do you see his laptop computer anywhere?"

The security man squirmed.

"If he did not sign for it, did you search the *waiguoren?*" He hardly paused. "No, I didn't think so."

The man's lips pursed and his eyes darted about.

"I mean no disrespect. But you see, my job is complicated by the laptop not being here."

"I said this man took nothing." The man's voice faltered.

"My mistake."

Now in the elevator, Knox handed over the two hundred *yuan*. Again, he spoke Shanghainese. "The *waiguoren* asked you to contact him if someone like me made inquiries."

The security man stood stoically.

"If you want to become further involved with the U.S. Consulate, then go ahead and make that call." He offered two more hundred-*yuan* bills. "As for me, I do not wish to be bothered, cousin. My government can make life hard for me. Same as your Party can make life hard for you. *Neh?*"

The bills disappeared.

Knox fixed his gaze onto the man for the rest of the slow elevator ride. The man stared straight ahead at their reflections in the polished metal. Then the doors opened and Knox left the building, his baseball cap brim held low against the eyes of the cameras as he entered the darkening dusk of Shanghai.

4:50 P.M.
CHANGNING DISTRICT
SHANGHAI

The door to Allan Marquardt's corner office was flanked by two ma-hogany desks occupied by efficient-looking twenty-something women with rigid spines and beautiful faces. Though most employees were gone for the weekend, not all had departed. Marquardt was not taking any days off, given the current crisis. Neither were his secretaries.

Grace checked in with an executive assistant named Selena Ming, who approved her visit and rose to open the office doors for her. Grace squared her shoulders and brushed her hands over her gray suit, double-checked that her collar was peaked properly, and fingered her modest string of pearls. Selena Ming trailed behind her with a steno pad in hand.

As the door closed behind them, Marquardt rose to greet her.

Grace wished he hadn't.

"Ms. Chu," he said. "It's nice to meet you! I've heard so much about you!"

Better, she thought.

The office was paneled in walnut, with hand-knotted rugs overlaying the parquet flooring. Crowded bookshelves gave it the feel of a private library. In the corner, a gleaming black lacquer tray held cut-glass bottles of colorful liquors and upside-down glasses. She felt as if she'd stepped back into Shanghai at the turn of the twentieth century.

"What a breathtaking view," she said, crossing the spacious room and shaking hands with him.

Marquardt indicated an armchair. It was covered in red raw silk embroidered with hummingbirds. The smell of sandalwood incense hung in the air. Selena Ming delivered green tea and there was five minutes of small talk.

Finally, Marquardt said, "You have filed a grievance with Human Resources."

His executive assistant took shorthand.

"A minor misunderstanding is all, I assume," Grace said.

"You are displeased with your accommodations?"

"I believe it is nothing. I was informed my residence would include lobby security and workout facilities."

"Yes?"

"In fact, my present accommodations do not."

"I am deeply sorry if there has been a misunderstanding," he said.

"No misunderstanding. It is in writing."

"We will resolve this immediately, Ms. Chu. With your permission, we will have your belongings transferred to a new residence"—he checked a note on his desk—"to the Kingland Riverside Luxury Residence serviced apartments in Pudong by the close of business today." He passed Grace a brochure. Selena Ming looked up from her steno pad, clearly intrigued, then lowered her head. "The keys will be on your desk before you leave for the day. I trust that will be satisfactory." His tone and demeanor were pitch-perfect.

"That would be lovely. Thank you."

"Now," he waved away Selena, "please allow me to show you the view."

Selena left, and Marquardt led Grace out onto a narrow balcony, closing the elegant French doors behind them.

She spoke softly. "I mentioned before that I need access to the end-of-year records—more than just the GA. I would appreciate the passwords required for access."

"You'll have them," he said.

Fifty floors below, the traffic crawled ant-like through intersections. The smog-encrusted skyline was broken by towering cranes, the air alive with the percussive sounds of construction and the steady drone of traffic.

He pointed. "To the right of the Jin Mao Tower, just past the World Financial Center. You see the building with the yellow crane on the very top?"

"Yes."

"That's ours—the Xuan Tower."

"Yes," she said.

Marquardt nodded proudly. "It's a beautiful building. And so far we've been tolerated by your government, though clearly our participation is unwelcome." He turned and looked at her. "We are Beijing's token foreign construction project, authorized only to show the rest of the world they don't favor their own. We've pissed off a lot of Chinese, Grace. I know we have. But just how far, I had no idea."

"It appears nearly finished," she said, noting the building's upper twenty stories were wrapped in a green fabric, strung over elaborate scaffolding, noting that he thought the kidnapping directly related to the construction of the tower.

"There's much yet to be done. Is it coincidence that as we near completion, Lu Hao is abducted and therefore the incentives stop, and we encounter problems? We're only a couple days into this and we're already experiencing costly slowdowns—materials, labor. Our vendors and suppliers aren't getting their payments." Marquardt paused to make full eye contact with Grace. "Our problem is, only Mr. Lu knew their identities. This is critical work you're doing, Ms. Chu."

"It benefits your Chinese competitors."

"If you go down that road, start with Yang Cheng. Yang's a devilish prick who has taken every opportunity for nearly a decade to remind me foreign builders don't belong here. He's never accepted our being awarded the Xuan."

"I will start with Lu Hao's apartment," Grace said. "The sooner I have the end-of-year accounts, the better. I can help keep auditors from realizing the exact nature of Lu Hao's work for you. Important should we fail in his recovery."

"Yes, of course," he said, though didn't sound at all certain.

Her BlackBerry vibrated.

"Take it, if you want," he said.

"I'm fine," she said, noting that the call was from her mother. She flushed slightly as she returned the device to its holster.

"Anything else?" he asked.

"Was there anyone within your company who served as a primary contact with Lu Hao?"

"Preston Song."

"I would like a meeting with Mr. Song. Not here. Not in the company building. Perhaps something social. But soon."

"I'll arrange it."

Before he opened the doors to the office, Marquardt said, "Please be careful, Ms. Chu. Yes?"

Grace nodded.

Back inside the office, Marquardt raised his voice slightly to make sure his assistants heard. "I trust you will find your new residence acceptable. If you have any more problems, feel free to bypass HR and bring them directly to me." He paused. "We are pleased to have you working with us, Ms. Chu."

Grace rode one of the elevators to the lobby and stepped outside for privacy. She returned the call to her mother, speaking Mandarin.

"Mother?"

"You come to Shanghai and do not tell me? What kind of daughter are you?"

Her mother continued berating her, but Grace was stuck on the fact that her mother knew she was in Shanghai.

"How can you possibly—? I only arrived *this morning.*"

"Third cousin by marriage, Teardrop Chang, was on a flight from Hong Kong. You do not call your own mother? Your mother who carried you for nine months? Your mother who suffered your birth?"

"Of course I was going to call," she lied.

"If you have returned for the sake of little brother Lu, please do not tell your father. He will most certainly have heart failure."

"Why would I return for the sake of Lu Hao?" Grace tried to sound naïve, her heart pounding now. Her mother could not possibly know of the voice mail she'd received from Lu Hao ahead of his kidnapping—a voice mail she'd ignored.

"Little brother Lu has not called his mother. Does not answer his mobile phone. Has not been seen. Do you know nothing, my daughter the detective?"

"Listen, Mother," she hissed into the phone, covering the mouthpiece with her free hand, "I am *not* a detective. I am an accountant. A contract accountant. And please, *no names* over the phone." Then more conversationally, "You must not speak of that which you do not witness yourself. Such mistruths are dangerous. *Do you hear me, Mother? Dangerous.* Think carefully of the well-being of your family." Appealing to the woman's sense of family was often the only way to get through to her—not a card Grace could play very often.

"If you can, you must help . . . our friend's son," her mother said. "He must have his medicine, the poor boy. His mother is vexed, although he looked fine to me at the party."

Grace had been told of Lu Hao's epilepsy, years before, by his older brother. But she'd forgotten until now, had not considered he would be on daily medication.

"What party, Mother?"

"His mother, Lu Li's celebration. Four years of the rabbit!"

"Lu Hao was at the party?"

"Of course. As was I."

"What day was that?"

"Sixteenth of September."

"You are certain?" Lu Hao had left the voice mail for her on Friday the seventeenth.

"Have I not known this woman my entire life? I'm as certain as I am of the shame you bring upon your father by not accepting the betrothal he has arranged for you." She never failed to rub salt into that wound. "For Lu Li's birthday, the families gathered."

"Lu Hao was there on the island that Thursday?"

"Are you listening? Do you doubt your own mother? Four day celebration!"

"I will call you later," she said and hung up. *Friday the seventeenth.* Guilt over never having returned his call wormed inside her.

Lu Hao's medical condition had not come up when she'd recommended him for the contract work for The Berthold Group. Along with the surprise that came with her mother's knowledge of her arrival was the news about Lu's condition, and the inescapable—and perhaps intentional—reminder of Lu Hao's older brother, Lu Jian, with whom she'd had a romance that had begun in high school and had ended nearly six years later with the announcement of her arranged marriage that had blindsided her. She'd fled Shanghai, joined the army, and had broken off communication with her family for the next two years. She had yet to speak to her father, and only heard from her mother periodically, when her father was not in the house.

Lu Hao was the black sheep of the family. A film student and ice-to-Eskimos salesman who had emotionally corrupted and manipulated his father to invest in his film project, Lu Hao had eventually bled the family savings dry and driven them toward bankruptcy and loss of face—the greatest disgrace of all.

Grace had known of the situation—through her mother—and had tried to use Los Angeles friends to circulate Lu Hao's script in Hollywood, but to no avail. Her second, more successful effort had been to win Lu Hao the contract with The Berthold Group. All this had less to do with

Lu Hao than it did her continuing feelings for his brother. She'd hoped that by trying so hard, she might renew contact with him. A hope that had yet to bear fruit.

Bringing Lu Jian's brother home could only help her cause.

The first step was to search Lu Hao's apartment for his accounts documents—and now, for his medicine as well.

Now. Tonight. With or without the man Dulwich said would be joining her. Grace was not waiting for anyone.

5:20 P.M.
CHANGNING DISTRICT
SHANGHAI

The man following her was a pro. Grace had changed into tight jeans and spike heels in a lobby restroom and then left by a side door eschewing the main entrance to the MW Building, home of The Berthold Group. She might have missed him completely had she not picked up a second whiff of him. But there it was, the same distinctive scent—a masculine musk, part pine, part perspiration—she'd first noticed while at an ATM, the stop used to scan the sidewalk.

She now knew he was back there—he'd passed close by her for a second time. The act alone showed nerve and confidence. While she reeled over how she might have missed sight of him in the first place, she contemplated her next move. She did not want to reveal her training, only to appear as an average citizen. At the same time, she would have to lose him once and for all.

Along with a column of hundreds of passengers crammed elbow to elbow, she took the stairs down to the platform. Glass partitions served as barriers to prevent the crowds from pushing someone onto the tracks. The hordes jockeyed for position, a regular part of any day, Grace along with them.

Flat-panel television monitors suspended from the ceiling counted down the timing of the train arrivals to the platform. *58 . . . 57. . .* Her skin prickled at the sight of a tan baseball cap she remembered from a window reflection back near the MW Building.

She shivered. Had he made her earlier, or only picked up on her at the ATM? Was he that good? Or was she that rusty?

She spotted the cap again, though she couldn't make out the face beneath it. Her nerves on edge, she moved down the line of the groups waiting to board.

26 . . . 25 . . .

Standing among a group of women, she withdrew a black scarf from her bag and pulled it over her hair. Then she donned a surgical mask of the kind worn by many city-dwellers to protect against the Shanghai smog.

10 . . . 9 . . .

The crowd surged toward the doors. A squeal of brakes cried from down the dark shaft.

Grace slipped out of the crowd and pressed her back against the escalator's retaining wall.

The ball cap moved with the crowds. It jostled for position. As the train arrived, it paused. Turned toward her.

Could he have possibly spotted her transition into the disguise? Impatient passengers shoved past the hat. It appeared the man in the cap wasn't going to board.

She turned and took the long way around the escalator, intent on leaving the station on foot.

A quick glance back: the tan cap was moving onto the train.

But the body language was wrong—a Chinese, and in that instant she realized the hat had been given away by the first man wearing it.

He was *very, very* good.

She caught him, hatless, in profile at the base of the escalators. He fit the description she'd been given by David Dulwich. Relief flooded through her.

"Losing the ball cap was a nice touch," she said from behind.

The man spun around. He studied her and smiled a kind smile. He was tall. A well-lived-in face, tanned and lined, under a sprinkling of gray in his short, dark hair.

"Nice," he said, glancing once more at the train and the doors about to shut. "Very nice."

"Grace Chu," she said through the mask. They shook hands.

"John Knox. The scarf and mask . . . I didn't see that one coming."

"Next time," she said, "you should pay more attention."

5:25 P.M.
PUDONG DISTRICT
SHANGHAI

Three men in coveralls carrying toolboxes approached the receptionist desk in the spacious lobby of building 4 in the Kingland Riverside Luxury Residence. The lobby receptionist was a round-faced girl of twenty wearing a crisp navy blue suit and a plastic tag that bore the name SHIRLEY, a word she could not pronounce.

The first of the men spoke Shanghainese. "Chu Youya. Home theater installation."

The receptionist double-checked her logs. "So sorry. I show no such appointment for Ms. Chu."

"Then you will please tell Chu Youya why we left, little flower, when she asks tonight about home theater installation. Good luck with finding a new job." He signaled the other two. "That is it." He circled his index finger. The three turned for the street.

"Wait!" the receptionist called. "I will make an exception."

With the lead man's back to her, the young receptionist missed the wry smile that crept across his lips before he turned to offer a shrug of indifference. *Yes or no?* he seemed to be asking.

She picked up the phone and he feared the involvement of a higher-up. Always a higher-up, and after that, another.

"You make this a committee, I am leaving," he stated, calling across the lobby. "I have not got all day. Your decision, little flower."

Reluctantly, she hung up the phone.

Five minutes later, the lead man dead-bolted the door to Grace's apartment. It did not escape them that luxury apartments such as this were often bugged by the government. That they were bugging an already bugged apartment was the source of great amusement.

They went about their business expertly. One handled the video while the other installed the audio. The team leader chose the placements. Five microphones, three prying eyes. A pressure sensor beneath the carpet at the front door capable of turning the devices on and off in order to conserve battery life.

The lead man used his mobile phone to log in to a secure website. Moments later, he was looking at a miniaturized color image of himself staring at the phone.

On the way out through the lobby, his men avoided looking at the receptionist, as ordered. The fewer recognizable faces, the better.

The leader raised his arm. "All is well, little flower. Hopefully we not see you again."

"Your card!" she called out, having overlooked this requirement earlier. She needed a record of exactly who had visited.

The lead man hesitated, then returned to the desk and handed her a business card. He could sense her palpable relief as she read the card from a Best Buy in the Changning District: a card he'd received from a show floor salesman on an earlier visit.

On his way out to the parked van, he lit a cigarette and dialed from his mobile phone.

"It's done," he said.

"Record everything," a man's voice said.

On the other end of the call, Feng Qi lowered his voice as he stood at the entrance to Xiangyang Park. Wiry, well-dressed and carefully manicured, he had not yet seen the Chu woman leave the MW Building. As the chief of security for Yang Construction, he was the man responsible for tracking The Berthold Group's new arrival in the finance department, the division in which the recently departed Lu Hao had worked. Feng Qi was deeply concerned by the woman's long absence and could only hope she was working late on her first night on the job. He continued into the phone: "I want full transcripts and video delivered by e-mail each night before midnight."

"You will have it. Transcripts cost extra."

"That is to be negotiated," Feng said. He got no argument and ended the call. In Shanghai, everything was negotiable.

6:30 P.M.
ZHABEI DISTRICT
SHANGHAI

As Knox and Grace rode the Metro toward Lu Hao's apartment building, Knox reviewed for her his search of Danner's apartment. Grace told him of Lu Hao's apparent need for medication, which Knox took as progress. The kidnappers might be forced to return for the medication, providing them an opportunity to identify one or more.

Together, they entered a corner tea shop with a view of Lu Hao's apartment building and Knox bought Grace a green tea.

"The intel on the medication," he said. "Is it from a trustworthy source?"

She blushed.

"What is it?" he asked.

"Lu Hao," she answered, "is the second son in a family close to my own. I recommended him for the consulting job at Berthold. This information about his medication . . . it comes from my mother. Unfortunately, I do believe it is reliable. Your mother is alive?"

"Dead."

"I am sorry."

"Sarge hosed us," Knox said, irritated.

"Excuse me?"

"Mr. Dulwich. This op is personal for me, too. Clete Danner, the other hostage, is a close friend of mine. He's my younger brother's godfather—his caretaker in the event anything should happen to me." The news

clearly surprised her. "Our personal relationships with the hostages ensure that we will make our best effort at recovery, and—"

"If we are caught by police there is an explanation for our involvement. Yes. Convenient for Rutherford Risk."

"Very."

"I assure you, Mr. Knox, I will not allow this to interfere with the ex-
ecution of my duties."

She sounded like she was reading it from a manual.

"I'm not worried about you," Knox said. "The point is, if the stuff hits
the fan, Rutherford Risk may not exactly have our backs."

"I cannot believe that," she said.

"Good. Let's hope I'm wrong."

She hesitated. "There is one thing more." The skin around her eyes
tightened. "I received a message from Lu Hao on the seventeenth of
September. A voice mail, to be precise."

By all means, let's be precise, he nearly said. *Who was this robot?*

"He sounded panicked. He said he had seen something. That he was
not sure where to turn." Now, she pleaded with Knox. "The thing is, Lu
Hao has an active imagination, and is always looking for others to take
care of problems he started. I was not going to get any more involved than
I already was. So typical Lu Hao. High drama. I was exceptionally busy at
the time, a job for Rutherford Risk. I never returned the call."

He said, "Don't beat yourself up over it," though he could see she was.

Knox changed the subject, detailing his search of Danner's apartment
with mention of the missing laptop and GPS.

"You think the police were there first?" she asked.

"A *waiguoren*, according to the security guy. I'm thinking it's a guy
I know at the U.S. Consulate. Makes sense for him to chase something
like this. I can't ask him outright, but I can nibble around the edges."

"Nipple?"

"Nibble. Small bites."

"Ah . . ." No blush from her, no embarrassment, he noted. "And us,
Mr. Knox? Our cover. Professional, or something more intimate?"

"Meet your new client," he said. "I operate an import/export com-

pany. For real. You just became my Chinese tax advisor and accountant."
He held out his hand and she stared at it. He withdrew his hand.

"Import/export always struck me as a rung above rug merchant."

"Accountants are the most boring people I know," Knox countered.

"Which is why I joined the army," she replied.

"Which explains why I didn't," Knox said. "I just supplied them with
bottled water and hand lotion."

"A mercenary, I believe you call it."

"Not exactly. More of an opportunist."

She had perfected the air of superiority. "Step one to finding the
hostages is Lu Hao's records. His accounting of the incentives," she said.

Knox snickered at the use of the euphemism.

"The records may lead us to someone motivated to abduct him.
Agreed?"

"I realize that's Rutherford Risk's plan, but Danny—Mr. Danner—
takes no prisoners. That is, if there was any lead up to this, any planning,
any indication it was coming, he'll have left crumbs for us to follow. I
think Danny's laptop is our most valuable player."

"We must work together, Mr. Knox."

"Agreed."

"So, Lu's accounts are first. I have my instructions."

"And I have this timer running down in my head. All things being
equal, I'd like to find Danny alive."

"We must not ignore The Berthold Group's Chinese competitors.
There is bad blood. These companies would gain a great deal from either
stopping the incentives or intercepting the list of recipients. A great deal,
indeed. Reason enough to kidnap and torture. Mr. Marquardt mentioned
Yang Construction. Yang and The Berthold Group have a colorful past.
Much competition. I am unclear how to approach this. But perhaps something will present itself."

"Yeah. Well . . . I'm still taking Danny and his research." He paused.
"You were given an iPhone?"

"Yes. Secure communications."

"We can text."

"Most certainly. As well as voice."

Despite her two years in California, there were times she still sounded like a language lesson CD.

"The next time we meet, I'll bring my financials," he said. "As cover."

"This is acceptable," she said in Shanghainese.

"The first forty-eight hours are critical in a kidnapping. No need to tell you that."

"No."

He glanced at his TAG Heuer knock-off out of habit. "We're well past that already. Sarge . . . Dulwich to you . . . is convinced Danny's presence is a game changer."

"Yes."

"That they'll kill him, maybe both of them, because he's American."

"Not if we kill them first," she said.

He hesitated. It didn't sound right coming from her mouth.

"Agreed," he said.

"And as to logistics. How we move, when we move. I will handle."

He opened his mouth to challenge that when she said:

"This is my city, Mr. Knox. Do not forget it."

6

Allan Marquardt waited behind his desk for the People's Armed Police officer to say something. Instead, the man seemed to be trying to make a point by looking out at the Xuan Tower as the work there continued through the night, illuminated by massive floodlights. The scaffolding crawled with ants—though Marquardt knew it was far fewer ants than the day before, a troubling development.

This meeting had been arranged abruptly, interrupting Marquardt's Saturday evening at the Shanghai Grand Theater. No great loss. He still had calls to place to headquarters in Boston and an engineering firm in San Francisco. It promised to be a long night.

But one did not turn down a meeting requested by the People's Armed Police. He thought of them as the Gestapo of China. Marquardt was well familiar with the term "Iron Hand," and now, looking at this man, understood it more fully. Inspector Shen Deshi was bigger than most Chinese by half, his face unreadable, eyes distant, like a man incapable of feeling. Marquardt had no intention of putting The Berthold Group on his bad side; he had trouble enough.

Having been coached by Brian Primer over the phone on his way here, Marquardt braced himself for mention of the kidnapping, to show no reaction, to deny it, reminded the police wanted such a situation no more than The Berthold Group. If not provoked, the officer would more than likely skirt the issue, giving Marquardt openings but not pressing him to take them. Failure to address the crime would be held against him at a later date, but appreciated in the near term. The complexities of the interwoven social and professional etiquette involving the Chinese required him to rethink his replies. The vaguer, the better.

"Any problems lately?" asked the inspector.

There it was, teed up. Marquardt needed to show respect while demonstrating his understanding of proper etiquette. Speaking adequate, though American-accented, Mandarin, he said, *"Shi shang wu nan shi, zhi pa you xin ren."* A Chinese proverb that literally translated: "You must persevere to accomplish seemingly impossible tasks."

"Yi ke lao shu shi huai le yi guo zhou," Shen Deshi tested him.

"Again, please? Slowly." .

The inspector repeated his proverb. Marquardt managed to translate it, though searched for the true meaning. The Chinese language had many nuances.

The man spoke passable English. "One mouse dropping ruins the whole pot of rice porridge."

"Thankfully, no mice around here," Marquardt said.

"Mice are everywhere."

"We guard against them."

"Have you? I am aware that there is some kind of documentary being filmed about your construction project."

Marquardt felt his tension release by a degree. Had he assumed incorrectly the inspector knew about the kidnapping?

"Ah, yes. It's a piece for our National Public Television in the States."

"You must enjoy dogs biting at your feet."

"We can tolerate it. We're used to it, actually. A free press is something you learn to tolerate."

"In China, we have no tolerance for unauthorized investigation."

Marquardt said nothing. He found it an interesting choice of words.

"Any problem with the film crew?"

"To be honest, I have little to nothing to do with them. You would need to speak with our Director of Communication."

"I am speaking to you."

Prick. "My dealings with the film crew have been positive. Nice enough people. We screened the first episode, but I haven't seen anything since. Why do you ask?"

"Visas for foreign press are quite specific," the inspector said. "This crew has approval to make film of Xuan Tower as well as your offices." He hit the arms of the armchair. *"Nowhere but this."*

"If they've overstepped their bounds, I wouldn't know. If you want to deport them, be my guest." Marquardt tried to calculate where all this was leading. It was a Saturday night. An inspector with the People's Armed Police was in his office. All this because of a visa violation? It didn't add up. "We are only the subject of the film. This crew does not work for us. Has no affiliation with us. Is there something I should know?"

"I believe you must be aware two of the cameramen have connections with World Life."

"The environmental group? Certainly not."

"Extremists. Militants," Shen Deshi said. "If they do not work for you, then I trust that I can expect your cooperation in this matter."

"I—ah . . . first, Detective—"

"Inspector."

"It must be understood that neither I nor anyone in this company has any knowledge of, nor control over, the visa status or operations of this *freelance* film crew." Marquardt was tempted to call in their chief counsel.

"I must account for each member of the film crew," Shen Deshi said.

"With all respect, sir, as I was saying—"

"And it must be now. Tonight."

Marquardt felt his temper flare. "Listen here. Tonight is"—*out of the question*, he thought—"unlikely," he said. "Our Director of Communication will be in by ten o'clock Monday morning."

"This is unacceptable," the inspector said.

"I repeat: The Berthold Group has no professional affiliation or business relationship with the filmmakers beyond an agreement to grant them access to our offices and construction site."

"You will please make contact with your communication direction tonight," Shen Deshi said, misspeaking. Marquardt wasn't about to correct him. "I wish to speak with the entire crew at once. Please," he added as an afterthought.

Prick on a stick! Barely able to control himself, Marquardt eked out, "Monday morning at ten o'clock."

Shen Deshi drew himself out of the chair heavily. He reached into his pocket, withdrew a leather wallet, and carefully passed his business card to Marquardt, both hands extended. Marquardt returned his card in similar fashion.

"If you are able to help me in this matter," Inspector Shen Deshi said gravely, "your present situation will continue to be overlooked. At least for the time being."

Marquardt swallowed dryly. *Your present situation.* The kidnapping.

"We believe one of the cameramen is unaccounted for," Shen Deshi said.

A member of the American press had gone missing? Was this man hinting at his knowledge of the kidnapping, or could there have been another—a second—abduction? A journalist?

Given what he now knew, Marquardt realized the man was on orders from the highest level of his government. The Chinese would want to get in front of the event before they lost face in the international community. Their unforgiving stance on foreign journalists was well documented. Not a pretty track record.

Christ, there must be heads rolling. Marquardt's next thought was whether he could leverage this to his advantage.

His hand felt small in the other man's as they said their goodbyes. But it was the determined, hardened look in his visitor's eyes that stayed with Marquardt.

This man will stop at nothing.

SUNDAY

September 26

5 days until the ransom

7

"The realtor will meet us in thirty minutes," Grace said, returning her iPhone to her purse.

"I love Shanghai," Knox said. "You make a call, on Sunday afternoon, no less, and you get a showing two hours later. Entrepreneurship at its best. In the U.S., we've become too complacent, too expectant of the good life. Here, everyone still earns it." His one accomplishment of the day had been walking the crime scene: the backstreet warren from where Danner and Lu Hao had been abducted. Lu Hao had ridden into an ambush, though why he'd turned into the narrow-lane neighborhood in the first place remained unexplained.

"You heard me, yes? Thirty minutes?"

"Yep. You look appropriately slutty, I must say. I, on the other hand, could use a quick makeover."

"Watch your mouth, John Knox."

"I mean it as a compliment. It's part of the plan, right?"

Grace was looking past him, across the street. "I spot two possible policemen," she said.

"The one working the trinket cart and the big guy inside the restaurant over there."

"Yes."

"I make the one with the cart as PSB. You?"

"Certainly police of some kind. Yes. We have many such bureaus and ministries here in China."

"The other, I'm not so sure about."

"Private security, I think," she said. "Would other foreign companies have an interest in Lu Hao? Of course they would."

"So maybe that's it."

"I do not know," she said, still sounding stiff. He was considering nicknaming her "Rosetta Stone." "The realtor said she would meet us out front."

"You should hang all over me. You know? Like we're shopping for a place to . . . you know. To carry out our torrid affair."

"Not a problem," she said.

"Seriously? Is it that easy for you?" He couldn't imagine this woman acting sexy or slutty. He couldn't wait.

"Think of it this way: when I am not serious, I will let you know."

Together they found a shop and Knox bought some dress pants and a pressed shirt. He changed and added his worn clothes to hers in the bag she carried.

"One thing I'm confused about," he said, studying himself in the shop's full-length mirror. "After all that education, why join the army instead of returning here and making serious money? And then, why Hong Kong?"

"It is complicated," she said.

"We make the complication. It doesn't make us."

"You may be good at whatever it is you do, Mr. Knox. But you are not much of a philosopher."

He narrowed his eyes.

"Have I offended you?" she asked.

"You would have to work harder than that," he said.

"Lu Hao has made much trouble for his family. Bad financial dealings. I extended the offer of employment to him in hope of assisting his situation—his family's situation. The Berthold Group was paying him extremely well. Now, he is in trouble—"

"Which reflects badly on you," Knox said.

She said nothing for several strides. "As I said: it is complicated."

Minutes later, they were on the sidewalk in front of Lu's apartment building.

A young, energetic Chinese woman approached them. She was in her mid-twenties, displaying unbridled enthusiasm and a lot of leg beneath a miniskirt. They introduced themselves. She two-handed them both her business card: SPACE—REAL ESTATE FOR TOMORROW.

The apartment building's lobby was clean and brightly lit.

"All latest qualities," the agent said, her English clipped and, at times, broken. "The high-speed Internet, the telephone and the highly technical security. Every residence have hot water and warming and colding of the environment."

They rode as a group to the fifth floor in the building's only elevator. The name of the vacant apartment being offered was labeled in Mandarin beside the door: "Five Fawns."

Knox crossed the small living room and looked out the window to inspect the view. First he saw the man in the restaurant window; then, a complication: the trinket cart was heading toward the apartment building.

Wondering if they'd been made, Knox considered aborting. Instead, he hoped to speed things up and get out of here.

Grace surprised him with a squeal from the bedroom. "Lover!" she called out. "You must come here this instant!"

Knox entered the apartment's bedroom, a space barely wide enough for the double bed. Grace was bouncing on her knees on the mattress like a five-year-old.

"So soft! You must try this!" she said, patting the mattress.

Knox waited for the agent's attention to return to Grace and he subtly tapped his watch. Grace's head went up and down as she bounced: she'd caught his cue.

"What do you think?" she asked. "You like it?"

"It's the *view* I'm concerned about, my little rose. We talked about this street being too noisy. *Too busy.*"

Grace threw herself back onto the bed, drew her knees up into her chest and hummed her satisfaction. "Always so practical," she said to Knox as she sat up. "Very well. You," Grace said to the agent, "will please negotiate on our behalf. Street noise is too much. Requires fifteen percent deduction."

The real estate woman said, "I am quite certain price is firm."

Grace laughed derisively. There wasn't a firm price in all of China. "Must I remind you: you represent both the landlord *and* our interests."

"Yes," the agent said. "Of course."

Grace patted the mattress again. Knox did not sit.

"The landlord is to install a mirror on the ceiling," Grace said. "Bedroom lights must be on dimmers." She reached over and took Knox by the hand. "Come on, Lover! Please, you must try."

Knox shot her a look.

The agent pulled out a small notebook and took notes.

"Flat-panel television," Grace said, "one hundred centimeters. Reading lamps on both sides of the bed. No compact fluorescent. Makes your skin look yellow. Disgusting."

The agent continued writing.

"Not that there is to be much reading," Grace said, mooning at Knox. "Hmm?"

Knox grinned. "Oh, you," he said, pushing her shoulder so hard she fell back onto the mattress.

"Ah! You want to play?"

"Later," Knox said in a suggestive tone.

Grace faced the agent. "Landlord is to pay utility, of course," she said. "Lover will pay for television cable channels."

Knox took Grace's hand as she reached over for him.

Grace glanced down at the floor demurely. "You will excuse my demands, cousin," she said in Shanghainese, "but this man, and his opinion of me . . . my time with him, all very important."

"Of course."

Knox played it as if not understanding a word.

"Now I will leave you two," Grace said, "to review the mechanicals, and discuss numbers. Yes?" Grace asked rhetorically. "Yes."

"Don't be long," Knox pressed.

"Cannot bear to be without you!" Grace said, popping up off the bed. She swished past the agent.

"Your phone," Knox said, making a point of handing her both the purse and bag containing their clothes. "I'll text you when it's time to leave."

The agent waved Knox toward the kitchen. "I believe you must be most impressed with features of the kitchen dining."

"Not really, cousin," Grace called back on her way out the door. "It is not like we will be doing much cooking."

minutes later, Grace arrived to the door marked "Seven Swans," having passed "Seven Lakes" and "Seven Gorges" on her way from the elevator. She drew in a deep breath, and knocked. Seven was a neutral number, but she took it as an ominous sign.

She was greeted by a gangly young man in his early twenties. His T-shirt showed grease stains, his right index finger a smoker's smudge.

"Where is he?" Grace asked angrily in Shanghainese.

She barged past the surprised young man, quickly taking in the three other boys reclining in front of a flat-panel television. Take-out wrappers, pizza boxes and Red Bull cans littered the low coffee table.

"Tell me where he is!" she shouted, not liking the look of Lu's living room. Clearly it served as a dormitory, housing the other men as well. The space was crowded with bamboo mats, pillows, blankets and IKEA furniture. Singling out Lu Hao's belongings from the mess would be next to impossible without a great deal of time, not to mention privacy. She continued on to a closed door and threw it open.

"Hiding in here?" she called out.

Better. This room was neater. A single futon occupied the corner, alongside which were a low bedside table and a crane lamp. An IKEA desk, part of a matched set with the dressers in the living room. A smaller flat-panel television, with a game box, a DVD player and a cable box. *Lu Hao's room*, she thought.

A bamboo rod hung from wires screwed into the ceiling, holding laundered pants, shirts and two sport coats on plastic hangers. She pulled open the armoire to find it stacked with suitcases and packaging for all the electronics.

A digital picture frame on the desk stopped her. A photo of Lu Jian came and went in the frame's slide show, confirming her suspicion. Her chest cramped. Lu Jian looked somewhat older than she remembered him, but even more handsome, if that were possible. The same warm eyes. For a moment she couldn't breathe.

She sensed a presence behind her. Without turning, she asked, "Where is he?"

"We haven't seen him for a couple of days," a roommate informed her.

She wheeled and moved toward him. "Another girl?"

"How should I know? He's a big boy. He doesn't need me looking after him. Maybe you should check his family home. It's—"

"Chongming Island. Yes, I know. Do you think I do not know Lu Hao? You child."

The boy did not appreciate the admonishment. "Some are saying the Triad got him."

But if one of the Triads, she thought, *then why had the apartment not been tossed?*

"Killed?" She made herself sound shocked.

He didn't respond.

"Kidnapped?" she said, letting emotion enter her voice.

"You know rumors."

"Tell me truthfully: have others been here asking questions? Do not lie to me!"

"I swear, no one."

She sniffled. "Please. I need a minute alone."

He seemed eager to leave her.

She saw him out of the room, and then closed the door behind him. Quickly, she entered the bathroom adjoining Lu's bedroom, pulled this door closed as well, and started rummaging through everything in sight.

F rom inside the galley kitchen, Knox had a clear view of the wall-mounted video display showing the apartment building's secure entrance. He kept one eye on it as he feigned interest in the pantry shelving and the cabinet water heater. The agent stood alongside, studying him, reciting the benefits.

Five people had left the building in the past few minutes. No one had entered. But when a heavyset male appeared in the security display, grabbing the closing front door, Knox took note of the black leather jacket. The man who'd been watching the apartment from across the street? On camera, his features were sharper and bolder than most Chinese. He looked bigger as well.

"I've forgotten if you told us," Knox said, addressing the agent. "How do I reach the building's manager if I need him?"

"There is direct dial on the state-of-art security installment entrance beside the entrance."

"He lives in the building?"

"Of course. On the lower level."

"Do I use the east or west stairs to reach him?"

She looked a little put off by the question; there was no figuring Westerners.

"West."

The manager would have the security camera system in his room. If a cop or agent, the man who'd just entered would check the videos first, trying to determine where he and Grace had headed. It gave them a few minutes, but not many.

He texted Grace:

```
abort
```

He had to separate himself from the real estate agent, get Grace clear of the building; then, if possible, he would tend to business.

G race cursed her mother under her breath, having found no prescription medication among Lu's toiletries. Back in his bedroom, she searched his desk, then the rest of his room methodically but hastily, pulling out drawers, crawling beneath the desk, checking for a hidden USB drive or external disk drive, any conceivable place he might have stored the desired documentation of his bribery. She patted down all his clothing, checked inside the toes of his shoes. A tennis racket cover. Two empty backpacks. The futon mattress and frame.

Her iPhone vibrated.

```
abort
```

She cursed aloud and then started snapping photographs of the room, including the empty desktop. Never mind the roommate's claim: it appeared the room must have been searched, the most important items taken. The digital frame switched photographs: Lu Hao on a lovingly restored motorcycle and sidecar; this transitioned into Marlon Brando also on a motorcycle; then Steve McQueen in *The Great Escape*, followed by Harrison Ford and Shia LaBeouf in *Indiana Jones*—also a sidecar and bike; and finally the Shanghai skyline before revealing a new picture of Lu Jian. Grace put her hand to her mouth as she took in the photograph: this time Lu Jian was smiling widely, his arm around another woman.

She fled the bedroom quickly. The kid had returned to his place on the couch.

"Where is Lu Hao's laptop?" she asked. "He had an address I need."

The boy shrugged.

"Was it not here the day he disappeared?"

Another shrug.

"Has someone been here before me?" she asked. "Someone asking questions, looking around?"

"Who are you?" the boy asked.

She marched over to him. "You know what they say about a woman scorned?"

The boy appeared properly terrified.

"That's me. You do not want to make me any more angry than I already am. So . . . who was here before me?"

"I told you: no one. I swear it."

"A woman?" she said, playing her role to the limit.

"No, I promise."

"What did she look like? What is her name?"

"I tell you: there has been no woman. No man. No one!"

"Liar! You tell Lu Hao to call Ling-Cha," she said, making up a name, "the moment he steps through that door. You understand?"

The boy nodded.

"By the gods, I'll have your balls in a vise if you forget."

She marched to the door, turned and glared at the other boys—they all looked both terrified and relieved that she wasn't haranguing them. She let herself out.

Knox stepped aside, allowing the agent to enter the elevator first. "I would like to take the stairs," he said. "I will meet you in the lobby."

The agent stepped toward the control panel to stop the car, but too late. The doors slid shut.

He assumed the Mongolian—for that was how he'd pigeonholed him: northern Chinese or Mongolian—would use the west staircase because, according to the agent, the west staircase was closest to the superintendent's residence.

In the event of an abort, Grace would take the west staircase—farthest from the building's main entrance. Knox texted:

```
take east stairs
```

. . . but moved quickly to intercept her in the event it was too late.

He reached the stairs and put his ear to the door: faint footfalls . . . *approaching* him. He slipped inside. Steel and concrete stairs in a concrete shaft.

Sounds from above and below: above being Grace; below, the Mongolian. He caught Grace as she rounded the upper landing, hand signaling for her to leave the stairwell.

The ascending footsteps grew louder and quicker.

Grace paused, heard the approach and left through the door.

The shoulder of a black leather jacket appeared. Knox stepped away from the railing, drawing in a deep breath to charge his system and purge the adrenaline.

Knox's SERE training had inspired in him an interest in, and study of, hand-to-hand combat techniques. Chinese soldiers and Shanghai police were trained in *sanshou*, a bare-fist close-quarters fighting technique. Russians were taught *sambo*, a martial arts style of fighting that combined hard-fisted blows and wrestling techniques. Within the first few blows, Knox would know where his opponent was from—information that might come in handy later.

Knox flew off the landing, catching the Mongolian midstride and plastering him to the wall. The man maintained his balance and postured a wrestling stance.

Sambo. So, not Chinese and therefore unlikely he was police. A game changer. Knox could do more than push and shove.

His mind raced. Russian? Mongolian? North Chinese? A foreign agent, or private security? Good either way, as he could fight the man without fear he was assaulting a Chinese officer.

He pivoted and kicked the man's chest. Followed with an open-fisted chop aimed for the man's throat. But the man countered with an effective forearm block and used Knox's forward momentum against him. He ducked under Knox's arm and head-butted Knox's ribs.

The wind knocked out of him, Knox teetered. The man stepped in for a headlock—again, a wrestling move.

Knox kneed him in the side and drove his elbow into the man's face. A bone cracked. The man's jaw looked like a jack-'o-lantern that had been dropped.

He cursed—not Chinese, not Russian. The man ran off a string of expletives. An agglutinative language. *Mongolian?* Knox had been to Ulan Bator only once.

In a matter of seconds, the fight was over, Knox pinning the man, pressing a knee to his groin while holding his right arm twisted to within a quarter turn of tearing his rotator cuff. His opponent remained conscious, but in a crippling amount of pain.

Knox removed a switchblade, a wallet and a cell phone from the man's pockets. He would overnight the phone or its SIM card to Rutherford for analysis.

He considered working the man for information, but the guy didn't look the conversational type, and Knox was pressed for time. He gave the arm a sharp twist—like taking a leg off a cooked turkey. But this was a big bird, and its cry, convincing.

Grace waited for him in the back room of Bliss, a bar on Jinxian Road decorated in 1970s retro. The cigarette smoke was thick, the recorded jazz smooth, and the waitresses very young and pretty. The sign listed twenty-two on the occupancy permit. Maybe it was a maximum age limit, Knox thought. There were five others scattered around at tables eating dessert or enjoying a drink. No one over twenty.

"Next time," she told Knox as he sat down across from her, "please let me pick the place."

"It's quiet," he said.

"I cannot breathe."

"If you jump the wall out the back door you're in a *lilong*," he said, explaining his choice. A lane neighborhood. He ordered a beer when a clear drink arrived for her. Vodka, rocks, he was guessing.

"So? What'd we find?" he asked.

"You are favoring your right side."

"I'm fine," he said. "Tell me about the apartment?"

She passed him her iPhone, on which she'd been reviewing the photographs she'd taken in Lu's room. In return, he passed her the Mongolian's wallet and produced the SIM card from the man's phone.

"He's carrying a national ID, so maybe not Mongolian. But he looked Mongolian."

"I found no medication," she said. "Troubling. No toothbrush. No laptop *or* charger. No mobile, or charger. No USB or storage device for files. No accounts, no files, nothing."

Knox looked up from the photos on the phone. "The kidnappers beat us there."

"The roommate says otherwise."

"How about clothing?"

"Nothing to say one way or the other. My mother was obviously mistaken."

"Mothers are never mistaken," he said. "Not if you ask them." He had hoped for a smile.

"Perhaps Lu Hao keeps his medication with him."

"Could be. But why take your laptop on a delivery run?"

She said, "In China, a laptop is a sign of prosperity. People carry them like handbags." She pointed across the bar to two young Chinese at their laptops.

"Yeah," he said. "I didn't say it meant anything."

"Your voice did."

"Know me that well, do you?"

She worked the vodka. "Well enough." She had the Mongolian's wallet open and was pulling out cards. A transportation card. A Chinese Resident Identity Card. "If a forgery," she said, "it is a very good one."

"He sounded Mongolian," Knox said. "Looked it, too. But maybe he's Chinese?"

"Possible. We get our share across the border."

Knox had never thought of people wanting to get *into* China before. "He was trained in close quarters combat. *Sambo*. You know *sambo*?"

"Yes, of course."

"*Waiguoren*," he said in Mandarin. *Foreigner*. It made Knox think back to the guard at Danner's apartment building mentioning a foreigner.

The beer was half gone. Knox ordered them both another drink. She didn't object. He liked that.

"I'm going to overnight the SIM card to Dulwich. But first, tonight, I'll hope for an incoming call. Or maybe we should call some of its recently called numbers?"

"Patience."

"My contact at the U.S. Consulate might run the national registration card for me. He's a good man. And if he's who took Danner's laptop, he might be willing to share."

"What about Lu Hao's motorcycle?" she asked.

"What about it?"

"Mr. Danner and Lu Hao were both on motorcycles when they were taken, correct?"

"Correct."

"So what happened to the motorcycles? Where did they end up?"

Danner's missing Garmin GPS, Knox was thinking. "You're brilliant."

She averted her eyes to the tabletop and reached out for the second drink as it arrived. Chinese had trouble taking compliments. Not him.

"Since the police do not yet officially recognize the kidnapping," she said, "perhaps neither motorcycle has been processed as evidence?"

Knox said brightly, "Lady Grace, you should drink more often."

"Excuse me?"

"Another compliment."

"Accepted."

Progress. He hoisted his beer and they clinked glasses.

A waitress passed. Knox's eyes strayed to her. He said, "Do you know the term "handi-capable"?"

"Afraid not."

"A person who's challenged, physically or mentally, but the challenge is viewed more as opportunity than limitation."

"That is nice."

"That is my brother," he said. "My business partner." The beer was wrestling with his tongue.

She sipped the vodka, looking across the rim of the glass at him curiously.

"Just thought I'd get that out of the way," he said, upending the beer.

She stared across, studying him.

"I actually would like you to review our books," he said.

"Then I will."

"Lu Hao?" he tested. "What's the family connection?"

"Not yet," she said, her lips opening to welcome the liquor.

MONDAY
September 27

4 days until the ransom

8

The U.S. Consulate occupied a former private residence on four acres at a prestigious corner in the heart of what had once been the French Concession. Having already copied and overnighted the SIM card from the Mongolian's phone to Rutherford Risk in Hong Kong, Knox walked in the shade beneath the plane trees, a warm breeze on his face. To his right rose the twelve-foot wall topped with razor wire that encircled the consulate. Phone booth–sized security booths stood at regular intervals manned by rigid, uniformed officers of China's Ministry of State Security. There had to be dozens of security cameras trained on the area. The Chinese captured and identified every face that entered.

Knox had originally met Steve Kozlowski through the man's wife, Liz, a statuesque blonde who served as an immigration lawyer at the consulate. Her love of all things Chinese had inevitably led her to Knox, whose reputation for procuring the best antiques and collectibles made him popular with the "trailing spouses."

He and Kozlowski discovered a shared love of American football, and with the consulate receiving the U.S. Armed Forces television feed, Knox had joined the ranks of corporate executives, university professors and a few select government workers handpicked by Kozlowski to watch live games with him and a few Marines, exactly twelve hours off the U.S. air time.

Over time, he'd developed a cautious friendship with Kozlowski, who, by reputation, got close to no one. Knox often wondered if the man were a spy.

Knox passed through the thorough security check and was greeted by Kozlowski. Tall and strikingly handsome, he had a receding hairline disguised by a nearly shaved head. Dressed in a tailored dark gray suit, a bright blue tie and with a consulate ID lanyard around his neck, Kozlowski looked more like James Bond than a bureaucrat responsible for the welfare of every American citizen in southern China.

Walking toward the century-old mansion converted thirty years earlier into consulate headquarters, the two discussed the NFL season. Knox asked after Liz. They passed sumptuous gardens where Chinese workers in blue coveralls toiled bent over in the shade.

They passed through an interior security desk. Knox was led into a large common area of pool secretaries and assistants that had once been a spacious sitting room. Kozlowski had the center office.

Knox immediately spotted an open folder on the desk: a gruesome color photograph of a—*man's*—severed right hand. *On Kozlowski's desk,* he reminded himself. He read the date upside down: nine days earlier. A ring with "OSU" running at an angle. He committed the design to memory, believing it either Oklahoma or Oregon or Ohio State. A dead American. *Correction,* he thought—*a butchered American. Too far back to be Danner's, thank God.* Knox felt a rush of relief.

Kozlowski must have seen him snooping. He shut the file folder and gave Knox an eye-fuck.

"So, what's up?"

Kozlowski moved like a piece of Claymation, all sharp movements; Knox had never seen the man fully relax.

"On the phone you said you had an offer I couldn't refuse," Kozlowski said. "Which, by the way, is not terribly original, you realize?"

Knox lifted his hands in mock defense. "The offer's legit."

"So talk," said Kozlowski, leaning back in his chair.

"I'm looking into exporting CJ750s," Knox said. "M1s, M1Ms and M1Supers. Pre–World War Two, BMW R71s. If it goes well, maybe even some *tuo la ji*." He referred to three-wheel tractors common in the farms.

Kozlowski, who adored anything with two or three wheels and a motor, leaned forward now. "Yeah? So?"

"So, the baby boomers are moving away from the Harleys and into some of the vintage bikes. There's a market there. The recession has pushed more boomers into early retirement, but they're far from broke and they've got time on their hands."

"I drive the Chinese equivalent of a Vespa," Kozlowski said. "You're trying to get me to upgrade? Liz is the shopper in our family, not me."

"Here's what I think: the Chinese police must impound hundreds of bikes a week. The bikes then sit there and gather dust. Now, I could go around putting up posters in noodle shops with my phone number on tear tabs advertising I'll buy junker 750s. Or, I could talk to the boys at the impound about the timing of their next auction."

"Who says they have auctions?"

"You know otherwise?"

"You want to pay off a cop to walk them out of the door right now. I know you, Knox. I cannot, will not, be part of that."

Knox didn't deny it. "All you do is make the introductions, Koz. We look over the inventory. If I return another day, I return another day. No dealing with you in the room, I promise. And for the introduction you get the pick of the litter."

"I don't accept gifts."

Righteous motherfucker, Knox thought. "At cost, then."

"I'll think about it."

"You know what you'll think?" Knox asked. "You'll think you died and went to heaven when you see it buffed out and rebuilt. The 750 has a sidecar, Koz. Think of you and Liz on a Sunday afternoon humming down Changle Lu. It's a thing of beauty."

Kozlowski admonished him with a look. But it wasn't a full dismissal. Knox's eyes wandered, searching for what might be Lu Hao's laptop. He saw nothing that qualified.

"So," Kozlowski said, "you arrive in Hong Kong from Cambodia on a private jet leased to Rutherford Risk, and reenter the country commercial the same day. And you're telling me that kind of urgency is all about antique bikes gathering dust?"

Knox fought for composure, surprised by the man's knowledge. "Do I look urgent? I'm flattered you looked me up." Neither Knox nor Dulwich had considered the ramifications of Dulwich having flown on the Rutherford jet into Cambodia. If Kozlowski could uncover such records, so could the Chinese.

"You've entered China six times in the past year and a half. You're constantly on the road in South America, Europe and Eastern Europe. A man busy building a company. Or a corporate spy."

The two men remained locked eye to eye.

"Wouldn't a guy like you," Knox said, "know if a guy like me was a spy?"

"You aren't a U.S. spy, but there are all sort of spies these days, Knox. What we see the most here is privatized industrial espionage. It's rampant."

"I thought the shoe was on the other foot," Knox said. "Consulate employee. Head of Security."

"Not hardly," Kozlowski said.

"Listen, I'm in the Laotian jungle bidding on hammered bronze and swatting mosquitoes the size of sparrows and the lightbulb goes on in my head: motorcycles! Picture this: Liz with a scarf tied on tightly, the wind ruffling her shirt. You with your sleeves rolled up. A trip to Suzhou on a warm, late fall afternoon. Tell me that isn't perfect."

"So you call Rutherford Risk for a ride."

"Ran into a friend."

"In Cambodia?"

"That's right. David Dulwich, an old buddy of mine. We both worked for a private contractor that served Rumsfeld and George the Second. He was my paycheck for two years. A good paycheck. He pops up in Ban Lung, sightseeing for all I know, and offers me a ride as far as Hong Kong on the company G5. What would you have done?" He didn't dare lie about the details; Kozlowski could know anything.

"You would have thought up a better story if you'd had the time."

"If it were a story, believe me, I could have done better." Knox waited. "Tell me you'll help me with gaining access to the impound. Like today, for instance."

"I'll consider it. But I'm warning you: no business discussed in my presence, and I want no gifts, no deals."

"I'll be a Boy Scout, promise."

"Uh-huh. Right."

Knox lowered his voice. "One other favor?"

Kozlowski's eyes hardened. "I doubt it."

"What if a friend of mine lost something—*something important*—and I came up with a SIM card, some phone numbers, that might help him find it?"

"I can't help."

"I can't believe you'd want the Chinese looking for my friend's lost package. An American package. That's bad for everyone."

Kozlowski's eyes found the folder containing the severed hand. He slid back his chair and stood. "That's it. That's all the time I have."

They walked out together. Knox took his time, letting Kozlowski digest his Rutherford Risk connection, and hoping they might get around to talking about Danner's missing laptop, as Knox had tried to instigate. But it had to come from Kozlowski.

Not wanting to push any harder on the Danner front, he slipped Kozlowski the national registration card carried by the Mongolian. "Run this past your boys and see if it's legit."

Kozlowski accepted the card and pocketed it. "Don't overestimate our relationship, Knox. I can't work miracles."

"Who's asking for miracles?"

"You go down that road, you may need a miracle."

"Which road is that?" Knox slowed to a stop, sensing they were close to actual trust.

"Rutherford Risk is forbidden from doing their kind of business here, just as my office is. Has it occurred to you they're using you?"

"It was a plane ride, nothing more." He hesitated. "But my friend's laptop would help." It just came out. He wished he could have it back.

Kozlowski's nostrils flared, but he maintained his composure. "Remember what I said."

"Vehicle impound," Knox reminded, wearing his disappointment openly.

"I heard you the first time."

10:15 A.M.

Knox walked up Huaihai Middle Road, rather than take a bus or taxi. He marveled at the traffic sorting itself out, the birdsong in the middle of such a large urban landscape and the beauty of its women. He stopped on a wide-open plaza in front of a bank, took a look around and placed a call using the secure iPhone.

Dulwich answered before the second ring. "Go ahead."

"You got my package?"

"I did. I'd have called if we had anything. Goddamn labs."

Knox said, "Were any body parts included with the ransom demand?"

"Negative. There's a video. A proof of life."

"Why didn't I see it?" Knox asked.

"It arrived at Berthold today. We haven't seen it either."

"I need to see it."

"We're on it."

Knox said, "I saw a photo of a hand just now. I was in the U.S. Consulate. It was not pretty."

"None of our business that I know of, but I'll look into it."

"A college ring: OSU."

"Got it."

"Turns out your jet comes back registered to Rutherford Risk, LLC."

"It's Flight Options. So what?"

"So, I'm made."

Silence. "My bad."

"You wouldn't happen to have someone keeping an eye on me?"

More silence. The phone made subtle sounds each time it switched carriers. Knox wondered why Dulwich was taking so long to answer.

"Negative," Dulwich said.

"A Chinese or Mongolian the size of a Sub-Zero?"

"Same answer."

"I've sent you a second package. A SIM card. I could use the three Ws on caller-ID coming and going."

"We'll try. No promises."

"I'm getting a lot of that."

"So see a doctor," Dulwich said. "You've met the girl?"

"Piece of work."

"I know it's against your nature, but trust her."

"There are a lot of moving parts," Knox said. "We're after his records. We get that, maybe it tells us who did this. We get that, then extraction."

"Keep it simple."

"TIC." *This is China.*

"That all? I've gotta be someplace."

Knox laughed. "The girl mentioned some competitors. We're going to look at them as well."

"Makes sense."

"The Mongolian, or whoever he is, is troubling," Knox said. "There was one guy trying to look undercover by pushing a trinket cart around. A cop for sure. But a Mongolian? Is this thing international? Is he private muscle for one of the competitors?"

"We'll look at the SIM card and tell you what we find out."

"Any more contact?"

"These things are fluid, Knox. We know what we're doing."

"We need more to go on."

"There's a surprise."

Knox ended the call, frustrated. Dulwich, with all his resources, and no one seemed to know anything.

Sichuan Citizen, only a few blocks from the MW Building, served a mixed clientele of Chinese and expats in a hip, urban atmosphere that included canvas paddle fans and a long-legged hostess in a form-fitting black silk pantsuit. The aroma was a pleasing combination of hot peppers, exotic spices and sesame oil. Mandarin mixed with English in a singsong of language, interrupted by French and Dutch.

Knox, who'd entered by the back door, sat down across from Grace at a small table for two. He laid down spreadsheets in front of her and anchored the corners with steaming black bowls of rice noodles, eggplant and ginger-glazed pork.

"You were followed," he said.

"By a Chinese. Late twenties. Scooter. Neatly dressed."

"That's him, yes." Impressed she knew of the tail, Knox said, "Certainly not Mongolian."

"Han," she said, naming the race of Chinese that accounted for over ninety percent of the population.

"You allowed him to follow you?"

"Of course. That way, when I need to lose him, he won't be ready for it."

"I copied and mailed the SIM," he said, speaking quietly. "One number was called six times in a row."

"To the intellectual," she said. She answered his curious look: "Our term for the leader."

He nodded. "Yes. The brains. You see the Chinese and Americans aren't so different."

"You want to call the number," she said. A statement.

"Of course I do. But once we make that connection, he won't answer it again. The phone will be tossed. We lose any chance of any contact or tracking. I think we keep that one in our back pocket."

"Agreed," she said.

He was about to point out he didn't require her approval when she spoke, interrupting his thought.

"Some interesting leads in Lu Hao's receipts," she said, lowering her voice. "I found these in his apartment." She passed a stack of receipts across the small table.

He studied the receipts. "Sherpa's?" he said. "What's so strange about that? Half the city orders from Sherpa's." The Sherpa catalog of restaurants participating in take-out service was in the kitchen drawer of every expat in Shanghai.

"You have not seen photographs of the ransom demand?"

He remembered Dulwich sitting across from him in Ban Lung. "The letter. The ransom demand. Yes."

"They were delivered by a Sherpa's delivery man to Allan Marquardt at The Berthold Group. Please notice the chop," she said.

Chinese used chops as their personal signatures: small, individualized stamps. Knox had one. He examined the square red stamp at the bottom of the receipts. "They're identical."

"All nine receipts, the same chop," she said. "The same Sherpa's *delivery man*."

"Nice catch."

"This cannot be coincidence. Impossible odds."

"A friend betrayed Lu?" Knox said. "Lu Hao places orders with Sherpa's so he and a friend who works for them can hang out. Someone gets to the friend?"

"More likely, the Sherpa's driver is a new friend."

"That's more interesting," Knox said. "This guy befriends Lu, gathers enough information to pull off a kidnapping." He worked it around in his head. Maybe they didn't think so much alike. "I like it."

"We must interview the Sherpa. There were all sorts of take-away food containers in Lu Hao's apartment. Maybe this man has been back to the apartment since the kidnapping. Maybe he took Lu Hao's laptop and medication."

Knox now recalled Dulwich saying something back in Cambodia about the take-out food carton used as the ransom delivery. He fought his fatigue.

"Notice the bigger chop on back of the same receipts," she instructed.

He flipped over one of the receipts. The chop carried the Sherpa's logo along with an address. He inspected several more: the same chop and address.

Grace said, "There are a dozen Sherpa's dispatch offices throughout the city. Yet all these deliveries issued from the same office."

"This driver is assigned there," Knox said.

She pursed her lips, staring at Knox.

"It cannot be a *waiguoren* asking questions at a local Sherpa's dispatch," she said. "Therefore, I must do this."

"I'm going with you. If this guy betrayed Lu, who's to say there aren't others there working with him? Maybe a bunch of Sherpa's guys."

"I can handle it."

"I'll keep my distance. We will be connected by the iPhones so I can listen in to what's going on."

Grace said, "I must return to the office. I will change clothes—so I may leave the building undetected. I do not wish to be seen trying to lose someone. Not at this early stage. We must be careful."

"Agreed."

"We'll meet in one hour," she said, "outside City Shop on Shaanxi Road."

"Take those with you," he said, pointing to his company's accounts. "I'd like you to look them over."

"As you wish," she said, gathering the pages.

9

Grace's change of clothes provided her a disguise so that as she left the MW Building her surveillant missed her entirely. To confirm her success, she took her time reaching Huaihai and Shaanxi and then spent five minutes in the aisles of the subterranean City Shop supermarket before ascending back to street level.

Precisely on time, Knox pulled up on a motor scooter that had seen better days. She accepted a scuffed-up helmet from him and climbed on. Hiding within the helmets assured them of anonymity on the streets.

"Did you steal this?" she asked.

"Borrowed. A friend of a friend," he answered in Shanghainese. "No worries." The scooter belonged to Fay's bookkeeper, who had rented it to him for what to him was a song, and to her a fortune. His to keep as long as he needed.

"Good friend," she said.

"You don't have to sound so surprised."

The traffic lanes were jammed, but the bike lane moved well. At a stoplight, Knox lifted his visor and turned toward her.

"Rehearse what you're going to say," Knox instructed. "It must not raise eyebrows."

"Eyebrows?"

"Suspicion."

"You believe me so incapable?"

"You went a little wild in Lu Hao's apartment. A mirror on the ceiling?"

"As only children, we Chinese are privileged. Pampered, even. We get what we want, when we want it. The agent expected such demands from this kind of girl. A mistress to a *waiguoren*. Leave all things Chinese to me, please. I know what I am doing."

The slow-moving river of vehicles flowed on. Ten minutes passed. Knox dropped her off.

"Call me. Now. For the connection."

Grace placed the call, strung the white ear buds and microphone around her neck—she needed only its microphone—and headed down the sidewalk toward the cluster of motor scooters and electric bikes bearing orange Sherpa's crates strapped above the rear fenders.

"If you do not hear me," she said, Knox hearing her clearly through his ear buds, "nothing we can do about it."

She paused in front of an unmarked storefront with gray, rain-streaked glass.

Knox waited her out.

"Ni hao," he heard Grace say.

"Ni hao," came the faint reply of a male voice through the ear buds.

Speaking rapid Shanghainese, Grace appealed to the manager to help her right a wrong. She claimed to have short-changed one of his drivers and did not want to get the man in trouble. The phone offered enough clarity that Knox could actually hear her proffering a receipt.

The manager thanked her and offered to accept the money on behalf of his driver. Grace apologized profusely, citing her own inadequacy and stupidity, while firmly insisting she pay the driver directly herself.

"It is most unfortunate," the manager said, speaking more slowly. "Afraid this is not possible. Lin Qiu has had misfortune, I am so sorry to say."

"Is he ill?" Grace asked. "Perhaps balancing his debts might cheer him up."

"An accident, I am so sorry to say. Badly injured. Many broken bones. Bad luck."

"I see."

"You will be kind enough to allow me to pass along your generosity." The manager was no longer asking. His patience had worn thin.

"I would so like to apologize in person."

"Not possible."

"And to think just yesterday I saw him riding on Nanjing Lu. It reminded me of the debt, you see?"

"Yesterday?" the manager inquired.

Knox was impressed that she attempted to nail down the date of the driver's injuries.

"I am afraid that is impossible, cousin," the manager said. "The accident occurred Thursday."

"Thursday?" she repeated.

"Exactly so. Late afternoon."

"But I was so sure."

"I think not," he said.

"Here, then," she said. "The debt plus a little something for his troubles."

"Generous, indeed."

"You will see he receives it?"

"By my honor, of course. I have someone going that way now. You needn't trouble yourself with it a moment longer."

Grace exited the storefront along with the manager, who leaned over to one of his riders and handed him what had to be the money.

Knox rocked the scooter off its stand and rode past, making sure

Grace had a chance to see him. They met minutes later at the far corner. She climbed onto the back of the bike, saying, "The driver's wearing a green tam."

"Saw him."

"Headed west on Xincun."

Knox steered the bike around the block.

"Hurry!" she said. "We'll lose him!"

"Seriously? Do you think I'll lose him?"

Knox gunned the scooter, forcing her to grab him around his waist. He weaved through oncoming traffic into the westbound bike lane.

They caught up to the delivery man and followed the bright orange box strapped to his rear fender. He collected a take-out order from an Indian restaurant on Dagu Lu near the Four Seasons Hotel and headed northeast. His next stop was at a Thai restaurant—a second pickup. They rode behind him for another fifteen minutes. His first delivery was made in Huangpu District, the second in Changning. From there, the driver headed to Putuo District and a crumbling lane neighborhood destined for the wrecking ball.

Knox slowed, allowing the rider a substantial lead.

"We're here," he said over his shoulder.

The old *lilong*'s lanes were narrow and cluttered with rusted bikes and scooters. Houses sagged, bowing to gravity. Roofs were patched together with corrugated tin and blue drop cloths. Such neighborhoods existed as islands bound within the clusters of newly erected apartment towers, the contrast startling.

Knox and Grace putted down the lane, passing three intersections with even narrower sublanes running off to the right.

She tapped him on the shoulder.

Knox braked and backed up using his feet.

"I saw him turn left," Grace said.

A moment later, Knox, too, swung the bike left at the end of the sublane. The delivery man was just pulling to a stop. He left his scooter and entered a rundown stairwell, reappearing briefly on the second-floor balcony.

"We wait," Knox said, sneaking a look at his wristwatch.

Grace absorbed every detail of their surroundings—the hung laundry, the decrepit scooters, the timeworn faces in the open windows. A minute later, the delivery man reappeared. He drove past them, the sound of his engine growing distant.

Knox and Grace climbed the dingy stairs. Sounds of people coughing wetly behind closed doors mixed with a baby's crying over a background drone of Chinese soap opera.

At the top of the stairs, a landing offered three doorways, all hanging open for ventilation. Grace thrust her hand out to block him—this was for a Chinese. She stepped through the first door.

A woman's weathered face looked back at Grace, a cigarette dangling from her lower lip. She said nothing, only stared. Grace bowed and left, keeping Knox back and entering the second doorway.

"Hello, cousin!" she said loudly. "I trust you have just received the money you were due. I desired to see you received it. I am forlorn to see you so indisposed."

The man lay on a bamboo mat beneath an open window wearing only pale blue pajama bottoms, his battered head on a folded rag. He had facial bruises and poorly treated lacerations on his arms. The purple and black marks on his bare chest bore the distinct shape of fists.

Knox stepped in behind her. He shut the door.

The man asked Knox to reopen the door. He spoke a dialect of Mandarin, *not* Shanghainese, Knox noted.

Knox, also speaking Mandarin, said, "I prefer to leave it closed, cousin," his tones just right: menacing and impressively Chinese.

The room was spare, a small tube television along the near wall.

"We come for a simple reason," Grace said, also in a chilling monotone. She approached the man. "We are simple people with simple needs." She hooked a three-legged cobbler stool with the toe of her shoe and dragged it alongside the man. She sat down upon it. Every motion was confident and bold.

"It is extremely important, cousin," she said, "that you do not lie to us."

The delivery man's eyes ticked between Grace and Knox.

"I want no trouble," he said.

Reciting a proverb, she said, "'The greater your troubles, the greater is your opportunity to show yourself a worthy person.'"

"Please."

She said, "Lu Hao is my cousin."

The man's already sickly face drained of nearly all color.

Knox thought, *Sometimes I love this work.*

"We know you visited him." She glanced over her shoulder at Knox, as if she needed his assistance.

"Seven," Knox supplied.

"At least *seven* times," Grace repeated. "Seven is a neutral number, is it not? Could be bad for you. Let me see your hand. Let me read your lifeline."

She took hold of the unwilling man's forearm. He lacked the strength to stop her.

She held his hand in both of hers, secured by the thumb in her left, and his pinky finger in her right. She lowered her voice to a whisper.

"This line is bad," she said, tracing his palm with her red fingernail. She drove the nail down intentionally hard. He grimaced as tiny beads of sweat sprouted on his upper lip and forehead. He tried to withdraw his hand but Grace only tightened her grip, spreading his fingers farther apart.

He grimaced.

"You will please tell me where we can find Lu Hao," she said calmly.

His eyes darted between Grace and Knox, measuring them.

Knox said, "I am not sure he heard you. Time is running short."

Grace spread his fingers farther.

"Lu Hao! Friend!" the man said sharply.

"What kind of *friend* drops off a ransom demand?" Grace asked.

The man's lips pursed gray.

"We have you on security camera," Knox lied. "Sherpa delivery to The Berthold Group."

"His location," Grace said. "Think clearly before you answer." She maintained the outward pressure on his fingers.

"I do not open food container before I deliver," the man complained. "I pick up. I deliver. How am I supposed to know what lies inside?"

Grace snapped his finger, breaking the knuckle. He screamed. The finger hung like a broken twig. She seized his ring finger.

"Let us try again," she said in an eerily calm voice. "Where is Lu Hao?"

"Please. I beg you—"

She threatened this finger.

The man spit out an address so fast it was indiscernible.

Knox did not trust it. A delivery man would not be given the hostages' location. He was just trying to stop Grace from hurting him.

Grace shot him an inquisitive look. Knox shook his head.

"Slowly, now," she said. "Speak clearly, so I can understand. But know this: you lie to me—to us—and your family will mourn your ignorance." Grace applied pressure to his finger.

The man carefully repeated the address in the Xinjingzhen neighborhood.

"You lie," she said.

"By the gods, I speak the truth!" He repeated the address twice more.

Grace held the man's hand secure. She spoke English to Knox. "It is not possible the ransom delivery man would know the location of the hostages. The intellectual would keep these pieces very much apart."

"Agreed. And Xinjingzhen is at least thirty minutes from here. He's trying to buy himself time to disappear."

"He cannot disappear with me by his side holding his hand," Grace said, also in English. "Call me once you arrive at this place. We will get to the truth. If he should be testing our resolve, I will test back."

Knox did not like the idea of leaving her alone, even with her so firmly in control. "Find out who did this to him. His beating."

She turned and looked into the man's terrified eyes. Holding fast to his fingers, she spoke Mandarin. "We do not take kindly to old news. 'A rat who gnaws at a cat's tail invites destruction.'"

"What rat? I tell the truth!"

"Then tell me who did this to you. You did not fall off your scooter."

"But I did!" he proclaimed, showing her the lacerations on his wrists and forearms.

"Who?" she repeated.

"They ambushed me!" he groaned. "Filthy *waiguoren*!"

"*Waiguoren* like him," she asked, pointing at Knox.

"No. A northerner, cousin. Autonomous region, perhaps. North of that for all I know. The filthy invaders."

"Mongolians," Grace said in English, glancing over her shoulder at Knox.

"You gave the Mongolians this same address you have given us," she said in Mandarin.

"I dare not lie," the man said. "It is true. *Do not punish me!*" he cried out to Grace. "I did only what any man would do!"

"The hostages will be long gone," Knox said in English, his disappointment obvious. "Providing they're still alive."

Grace flushed behind anger. "I would like to break every last finger," she said, not letting go of the man's hand.

She said threateningly, "Who took Lu Hao? Who are these people who took my cousin? These people to whom you betrayed my cousin?"

"Do I know one face from another? I tell the *waiguoren* the same thing! I am told to pick up and deliver a meal. I pick it up. I deliver it. A face is a face, nothing more."

"You lie poorly," Knox said in perfect Mandarin. "You *knew* this man, Lu Hao. You are no simple delivery man."

"How did the northerners find you?" Grace challenged.

"No idea! They appeared after delivery to The Berthold Group. Arrive on all sides out of nowhere."

Grace shot Knox a look: the northerners had been watching the MW Building?

"I gave you the address," the man said. "I was to report there. This is all I know." He cowered.

"Who are your partners?" Knox asked. "You mean to lie to us again?"

"Lu Hao, Lu Hao, Lu Hao," the man chanted, dismayed. He sounded as if he was calling for his help.

"Your partners?" Grace hollered.

The man trembled with fear and passed out.

Knox took the man by the chin and shook him. "Who knows? He could be out awhile."

"If we leave here, we will never see him again," she said.

"If we stay," Knox said, "who knows what trouble the neighbors will bring us? He was pretty loud."

"I should have gagged him." All business.

Remind me to stay on your good side, he thought. "We have to leave now," he said.

"There is more he can tell us. I can feel it."

"These others—Mongolians?—are out in front of us," he said. "I hate playing catch up."

She let go of the man's arm. It bounced lifelessly against the bed.

"The way you handled yourself," she said. "You are part Chinese, you know?" she said.

"Thank you," he said.

6:45 P.M.
CHANGNING DISTRICT
SHANGHAI

Knox took precautions to identify motorized surveillance—executing four consecutive right turns; slowing down, speeding up; reversing directions. Grace kept a lookout as well.

"Do you have him?" she asked, leaning her chin onto Knox's shoulder, their helmets bumping. "Black shirt? Shaved head."

"Yes. I haven't seen anyone with him." Knox shouted above the roar. "No."

"Doesn't that seem a little odd?" Vehicular surveillance nearly always came in pairs or trios.

"Uncommon," she said. "Yes. Maybe their numbers are small."

"About to get smaller. Can you drive one of these?" he asked.

"Of course."

"Hang on!" He felt her hold to him tightly. He abruptly directed the scooter down the next lane. He turned right at the first sublane, and leaned over, allowing Grace to grab the scooter's left hand-grip. Knox then slipped off the seat and his shoes met the concrete. He ran with the momentum to keep from falling.

The scooter wobbled but Grace gained control. She continued down the sublane. Knox hid in a doorway, peering out. Breathing hard. Adrenaline running hot.

An older Chinese couple passed, arms hooked, strolling down the *lilong*'s main lane.

Grace and the scooter disappeared to his right.

The idling bubble of a small-cc motorcycle engine grew louder. Closer. Knox ducked back into the doorway. He reached for a bamboo broom as the scooter driver goosed the throttle to make the turn.

The man was big, with sharp, high cheekbones. Another Mongolian?

Knox lunged and drove the broom handle through the front wheel. He slapped his hand over the rider's and gunned the throttle. The bike lifted over its front wheel. The helmetless driver sailed over the handlebars and smashed down onto the concrete, the bike slamming on top of him.

Knox sprang, kicking the bike out of the way. He removed a Russian Makarov 9x18mm from the man's lower back. Knox took the man's mobile phone, noting it was the same make and model—the same color!—as the man's he'd attacked in Lu Hao's apartment stairwell.

He pulled the man free, drove his knee into his groin and watched the man recoil. He found a Resident Identity Card and some *yuan* in the front pocket of the man's jeans. He kept it.

"Where is the hostage?" Knox spoke slowly in Mandarin. "Where is Lu Hao?"

The vacancy in the man's eyes told Knox he either didn't understand Mandarin, or was ignorant of the information.

He struck him hard in the face.

"Lu Hao!"

The man spoke, and this time there was no question: not Russian, but Mongolian.

"Who the fuck *are* you?" Knox said in English.

"Fuck you," the man returned in English.

The *thwap* of the man's skull smacking concrete was slightly sickening. He was out cold.

Knox checked the man's hands for calluses—right-handed. He broke the man's right elbow across his knee.

He was interrupted by an old woman's shouts of distress. Knox looked up, his temper boiling. Looked right into a surveillance camera high on the building's corner.

The scooter reappeared, Grace's timing, impeccable.

Two Mongolians, he thought, wondering, *what the hell*. Private muscle? For whom? Berthold's construction competitors? Foreign agents? Chinese cops?

The bike sped off, Knox wrapping his arms around Grace's tiny waist.

7:25 P.M.
XINJINGZHEN NEIGHBORHOOD
SHANGHAI

Grace steered the scooter in a U-turn across the wide, empty road and returned, having driven past the address supplied by the Sherpa delivery man. The scooter's light found the light industrial compound's entrance. Blocked by a padlocked steel cable, the interior roadbed was packed dirt, litter-strewn and weed-infested. It led to a group of six flat-roofed concrete-block buildings that looked decades old but had been built just five years earlier.

The cable was there to stop cars and trucks. Grace slipped the scooter past a stanchion and into the compound. Building 3's north side looked out on a field of weeds and heaps of rusted junk. She killed the engine, and together she and Knox listened, looked and learned.

Knox double-checked the designation: 3-B. He stacked some cinder blocks and climbed up to have a look through a gray glass window.

The interior space was dark, but looked empty. As Grace parked the scooter, Knox found a length of rusty wire and hooked it through the door's gap and tripped open the lock's tang. They were inside.

A typical warehouse space with floor-to-ceiling metal posts. In the near corner were three plastic lawn chairs and some overturned cardboard boxes along with empty pizza boxes, beer and soda cans.

Grace stepped forward, but Knox blocked her advance. He took photos using the iPhone's flash.

Wads of discarded duct tape lay on the concrete floor by a wooden chair. Knox pointed to the chair and held up a single finger, eager for quiet until they'd cleared the space.

He hand-motioned Grace to the left. He circled around the right. They checked nooks and corners.

"Clear," she said softly.

"Here, too," Knox said.

They returned to the area by the door, where a balled-up rag lay among the duct tape.

"One chair," Knox said, making his point again.

"So they divided up," she said.

"Yeah," he said, gut-punched. They both understood the other possibility.

"We work the evidence," he said. "You take the food and those lawn chairs. I'll stay here, on this."

"Sure," she said, sensing his anxiety over having possibly lost Danner.

As she worked behind him, Knox tried to make sense of the scene, to see people in the space instead of a space void of people. He put Lu Hao in the chair, bound by duct tape—confirmed by sticky adhesive on the front legs at ankle height and on both arm rests. He noted the stains and the sour smell, suggesting the hostage had urinated, soiling himself. Then he spotted a shallow plastic tub leaning against the wall—a makeshift bedpan. He put the hostage-takers in the lawn chairs, smoking and eating and killing time. Squatting, he moved like a frog around the chair, then stopped.

What he saw caused him to reassess. Not Lu Hao in the chair but Danner. Alongside the leg of the chair were three straight-line, black smudges: Danner's message—*three hostage-takers*. Knox felt a spasm of release in his chest.

"It wasn't Lu," he said. "It was Danner. In the chair. Three men covering him."

"Three. Yes. That is what I have got," she confirmed. "One a smoker. Another, left-handed and a vegetarian. The third, nervous and fidgety."

"Seriously?"

She glared at him. "That chair," she said pointing. "Cigarette ash and butts. Center chair: beer can on left side, not the right—left-handed. The pizza there is no meat, only vegetables—vegetarian. Last chair, napkin shredded, folded, pieces rolled up and tied in small knots. Nervous disposition."

"I'll take your word," he muttered.

He didn't need DNA results. He felt confident it had been Danner in the chair. He studied it more carefully, using a pencil light, paying special attention to where the man's hands had been taped. It took a different angle to see the grooves pressed into the wood of the arm.

"The number 'forty-four' mean anything to you?" Knox asked. He tried to get a photograph of it, but failed.

Grace looked over, but didn't speak.

"How about forty-one?"

Grace stepped closer, gravely. "Forty-four?" she inquired.

Knox pointed out the impressions in the armrest's wood.

"What is it?" he asked.

"Nothing."

"Grace?"

"Four sounds like—*si*—death."

"Danner or Lu?" he wondered aloud. "Danner could be wounded. Lu Hao could have had a seizure."

"Only the one chair," she said.

He pointed out the scuffmarks. "It was Danner in this chair. Count on it." He dug into the balled-up duct tape, peeling it apart. He found a patch with whisker hairs and torn skin in the rough shape of lips. The whiskers were faintly red under the pencil light. "Danner," Knox whispered. "For certain."

"Where's Lu Hao?" she gasped. "Dying and dead?"

"No jumping to conclusions," he cautioned. "We've got no blood. No sign of trouble. Chances are these guys are pros and kept the hostages separated. SOP. If they lose one to the cops or escape, they still have the other. Nothing to worry about. Not yet."

"You sound like you are trying to convince yourself, not me," she said.

Do I? he wondered. *Guilty as charged.* "A left-handed vegetarian?"

"He left a partially eaten pizza slice behind. Ate off the left side of the slice. You are trying to change the subject. Why would a simple delivery man know this address, yet it is not the address for Lu Hao? That does not make sense."

Not to Knox either. He was surprised how quickly she jumped to the same place he did.

"We can't get ahead of ourselves," he said. "We have Danner alive. Moved not too long before we got here, judging by the smell of the place." Sweat and smoke hung in the air. Someone had been here in the past several hours. "We have the Sherpa's driver, but he operated as an independent."

"The Mongolians?"

"Hostage-takers survey the payee of the ransom demand. We have the Mongolians watching Lu Hao's apartment. That could fit. Or, like us, they could be wanting Lu Hao's records."

"But I've seen well-dressed Chinese watching the MW Building from Xiangyang Park," she said. These were the men she used her disguise to be rid of.

"Yes. Maybe working with the Mongolians, maybe separate. If we forget the Sherpa's guy, that gives us the two groups to deal with."

"The well-dressed ones could be PSB, perhaps," she said. "Or independents. Or the kidnappers themselves."

"And if the kidnappers, then we have to explain the Mongolians. Listen, this was a lead we had to follow, but the gold ring is still Lu's records."

"Gold ring?"

"The prize," he said, clarifying. "We know from the Sherpa's man that it was the Mongolians who attacked him. They hit him after he made the ransom drop at Berthold, so they were watching either Berthold or the driver himself. They aren't the kidnappers. They got this address ahead of us. But by the time they got here, the place was empty."

"Because?"

"No sign of a struggle."

She nodded. "So the Sherpa's driver must have been expected to call in a code or message once he was safely away from the Berthold ransom drop. He never got time to do so because the Mongolians attacked him."

"And the kidnappers packed up and moved at least Danny. Yes. It makes sense. But if true, it also means the intellectual made an amateurish mistake in giving the Sherpa's man the hostage location. Why would he do that?"

"Maybe not a Triad," she said. "Someone less experienced at kidnapping."

"Like a competitor of Berthold," Knox said.

"We come back around to needing Lu Hao's accounts of the incentives."

He bristled at the use of the euphemism. "One step forward . . ." he muttered. "But who are they, these Mongolians?"

"Perhaps we should inform the PSB about this place," Grace said. "The PSB is efficient. They can lift fingerprints. DNA. This evidence could help a great deal."

"If the PSB finds Danner ahead of us," Knox reminded, "he's worse off than in the hands of the kidnappers. Lu, too, more than likely."

She looked ready to argue. Instead, she exhaled and settled herself. "Three days," she said.

TUESDAY
September 28

3 days until the ransom

10

"You asked I show you everything," Feng Qi said, sitting uncomfortably in a dynastic armchair seven centuries old. Across from him, occupying an ornately carved chair and looking like a feudal lord, was Yang Cheng. The expansive desktop was a museum piece: exotic mahogany inlaid with ivory, ebony and mother-of-pearl.

Yang Cheng was everything Feng Qi longed to be: rich. Not that a security man could get rich off the salary he was paid, but the stock market was another story. Along with the old toothless geezers in their pajamas, Feng stopped into the public trading rooms whenever possible, buying and selling on rumor and instinct. He was up eleven percent in the past two months. He invested every dime he earned, a good deal of it in Yang Construction.

"Let's see what you've got," Yang said. He ran the DVD player, and the four-quadrant screen came alive with security camera images of Grace's apartment.

"It is interactive. You may select any image at any time." Feng had no doubt what image his boss would select. He had personally cued the DVD for the occupant's entrance into the bedroom from the bathroom. The woman was naked. Feng knew on which side his bread was buttered.

Yang Cheng replayed the full screen image several times.

"*Oh, my!*" Yang Cheng said. "That puts some cayenne in the old stalk!"

"She is very clever, this one," Feng said. "We see her entrance, but have yet to spot her *leaving* the MW office building. This, while watching every exit carefully."

"Disguise?"

"Yes. It is the only explanation."

"This tells us she is up to no good. Also that she spotted you! You are an idiot!"

"Or she was told by Berthold about the kidnapping and to take no chances."

"Why her and no other employees?" Yang asked.

Feng looked stumped.

"We must now consider that she is aware of Tragic Lu's current situation. I imagine Berthold employees are not the happiest right now. This gives me a good idea."

"One thing of note: she made no attempt to disguise herself for yesterday's lunch with a *waiguoren*." He paused. "Canadian. American, possibly."

"This I find even more interesting. No. Listen to me . . . I told you: she is up to no good. Her arrival is no coincidence. Her precautions? She fears the government, of course—the Ministry of State Security. What else? That they are aware of the kidnapping and may be interested in any newcomers. Of course! I knew it! And the fact that she takes such precautions? A windfall. She acknowledges her importance to us. Leading us to the American? She is engaged in the highest form of deception. She is challenging us to take the bait, or let it go. Thankfully our resources are many. We can play both sides to our advantage." He was excited to the point of arousal.

"The two appeared to have reviewed financial statements."

"Lu Hao's accounts?"

"In public?" Feng said. "No. Their waitress, Sweet Lips Woo, said it was an expense account, maybe."

"You paid the waitress? You are a smart man, Feng."

"It's what I do."

"Did you follow the foreigner?"

The question put Feng in a difficult position. If he admitted his man had lost the foreigner, he, Feng, would be held responsible. If he tried to pretend he'd been shorthanded and had not followed, he would be declared incompetent.

"I deemed it more important to stay with the woman," he said.

"Next time, get your head out of your ass and wipe the shit out of your eyes."

"But if anyone is to lead us to Lu Hao's bookkeeping, it is this woman. I have it on good authority she has spoken directly with Marquardt himself."

"All important. Absolutely. But I want the name and employment situation of the *waiguoren*. Your job is information. Bring me the information!"

"Yes, sir."

"You must do better, young man."

"Of course," Feng said, having no idea how he might go about finding the man again. "I endeavor to serve your every need."

"Your needs as well. There's a bonus in it for you."

Feng thought there was no more sweet-sounding word. Yang was known to hoard his profits, but he could be generous with his mistresses and held much *guanxi* with his business partners.

Yang stared out at the Pudong skyline, envious of the Xuan Tower. It stuck in his side like a thorn.

Feng said, "If I might make a suggestion?" Yang Cheng didn't take kindly to suggestions. This was dangerous territory.

"If you must."

"Perhaps, if you were to invite the accountant, Chu Youya—the one they call 'Grace'—to this evening's festivities? Perhaps encourage her to bring a companion?"

"The *waiguoren*?"

"If we get lucky."

"I am always lucky. I was born lucky. Eighth day of eighth month."

Feng suppressed a gasp. It explained so much about Yang's ability to amass such a fortune so relatively young. Double eights. What more could any person ask?

"It's a good suggestion," Yang said. "A fine suggestion! This is exactly why I pay you so well."

Feng coughed, keeping his sarcasm at bay.

Yang passed the invitation along to an assistant by phone. When he hung up he said to Feng, "Should she refuse my invitation, perhaps her employer or the PSB would be interested in her contact with this *waiguoren*. Perhaps she lacks the proper licensing to do such business. I leave the details to you."

"You are a brilliant and cunning strategist."

"You will join me tonight. The nineteenth hour. Place two of our men outside number twenty Guangdong Road. At the ready to follow. You will be inside with me."

Feng's chest swelled with pride. "My pleasure."

"This isn't about pleasure, you fool. Keep your wits about you. It's about laying a trap. It's about outwitting the competition. Have you learned nothing?"

"My apologies."

"Go now. Leave the DVD with me." He had freeze-framed the naked image of Grace striding across the bedroom. "If you get any more like this, I want to see it."

"Of course." Feng suppressed a grin. The bonus couldn't be far off. Eleven percent in two months, he thought, already doing the calculations.

8:45 A.M.
CHANGNING DISTRICT

Grace had no intention of showing up for work, her full attention on obtaining Lu Hao's records of bribery. The three days remaining until the ransom drop felt more like three hours. She and Knox had a few sketchy leads: the existence of the Mongolians, their phone records and their Resident Identity Cards. They knew Danner had been held alone. A return to the Sherpa's driver had found him gone, as they'd expected.

Knox had called to nudge Kozlowski once again about making a connection to the police motorcycle impound, while dropping another leaden hint that he needed the contents of Danner's laptop.

So they waited, the one thing Grace was not particularly good at.

She was sipping a coffee at a bakery/café, when her phone rang—not the iPhone, but her private mobile. She reached for it tentatively, fearing another battle with her mother.

"Ms. Chu? Hello." A woman, definitely Chinese. She spoke English. "I am calling for Yang Construction at the request of Yang Cheng, our president and CEO."

"Yes?" she said politely, her chest suddenly tight. Yang Cheng calling her? On this number? How did he even know about her?

"Mr. Yang invites you, and a guest if you like, to a cocktail reception at the Glamour Bar this evening. Seven P.M. Business casual."

"I am . . . flattered," Grace said. "Honored. But—"

Perhaps anticipating her hesitancy, the woman said, "Mr. Yang like to welcome your return to Shanghai."

"My return?"

"Y . . . es. This is Chu Youya?"

"Yes. Exactly so." They'd done their research.

"Can I put you down for a party of two?"

"Thank you."

"I apologize for such short notice. Entirely my fault, I assure you."

"No apology necessary."

"We would be happy to send a car for you if—"

"No need." So they wanted to know where she lived as well. "Seven. Business casual?"

"As you wish."

"See you tonight, then, Ms. . . ."

"Katherine Wu. I so look forward to meeting you," the woman said. "Should I put you down for plus-one?"

"Yes. I will bring a client with me. Thank you."

As Grace hung up, a throat cleared behind her. She looked over her shoulder wondering how much Selena Ming, Allan Marquardt's assistant, had overheard.

An awkward moment, as neither spoke.

"Congratulations on the new apartment," Selena said.

"A promise is a promise. Certain arrangements were made at the time of my hiring." Grace knew that only executives of vice president and above were provided such luxury housing. She wondered how this might sit with the other Chinese employees. "Join me?" Grace motioned to an empty chair.

"I could not."

"Please."

Selena sat. "It is nice? The apartment?"

"Very nice." It took Grace a moment to catch on. "Would you like to see it sometime?"

"Oh, please, I do not wish to trouble you."

"No trouble. In fact, Mr. Marquardt has meant to deliver the EOY— the end-of-year—financials to me. Perhaps you would be so kind as to bring them along?"

"I can check with Mr. Marquardt. But if he clears it, most certainly."

"Good! Thank you very much." Grace had hoped to avoid that hurdle, but by putting the request to a third party, it pressured Marquardt to either deliver the accounts or explain to Brian Primer of Rutherford Risk why he would not.

The girl's face brightened. "Yes. And thank you," she said. Selena walked off, practically floating.

Grace reread her note about the cocktail party. She needed to reach Knox. Then, a new dress.

10:25 A.M.
HUANGPU DISTRICT

The air was guncotton gray, visibility less than five blocks. Commuters and pedestrians wore surgical masks against the smog.

Kozlowski waited at the entrance to the police impound, a door marked with a small plaque.

"If this works," Kozlowski said, "I get my pick of the litter. But at your cost. No gifting."

"Agreed."

"As to your not so subtle requests. Let me drive home this point: tread lightly, friend."

"An Inspector Shen shook down Berthold Group's Allan Marquardt about a film crew and a missing cameraman," Knox said, relaying what Dulwich had told him in their daily wrap-up conversation the night before. He knew quid pro quo was his best shot at winning favors—possibly Danner's laptop, if Kozlowski had confiscated it, which Knox suspected.

Kozlowski did not break his cool, did not allow the slightest indication of any kind of knowledge to cross his face. It was new territory for their friendship.

Kozlowski was focused on Knox's barked knuckles. He could easily have been informed of a Westerner having assaulted a man in an apartment house stairwell, or having dumped a motorcycle in a back lane of a *lilong*.

Knox said, "Given the restrictions our government faces concerning investigation inside China . . . If you ever needed an errand boy . . ."

"Shut up," Kozlowski said softly. He took Knox firmly by the arm. "I ran that registration card as you asked. It's legit. Issued in Beijing."

Knox had been convinced the card would turn out to be a forgery. "Legit?" he said.

"Correct. So he's either a Chinese, or he's very well connected," Kozlowski said. "As in: don't go there."

"I'm already there," Knox said. "Who could get a legit registration card made for his hired muscle?"

"I don't even want to think about that," Kozlowski said.

"I do."

"No, you don't." Kozlowski opened the precinct's door for Knox and they entered. Kozlowski showed the receptionist his U.S. Consulate identification tag. She clearly recognized the name. He showed them into the back where a chisel-faced man in his forties with greasy hands welcomed them. Superintendent First Class Gao.

Following some small talk, all in Mandarin, Kozlowski presented Knox's wish to be included in any auctions.

"Prior to auction," the superintendent said, "station officers get first pick of litter."

Knox recognized an opening. He said, "How many officers might there be in the office?"

"Fifteen, including myself. We each may advance bid on one vehicle per auction."

"Perhaps one or two might be willing to serve as my proxy?" Knox said.

"I would be most pleased to present your card by way of introduction." Gao was no stranger to exploiting loopholes. By working with Knox, he could pad his officers', and his own, pockets; establish valuable *guanxi* with Kozlowski; and reduce his inventory.

They accepted the offer to tour the back lot, a mud yard surrounded by a rusted cyclone fence. Hundreds of motorcycles, motor scooters and electric bikes were chained together through their front wheels in ungainly lines. Some looked salvageable; a few looked interesting. All were rain-scabbed and filthy.

It took Knox less than a minute to spot a beautifully restored CJ750 and sidecar that matched Grace's description of what she'd seen in Lu Hao's apartment. Five bikes farther down the line, he identified a dark green Honda 220 street bike, reminding him of the owner's manual for a 220 in Danner's desk drawer.

"Beautiful," he said in Mandarin, approaching the 750. He rattled off the bike's specifications and caught Kozlowski staring at him, not the bike.

"A recent addition," the superintendent said. "This one will not last. Will be reclaimed for certain."

"This model, and ones like it, interest me greatly," Knox said.

The superintendent wandered the lines, searching out other antiques.

Knox meanwhile moved closer to Danner's Honda.

An agitated Kozlowski, hands in his pockets, didn't know what to do with himself.

"It would be impolite to leave the captain alone," Knox told Kozlowski, who glared back at him.

Knox reached Danner's bike. Its right side was badly scarred. It had been dumped and had skidded a good distance.

Reaching it, he called out, *"Hen hao!"*—very good!—so that his spending time with it could be explained.

The superintendent hoisted a thumbs-up from across the yard—he could smell the *yuan* flowing.

Knox observed a bracket attached to the handlebars, its black plastic stamped GARMIN. He checked over his shoulder. The superintendent was busy searching for a similar prize.

Kozlowski watched Knox from a distance, like a worried parent.

Knox screened his opening of the motorcycle seat's storage, and he rummaged its contents: a pair of foam earplugs, leather gloves, a cable lock, a small plastic funnel, bungee cords. And a black, faux-leather drawstring bag. He lifted the bag—the weight and shape making sense for a GPS—and he zipped it into one of the ScotteVest's lower pockets.

The superintendent shouted as Knox was zipping up the jacket. "Do not make a mistake!"

Knox's blood ran hot. It was too late to return the GPS. He got the seat compartment closed, believing he'd been caught in the act.

"That one may look pretty," the superintendent said in blistering Shanghainese, "but the older ones run far better."

Knox shouted at the superintendent. "I do not doubt! The young, pretty girl has nothing on the older, experienced woman!"

The superintendent howled. Kozlowski bristled. The superintendent indicated a beat-up 750 that lacked its sidecar. Knox moved in that direction, passing what looked like a vintage BMW or a good Russian copy of one.

They identified six bikes, including Lu Hao's. The superintendent wrote down the plate numbers. Gao would talk to his men and be back in touch.

Out on the street, Kozlowski said, "If you're lucky, they put you in a six-by-six-foot cell and slowly starve you. Within a week, you'll say anything into the video camera they want you to say, and it won't help you one bit to say it. If you're unlucky, you never get as far as the cell."

"He liked me," Knox said.

"You do not want to get into this."

"I'm buying a couple motorcycles."

"Listen, I know who lives in the apartment building in Zhabei where the man was beaten—a man, by the way, who has not been seen since. He should have visited a hospital; he did not."

"Health care these days."

"I also know which private security companies are contracted to which U.S.-based corporations with offices here. I know whose jet carried you into Hong Kong. I will say this, Knox: I'm very careful about running background checks on the people I drink beer with. Break bread with. The people I admit into the consulate for Monday Night Football. Extremely careful. So either I missed something—unlikely—or you're a sleeper—also unlikely—or you're into something you shouldn't be. But I'd gotten to like you, and that opinion is quickly changing." He waited a moment for people to pass them on the sidewalk. "I help people I like. But not the stupid ones."

Knox considered entering full denial mode—his knee-jerk reaction to such lectures. He caught himself and said, "I need the laptop or its contents. I need a heads-up if the heat joins the game. And I need some slack from you."

Kozlowski said, "You think? Really?"

"Time's against us here," Knox said. "I'm staying at—"

"The Jin Jiang, room five-forty-seven. I know that. Shit, Knox, what do you think I do all day?"

Knox swallowed dryly. He didn't like the thought that Kozlowski was keeping tabs on him. He wondered if Kozlowski knew about the room at Fay's as well.

Knox shook the man's hand and thanked him. "You've been a big help."

"Whatever you took out of there," Kozlowski said, "I wouldn't mind it landing on my doorstep in a basket with no note. This street is two-way or it's shut down," Kozlowski said.

"Understood."

Knox looked up in time to spot the distinct shape of a face among the hundreds of Chinese looking his way. A man on a green motorcycle, nearly the color of Danner's.

A Mongolian.

10:45 A.M.

Up the street, a wide-shouldered man loitered on his motorcycle by a cart that sold *cong you bing*—green onion pancake. He watched the two Caucasians leaving a nondescript entrance.

The man's parents had created his name, Melschoi, by way of a cruel acronym: Marx, Engels, Lenin, Stalin and Choibalsan. He'd taken heat for it in the schoolyard, but by the time he'd signed with the police in Ulan Bator, no one murmured a critical word in his company. Melschoi had developed into an imposing force: physically oversized, mentally resilient and morally strong.

After six years, on a police force fueled by corruption, Melschoi's attempt to stay clean proved his ruin. In failing to bring down a cabal of officers, he and six police loyal to him—four of whom were with him now in Shanghai—had been betrayed. Two of his team, including his younger brother, had been abducted, tortured and brutally killed. He and his remaining four officers had been forced to run, stowing away beneath a winter train bound for Beijing, an experience that accounted for the two missing fingers on Melschoi's left hand.

Disgrace had left him disfigured. He and his men planned to return to Ulan Bator with enough money to move and protect their families before finishing what they'd begun.

Now he'd lost two of his men to injury at the hand of an *eBpon*—a foreigner. He'd witnessed this same *eBpon* visiting the Sherpa's driver. Now he was with Cold Eyes—the U.S. Consulate's security chief. As far as he was concerned, it confirmed the *eBpon* was a spy, a foreign agent. This discovery irritated him, because it meant that the man was hands-off. His client would not tolerate an act against the U.S. government.

Melschoi understood the guidelines imposed. But he understood the rules of a street fight better. The foreigner would pay for cutting his team in half, though the man's ability to take out two of his men did not go disrespected. Melschoi had long since proved himself to be a patient and careful adversary. Accidents happened.

He left the motorcycle and hailed a taxi, prepared to switch cabs several times if necessary.

The *eBpon* would never know what hit him.

11

Heading up Guangdong Road toward the Huangpu River, the buildings grew older and more imposing. Some of them dated back to the nineteenth century, when this area was an enclave of foreign privilege, and Shanghai thrived on trade in tea, silk and opium. Where once the flags of many countries flew from these rooftops, now hung the distinctive scarlet Chinese flag.

The wide avenue paralleling the Huangpu fronted a river walk that held ten thousand or more Chinese tourists on a given night. Weekend nights, there were even more. There was a European grandeur to the Bund, like Grand-Place in Brussels, or the Champs-Élysées in Paris, an architectural nobility. The air buzzed with an intoxicating mix of human excitement, ships' horns and the whine of vehicles.

Arriving at a group of valets, Knox had a glimpse of the teeming quay and beyond it, the neon- and LCD-charged Pudong skyline. The Pearl Tower flashed pink and turquoise through the evening darkness. Ten-story screens on the sides of high-rises played advertisements for Coke and KFC. Tens of thousands of tourists jammed the elevated quay, all jostling for a piece of the famous view.

Grace waited on the steps, pushed back against a handrail while watching guests being dropped off by their drivers. Mercedes, Lexus, BMW, the ubiquitous chauffeured blue Buick minivan, a symbol of the corporate expatriate life.

She looked ravishing in a short purple raw silk jacket over a black tea dress with a high neckline. A string of turquoise and red coral complimented her long neck. Her hair, not a strand out of place, was pulled back into a bun stabbed into place by a length of tortoiseshell.

She leaned to kiss Knox on the cheek, ever the role player. "You will find, unlike our American counterparts, Chinese women are *always* on time."

Knox checked his watch. Five minutes late.

"You look . . . lovely," he said.

"And I would take this as a compliment if I heard conviction over surprise."

He took her arm, his grip strong on her elbow, and guided her up the marble steps.

Grace resisted. "I would prefer a drink, alone, before we go up." She seemed hyperaware that anything and everything said between them might be heard. She angled her head across the street.

"Your wish—" he said, escorting her through a break in traffic.

They rode the elevator to New Heights, a seventh-floor restaurant and bar that also overlooked the river. They had a view across Guangdong Road and through the windows into the Glamour Bar where Yang Cheng's party was already underway.

The bar itself was made of thick, frosted slab glass, the liquor bottles reflected off shiny shelves of black lacquer. He ordered a beer, and she a glass of Champagne. With no seats to be found, they stood at a chest-high drink counter.

"So?" Knox said.

"Before we go upstairs and into that," Grace said, pointing toward the Glamour Bar, "where honestly we must play our roles to perfection—I wanted to know when you were going to tell me about what you are carrying in your coat pocket?"

Knox leaned away.

"I felt it when you kissed me on the steps. You don't smoke. It is not a cigarette case. It is too heavy, and too big for a phone. Too light for a handgun, too bulky for another kind of weapon—a knife, for instance. It is in your right pocket—you are right-handed, so you obviously wanted it close."

"Obviously." He swallowed dryly and looked for the beer.

"A video camera?" she asked.

He glanced into the reflection off the glass, admiring her. Small, but beautiful. Fiercely put together into a showcase of fashion and femininity, giving no hint of the physical power she no doubt contained from her army training. Her focus. Most of all: her control. Lowering his voice, he said, "My friend's GPS."

"*Ayee!*" she let slip.

"It was your suggestion: the impound."

Grace snarled. She clearly didn't want compliments or small talk.

"I can follow its moving map. But I don't know the city well enough to know if a *waiguoren* will stick out. And as much as I don't care who's there to greet me, I don't want to put Danner at risk. We can't afford mistakes. Not with only a couple days to go. We know they've moved at least once. I don't want them moving again."

He passed it across to her. "There are seven saved locations. It's got to be Lu's payout route. Danner follows Lu Hao and marks each location where he leaves a bribe. It's better for us than his accounts."

"We do not know what these locations are."

"I know how Danner is," he said. "Trust me: this is the money trail."

Grace said, "It could be nothing but his favorite restaurants or massage parlors."

"Then let's go get a bite and a rub and see what kind of tastes he has."

She turned on the GPS and scrolled through the saved locations.

"It is an interesting mix of neighborhoods," she said.

"I'm listening."

She looked across at him as if she considered this a rarity.

"Some are poor," Grace said. "Others, upscale."

"Both fit for kickbacks," he said, "depending who's on the take."

"The riverfront compound across in Pudong," she said. "Luxury condominiums for Chinese. Party officials. Businessmen."

"You see?"

She softened and then said, "We do not want to accuse such people. We must leave this to others. Very powerful. Very connected, such people."

"I have no intention of accusing anyone. I want to have a nice, quiet sit-down with them all."

Grace flashed her disapproval.

"You want to involve accusations and lawyers?" Knox asked. "We have two days."

"I want Lu Hao's accounts," she countered.

He threw up his hands. "I'm open to ideas, but this," he said, tapping the GPS in her hands, "this is the closest thing we have to a lead."

"This is not a good idea."

"Help me with the neighborhoods, please. Danner bookmarked these locations. I need to have a look."

Grace switched off the device and slipped it into her purse.

"Give me that!" Knox drew some looks.

"You must trust me," she said.

"You're not working real hard to earn it. Give it back, please. Or I'll take it from you."

"It is no good at night, this kind of thing. *You must trust me*. You ask for my advice on Shanghai. This is my advice. We must plan double egress for each location. Establish rendezvous. We will meet early tomorrow morning, at six A.M. First light. We will do this together. Early morning, the traffic is not as bad. This is a good time for us, John Knox."

He attempted to cool himself down with the beer. He failed. His attention remained on her purse and the GPS it contained, but his eyes did not. He didn't want her playing defense.

"To absent friends," he said, hoisting the bottle and waiting for her Champagne glass.

7:30 P.M.
THE BUND

The Glamour Bar's lavish Art Deco interior was a throwback to the heyday of Shanghai in the 1930s, when commerce, intrigue and opium conspired to form the most unique and magnificent city in all of Asia.

Knox and Grace were checked against a guest list and then welcomed by a gorgeous twenty-something hostess. The bar was a black granite island in a central room off which hung two sitting rooms and an elevated lounge that overlooked the Huangpu River. Pudong's neon-trimmed highrises flashed colorfully. River tour boats, tricked-out in neon and more video screens, slipped between coal-laden barges. It was Times Square times ten, with Broadway a quarter-mile-wide black water river.

The bar crowd was a mixture of Chinese and expatriates, the Asian women breathtaking, the men overconfident. The Euro waitstaff circulated with trays carrying Champagne, sparkling mineral water and pineapple juice. Big Band music fought against the din of voices. Knox choked on the cigarette smoke.

He caught Grace appraising the other women. "You needn't worry," he said. "They're all eating your dust."

She looked down. "Dust?"

"You look fine."

"Fine?"

Before Knox could rectify the moment, the two of them were interrupted by a young Chuppy—a Chinese upwardly mobile professional—

bulging out of a low-cut bustier and wrapped in a dark gray jacket and skirt. Her chic eyeglasses reflected the glow of an iPad she carried with authority.

The woman introduced herself by her English name, Katherine Wu, and her position as Yang Cheng's executive assistant. Grace introduced Knox as a business client. The hostess had greeted Knox with an openly coquettish expression, though it turned quickly churlish: import/export was regarded as unglamorous and "last century."

"Allow me to introduce you to our host," she said as she led them through a choking crowd around the bar and up three small stairs to the view lounge.

The lounge consisted of clusters of well-heeled guests randomly grouped. Yang Cheng stood at the top of the steps welcoming and chatting. Slightly balding and of an indistinguishable age, Yang wore a tailored suit, Italian leather shoes and a red tie. His wide-set eyes suggested a man overly pleased with himself.

Knox identified the fit man in the cheap suit as the bodyguard or security man. This man lingered a little too long on Grace for a complete stranger. There was something smarmy about the look. He then took in Knox like a full body scanner. Knox distilled this man's reaction and quickly analyzed it: he knew Grace; he didn't want to forget Knox.

Then something strange happened as Yang spotted Grace. He offered a smarmy look at his security man. It was a locker room exchange: one man to another, a look Knox knew well and had trouble processing for its content. It went beyond "She's hot" to something more licentious. It was, in particular, personal, not simply suggestive. Knox was right on the edge of understanding it when he was jarred by introductions. The meaning escaped him.

The provocative young assistant introduced them. Yang had the enviable ability and grace to make them both feel it was only the three of them in the room. Knox caught a tick to Yang's eye and Katherine Wu gently took Knox by the arm, following an obvious script. For now, Knox agreed to play his part.

"Please, Mr. Knox, allow me to show you the view." She eased Knox away from Grace and toward the windows. Grace and Yang Cheng descended into the bar area.

"You have been to the Glamour Bar before?"

"Many, many times," Knox replied. "One of my two favorite views in all Shanghai."

"And the other?" she inquired.

He turned his gaze onto her. "Why, you, of course."

"Ah!" She blushed involuntarily.

"But alas, views are only for looking. You'll please excuse me, Ms. Wu," he said cordially, wanting to keep track of Grace. "I'll be right back. I just need a beer."

Her grip tightened on his elbow. She lifted her other hand and miraculously, a waiter appeared like he'd come through a trap door. He took Knox's order.

His hostess said something, but Knox didn't hear. He'd lost sight of Grace.

7:48 P.M.

Being led by Yang Cheng into the main bar, Grace couldn't help but see eyes following them. Yang demonstrated his knowledge of her, reciting pieces of her CV. Thankfully, he referred to her most recent employment as an independent accountant based in Hong Kong; there was no reference or insinuation of any work being performed for Rutherford Risk. The take-away for her was that she was a person of interest to him. This, in turn, made him more interesting to her. Was he calculating enough to have had Lu Hao kidnapped? Was her invitation to the party related to the kidnapping?

He continued greeting guests and shaking hands on the way to a table reserved for them. She declined the offer of Champagne, as her head was already spinning.

"My father," he said, "began this business with a single handcart and a shovel."

"Yang Construction has a fine reputation as the number-one construction company in all of Shanghai. All of China."

"You flatter me."

"I repeat only that which I have heard," she said.

"We are honored to do business in such a great and charitable nation. We employ over twelve hundred in management positions, and many thousands in the workplace. All Chinese. No foreign blood other than a few consultants for appearances." When he smiled, his eyes became quiet. "For nearly twenty years now, our chief competition is The Berthold Group, your new employer, Chu Youya. Their presence has grown from consultant to major player. My father first did business with BG in nineteen eighty-two. Now look: they are building the Xuan Tower. Foreign firm, not Chinese. This is not right. I make no secret of my wish to see Xuan Tower completed by a Chinese firm, such as ours."

"I have just recently arrived in Shanghai," Grace replied. "I am sorry to hear of your differences with The Berthold Group."

"It is not your concern. Forgive me." He paused and offered her a drink for a second time. She declined. "I would like to come straight to the point, Chu Youya," he said. "I have the burden of many guests I must entertain. So you will please forgive me."

"Of course," Grace said, concentrating on keeping her face calm. Yang Cheng would never begin the ransom negotiations himself, but she prepared herself to look behind whatever his point was.

He lowered his voice. "The house of Allan Marquardt is destined to fail, Chu Youya. It is a foreign company, after all. No matter the lip service paid by our great country, a foreign company will never be allowed to attain the position of a Chinese company within her borders. Never! You and I both understand that. When Berthold fails, many people will be seeking employment. Accountants—even brilliant, young accountants— will be like ants after the same sugar. Great challenges present great opportunities," he continued, as if quoting a proverb. "Such an opportunity now awaits you, Chu Youya. You are Chinese like me, not foreign blood like them. You come work for me now, I will pay twenty-five percent more than Allan Marquardt, I will offer better benefits, and you will honor your family by working for a Chinese company."

"You do me a great honor, Yang Cheng." Grace hung her head, wondering if this was indeed the point of her invitation, or was he seeking to explore the possibility of negotiation by erecting the pretense of an employment deal between them? "I am deeply humbled. You will forgive me if I must take time to consider your generous offer."

"Time is sometimes a blessing, sometimes a curse. Use yours well. I am not the one in a hurry. You . . . on the other hand." He paused, tellingly. She thought the implication had to be connected to the ransom situation, but then became confused as he continued. "The Xuan Tower nears completion. Mark my words: it will not bear the name of Berthold Group at the time of its ribbon ceremony. It was never to be."

"In defense of my current employer," she said, letting it hang there, "certainly dozens, maybe hundreds of buildings in Shanghai have been financed and built with foreign money, whether in part or in whole. So many Western architects have made our skyline all the more interesting. The French. The Germans. The Arabs. Shanghai is truly metropolitan."

"Of this there is no doubt. Americans, too. Yes. But Xuan is to be the tallest building in world. A point of great Chinese pride. Chinese pride, not American pride."

"Yes, of course."

"There will be no confusion on this point. Do not fool yourself. Allan Marquardt's reach will stop here in Shanghai, and before the Xuan is open." His face grew red. The whiskey? She doubted it. Perhaps he'd had a promise from the government from the start. Lu Hao's kidnapping might be but a single mahjong tile pushed to send others falling. Financial conspiracy was an art form in Asia, practiced by all—from the street sweeper to people like Yang Cheng. He said, "Chinese profits are reinvested. Foreign profits travel across the oceans and never return. Enough is enough."

. . . *will stop here in Shanghai*. The Berthold Group had construction projects in cities all over China. Yang Cheng had slipped up. Was there a

bidding war underway for a Shanghai project that Yang Cheng was determined to win? Was confident he'd win? If he knew about Berthold's
secret payments to inspectors and subcontractors he could instigate an
investigation and immediately disqualify Berthold from any future bids,
ensuring his own success. Lu Hao's off-record books would play a critical
link in any such attempt to paint Berthold as corrupt.

"Please," he said, signaling a passing waitress. He snatched a glass of
Champagne for her and lifted his glass. She took a small sip.

"I await your decision," he said. "Before the dismissal for the National
Holiday, if you please." He'd named the same deadline as the ransom. Was
she to make that connection? Was she supposed to acknowledge it? "Will
you be joining your family on Chongming Island for the holiday?"

Every muscle tensed. His knowledge went well past her CV.

"If time permits," she said, lying. She had no intention of seeing her
father.

"Family is everything."

A threat? Or a simple reminder of her Chinese roots and where her
loyalty belonged?

"Country, ideology, family," she said, reciting priorities established in
her early schooling.

Yang Cheng's eyes went beady as he forced a smile. "Yes. And of all
these: family."

8:00 P.M.

Knox took issue with a person wearing a Bluetooth headset in public.
Alone behind the wheel, fine. Around the house, maybe. But it struck him
as pretentious, insular and ridiculous looking. If God had intended for man
to have a plastic horn protruding from one ear, he'd have put one there.

Katherine Wu kept touching her ear and going off into conversations
that didn't include him. She looked and sounded like a robot while her
body sent much different signals.

Knox forced a word in. "I understand The Berthold Group has encountered workforce slowdowns this week." A stab in the dark, but an educated one. Dulwich had told him as much. "Problems with materials delivery. Some trucking issues."

She flushed. "I manage Mr. Yang's schedule, Mr. Knox. You overestimate my position, I am afraid."

There was that word again; he wished she would stop that.

"Oh, I doubt that," he said. "It's all over Shanghai."

"Is it? And I am the last to hear. So typical. I wouldn't believe every rumor you hear."

"I thought that was you!" A Chinese woman's accented voice from behind Knox. A voice he knew. A voice he'd heard in many incantations, from joy to ecstasy.

Amy Xue, a petite beauty, wore a loose-fitting raw silk off-the-shoulder top and a pair of jeans that threatened her circulation. Her hair was done in an asymmetrical cut, with bangs slanting high to low, right to left. She wore no visible makeup, a gorgeous pair of black pearl earrings and a matching necklace. Her face was girlish—ageless—with long narrow hooded eyes that had first won his attention three years earlier.

Knox kissed her on both cheeks. "Help," he whispered. They held arms tightly as he introduced her.

"Amy Xue, this is Mr. Yang's assistant, Katherine Wu. She is showing me the view." He faced Ms. Wu. "Amy is one of my original trading partners," Knox said, "and a close friend. She has the finest pearls in all of Shanghai. But often, too expensive."

"Americans always want cheap, cheap, cheap," Amy said. "Like sound of bird."

"Sounds as if you two have been *trading* together for a long time," Katherine Wu said, intentionally impolite.

"As I said: old friends," Knox said, having not taken his eyes off Amy. Glad she'd confirmed his occupation without prompting.

"*You* may be old, John Knox, but not me. You come to my city, not tell me in advance?" Amy said. "How am I to hold best pearls for my best customer?"

"If you don't mind," he said to Wu, taking Amy by the elbow and leading her away.

Katherine Wu allowed them a fifteen-foot lead and then followed on a leash. Knox steered Amy toward the bar and finally caught sight of Yang and Grace at a table in the far corner of the cocktail lounge to the right. He felt an enormous sense of relief.

Amy didn't miss much. "Friend of yours?"

"My accountant."

"I've always thought spreadsheet a dirty word."

"Not like that, Amy. You know better than that."

"I know my favorite customer when I see him. I know you did not send e-mail telling me you were coming."

"It was a last-minute decision, this trip."

"Tell that to your accountant."

He ordered drinks for them both. A kir for her. Beer for him. The smoking at the bar bothered her, so they moved closer to a marble slab holding satay, egg rolls, pot stickers, *bao* and fruit. Knox ate the pot stickers and satay. Amy stuck to the fruit.

He thought about Danner. What he was eating, where he was sleeping. He felt shitty about his own present surroundings in the lap of luxury. The GPS burned a hole in his coat pocket. He'd slipped it from Grace's purse as they'd boarded the elevator. He hoped she wouldn't discover it missing before they separated for the night.

"Did you like last shipment?" she asked. What he liked was the way she slipped the chocolate-dipped strawberry between her lips and sucked on it.

"We could use more of the stone boxes and the black pearls. We're getting squeezed on the cultureds by other online sites. Fewer of those."

"We will give you what you want," she said, making him suffer through another strawberry.

"More of the custom designs. We can't compete on unstrungs. It's your beautiful designs that separate us."

"You flatter me, Knox."

"The bracelets are popular. More bracelets."

"Black pearls. More bracelets. Not a problem."

He considered asking Amy what she'd heard about the kidnapping. Rumor spread fast on the street. But self-preservation was about containment. Loyalties changed here as quickly as the weather.

"Amy, would you help me with something. Kind of like translating," he said, thinking about the GPS.

"You speak better than most Chinese."

"Your beauty is exceeded only by your exaggeration," he said in Mandarin. Then, returning to English. "Shanghai neighborhoods. Which are trickier than others for *waiguoren*. These are business addresses for possible suppliers. As safe as this city can seem, I don't want to end up somewhere I don't belong."

"Suppliers?"

"I promise: no pearls. No jewelry."

"You know this city well, Knox. You do not need me." She'd teed one up for him to ask about Lu Hao and Danner.

"I hear the city has become more dangerous for a *waiguoren* in recent days."

"Is that so?" she said, her voice as smooth as the surface of a fine pearl. She offered no way for him to judge her knowledge.

Knox spotted Bruno, the bar and restaurant manager, and signaled him. Bruno's size and comportment befit his name: he had a wide, serene face and a boyish smile, all tucked into a six-foot-one, two-hundred-and-eighty-pound body.

At Knox's request, Bruno led them into his back office and left them alone.

Knox took out the GPS and showed Amy the bookmarked locations.

She worked through descriptions of some of the areas where a *waiguoren* would stick out. "Not that there is any risk to you. No physical risk. This is Shanghai."

Knox memorized the map with her comments in mind. He wondered if she had possibly not heard of the kidnapping. She gave no indication otherwise. He thought all of Shanghai knew.

"You saw this, yes?" Amy asked, pointing to a tiny red dot the size of a pinhead alongside the character notation.

"I might have missed that," he said, having no idea what it was.

"It is a voice note." She scrolled along the bookmarked route. "Each location, a voice note."

Knox studied the device, thinking: *Voice notes?*

"Friend in International Pearl City try to sell me this same GPS," Amy said. "Gar-min," she said, making it sound Chinese.

She worked the device through some menus and Knox's breath caught as Danner's voice—calm and restrained—spoke. He had trouble concentrating on the actual message.

"Second floor, second door from the south corner. Husband and wife. Mid-forties—out of shape. No children."

Knox wanted to replay it just to hear Danner's voice.

"A note for each location?" he said, rhetorically.

"Evidently."

"Okay, then." He accepted the device back and pocketed it. A note for each location. It might prove a shortcut to nearly the same information they sought from Lu's accounting of the bribes: the precise location of each bribe recipient.

She said nothing more about it, showed no outward sign of interest or curiosity—as discreet as one could ask for.

"Here," she said, kissing him just off his lips, and catching his hand as it came up. "Do not wipe it off."

"Who's going to see us?"

"Everyone already has. If you do not want them asking the obvious questions, then leave it."

She was testing him. Her way of asking him what this was about while saving herself face.

He searched her exquisite eyes. "What are the obvious questions?"

"*Xing xing zhi huo ke yi liao yuan,*" she said. *A single spark can start a prairie fire.*

"*Shu dao hu sun san,*" he returned. An equally well-worn proverb. *When the tree falls, the monkeys scatter.* He warned of fair-weather friendship.

"I am no monkey," she said. "You must be careful, John. You never fail to surprise me. This makes me warm for you."

"It's not what you think," he said. All *waiguoren* were considered spies first.

"Have you no idea what I am thinking about?" She placed his thigh between her legs and pressed, letting him feel her heat. She craned up and whispered, "Maybe you can guess."

They kissed.

"Enjoy your accountant," she said, pulling away from him, making a show of her muscular backside.

Reentering the bar, he was hyperaware of the dozen eyes that found him—including Grace's.

He arrived at her table and addressed Yang. "If you are seducing my date, I will have to cry foul. As the host of such a perfect party—the drinks, the food, the guests—you outclass any man in attendance and play to an unfair advantage."

"The older the ginger, the hotter the spice," Yang answered. "He who pays the piper calls the tune." He glanced over to Grace.

"Only a fool would argue with such wisdom," she said.

"We were just wrapping up," Yang said. He moved to draw Grace's chair back. Grace stood, thanking him.

Katherine Wu appeared, seemingly out of nowhere. Knox noted how well she'd been trained, and kept his mind partially on Yang's security man, wondering if that training spilled over to him; wondering if he happened to know some Mongolians.

"I trust you will enjoy yourself," Yang said to Grace.

"The rest of the evening will pale by comparison to these few minutes in your company," she said.

Yang bowed ever so slightly. Together, he and his assistant moved toward the bar.

"Had enough?" Knox said.

"You can leave any time you would like."

"If I want permission, I'll ask," he said.

She indicated her own chin and passed him a napkin from the table. Knox wiped off Amy's lipstick.

"Part of my cover."

"You do not have to explain yourself to me," she said, sarcastically. "I wish to stay a while longer to see if I can get our host alone once more. I worry for Lu Hao. I do not doubt a man like this could be behind it."

"Did he offer to negotiate the ransom?" he asked, aiming for specifics.

"Leave when you wish. Perhaps we make a small scene and I am left on my own. Men can be so predictable."

"You could slap me," he said.

"Happily," she whispered.

"Six A.M.?" he asked.

"I don't forget so quickly," Grace said, her eyes lingering a little too long on the smudge still clinging to the corner of his lips.

"The corner of Huaihai and Maoming," he said. "Near the entrance to the Metro station."

She cracked him across the cheek, everyone nearby interrupted by the slap.

Knox nursed it and moved away, cutting through the crowd. She had a hell of a right hand.

9:10 P.M.

Knox took repeated precautions to avoid being followed, including arriving at the Jin Jiang Hotel, where he was officially registered. He went through the motions of riding the elevator to his room, both for the sake of his cover, and to try to trap anyone behind him he might have missed.

Once inside the room, he stopped short at the sight of a brown padded envelope on his bed. He felt through it before opening—something hard, slightly smaller than a paperback book.

He spent a minute giving the room a lived-in look. Kept one eye on the package, which was both stapled and taped shut.

Finally, he tore it open and slid out the contents revealing the smooth aluminum of an Iomega portable hard drive. He double-checked the envelope. No note.

Kozlowski. Had to be. Before calling Dulwich to deliver his daily briefing and inquire if the delivery of the hard drive was somehow his doing, Knox pulled out the GPS and listened to Danner's seven voice notes. Used as a dictation device, the notes were brief and cryptic, unemotional and nearly without personality. But Knox held on to the sound of the man's voice, replaying several of the messages just to hear him speak. He suffered nostalgia, a condition he thought he'd been cured of permanently following his contract service with the military. The last real friendships he'd forged had been in Kuwait, now too many years ago to count.

He needed to listen to the last voice memo several times to decipher Danner's verbal shorthand.

"Late addition to route. Heavy duffel left behind. Choke point. Civi guard took off, leaving two Huns as gatekeepers."

Huns . . . Mongolians? On Lu Hao's payout route? Added late in the game?

Knox mulled it over as he rode the elevator to the mezzanine and used his card key to enter the empty business office. Connected the hard drive by USB cable and studied the drive's directory. He tried search strings for "Lu," "bribes," "payoffs," "incentives," "Berthold." Nothing. The most recent Word files were letters written to his wife, Peggy. Reading the letters stirred guilt and anger in Knox. He owed Peggy a call. Something reassuring but vague. He found the most recently opened Excel files, also of little use: expense accounts. Nothing that pointed at Lu. Maybe Grace could find some files of significance, but at first blush, Knox doubted Lu Hao's books were anywhere on Danner's drive.

He disconnected the drive, hit the street and bought a second external drive and had the teenage clerk copy it. It took forty-five minutes; he tipped the kid a week's salary. He returned to his room and placed a call.

"Go," Dulwich said.

"Are you behind the package I found on my hotel bed?"

"Negative. What kind of package?"

Knox explained the package. Dulwich knew nothing of any hard drive, but clearly wanted to get his hands on it.

"I can't see Kozlowski helping me out," Knox said. "Too big a risk for him to take."

"Consider that he wants Danner back as much as, maybe more than, any of us. FYI: I was about to call you. DNA is a match. Good work. But listen, an American gone missing? This is on Kozlowski's watch, don't forget. If you get Danner back before the ransom's paid, the kidnapping will never be officially recorded. No black marks on anyone's service record. The government escapes a tricky one. The Party, and Kozlowski and the consulate, too."

"But I have no doubt—zero—that he's connected me to you and Rutherford. So why not just overnight it to you directly?"

"There would be records of that. You, on the other hand, just discovered something on your bed. He probably paid off a chambermaid or doorman. No legs. Now you're the one in position to do something with whatever's contained on there. He knows that. And if he found something on there, it makes all the more sense because his hands are tied. You become the sacrificial lamb. You say he's made the connection to us. He knows who we are, knows we're major players. Knows we specialize in kidnapping resolution and extraction. If you're him, who would you want on your side?"

"I suppose," Knox said.

"And consider this: that laptop was encrypted. Count on it. So your consulate buddy broke the encryption. That means he's got whatever you've got. He might have even removed a few files before giving you a copy. But who knows? Maybe it's a matter of making sense of it. Maybe there's something on there but he needs a second set of eyes."

"I can pass it on to Grace," Knox said. "But with two days to go, I'm not putting my nose into a computer screen."

"Understood."

"Is the date still firm?" Knox said.

"Yes."

"And?" Knox could hear it in the man's voice.

The line remained open, but Dulwich wasn't speaking.

"Sarge?"

"A finger."

The open line sparked with static.

"Whose?" Knox said, knowing already.

"Look on the bright side," Dulwich said. "We know Danny was alive as recently as yesterday. And within city limits."

The finger had retained warmth—the only explanation. Knox swallowed dryly. "Which finger?"

Silence.

"Which finger?" Knox repeated.

"Middle finger, right hand."

"Oh . . . shit." The kidnappers had seized the opportunity to send a message within the message. Knox's stomach turned. No DNA swab this time. He tried for air. "I'll kill these guys," he said.

"You and me both."

"Peggy?"

"No need to bother her with details."

"She has a right to know he's still alive. That is not a detail."

"This is what we do, buddy boy. We're on it."

"Any renegotiation?" Knox asked. Ransom sums were always reduced the closer to the drop.

"Marquardt handled it very well. It's down to a quarter million USD."

"Two-fifty K? For two hostages including one American? Are you shitting me?"

"We've adjusted our game plan to consider them amateurs," Dulwich said. "Berthold was prepared to go as high as ten million."

Knox filled him in on the Sherpa delivery man knowing a valid address and how this supported the amateurs theory.

"Game changer," Dulwich said. "If not a Triad, then maybe a co-worker or a competitor. But our modeling continues to suggest one of the bribe recipients. We need those people identified. You need to bring me Lu Hao's accounts."

The Mongolians did not strike Knox as amateurs. Yang Cheng's men perhaps.

"FYI: We followed up on Inspector Shen's inquiries with Marquardt about the American documentary film crew."

Knox said nothing, his mind back on the Sherpa and Danny's severed finger.

"We've confirmed one of the film crew is missing," Dulwich continued. "We got it from the head of housekeeping at the Tomorrow Square Marriott. He's a cameraman. Neither he nor his camera has been in his hotel room for over ten days."

"And this pertains to us how?"

"Listen, they're filming The Berthold Group. Right? The tower construction? Now the Chinese are all over it. So that means we're interested. It's a missing person. We've got a couple of those ourselves."

"Also kidnapped?"

"Who knows?"

"They sent a hand instead of a finger?"

"No one sent anything. That hand was fished out of the Yangtze."

"Dead?"

"How would we know? Hotel security can track key-card usage. Only housekeeping has been in and out of that missing guy's—this cameraman's room—over the past ten days. Sounds like he's toast."

"Again: why do I care?"

"You're a cold-hearted bastard. A man's missing." Said one of the coldest-hearted bastards Knox knew. "Inspector Shen pays Marquardt a visit a couple days after a kidnapping of a Berthold employee and is clearly investigating a *different* missing persons case. He's letting Marquardt know they can share the wealth—that one investigation may inform the other."

"Or he's threatening him not to investigate anything himself. Which means me."

"That would be you," Dulwich agreed. "Another reason it's worth discussing, don't you think?"

"Would the People's Armed Police, a guy like the inspector, ever employ Mongolians as muscle?" Knox asked.

"I'll tell you something: the Ministry of State Security would employ goddamn Attila the Hun if it suited their purpose. Why?"

"I've dropped a pair of guys," Knox said. "Both apparent Mongolians but holding legit National Residence Cards. They're all over this like flies. They were in the incentive loop."

"I'm interested because . . . ?"

"I recovered Danny's GPS. He left himself voice notes at each of Lu Hao's drop points."

Dulwich whistled.

"The latest addition to Lu Hao's payments could be these Mongolians."

He heard Dulwich's labored breathing. That comment had gotten his adrenaline pumping. "I can have Primer ask Marquardt about any Mongolians, any blackmail or extortion that predated the kidnapping, but I've got to think he would have volunteered that. We're working for him, after all."

Knox said, "The Mongolians beat the shit out of the delivery guy who left the ransom."

"You do work quickly."

"Their whole focus appears to be finding Lu. I don't see them behind this. More like 'way behind,' like we are."

"If they're proxies for the Chinese, you're fucked. Those boys will take you behind the shed and put one between your eyes."

"Thanks for that."

"I need you to make a second copy of Danny's hard drive," Dulwich said. "I need my tech guys here to get a look at that."

"Maybe the GPS and Danny's voice notes get us around needing Lu Hao's records."

"You have names? Amounts?"

Knox didn't answer.

Dulwich said, "Stay focused, Knox. Those books remain the brass ring."

"I thought getting them out alive was the brass ring."

"I'm just saying."

"And I'm not liking what you're saying." The Berthold Group being more concerned with creating a cover-up than winning extraction made corporate sense. "Am I supposed to read between the lines, Sarge?"

"There are no lines. The priority is human life," Dulwich confirmed. "That hasn't changed."

"If it does, I'm out. I'm solo."

"No argument from me."

"I wouldn't suggest overnighting the hard drive."

"No."

"Or sending it electronically."

"No. We'll put a courier in place."

"I thought you couldn't put people in place over here."

No immediate response. Then, "We need that drive today," Dulwich said. "We need to move the ransom's USD in-country. Marquardt doesn't have access to that kind of U.S. cash. You take care of your shit, I'll handle mine."

"If I'm giving this drive to someone, make it someone I know by sight. Send me a picture or something."

"Don't go all Pierce Brosnan on me."

"Daniel Craig. You gotta keep up."

"Fuck you." The line went dead.

Knox rode the scooter out onto Changle Lu and took as many precautions against tails as possible.

Twenty minutes later, he'd made the five-minute ride.

As he eased the guesthouse's back door closed, he heard the steady murmur of voices, the fill of background music and the clinking of glasses and tableware. He decided to bring a beer to his room. He would dress, and drive the GPS's bookmarked route as an intelligence gathering before doing so with Grace in a few hours.

He passed into the tiny dining and bar area. An off-the-shoulder raw silk blouse caught his attention. Amy Xue nursed a kir, her back to him. He approached and paused behind her.

"Join me," she said, patting the stool beside her. They met eyes in the bar mirror.

Knox slid onto the stool and ordered a beer.

"You have words with accountant?" she said in Mandarin.

"A slight misunderstanding," he said, also in Mandarin. So the ruse had fooled even Amy, he thought.

She switched to English. "I worry for you, John Knox. You snooping around."

"Who said I'm snooping?"

"You have money problems, you should say something."

"No money problems."

"If you need extension of credit, why did you not ask your friend?"

"Am I missing something?" he said. "Why would I need an extension of credit?"

"I ask myself same thing."

The Chinese could never face a request or a favor head-on. It always went around the block before arriving at the destination, or a middleman was used to save face for both sides.

"This has to do with my payment?"

"Yes, of course. I do not charge my friend interest," she said, "no matter that it is within my rights."

Interest? "Why would I owe you interest?" Knox asked, taking the more American route.

"You have spoken to your brother?" she asked.

What did Tommy have to do with this? Do not involve Tommy! "About?"

"John," she said, "last payment not received. I do not charge interest for valued customer."

It took Knox a moment. "Our last payment?"

"If you need more time, this can be negotiated."

"That was months ago."

"Two months, sixteen days," she said.

"You didn't get the wire? You should have said something."

"I am saying something. Did not receive wire transfer of funds. Did not receive any funds."

"You should have said something *sooner*. We issued payment, Amy. A wire transfer to your bank in Hong Kong, same as always. My brother . . ." Evelyn, their bookkeeper, never made such mistakes. Tommy, maybe. It wasn't impossible, given his condition, but it wasn't likely. "I'll look into it immediately."

"You are a good customer, John Knox. *Favored* customer." Amy considered every customer her best customer, but there was something more that she wasn't bringing up. Still, it hung between them. "You miss a payment, not a problem. But when you did not mention it tonight . . . well, this is not like you. Not like a most valued customer."

"We paid," he said.

"And the wire cleared?" she asked.

"I'll talk to my brother and my bookkeeper. Please forgive this failure, Amy. This dishonors me greatly." Contrition was an important part of business relationships with the Chinese.

"You can make it up to me," she said, coyly. "Show me interest, not pay it."

"No shortage of interest."

Knox wrote GRAND CATHAY in block letters on the bar napkin—the name of his room. He pinched it beneath the base of her Champagne glass. Amy kissed him and slipped off the bar, taking precautions in a city where the rumor mill spun faster than a turbine.

Having left the guesthouse by the front door, she circled around to the back door and joined him in the guestroom. Joined him without a word spoken between them. Joined him in a sweaty, athletic indulgence that ended with her straddling him, their eyes locked, their shared rhythm near perfect, their needs fulfilled.

"Sometimes I wish I still smoked," she said, lying on her back.

"Oh, you smoke," Knox said. And she hit him.

Knox rose up onto an elbow to enjoy the look of her. He could see her heart beating quickly at the V of her ribcage.

"If a body could be put into words," he said, "yours would be poetry."

Her smile widened. "Silver tongue, cold heart."

He took her hand and placed it on his chest. "Does it feel cold to you?"

She shook her head, still smiling, and staring at the ceiling fan. "It is an expression is all." She hesitated. "I am worried for you."

He turned on the television and cranked the volume. He trusted Fay not to bug his room, but believed in taking precautions. "No worries," he said softly.

The iPhone rang. He scrambled to get to it and then considered not answering it. But he couldn't help himself. "Yeah?"

"Who do you think you are?" Grace's shrill voice caused Knox to distance the phone from his ear. He moved away from the bed and made a face to indicate his surprise. "I will tell you: a common thief. A liar. A cheat. Worse than all: a man whose word cannot be trusted."

"Listen to me a minute," Knox pleaded.

"The GPS is the key to our success. We are partners. And yet you steal it from me. *Steal it!* A common thief! You delay our efforts. You cost me panic and fear when I cannot find it. How dare you treat me with such disrespect!"

"If you would just . . . listen."

The line went dead.

"What have you gotten yourself into?" Amy asked.

"An unhappy customer," he said, returning to her.

"You see? You have problem with customer, too."

"It's true." He'd known Amy long enough to believe he could trust her, though trust was more of a concept here than a practice. Together they'd bent enough export laws to hold weight over the other.

He nibbled her tenderly and she startled.

"Oooh. I like that."

The television continued to blare, though the sounds it covered were no longer of conspiracy and collusion. Instead they were the sounds of secret touches, pressures and timing. Of instruction and direction. Of a woman's cries muffled by a pillow and a man's growl as skin slapped skin and traffic hummed. Of shared guilty laughter between two people who knew no one deserved something so good.

When she had gone, Knox called down and ordered an espresso. He showered and dressed and double-checked the knife he carried, as if by looking at it he could hone its blade.

Then, he placed the call he'd not wanted to make. He used the iPhone, allowing Dulwich to pay for it—knowing it could not be eavesdropped upon.

Tommy answered on the third ring. Detroit sounded next door.

"Hey, bro," Knox said.

"Johnny!" Tommy was the only person Knox tolerated using the nickname. His brother sounded as excited as if an ice cream truck had just pulled up in front of the house.

With proper medication, supervision and a solid routine, Tommy did all right. He could handle the responsibilities of their partnership. He indulged in video games. He'd pretty much conquered public transportation. He had a start on adulthood, if not there yet. Thankfully, he wasn't inclined to look for the man behind the curtain. Knox played his role close to the vest.

The missed payment to Amy was a red flag. Knox did not want to access any of their online bookkeeping from China. He didn't want to give the Internet-sniffing Chinese authorities a leg up.

"How goes it?" Knox asked.

"Just fine," Tommy said.

"Business good?"

"Couldn't be better."

"Small problem over here."

"Where?"

"Shanghai. Amy never received her wire."

Silence.

"The pearl lady."

"But that was months ago," Tommy said.

Impressive, Knox thought. "Yes, exactly."

"Wouldn't we know if a wire didn't go through?" Tommy struggled with the concept of moving money electronically.

"We should, yes."

"You mean *I* should," Tommy said.

"I didn't say that."

"It's what you're thinking."

"Don't go there, Tommy. It's *not* what I was thinking."

"You think I screwed up."

"If you screwed up, I'd say you screwed up. Since when do I mince words?"

"Then what? If not that, why are you calling?"

"Because we owe a lot of money to an important supplier and I want to get on it. That's all there is to it. Don't make this bigger than it is."

"I'll have to check with Eve." Evelyn Ritter, their bookkeeper and accountant.

"Yes. That's where we start. Exactly. A record of the wire and, if for some reason it didn't go through—"

"We resend," Tommy said, agreeing.

"Are you writing this down?"

"I'm not stupid. Of course I am."

"We'll need to check other payments as well. Eve can help. I don't get how she could have missed this one, but stranger things have happened. Bet you anything it's on this end: you know Chinese banks."

Tommy had a schoolboy crush on their attractive bookkeeper. Knox did not like the way the relationship had developed—he didn't know if he was jealous of Eve for winning Tommy's attentions, or if he questioned why an attractive, smart woman would express interest in someone with Tommy's limited social skills. But Eve spent time with his brother—quality time—and that was a blessing he wouldn't discourage.

"How are things otherwise?" Knox asked.

"Tigers suck."

"There's news."

"How about you?" Tommy asked.

"Looking into importing vintage motorcycles." He'd lived with the lie long enough to begin to buy into it.

"Seriously?"

"They have some real beauties over here. They copied BMW and Russian designs for years. Better than the originals. We can get 'em for a song, bring 'em up to standards and sell them for five, maybe eight-X."

"I thought I'm not allowed to ride motorcycles," he said, sounding younger all of a sudden.

"Some of them have sidecars. Maybe we'll make an exception."

"An exception," Tommy said, mimicking. A signal he was tiring. Phone calls were harder for him than face-to-face. Tommy's doctors could not explain half of what went on—or failed to go on—in his brain.

"I'll sign off," Knox said.

"Expensive call."

"E-mail me what you find out from Eve."

"I'll e-mail you," Tommy said.

"You're a good man, Tommy."

"Miss you, Johnny."

He hung up. Knox kept the phone to his ear a little longer than necessary, his heart working like timpani. He trod softly as he descended the stairs, heeding Fay's warning about the night watchman, and slipped outside, carefully shutting the back door behind him.

"Enjoy yourself?" Grace's voice at his back.

Knox didn't miss a beat. "That's the general idea."

He turned and she stepped out of shadow. It wasn't Grace's presence that shocked him, but the fact that he hadn't spotted her.

"She is pretty, in a slutty kind of way," Grace said.

"I didn't know you cared," he said.

"You are going out on the route," she said, seeing the helmet.

"Yes."

"Without me."

"That was the plan," Knox admitted.

She crossed her arms defiantly. She couldn't bring herself to look at him.

"This is not what we agreed to," she said, speaking to the lane.

"No."

"Then why?" she asked.

"It's what I do. The way it's done. It's called advancing."

"Do not patronize me, John Knox."

"That's all it was going to be: ride the route. Make sure it's safe. De-termine multiple points of egress. I was not going to ride you—us—into a possible ambush. My friend . . . this was his job. It's what he did for me. I'm doing the same thing."

"'For me'?" Loaded with sarcasm.

"Nothing more, nothing less." He told about Danner's hard drive, about his wanting—*needing*—her to look over its contents. Admitted it was beyond his current patience level.

"I agree to this," she said, softening some.

"I would have been there at six A.M.," he pleaded. "Believe that or not, that's the truth." He hesitated. "As to the woman—"

"No!" She moved toward the scooter. "We do this tonight. Now, when these . . . criminals are in their homes."

"We drive it first," he said. "The entire route. We don't approach any of them until first light. Any of these people—all of them—know their neighborhoods. They can navigate in the dark far better than we. Patience and planning, or we don't do this at all." He motioned toward the scooter.

She stood there immovable, intractable and willful.

"Please," he said.

Two motorcycles turned into the mouth of the lane, racing toward them at a high-pitched whine. Knox saw apology and regret in her eyes: she'd allowed herself to be followed.

Both bikes veered toward Knox, skidding out from under the riders, who leaped off and dumped them toward Knox like bowling balls aimed at pins. Knox timed his jump well, though was tripped up by a rear fender as he came down. He sprawled onto the concrete, a boot heel aimed for his face before he could recover.

Grace took him out. The boot missed Knox's face.

The other rider had gone down onto a knee while dumping his bike. Knox rolled toward him, stood, and kicked him in the groin. The man lurched forward reflexively. Knox kneed him in the face and he was out.

Grace's opponent suffered. Her first kick had thrown him into the back wall of the Quintet and off of Knox. A moment's hesitation on his part—disbelief such lethal force could come from a hundred-pound woman—cost him. She went after him like he was a punching bag, and he sank.

"I know this one!" she called out to Knox as she continued to deliver a volley of blows to the man's abdomen, reducing him to the fetal position. As the man sank, she searched his pockets and came up with a wallet.

"Overconfident fools," she said.

"Know him, how?" Knox asked.

"Yang Cheng's cocktail party."

Knox got a closer look. She was right: the bodyguard type never far from the party host.

"Damn," he said, impressed.

He got the scooter going and aimed for the street. Grace threw a leg over the seat and wrapped her arms tightly around his waist and they were off.

WEDNESDAY
September 29

2 days until the ransom

12

The first pass amounted to a surveillance run. Knox drove with Grace directing him from behind while holding the GPS. He replayed Danner's voice notes in his head and relayed them to Grace. Afterward, they killed an hour in Jing An Park awaiting the sunrise.

"I want you to keep this," he said, passing her his copy of Danner's hard drive. "Insurance. Also, we're going to need a laptop. We need to study the contents of that drive A-SAP."

She looked somewhat confused.

"As soon as possible," he said.

"Is not a problem. Laptops are for sale on every block in Shanghai. And cheap."

Knox laughed, and she followed, covering her mouth as if ashamed. Knox wanted to tell her to show her smile; he said nothing.

"Do you love her?" she asked.

He considered the question thoughtfully, and how to answer. "Do you know particle physics? You accelerate a proton or neutron and smash it and it gives off energy and breaks into smaller particles, which you then capture? That's how I see love. I've experienced the breaking up thing, the energy. I'm still waiting for the capture." He added, "Back at my place . . . it wasn't what you think," he said.

"You do not know what I think," she said.

"We don't control these things," he said. "Do you understand? Some things control us."

"I understand perfectly well."

"What controls you?" he asked.

She snorted.

"The connection to Lu Hao's family," he speculated, having tried before.

She flashed him a penetrating look. "Lu Hao's older brother is called Lu Jian."

He waited her out.

"I was responsible for Lu Hao's placement with Berthold."

"You feel responsible. Tell me about Lu Jian."

It was more than that. His comment drove her to silence. "I do not think so."

"A romance."

She didn't deny it.

"Current or past?"

No answer.

"Or both," he said. "That's part of this for you."

"There are family obligations."

"Face."

"What would you know of face?"

"My brother. I told you about him. Perception and reality are two very different things. Maybe I know more about face than you might expect."

"I doubt it."

"You're hoping for a second chance," he speculated. "You save the little brother, maybe you save the romance."

She shot him a vicious look. But she didn't deny it.

Not long after, the sky lightened and they returned to the scooter. Street traffic was sparse, though the corner *bao* shops teemed. The smell of charcoal and grilled pork filled the air.

The routes and destinations were more familiar to them now. Knox slowed the scooter as they neared the first location. Danner's voice told him it was a childless couple in their forties. He pulled the scooter to the curb.

Grace jumped off the back and threw her helmet to him.

"You need to stay here!" she said in Mandarin, for the sake of the people passing on the sidewalk.

Knox did not want to make a scene. He knew any *waiguoren*—any American accent, no matter how good—would stand out. But he had no intention of standing by and leaving Grace alone.

He slipped off his helmet, pulled on a ball cap and hurried across the street chasing her.

"Foolish!" she said, refusing to look at him.

"The way we talked about," he said. "The way I laid it out."

Together, they hurried up the darkened exterior staircase to a second-floor balcony and around the corner to the second door from the street side of the apartment building. Knox put his back to the wall, out of sight of the door.

She knocked and a moment later the door came partially open.

"*Wei?*" a woman's voice speaking Mandarin. *Yes?*

"I have the delivery you've been expecting," Grace said.

The door swung open farther as the woman called out, "*Laogong!*" *Husband.*

The sound of shuffling slippers announced the husband's arrival.

Grace threw open the door. Knox stepped through, shoving the unsuspecting man back. Grace shut the door. Knox drove the husband onto a stool that overturned as he fell, and Knox followed him to the floor on one knee. The room was sparsely decorated but well kept, with a tile floor and a low coffee table surrounded by wooden stools.

Knox spoke an angry, unforgiving Shanghainese. "I will tear your sack off your body, my friend, and give it to your wife as a souvenir."

A plastic ID and lanyard landed on the floor next to Knox. Grace had tossed it to him, from a hook by the door.

"Steel inspector," she said.

"The man who paid you—" Knox said.

His victim shook his head frantically shouting, "No good! No good!"

"We have come for him."

"Bu xing!" The man backpedaled, trying to get Knox's hand off his throat. Then: "I do not know!" Repeatedly. His face had gone the color of an old bruise; his eyes occupied a third of his face and were growing.

"You tell me now," Knox said, reaching between the man's legs, "or you piss blood for a week."

The color in his face deepened.

"He paid you, my friend," Knox said. "Do not lie to me!"

"I take the money! It is true. Each week, I take the money. For this I give favorable quality standard reports. May Buddha forgive me. I know nothing more than payment did not come this week. Nothing more, I tell you!"

"Enough!" Grace called out.

Knox released him and shot her a look that warned her not to interfere.

"And this week?" Knox asked the man. "Did you still give favorable report?"

The man flinched and recoiled as Knox lifted his hand toward him.

"I did not think so," Knox said. He scooped up the man's ID and pocketed it. "If you ever take so much as another *fen* for such a favor, your family will pay for generations." Knox knew a threat to a man's lineage was the most serious of all.

"I told you!" cried the wife. "I warned you nothing good came of such greed." She, with both a new refrigerator and a dishwasher in her kitchen. Not even expats had dishwashers.

"Your phones," Knox said to the man.

He glared back, puzzled.

"Both of your phones," he said to the couple.

They produced them. Knox collected the SIM cards and crushed what remained.

He grabbed Grace by the arm and they backed out, pulling the door closed behind them.

"Walk calmly," Knox said.

Grace was unfazed. Knox's right hand was shaking.

"We might have handled that differently," she said, accusingly.

"That's how it's going to be," Knox said. "Exactly like that until we're convinced the person's telling the truth."

"And if they know each other? If he should call ahead to warn the others?"

"That's partly why I took the phones," he said.

"I think you took the phones to look at who he calls, who he knows."

Knox said nothing. She was too smart by half.

"But if he should call ahead," she said, repeating herself, provoking him.

"What do you want me to say?"

She didn't answer. Together, they climbed onto the scooter and drove off, Grace holding Knox around the waist. She read directions from the GPS while Knox recalled everything Danner had recorded as if it had been left for him personally.

They moved between districts and neighborhoods, honing their interrogation skills with each stop. Grace was forced into the fray twice, responding with a technical precision and efficiency to her movement and force. Together, they manhandled and subdued three more recipients of Lu Hao's bribes, bringing the total to four, when they found themselves facing a cluster of impressive high-rise apartments overlooking the Huangpu River.

Danner's voice notes had the floor and apartment numbers as well as comments about the lobby security.

Knox passed Grace a ball cap for the sake of security cameras.

"These buildings," she said. "No expats. All Party officials, Chinese businessmen. Important people. Everyone in Shanghai knows this address."

"Construction inspectors?"

"We do not know for certain, *neh*? Not until we find Lu Hao's accounts."

She pushed this on him, reminding him he had failed to secure the accounts. She couldn't analyze what she hadn't yet seen.

"Every kind of successful person lives in this compound," she said. "Inspectors? Perhaps. Also city planners and regional supervisors. Architects. Engineers. Decision-makers."

"It's early yet," Knox said. "Every reason to believe they will be at home."

"Two are in the same tower," she reminded him.

"Yes. The fifth floor and the twelfth."

"Once we have visited the one, it is highly unlikely—*not likely at all*," she emphasized, "that a second interview will be possible in the same building."

Interview, he was thinking.

With each stop, Knox sunk into a darker place. He'd begun to enjoy the punishment he delivered, to transfer his anger over Danner's situation into his fists. To look forward to the next stop. He'd failed to fully consider the conflict this building presented until he heard her voice it.

"That is a problem," he said. "We can't pick one over the other. People in power—the way you describe these people—these could be the people we're looking for."

"Yes. We must coordinate our efforts. Time this perfectly."

"You're suggesting we split up?" he said. She'd been complaining about his techniques.

"Is there a choice?"

He imagined her gloating. "There's always a choice," he said.

"Then I will take the fifth floor," she said. "If they throw me out the window, it is shorter to fall."

"You're going to joke about this?"

"I am learning," she said.

Knox laughed aloud.

"You understand—" he began.

Grace put her fingers to his lips, stopping him. "Much more than you can possibly convince yourself of."

She removed her hand just as fast as she'd used it to silence him. There was no hidden meaning to be read into her touching him. There was nothing suggestive implied by it. Yet Knox felt his lips tingle well after her fingers were gone, reminded for the first time since the cocktail party of her femininity, and the power women wielded over him, intentionally or otherwise.

He said, "We have two choices for gaining entry—subterfuge or power."

"You leave this to me," she said. "We will go to the twelfth-floor apartment together. From there, I will leave you and take care of the fifth."

They made it past two doormen in the lobby by Grace holding on to Knox's arm and acting incredibly sexy. She turned it on so quickly it surprised him, which was her intention. She ran her hands all over him, while giggling and purring. She pulled his hand onto her backside and he held it there. The boys—for that's all they were: boys in gray suits— couldn't keep their eyes off her and weren't about to interrupt such a woman with a *waiguoren* involved.

They rode the elevator to the twelfth floor with Grace continuing to act her part, well aware the security boys would be attempting to follow them using security video.

Grace gambled correctly that a maid—the *ayi*—would answer the door. Taking a cue from Danner's voice note, she mentioned a teenage boy to the Chinese woman at the door, saying she had important information that could keep the family from embarrassment. The door came open.

Knox swept inside. Grace pulled the door shut, leaving Knox cupping the unsuspecting maid's mouth as he dragged her to the telephone and pulled the phone off-hook, engaging the line and ensuring an outgoing call could not be made. The maid went limp, having passed out from fright. He left her on the floor and hurried down the hall. Grace stayed behind to tie her up.

The first bedroom belonged to a sleeping teenager who didn't move— wouldn't move. "Only child, male," he recalled Danner saying. Next door was an empty guest room, and finally the master suite.

He moved for the bed, but was jumped from behind—*a stupid mistake!* he realized. He'd made too much noise with the *ayi*. A male with a knife, and he knew how to use it. Knox turned, but too slowly. The knife punched for him. Knox blocked the second lunge. He was a fat Chinese man in checkered pajamas, sweating from nerves in the glow of a green nightlight.

Knox wrestled the knife free and kicked it across the floor. The man kidney-punched him. Knox slumped, surprised by how much it hurt.

He recovered to block another attempt and then, with an opening, he kneed the man in the groin, and a fist to below the ribcage. The man sank to the floor. The wife came screaming out of bed carrying a sheet. She tripped on the sheet, exposing her nudity, tripped again and fell.

Knox, now in full control of the man, punished him with a flurry of fists.

"You have taken money on the Xuan Tower project," Knox said in steady Mandarin. "Do you deny it?" He clenched the man by the throat.

"You are wrong!" the man wheezed.

Knox leaned his weight into the man's throat.

The wife tried to hide herself with the sheet, failing miserably. She skidded back on her bottom toward the wall, sobbing.

"I seek information about the one delivering your money," Knox said.

"Fuck you."

Knox dragged him toward the French doors. "All men fall at the same speed," Knox said, "as you are about to find out."

"Husband!" the wife called out.

He heard Grace before he saw her. She was craning over the cowering woman.

"You keep your tongue in your hole, or I will tear it out," Grace said. She moved across the room and opened the French doors for Knox.

Knox's victim saw he was outnumbered, saw the doors swing open.

"Shi de!" he cried. *Yes!* "It is true. All true!"

Knox squatted and questioned him. Grace crossed the room to gag and tie up the wife. She then took off down the hall.

The man confessed to accepting the bribes in exchange for "harmony on the construction site," but claimed to know nothing of Lu Hao's disappearance or whereabouts.

Knox told him if he reported their visit, even to security within the building, it would result in news of the bribes going public.

By arrangement, Knox did not go to the fifth floor, just as Grace would not return to the twelfth. Instead, he left by a stairway door and returned to the scooter, awaiting her. She met him less than five minutes later, her face flushed and shining with perspiration.

"Anything?" he said.

"Nothing," she said.

"One left."

"Getting late."

"Or early," he said. "Yes. But worth a try. Is it okay with you?"

She looked surprised he would ask. "Yes. Okay."

The final stop came with an ominous note from Danner: "Recent addition to route. Extremely narrow alley. Ground floor, second or third door. Choke point."

No mention of an individual. No exact apartment. Of greater concern, and explaining Danner's lack of specificity, was his categorizing it as a choke point—a funnel with limited access, making anyone who entered vulnerable.

"This one is not good," Knox said at a stoplight as they followed the GPS track. "Not enough information. Danner didn't like it."

"Latest addition to Lu Hao's stops," she said, reminding him of Danner's voice memo. "If we had an exact date this could help me with the Berthold financials."

"If I ever get you Lu's books."

"We will get them."

The Muslim neighborhood was small but heavily populated. Dress changed, as did the smells of the street food.

Once again, Knox studied the entrance to the narrow alley off Ping Wang Jie Road. Once again, from a distance. Danner's description was accurate: a choke point.

"Let me walk it," she said. "Alone."

"No."

"I will not stop, will not ask questions. Just a walk-through." She handed him the GPS indicating the lane, which appeared on the virtual map as a shortcut between two parallel streets. "A *waiguoren* cannot do this, Knox."

At that moment Knox spotted an expressionless man coming out of the alley and looking toward them. *Civi guard took off,* he recalled Danner saying. A lane guard, a Party employee assigned to a neighborhood as a security detail. Not police, but someone gaining experience ahead of the application process; typically, a person eager to prove himself. Knox knew Grace was right.

"Go," he said. "I'll meet you around the other side. But if I don't see you in five, I'm coming in after you."

"Please. I will be fine."

She slid off the scooter, handed him her helmet and disappeared through the traffic.

Grace noticed the lane guard turning to follow her. She kept up a brisk but unhurried pace. She would not give him anything to feed on. Behind her, she heard the scooter head off.

The lane was nearly narrow enough to touch walls with her arms extended. Stucco walls raised three stories overhead, interrupted by rusted wrought-iron balconies. It felt cloistered; the air smelled stale. She passed a series of doorways on her right and then caught herself staring at a green motorcycle. It was the combination of the unusual deep green color and the basket on the back fender. She'd seen it in the lane outside the Sherpa's apartment. The Mongolians had been watching him. That, in turn, meant they'd seen her and Knox enter the residence.

The guard followed down the lane behind her.

A choke point, she recalled.

She walked past the motorcycle, committing its tag to memory. Stole a glance toward the small window by the door to her right: curtained shut. Passing the next apartment, its door hung open. She absorbed the layout: a single room of perhaps nine square meters. In this case, limited furnishings—a pair of bamboo mats on the floor and some stacked aluminum bowls. A slightly larger window in the back wall.

The footfalls of the guard suggested he'd closed the distance with her, now only a few meters behind. She continued walking, neither fast nor slow, knowing that had it been Knox in this lane the guard would have confronted him.

Two doors down, she saw another open door. Despite what she'd told Knox, she stopped and called inside, in part as an act for the security man. A Muslim woman met her. Grace lowered her voice, taking a chance.

"Hello," she said in Mandarin. "You are familiar with the northerner two doors down?"

The woman nodded. "A Mongolian. And not the only one!"

Grace nearly cried out with the confirmation.

"One of his friends owes me money," Grace said.

The woman's eyes hardened. "I would forgive the debt, cousin."

"Do you see his friends often?"

Another slight nod. "Yes," the resident said, in an even softer voice than Grace was using. Her voice brought chills up Grace's arms.

"Do they live with him, these other men?"

"Down the lane," the woman answered. "Two to a room."

A choke point.

"How many?"

"Five, all told."

That left three in good health. "The reason I ask," Grace said, "is that I would rather not be seen by the one that owes me. He is not pleasant."

"All rough men."

"Yes," Grace said. "Mongolians are rough."

The woman did not contradict her. "In pairs," she said. "Roommates. The leader lives by himself."

"Leader?"

"They travel like a pack of dogs."

"Yes." Grace assembled the data, wondering how far to push it. "Two rooms," she proposed.

The woman's icy stare was difficult to read.

Grace sensed she'd overstayed her welcome. "You have been generous with me, dear lady."

"Not at all," the woman said.

Grace backed away. The woman stopped her.

"Again. My advice? Forgive the debt. Do not deal with these dogs. We—those of us in the lane—leave them to themselves."

Grace nodded. "Peace be with you."

"And you."

The woman pushed the door shut.

The lane guard had lit a cigarette and sat himself down on a stool by a pair of potted plants and smoked. He'd been watching, but out of earshot.

Grace moved on, a moment later leaving the lane and entering onto a busy street. She walked a block before crossing and joining Knox on the scooter.

"Well?" Knox said.

"Drive," she ordered. "I'll tell you as we go."

Knox pulled out into traffic and Grace wrapped her arms around him. She let go, jerked back and cried out softly.

"Knox! Knox!" Her left hand was smeared with his blood. She held it out to his side on display for him.

"I'll be damned!" he said.

"You are bleeding."

"I know that."

"You did not tell me!" She shouted to be heard over the engine.

"Adrenaline," he said, as if that explained anything.

"We go to your place at once."

"We can't," he said. "Our visitors. Remember? In the lane? They know that location now. Eight-oh-eight is out. I cannot return. And we can't go to your place either. You were compromised when we fought them. They followed you, possibly from the party, but you went back to your place." She didn't contradict him. "So they have your apartment. They have the guesthouse. They want us, or they wouldn't have come after us like that. Neither of us is going home."

She considered what he said for several long seconds. "I know a place," she said. "We can go there and decide what to do later."

"It can't be a friend."

"It's a service apartment rental. But not with the best reputation."

"But you know it, first hand?"

"I know it. I have stayed there." She thought back to Lu Jian.

Service apartments, with kitchens and maid service, were used for long-term stays by traveling businessmen in lieu of more expensive hotel rooms.

"That could work," he said.

"We must hurry," she said, panic rising in her voice. "You are bleeding badly."

He had her trigger now: the sight of blood. Everyone had one. His was abuse: the strong taking advantage of the weak. It left him sick.

"Honestly," he said, leaning back to call out to her, "I didn't even know it was there. I'm fine."

"You are bleeding, John. Bleeding badly. Pull over. I will make a call. Then I drive."

She'd called him by his given name for the first time. He smiled through an unexpected wince of pain as she held to him tightly while he pulled the scooter to the side of the road.

8:00 A.M.
JING AN TEMPLE
JING AN DISTRICT
SHANGHAI

Melschoi paid a sorry-looking vendor seven *yuan* for a bundle of incense, cursing the amount under his breath, and entered the dimly lit temple. The cross-legged, gold-leafed Buddha rose thirty feet high, surrounded at the knees by pomelo fruit and fresh flowers. The fragrant smoke hung heavily in the air, wrapping the idol's shoulders like a scarf.

Melschoi was not there to worship, but because one of his two remaining uninjured men was assigned to survey Yang Construction's security man, No Nuts Feng. His man had followed Feng into an alley behind Quintet and had watched as a woman and an American had pummeled both Feng and another man.

Melschoi's spy had held back but had subsequently lost the two in traffic—in Melschoi's mind a punishable offense. That left him Quintet, and the night watchman Melschoi had just followed to the temple.

There was probably a Chinese proverb about there being more than one way to skin a cat, but Melschoi didn't want to hear it.

His Beijing boss was so well connected that he had ears in every keyhole. How long until he learned of the compounded mistakes Melschoi and his men were making? How long until he cut bait? And what then? A bone crusher sent for him in the night? Police? Arrest? Melschoi had no leverage over his Beijing employer—knew nothing but that the money was good and it kept coming.

Despite his agnosticism, Melschoi took a moment to pray for the opportunity and funds to return to his homeland and make things right for his family.

The subsequent talk with the night watchman came down to what everything in this city came down to: money. Melschoi offered five hundred *yuan* and the man was ready to give him his first-born.

The foreigner had had a lady visitor at the guesthouse that same night. The woman had waited for him and had engaged in typical bar conversation with the barmaid. The conversation had centered on jewelry because the guest owned a pearl shop in International Pearl City in Hongqiao.

Melschoi would have words with this woman. He would know all she knew about this American and what the man wanted with Lu Hao. She was all he had. She, not this gold idol, was to be his savior.

And everyone knew the fate of all saviors. They were sacrificed.

9:00 A.M.
CHANGNING DISTRICT
SHANGHAI

"Wo de tian!" Grace led the way into the furnished service apartment, having secured it as easily and nearly as quickly as a hotel room. The biggest threat came from having to show identification; Grace had gotten around this by implying she and Knox were having an affair. For a negotiated price, the landlord had supplied the ID. She carried several shopping bags with her, having made stops along the way.

The floor was a hideous marble tile; the furniture, black leather and aluminum; the lighting, recessed halogen. The view was of another tower across a lane.

Grace pulled the drapes and blinds.

Blood caked his hand as Knox slipped out of the ScotteVest, his shirt damp with it. "I could use your help, if you have the stomach for it."

She backed up a step, repelled by the sight of his bloody shirt.

He pulled off his sticky T-shirt with some difficulty. Grace stepped up to help him. She turned away at sight of the wound.

"It looks worse than it is."

"You've been stabbed."

"Yes," Knox said, fingering it. Two older scars, one on his chest, one across his ribs, looked much worse. "The guy jumped me. He landed one before I reacted. My bad. Can you help?"

Knox moved into the bathroom and she followed, carrying one of the bags. With her looking on, he washed the wound and dried it. He grimaced as he stabbed an antibacterial pad deep into the wound and left it there for a count of thirty. Squeezed a bead of gel into the edges of the wound and turned to Grace. Her color had returned; she didn't look the least put off.

She snipped the applicator on the end of a tube of Super Glue.

"You hold it closed for me," he suggested.

"I will apply the glue," she said. "You hold it closed. You need stitches."

"This will work." He pointed out his two scars. "Stitches. No stitches, only glue." The glued scar was gnarly and thick.

He pinched the skin together as tight as he could get it. "Go." He held it as still as possible for five minutes. Some of the two-inch wound held shut; some pulled back open. Three applications later, he was sealed shut.

"How did you get these scars?" she asked.

"Most are shrapnel. Dulwich and I . . . we were in convoy when an IED, a bomb, took out the road. Sarge's vehicle took the brunt of it. I caught some metal."

"You went after him." She made it a statement.

"Those two years . . . that's most of my scars. You start out that kind of work thinking you're bulletproof. You end up waiting for your contract to expire."

"So Mr. Dulwich owes you."

"It doesn't work like that. Americans don't think like that."

"Everyone thinks like that."

"Tell me about the Mongolians," he said.

She seemed tempted not to change the subject, but relented. "Five, all living in the lane."

"And Lu Hao paid a visit to one of them."

"So it would seem," she said.

"For a large payoff, according to Danny."

"No way around needing Lu Hao's books," she said. "We must not lose focus."

"It's a work in progress. Danny's hard drive may help us there. But the Mongolians mean something. Are they just after their share? Could it be that simple?"

"Why not?"

"Or are they working for the police? Or State Security? Someone who could obtain the proper documents for them."

"Freelance? It is possible. In that case, for what you've done to them . . ."

"It would explain their watching Lu's apartment," Knox said. "They're keeping tabs on you and me because we showed up there. Maybe they think you're the next Lu Hao and they want to make sure you know they're due their share."

"It would be easier to speak with me. No need to follow."

"Yeah, I know," Knox said. He didn't like it either.

She'd already told him about the green motorcycle.

"So they beat the crap out of the Sherpa."

"Hoping to find Lu Hao."

"But like us, it's just an empty warehouse. So they keep an eye on the Sherpa and we come along. By now they know an American has taken out two of them. That makes us persons of interest to them."

"Or targets."

Knox moved only slightly and winced with the pain.

"The incentive budget would have increased to account for the Mongolian payment. Your Mr. Danner said it was a recent addition. That money must be accounted for. The Berthold EOY records should account for it."

"There's always just asking Marquardt about it."

"He would not know such details. He is insulated from the particulars. Preston Song, perhaps."

"Can you talk to Song?"

"I would prefer to see the company financials first. The more I know, the more hard information I have, the more leverage."

He heard the frustration in her voice.

"Lu's books," Knox said.

"Yes. His accounting of the incentives should answer many of our questions. His accounting is currency. Whoever has that information, whoever controls it, has the real power."

"So, if nothing else, we get it for that reason: to protect it."

"To keep it from others," Grace said.

"Works for me."

"Mr. Marquardt has yet to provide me the end-of-year accounting. I do not know if this is intentional or simply neglect. Perhaps it is significant. Perhaps not."

"Above my pay grade," he said, feeling his wound. He wanted sleep. "If I had to bet, Danny got himself a copy of Lu's payouts within the first week of his covering Lu. It's how he rolls."

"So it makes sense for me to do a thorough study of the hard drive's contents," Grace said. "I am an expert with such data. But, unfortunately, I'm not finding the data on the hard drive in the first place."

"We can find somebody to help."

"Your friend," she said, disgustedly.

Knox remained motionless to allow the Super Glue to set.

"Did you get beer?"

She returned with two open beers. They drank together.

"I must attempt to engage Preston Song. Also, Mr. Marquardt, if possible."

"You must take every precaution," he said.

"Yes. Of course. Off site, if I can manage."

"We have three known groups we're dealing with: the Mongolians; Yang's boys; and this government cop, Shen. That's a lot of possible eyeballs on you."

"Understood."

He liked the way her throat moved as she drank.

He said, "And only one of me watching your entrance and exit. Our best and only real shot at identifying your surveillants."

"I will arrange off site," she repeated. "Away from the office. I arrive early, leave late."

He was going to point out that her earlier mistake had led to the attack in the alley, but she didn't strike him as a person who wanted or needed such reminders. Still, as he pieced it together, he couldn't help himself.

"Yang's men must have overheard your ranting about me taking the GPS from you," he said.

She looked struck. "I had not considered."

"Nor I. But that's why they hit us with force: they knew we had Danny's GPS."

"My apartment," she said.

"There's something I haven't mentioned," he said. "A guy thing. The way Yang Cheng and his bodyguard looked at you at the cocktail party. It wasn't casual. It was . . . all-knowing."

She stared at him. "I do not understand."

"There's checking out a woman, and then there's the X-ray vision thing. The full body scan. The snicker. Boys in the treehouse. These two had seen you."

"Of course. They were looking at me."

"Had seen you in . . . private. Your apartment, I'm thinking."

She pursed her lips.

"Listen. They were ogling you."

He saw her shiver.

"We might be able to use that," Knox said.

Her eyes pleaded for him to stop.

"I need to call Sarge and let him know we're blown," Knox said.

"And injured."

"He can inform Marquardt."

"I will take care of that when I see him and Preston Song. John, I am sorry for this. It is my fault."

He didn't disagree with her. "The assault. After the hurt we put on Yang Cheng's guys . . . even though they won't report it to the police, there's a good chance the police will hear about it. Way too many eyes in this city. So we can add the police to the list of people to avoid."

He chugged down half his beer. "Face recognition." He burped. "Sarge warned me. We need to take care."

She sipped from the bottle. "When he hears of your injury, Mr. Dulwich will order you back to Hong Kong."

"So he won't hear. Besides, I don't answer to Sarge."

"We both answer to Mr. Dulwich," she corrected. "He is our immediate superior."

"It's a cultural thing," he said.

"I believe we will be recalled."

He scoffed. "Let me ask you this: if they 'recall' us, are you going to leave Lu Hao behind?"

She nursed the beer, eyes probing over the curve of the bottle.

"Me neither," Knox said.

13

The White Lotus, located on the twenty-seventh floor of the Marriott Tower in Tomorrow Square, had a dozen private rooms off its central dining room. Each private room had an expansive view of the city. A private waitstaff came and went; only the headwaiter remained in the room, arms behind his back, standing rigidly in the corner.

Allan Marquardt dismissed him. The round table could accommodate ten. Three was somewhat awkward. Preston Song sat slightly closer to Marquardt than to Grace, isolating her from the center of power. A soft forty-something with piggish eyes, Song wore a glorious blue suit, a gold tie pin and a leering look of displeasure.

Grace updated them on the Sherpa's connection and her possessing Danner's GPS locations all in an effort to gain the elusive end-of-year accounting.

"From what you've told us, you've clearly made progress," Marquardt said. "We're encouraged by that."

"I understand you have done well with negotiations," she said.

"Yes."

Preston Song studied her distrustfully.

Grace collected her thoughts and sought a professional and confident tone. "In our pursuit of Lu Hao's accounts, and location, my associate and I have questioned those people on Lu Hao's route—those receiving incentives. I am afraid none is a candidate for Lu Hao's kidnapper. During this process, we were made aware of a recent payment added to Lu Hao's route." She watched for reaction. Marquardt smirked. Preston Song revealed nothing.

"If we are to be effective, we need to know who these people are, and the purpose of the payment." She paused, waiting.

Song was too practiced to allow anything to show on his face.

She said, "The first of two payments occurred on or before the tenth of last month," having gleaned the date from the voice memo on Danner's GPS.

Song's eyes were fixed as she imagined him working out what to say.

"My dear girl," Song said, "as we approach the conclusion of a project the size and scope of the Xuan Tower, it is only natural that unforeseen expenses arise."

"Additional incentives must be paid. Understandable," she said, knowing then that Song oversaw the payment of incentives for The Berthold Group, and acted as a buffer, protecting Marquardt.

"The point is," she continued, "these men have taken an active interest in our efforts to find Mr. Lu. Knowing their exact role is crucial. If I may be direct: we need to know if they are friends or enemies. To date, they are behaving much like enemies."

A knock on the door interrupted her. Song wore an irritable expression as a wave of servers delivered dim sum. Tea was poured. As quickly as the servers arrived, they were gone. The food moved around on a lazy Susan, propelled by Marquardt's hand. Plates were filled.

"What was the purpose of these payments?" she asked.

Marquardt rested his chopsticks on the small porcelain lift alongside his fork, his appetite apparently gone.

"Your line of questioning is growing impertinent," Song said.

"This information is central to our task and to our safety," Grace said. "Extortion? Blackmail? Might it have to do with the documentary being shot? The missing cameraman?"

Marquardt looked up quickly, his eyes piercing. Song never skipped a beat, eating the dim sum before it went cold.

"The first I heard of the matter was a few days ago," said Marquardt. "I promise you, we have nothing to do with this."

"And these most recent payments?"

"As Preston has said: end of project stuff. The usual unforeseen complications." He paused deliberately for a breath. "We have every hope and intention of getting Mr. Lu back safely. With your help, that is. Certain financial matters need to remain confidential. There are millions of dollars at play, as you can well imagine. If these matters had anything to do with Mr. Lu—anything at all—we would not hesitate for a moment to share them with you. Do you understand? We're not fools. We want the same thing as you do."

It occurred to her that Lu Hao might have discovered the film crew. He could not resist anything to do with film. His passion was the reason he—and everyone else—was in this mess. He had put his family on the brink of financial ruin because of his passion.

Song said, "This most recent increase to our subcontractor's invoice was approved and paid out. Nothing more. The reason we hire such subcontractors is so that someone else handles these complications."

She knew very well why they hired such subcontractors: so their criminal acts of bribery fell onto others. She bit her tongue.

"Very well. Thank you," she said.

Marquardt said, "Listen, I'm not going to lie to you: Lu Hao's accounts of the incentives going public could pose difficulties for us. We want and need to recover those records. But let there be no question about it: first and foremost we want to get Mr. Lu and Mr. Danner back safely, as I've said. To that end, we are at your disposal."

"I would appreciate the end-of-year accounts."

"I do not see how that will help," Song said, his mouth full of chewed food, his plate held to his lips.

"I asked for this before," she said to Marquardt.

"Indeed. I would have expected you to have that by now. Preston, I asked Gail to take care of this. What's the holdup? You'll look into this for me, yes?"

"Of course."

Marquardt sounded legitimately put off. Song worked eagerly on the glass of beer. The man shouldn't have tried for the *shao mai*. The tips of his chopsticks shook considerably as he pinched the piece of wonton-wrapped pork and slid it between his wet lips. It was the first sign of cracks in his demeanor.

Grace reveled in the moment. Preston Song had no intention of her seeing the EOY accounts—which made her all the more eager to do so. Marquardt, on the other hand, felt like an ally.

12:50 P.M.
CHANGNING DISTRICT
SHANGHAI

Knox awoke with a start and answered the ringing iPhone.

"Yeah?" he said, looking around for Grace. She'd slept on the couch, where a blanket was now folded. No sign of her. It had to be around noon.

"It's me." Dulwich.

"Surprise," Knox said.

"There's a wet market on the north side of Julu, east of Xiangyang Road. Bring the hard drive. Ten minutes."

"More like fifty," Knox said. "I'm nowhere near there. Had to move."

"We'll talk. Bring the hard drive."

"We?" Knox said. But the call was dead.

A light rain discouraged use of the scooter and made finding a taxi difficult. Knox was late before he started. An hour after the call, he walked past the wet market on Julu and stole a glance inside. No Caucasians. He wore the ScotteVest, the stain scrubbed clean from around the small slit in its left side. He kept his right hand on a knife in the pocket.

Entering the market, he circulated down aisles of bubbling plastic tubs containing live eel, catfish, perch, jellyfish, minnows, myriad crustaceans; displays of rabbit, pigeon, chickens and carcasses he could not identify.

The market jogged to the right into another, smaller room unseen from the entrance. It appeared empty until Knox spotted a man looming behind a tank thick with a moving coil of fish. The fish spooked and parted. The man's face appeared.

Dulwich.

He stepped around into the open.

"I didn't expect to see *you*," Knox confessed. "I thought the reason I'm here is because you couldn't be?" He felt the sting of dread—had Dulwich set him up all along?

"Don't worry," Dulwich said. "Technically, it's not me." He patted his chest pocket. He was on an alias passport, but still at great risk.

Knox did worry. If Dulwich had been able to enter China, then why recruit him for the job in the first place? As a fall guy, obviously. Someone expendable. So why would Dulwich enter now, when it seemed the risk was heightened over even a few days earlier?

Dulwich took Knox by the arm and led him into a room farther from the street. Gurgling Styrofoam tubs held soft-shelled turtles, frogs and sea urchins. Knox winced with the tug and Dulwich shot him a suspicious look.

"Pulled a muscle," Knox said.

Dulwich extended his open hand. "The hard drive."

Knox hesitated. "Seriously: what are you doing here?"

"The drop is still set for the day after tomorrow. We've requested a final proof of life just before the drop. You and the girl will make the drop."

"That's fine, but it doesn't explain your being here," Knox said.

"Since when do I answer to you?" Dulwich said gruffly.

"Since now."

"I'm here to help you," Dulwich said.

"You're here for the hard drive. But last time I checked, you needed me because you couldn't enter safely."

"Who said I'm here safely?" Dulwich said. "'Desperate times, desperate measures,' and all that shit. I'm here because of Danny. Because of you."

Knox wasn't buying it. "Tell me you've got my back."

"I've got your back."

"The Berthold Group doesn't want a second copy of Lu Hao's books out there. That's why the hard drive interests you. Yes?" Knox considered his own comment. "Are you so convinced the hostages will be killed because Danner's an American, or because The Berthold Group is more interested in getting Lu Hao's books back than the hostages?"

"Let's just say I'm playing percentages," Dulwich said. "Marquardt seems like the real thing to me, but who knows? These fuckers are in it for the money. Right? Danny is not expendable. Not to me. Not to you. That's why you're here. Am I right? What do I know? As to why I risked being here? My boss, Primer, raised the ransom cash for Marquardt. The two-fifty USD. It's coming into Guangzhou by container ship tomorrow. I'm the courier. Primer will not trust freelancers with that kind of cash. Who put the free in freelance?"

"You could have headed straight to Guangzhou," Knox said.

Dulwich bristled. "Coulda, shoulda. But Danny's hard drive's a priority."

"You got the SIM card I sent?"

Dulwich nodded. "Yeah. Your guy made repeated calls to another pay-as-you-go China Mobile phone. At first, we thought it might be the intellectual fielding those calls."

"The Mongolians aren't the kidnappers. They're on the receiving end of the incentives."

"Interesting," Dulwich said.

"Added on late in the game."

"Well, whatever all that means, the guy taking those calls appears to report daily to someone in Beijing. A Party member? Government? A businessman? Who the fuck knows? But he's a priority to you and me both."

"These Mongolians are muscle for some Beijing bureaucrat?"

"Or middlemen for the incentives," Dulwich proposed.

"That works for me."

"We've been following GPS locators on both phones—the Beijing guy, and the Shanghai phone that apparently reports into him daily."

Knox thought they were getting closer to the truth of why Dulwich had made the trip.

"You're tracking them? Nice of you to tell me."

"I'm telling you now. Right? The Beijing guy is smart enough to turn it off, and leave it off most of the time. Making tracking sporadic. The Shanghai guy, not so smart. You want to meet him?" Dulwich handed Knox his iPhone. "The blue dot. That's him. He's up the block from us."

Knox studied the moving map. "You've got a bead on the Mongolian? When exactly were you going to tell me?"

"He came straight here the moment you arrived. I watched the dot cross the city."

Knox tried to make sense of it. "He must have followed *you*. Is that possible?"

"You took a cab," Dulwich stated, as if Knox had committed a crime.

Knox explained, "I was short on time."

"We know this guy is connected to Beijing, right? You've actually helped us out by confirming the level of that connection. He didn't follow you, Knox. He just headed over here. That tells me this Beijing guy swings a big enough stick to have the Shanghai cabbies looking out for you."

"The run-ins with the Mongolians," Knox said. "The cops contacted Kozlowski at the consulate about an American wanted for assault."

"So they've been onto you. Makes sense. They lifted your face off camera footage, fed a photo to city cab drivers, and here you are. I'd keep my hat low from now on."

An elderly Chinese man entered the small space, scooped up some live eels into a plastic bag and left.

"What about him? I've got to lose him," Knox said, pointing to Dulwich's phone.

Dulwich grinned. "I thought you'd never ask."

1:20 P.M.
KINGLAND RIVERSIDE LUXURY RESIDENCE
PUDONG DISTRICT

"I wondered if you'd taken your lunch?" Grace said over the secure iPhone, knowing Marquardt's assistants rarely took a lunch break beyond a *baozi* from the corner.

She considered her lunch with Marquardt and Song a draw: not a total failure but not the results she had hoped for. With any luck, Selena could be manipulated to correct that discrepancy. Grace had learned from the best: her manipulative mother.

"Not yet," Selena Ming said. "Quite busy today."

"I thought you might enjoy a look at my apartment."

A moment's hesitation, then Selena replied, "Yes! Very much!"

"I am taking my afternoon here in order to focus on some accounting personally requested by Mr. Marquardt. Do you like sushi?" An extravagant meal for an office worker like Selena was KFC. Because of its price, sushi was considered fine dining—take-away or not.

"My favorite!"

"I will order some take-away."

"I can pick this up on my way."

"Would you? How kind of you!" Grace supplied the name of a shop less than a block from her Pudong apartment.

"Oh!" she said, as if just thinking of it. "Mr. Marquardt would like me to check the EOY financials. End of year. I may have mentioned that before." She knew she had, and Selena had been reluctant to help her obtain them. But now she came at it from a better angle. Selena had seen Grace win on the apartment issue. Her impression of Grace's power within the company would have greatly improved. "I left them on my office computer," she lied. "I wonder if I gave you my password, if you could bring me a thumb drive? I do not wish to trouble you." As Marquardt's executive assistant, Selena would be able to obtain nearly anything. Grace did not have the files on her machine, but knew Selena would never agree to access another employee's computer.

"We have a printout here in our files, if that would suffice? I would be most happy to deliver these for you, Miss Chu."

"Call me Grace, please." The final hook: first name basis with a junior executive. "Mr. Marquardt would like me to complete the work as quickly as possible. You know how he is."

"I will bring them with me," Selena said.

"Thank you. And I would just as soon he not know how forgetful I can be."

"Of course."

"See you soon, then," Grace said. She chortled upon disconnecting the call, proud of herself. Keeping in mind that her apartment was likely bugged, she and Knox planned to use Selena's visit to ferret out whoever was behind the surveillance—to offer up just enough juicy content to tease a reaction from either Yang Cheng or Allan Marquardt.

Grace fetched a scarf from her bag and covered her head. She entered a sister tower to her own residence and rode the elevator to the tenth floor where a sky bridge connected the two. If anyone was watching her tower, they would not have seen her enter.

Once into her apartment, she was mindful of the electronic ears and eyes. Eventually, Grace was buzzed by lobby security and Selena was announced. Marquardt's secretary failed to conceal her reaction to the apartment's opulence. She covered her mouth, moving room to room, her eyes giving away her astonishment. Following the tour, the two sat at the dining table and shared the sushi that Grace had put out on a plate. Grace positioned them both with their backs to the room as if to admire the view. In fact, it was for the sake of the possible cameras, hoping the open drapes would place them both in silhouette and make them less easy to read.

"I was unable to download the spreadsheets you requested," Selena said.

Grace's shoulders slumped in disappointment. "I see."

"But I was able to bring you these." Selena withdrew a pair of heavy binders from her backpack and slapped them onto the table. "I cannot give them to you, but I can leave them with you for a day or two. You can perhaps look them over and return them to me at that time?"

"Yes. Of course." Grace did her best to contain her excitement. These binders and the end-of-year accounts they contained represented a complex numeric crossword puzzle, as entertaining to her as it was challenging. She flipped open the first of the two, delighting at the sight of all those numbers. Somewhere in these pages was a record of every cent paid out as bribes through Lu Hao. Dates. Internal transfers of funds. Budgeting.

"It is what you expected?" Selena asked between bites.

"Yes. Perfect. Thank you."

"What exactly is 'forensic accountant'?"

"We are like surgeons. We cut into the body and find out what is wrong . . . how to fix it," Grace answered. She fictionalized her role for the sake of the surveillance, according to her and Knox's plan. "The firm believes there is an audit imminent from the U.S. tax authorities. Broadly speaking, my job is to make sure everything adds up."

"You will, no doubt, be troubled with Mr. Marquardt's travel expenses, then?"

Grace was typically focused on five or six figures and above, but she was tempted by Selena's concern.

"If you have had trouble balancing an expense account," she said, "I would be pleased to be of assistance."

"I just wish to make it known that it was not my idea to redact lines from his credit card bill. I would like very much for that to be understood. Is this a crime?"

"Happens all the time, dear girl. Not to worry." Inside, Grace was churning. Why should Marquardt want his assistant to redact line items from a credit card bill? Buying a gift for the wife on the company card? Had he lied about a mistress? Did any of it matter? "There is no blame that will result from my work. I find problems and make suggestions for how to fix them, to institute proper accounting practices."

"I removed the lines because of security concerns," she said, offering up the excuse. "I was told to by Mr. Song."

"Indeed?"

"He said our competition would go to great lengths to secure such information."

"Yes. Of course. I suppose the travel of the boss would be of interest to many." Grace couldn't allow herself to appear too hungry for more information, but her heart pounded. Ever mindful of the electronic eyes and ears, she considered how to end the conversation for now. "What were the dates of the trip? Or a particular charge? That might help me locate it within the accounting."

"A hotel and some meals in Chongming. Golf, you might think. Mr. Marquardt charges golf to the company card plenty. But not golf. He was with Mr. Song. So, business, *neh*? No pleasure trips with Mr. Song."

"It is nothing to worry about, I am certain," Grace said. "Perhaps, if you provide me with the dates . . ." she tried again, "I can take a look to make sure."

"As to that, it was mid-September. I don't recall the exact day. Second weekend, perhaps. Not during the workweek—I remember as much. Even more curious, given Mr. Song was traveling with him! The two together *on a weekend*! I would never have expected that," Selena chuckled.

"Business only," Grace said, simply to keep the conversation going while her mind sorted out what she was hearing. Danner had voice-dated the GPS bookmark for the Mongolian delivery for September tenth. She'd had the call from Lu Hao left on her cell phone a week later, the seventeenth. Marquardt's Chongming Island trip had to be tied to Lu Hao—Lu Hao's family lived on the island, as did Grace's. Did this trip explain Marquardt's reluctance to show her the more detailed account-ing while cooperating with her other requests? Did it somehow account for Lu Hao's kidnapping?

Selena gauged the moment, sipped tea and then marveled at the view, briefly changing the subject.

"Mr. Marquardt does not like Mr. Song," she said. "I cannot imagine him traveling with Mr. Song for pleasure. A weekend together at the same hotel? It must have been business."

"What kind of business?"

"Mr. Song conducts due diligence on our upcoming projects." Selena proudly showed off her in-depth knowledge of the corporate big men.

"Easily explained then!" Grace said cheerfully. "And the Chongming Island project is . . . ?"

Selena's eyes grew sharp.

"I do not wish to pry," Grace said. "I simply want to do my best to keep you out of trouble with the U.S. tax authority. If you are not the one in charge—"

"Of course I am in charge. I handle all of Mr. Marquardt's itinerary."

"All but his trip to Chongming Island . . ."

"This trip . . . this is the first it has appeared on his schedule."

"But the billing statement has been redacted," Grace reminded. "So there's no proof of it anyway."

"Of course there is proof! There is the original billing. A duplicate can always be requested."

Grace worked to appear surprised.

"I can request the records the moment I am back into the office," Selena said. "I will send them to you the moment I have them."

"What a clever girl you are," Grace said.

14

The wet market was less than three blocks behind him when Knox used a reflection off a storefront window to spot the dark green motorcycle at his back. It started to rain lightly. He walked quickly south and the Mongolian followed. Dulwich's explanation about the taxi driver reporting him seemed plausible if unlikely; more probable was that the Mongolian had spotted him and Grace on the scooter in his *lilong* and had then traced the scooter's registration back to the employee at Quintet from whom Knox had rented the scooter. He made a mental note to follow up with Fay about that.

Knox headed to the Modern Electronic City, a funky, three-story shopping complex at the intersection of Xiangyang Road and Fuxing Middle Road. Inside was a congested rabbit warren of narrow aisles and shop stalls crammed with anything electronic as well as the ubiquitous clothes and kitchen supply stalls.

He was met with the roar of negotiation. He climbed a moving escalator, turned right at the top and slapped a hundred-*yuan* note onto the scratched glass countertop. He punched "Kenny G" in the shoulder and, in halting Mandarin, told the shop booth attendant he was being followed by a Mongolian asshole who thought all *waiguoren* were fair game. "A common pickpocket, no doubt."

To be called "common" was among the gravest insults.

Kenny cursed. Knox, a regular customer when in town, stepped into shadow, wedging himself into a corner. The emergency exit he wanted was at his back.

Two minutes and the Mongolian had not entered.

Knox saw across to a stall selling digital cameras. On its counter stood an array of digital frames—electronic LCD screens that could display a slide show. One of the frames scrolled through images of the Great Wall and the terra-cotta soldiers. Another advertised across the screen in a steady scroll:

Join the revolution in digital storage!! Holds over 1,000 photos and 5,000 songs!

Grace had photographed a digital picture frame in Lu Hao's apartment. It had not occurred to her to collect it. But it being digital implied internal memory. The frames accepted images from USB connections.

Lu Hao had hidden his off-the-book spreadsheet *in plain sight*.

Knox was suddenly far less concerned with trapping and working over the Mongolian for information—Dulwich's current plan—as he was with returning to Lu Hao's apartment to grab up the digital frame.

Knox spotted Dulwich wandering the lower level. After allowing several minutes to pass, Dulwich rode the escalator upstairs and joined Knox around the corner at Kenny G's. They quickly swapped jackets and hats, Dulwich now dressed in the ScotteVest, jeans and ball cap, Knox in Dulwich's pale gray canvas airman jacket—candy bar wrappers in both pockets. Given the rain, the substitution might work.

"Forget working this guy," Knox said. "I've got a new lead to follow."

He explained how Grace had seen a digital frame in Lu Hao's apartment, how they'd overlooked that as a possible digital hiding place. "All I need is to get this guy off my back."

"The plan is still actionable," Dulwich said. "He's out there watching. We hit him. Now."

"He doesn't know shit," Knox said. "That's why he's following me."

"He knows something we don't. Beijing. That makes him an information asset."

"Just lead him away. Get him off me. You've got his location on your phone. We can take him anytime we want him."

"There is no 'we.' I have a train to catch. It's now or never."

"Then never," Knox said. Adding, "Not now. This frame is more important."

"Your call. Stay tough," he said. He turned and headed for the escalator.

Knox worked his way across the third floor to a stall selling rice cookers, blenders and hot plates. At the back of the stall was one of very few windows on this floor—a fixed-pane window six inches wide and three feet high. Knox put his face to it.

Through the blurry smudge, Knox spotted the Mongolian across the intersection on the motorcycle, oblivious to the rain; they both watched Dulwich—now wearing Knox's jacket and hat—dodge his way through umbrellas to the curb where a taxi was waiting. Dulwich opened the back door and climbed in. The taxi pulled out into slowly moving traffic.

Knox celebrated their success: the short distance to the taxi had made the substitution work perfectly. The Mongolian rose to kick-start his bike but held up on the curb watching as the taxi moved off.

Why was he not following? The idea had been to lure the Mongolian away, following Dulwich the impostor. So why give the taxi such a lead? Taxis all looked the same—they were difficult to follow.

Knox peered down the street. Was there a second Mongolian in place? Had they screwed this up?

Panic flashed through him. *A heavy rain in Shanghai.* Snagging a taxi in this weather could take fifteen minutes and yet . . .

The taxi had been waiting at the curb. Improbable on a sunny day. Impossible on a day like this.

Knox rapped his knuckles on the window as if he could stop the taxi, already moving. He fumbled with the iPhone; dropped it; stooped to recover it. Dialed as he stood.

His face back to the window, he saw the roofs of vehicles as traffic moved around Dulwich's taxi—another anomaly. Dulwich's taxi was clearly positioning itself toward the right lane.

"Yeah?" Dulwich said, his voice slightly altered by the ever-shifting signal embedded in the phone's security.

"Abort!" Knox said. "We were set up! That taxi was waiting for *me*!"

Knox heard Dulwich say, "Hey, pal, pull over," in English. *"Ting!"* he hollered. *Stop.*

Knox heard the breaking glass and twisting metal a millisecond before the same sounds found their way through the wireless phone network.

The taxi was T-boned by an old-model gray Toyota, pushed clear through the intersection and slammed into a tree.

The drivers of both vehicles hurried out and staggered toward the curb.

Now the Mongolian headed up the sidewalk on his motorcycle. He hopped off and reached through shattered glass as if trying to help. Knox knew better.

A massive throng of onlookers immediately surrounded the wreck. Everyone loved a good collision.

Knox made it to the ground floor before his brain fully kicked in. Protocol dictated he walk calmly in the opposite direction of the wreck.

Instead, he ran to the wreck and challenged the crowd, pushing and shoving and shouting curses in Mandarin. The Mongolian was back on the bike. He throttled up and swung left around the corner—out of sight.

The crowd owned Knox. He moved toward the wreck where a smear of blood stained the frame. The *whoop-whoop* of a siren cried out: an ambulance from nearby Huashan Hospital or the police. Either way, Knox couldn't stick around. He'd be questioned. Involved.

He pushed forward and tugged open the bent back door. Dulwich was unconscious, his face bloodied. Knox hooked him beneath his arms and pulled him out. As he did, his hand found the hard drive. He was searching for the iPhone when an old, nearly toothless woman slapped his hand and shouted, "Thief!"

Knox called her an old cow, but hurried off down the street before the crowd decided to make an example of him.

3:20 P.M.
JING AN DISTRICT
SHANGHAI

Knox called Rutherford Risk in Hong Kong and then waited ten minutes for the company's head, Brian Primer, to return the call to the iPhone. As they talked, he walked up Changle Road toward Huashan Hospital.

"Go ahead," Primer said, with no introductions.

"Sarge—David Dulwich—is down. Traffic accident. Looked serious to critical."

"You escaped unharmed?"

"Wasn't in the cab. What's the call? I can have him out of there within . . . two hours, at the outside. Request a safe house with medical, or an evac team."

"I appreciate your . . . loyalty. His identification is good. It should hold. No need to put the operation at risk. Not yet."

"But the ransom money," Knox said.

"Yes, I'm aware of the situation, believe me."

"You want me in Guangzhou?" Knox asked.

A long pause on the other end of the call as Primer weighed his options. Perhaps Knox had surprised him with his knowledge of the operation.

"I need a few minutes. An hour. Do you have the hospital?"

"Approaching it now."

"Survey for arrival of interrogation team, or anything suggesting compromise."

"Can do. I won't let him be taken," Knox stated.

"Settle down," Primer said. "We've managed a lot worse than this."

"It was intended for me. The crash."

"Knowledge or speculation?"

"I spotted an adversary in the area. Both drivers fled the scene."

"Good to know. Then I'd keep my head down if I was you."

"I want him out of there." He paused. "I need the ransom money."

"I said: settle down. This is what we do. Let us do it. You handle your end. The accounts?"

"A work in progress."

"And is there progress?"

It struck Knox that this was Primer's focus. "Guangzhou?" Knox said. He wondered if Primer would authorize a quarter million dollars in cash to be picked up by a relative stranger.

"That drop required Dulwich. We'll figure something out. Not to worry."

"Worry? We've got two days! Less, now. I can get him on a plane. A boat."

"You handle the accounts. The exchange."

"There won't be an exchange without that money!"

"Then extraction. We've got Dulwich covered."

Sure you do, Knox thought, wondering how expendable Dulwich was to a man like Brian Primer.

"Keep this phone close." The line went dead.

Knox had reached the street corner. Looking left, he saw the blockish white buildings of Huashan Hospital. In the first few hours of care it would be difficult to get to Dulwich. But after that . . .

He kept vigil, waiting for the arrival of police that never came. An hour passed. Primer was right: Dulwich's "accident" was being treated as just another civilian casualty.

For how long remained the question.

6:20 P.M.
CHANGNING DISTRICT
SHANGHAI

"The wheels are coming off this thing," he told Grace, having returned to the safe house apartment. "We have to get Sarge out of there. Priority one."

"The company will take care of Mr. Dulwich."

"The company will pretend he doesn't exist."

"Not Mr. Primer."

"Believe it," Knox said. "In truth, Sarge probably doesn't exist. He's probably an independent contractor, like you. Like me, now. Nowhere on their payroll despite his working there. It's an insidious arrangement set up exactly for moments like this."

"Like Lu Hao," she said solemnly.

"Yes. Like that," he agreed. "It all depends how good his documentation is. There are ways."

"You cannot possibly be considering removing him from hospital."

"Can't I?"

"We cannot care for him! The way you described his condition—"

"Don't get your panties in a knot."

"Excuse me?"

He didn't translate it for her. "At some point they'll determine he's an American. His teeth—dental work—will tell them that much. X rays. Tattoos. There are ways."

"We must focus on Lu Hao and Mr. Danner."

"Sarge was the source for the ransom money." He relived their conversation in the wet market, including the pickup in Guangzhou. A pickup that would not happen. "No Sarge, no ransom drop."

Grace hesitated before speaking. "Extraction."

"Right," he said. "As if."

He looked over at her. She needed sleep. They both needed food.

"Okay. One step at a time," he said. "Maybe the frame has Lu's files. Maybe the numbers tell us something we don't know." He no longer believed it. He suddenly saw them instead as a means to an end. "We're looking at this wrong."

"How so?"

"Everyone seems to want Lu's accounts, right?"

"It is possible," she said. "Yes."

"So whoever possesses his files has power over the others. Power means leverage."

"The numbers always reveal more than anyone suspects," said the forensic accountant.

Knox yawned. "You're missing the point."

"Which is?" she said angrily.

"We need to raise money in order to pay the ransom."

"I am aware of that predicament."

"So now maybe we have something to sell," Knox said.

Twenty minutes later, he sat in a wheelchair outside a changing room in a boutique clothing store.

"Do you know the expression, 'Take no prisoners'?" he asked, as Grace tried on clothes on the other side of a black silk curtain. He could see her bare feet. The petite woman who ran the store was in the front dealing with a customer.

"I have heard it before."

"Tie up every loose end."

"Yes," she said, impatient with him.

"That's why the change of clothes for both of us, and my condition." His hands on the wheelchair's wheels. "In case any of those cops are still watching the building."

"The police," she said.

"We don't know who they are. State Security? Private muscle?"

Grace drew back the curtain. She wore a gray business suit with black pinstripes, and a sheer white blouse unbuttoned to show a good amount of skin. She looked older. She carried a tote over her shoulder. *Just right,* Knox thought: *slightly slutty.*

She said, "How do you know those men who attacked us are not because of this woman you slept with?"

They both knew Grace's carelessness had led Yang's men to them in the alley, but he kept his mouth shut.

"How do you know Lu Hao isn't a blackmailer?" Knox said. "That he wasn't blackmailing some Beijing minister who then sicced the Mongolians on him to clean up loose ends?"

She studied him. Disappointment and disdain mixed with a hint of curiosity.

"Not Lu Hao," she said.

Knox rode in the wheelchair head down, a blanket across his lap. He wore a woven bamboo hat and a collarless blue cotton jacket typical of retirees, his shoulders hunched, his head drooped against a lightly falling rain. Wheelchairs were rarely seen on the streets of Shanghai. Wherever Shanghai's elderly or handicapped were kept, it wasn't on the busy sidewalks. But Knox fit the mold for those that were occasionally seen—old and decrepit, sad testimonies to the ravages of age.

Guiding him was an upscale office worker, a woman with a nice figure wearing high heels. She pushed the chair with one hand, and with the other clutched her purse over her head against the rain.

Grace said, "Pushing this is a lot more difficult than it looks."

Knox barely heard her. For the past several hours he'd brooded over the loss of Dulwich, intent on rescuing him from the hospital. He wished he'd secured the man's iPhone and its ability to track the Mongolian.

Now, less than thirty yards from Lu Hao's apartment building, Knox peered out from under the hat, looking for signs of the police and surveillants they'd encountered their last time here. They reached the entrance to Lu Hao's apartment building and Grace backed him through the door.

Inside, they acted quickly, having talked through it. For the sake of any cameras, Grace pushed Knox and the wheelchair into the elevator. She reached in and touched "7."

Then she headed toward the stairs, leaving him behind.

Down the hall she found a door marked BUILDING SUPERVISOR in both English and Mandarin. She descended the stairs into a dank-smelling but well-lit basement. The seconds ticked off in her head.

Knox's former assault of the Mongolian in the stairway meant the police had questioned the supervisor, residents and the real estate agent. Grace needed to take the supervisor's attention off her face, despite her attempts to disguise herself. She paused on a landing, bent down and tore her skirt. She did the same to her blouse, popping buttons and revealing her bra. She wet her finger and smeared her eye shadow. Hyperventilating, she approached the partially opened door that discharged cigarette smoke and the strains of a Chinese television melodrama. She knocked loudly and pushed inside without invitation.

"Help me!" she cried out in Mandarin.

Knox's plan was designed to work no matter what the manager's gender. By exposing herself, there wasn't a man alive who wouldn't jump to his feet to come to her aid; and the implication of sexual assault would bring sympathy from any woman. If a married couple—often the case for building supervisors—Grace would have her work cut out for her.

It was a married couple.

Early forties. He, with thinning hair and a bad complexion, all skin and bones; she, in a blue jumpsuit, her face oily, her hair clumped and pulled back in a bun.

Grace entered a small space, every inch used efficiently. A narrow futon, two stools with an improvised table between them. A small cathode-ray color television flickered between neat stacks of clothing on a shelf. To her right, another smaller black-and-white television sat next to two VCRs. Exactly as Knox had described.

She plopped down on the empty bed without invitation.

"He . . . I . . . he tried to . . ." She pleaded with her eyes to the woman. "Please."

She saw the gravity register on the man's face. Unless he could quickly control the story, he would be out on the street looking for work. There had already been one assault in his building in the past few days. Another would be the end of him.

"Tea, my dear," the woman said, shooting a look at her husband telling him to do something. The kitchen was behind a maroon blanket. With the clatter of pots and pans, Grace went to work.

She reached for the perplexed building superintendent. To her relief, he reached back for her.

6:40 P.M.

Seven Swans—Lu Hao's apartment.

Knox, wearing the hat to screen his face from the security cameras, used his knuckle to ring the doorbell, avoiding fingerprints. He kept watch on the glass peephole in the center of the door. As it briefly flashed dark—indicating its light source was blocked—Knox kicked open the door, taking the doorjamb with it.

As it swung open, he hit it again with a shoulder, making sure to crush the man caught behind it. He took two great strides into the center of the room, dispatching a greasy punk who rose up from the couch, and a second, sturdier kid who was apparently slow off the mark. Neither was unconscious, but they'd be wishing they were for the next several minutes.

Knox pivoted on his right heel. The man behind the door held up his hands in resignation.

He wasted no time getting into Lu Hao's bedroom. He grabbed the digital frame.

In and out of the apartment in less than a minute, he rode the elevator down, willing it to fall faster.

6:42 P.M.

Grace took the supervisor's hands, allowing him to help her up from the bed. As she came to her feet, she spun him and threw a chokehold, silencing him until he went slack and unconscious—the man's wife less than ten feet away. Grace eased him to the floor.

She hit Eject on both VCRs and they discharged their cassettes. They could not afford to be identified; Knox had been adamant about this. She took these as well as other cartridges from a neatly ordered stack and filled the tote.

The wife came from around the curtain, pulled by the sound. As her face filled with horror, Grace slapped a hand over her mouth from behind.

"He is fine. You do not move. No police. This never happened."

Knox's plan counted on the couple not wanting another report against them.

"The problem upstairs was drunken tenants. The usual youngsters. Do you understand?"

The woman first shook her head, then nodded, tears running onto Grace's hand.

"I regret the intrusion," Grace said. "Please accept my apologies."

She was back up the stairs in a matter of seconds.

6:44 P.M.

Knox wheeled himself out of the elevator, counting down the seconds. He would give her another minute, no more; then, he would go after her.

Grace arrived with her shirttails crossed and tucked in at the waist, her torn skirt rotated so that the slit ran all the way up her leg revealing the thin black band of her bikini underwear. She said nothing, only nodded at him before pushing his chair out the doors.

Knox reached over and deposited the digital picture frame and power supply into her bag.

Two blocks later, an empty wheelchair and a damp blanket collecting rain won the attention of the occasional pedestrian. It looked sad, as if it held a disheartening story.

Fifteen minutes later, it was gone.

An hour later, it had already been resold, twice.

THURSDAY

September 30

1 day until the ransom

15

"Can you hear me?" The rugged-faced man standing by the hospital bed cupped his hand, shielding the patient's eyes from the overhead tube lighting. "My name is Kozlowski. U.S. Consulate."

David Dulwich looked around the hospital room without moving his head or neck, which was held in a foam collar. He wanted a way out. There were slings and weights and pulleys attached to him; he felt stretched.

"You happen to be in luck," Kozlowski said, a little too cheerily. "Believe it or not, you have Formula One racing to thank for it. Ten years ago, the city wanted to bring in Formula One for a sanctified event. But event organizers require the availability of top-shelf Western medicine before authorizing an event. The result is this," he said, sweeping his hand, "umpteen millions of dollars spent on a state-of-the-art, fully staffed hospital ward for expats. You, my friend, are the beneficiary. From what I'm told you're lucky to be alive. If you'd been wearing a seatbelt, maybe you'd have walked away from it, but then again show me one Shanghai cab in which you can find the back-seat seatbelts. Am I right?"

He walked slowly around the bed. "In case you're wondering: it was the pins in your ankle that stamped you 'Made in U.S.A.' Though don't ask me how."

In a convincing Australian accent, Dulwich said, "They got the work right, mate, but not my country of origin. I'm Aussie. And it's 'sanctioned event,' not 'sanctified.'"

Kozlowski didn't look like a man who tolerated correction. "There was a time in my career when a guy like you would have confused me, or maybe even fooled me completely." Kozlowski held up a small white 4 x 6 card with boxes across the top. Each box contained a fingerprint.

"The Australian passport is good," Kozlowski continued. "Very good. Too good. Maybe even authentic. That tells me more than you want, believe me."

Kozlowski moved to the end of the bed, hoping for eye contact. Dulwich wouldn't give him any.

"Both drivers walked. One car was stolen. The nephew of the registered cabbie drove the taxi. On the outside, it looks like a U.S. citizen in the wrong place at the wrong time. But the passport; and iPhone the likes of which my tech guys have never seen; a plane ticket from Hong Kong booked an hour before takeoff yesterday morning; a first-class train ticket to Guangzhou?"

"Yesterday?" Dulwich said, trying to sit up. No use. "The date?"

"It's September thirtieth." Kozlowski pulled up a chair. "Mean something to you?"

"I never like losing track of time."

"By the end of the day I'll have confirmed your identity. I'm not going to get all *Law and Order* on you and tell you you're better off talking to me now than later. We both know that's bullshit. You're better off not talking to me at all. You're better off walking the hell out of here when no one's looking. But in your condition, I don't think that's even possible.

Maybe you could crawl. Honestly, I probably don't want to know why you're here. You smack of a ton of paperwork just waiting to happen."

Dulwich winced painfully again as he tried to sit up.

"There are plenty of individuals like you in this city. Don't think you're all that special. Trouble is, Americans like you are my responsibility. I'm supposed to keep your nose clean. Or at least mop up the snot after it's spilled. Maybe you're here stealing somebody else's secrets, keeping track of his sins, looking for a missing person, or trying to lead a revolution. I don't care. I need you gone. There is only one way you can gain my favor." Kozlowski withdrew and unfolded some photocopies. He held the first in front of Dulwich's face.

"No," Dulwich croaked out, seeing a photo of Lu Hao.

"Strike one. Him?" Kozlowski said, producing a second photo from under the first. Clete Danner.

Dulwich swallowed dryly. "No."

The medication belied his intentions.

Kozlowski noted the twitch, but said, "Strike two." He proffered the third of three: a security photo of a Chinese man. "And?"

Dulwich said, "He looks nasty, mate."

"You think you're going to outsmart the Chinese?" Kozlowski asked. "They're all over this."

"All over what?"

"Really?"

Dulwich had the twitch under control, giving away nothing. He was thinking: *the Iron Hand. The missing cameraman.* Kozlowski could easily be part of that investigation, could easily believe Dulwich was involved in that investigation.

"You'd better have some serious support in play, friend. Because from what the doctors tell me, you're not going anywhere soon. You're a sitting duck here—that's an American expression, but I think you'll figure it out. If you want help—protection, maybe a transfer, that's all there for the asking. If there's a bone in your body that isn't broken, they haven't found it." He waited. "Nothing? Seriously?" Kozlowski took a deep breath and stepped back. "Enjoy Chinese prison. I hope you like rice."

9:20 A.M.
CHANGNING DISTRICT

Knox and Grace spent the night working in the safe house. Grace reviewed Berthold's financials with special attention given to Marquardt's travel expensing, while security video of Lu Hao's apartment building ran in the background. If the Mongolians had a prior relationship with Lu, maybe they'd be seen. Or if the kidnappers had returned for Lu Hao's medication and laptop, perhaps they could be identified.

Knox confounded himself attempting to find any hidden files in the memory of Lu Hao's digital frame, a process well above his pay grade. He determined that the frame's memory was partitioned into two virtual drives—like two separate file cabinets. He'd been able to retrieve the images from one of the virtual drives, but as far as he could tell, the other was blocked by a password.

"If anything's on this frame other than the photos, we're going to need an expert," Knox finally confessed.

Grace said nothing.

"Did you hear me?"

"I heard you."

He glanced up at the fast-forwarding security footage. They shared this task.

"Anything?" he asked. She had the two volumes of endless spreadsheet pages in front of her. She'd placed bookmarks of torn napkin throughout both, making the printouts look feathered.

"I put Selena at risk," she said, not looking up.

"You had no idea she was going to guilt-trip off her boss going to some island and start blabbing about it."

"I have made her an unknowing accomplice."

"Sometimes you sound so cold-hearted," he said. "Not today."

"And nearly all the time you sound pig-headed."

"I think we could both use some sleep," he said.

"I need Lu Hao's records."

"I think we've established that."

Grace looked up at him, her face lined with fatigue.

"The Berthold Group's accountants consolidated the payments to Lu Hao's consulting firm in the GA—general accounting. Trying, I suppose, to make the payments appear like business as usual, when they know otherwise. The problem with that practice is that when those payments change substantially, as is the case recently, it is a red flag." She showed Knox the pages of numbers; he pretended to follow along. "In this case, an additional two hundred thousand U.S. was paid out to Lu Hao's consulting firm. The timing is significant, John. First, the added two hundred thousand," she switched volumes and drew her finger down a column, "then, less than a week later, Marquardt's redacted trip to Chongming Island," back to the original ledger, "then a second overpayment of two hundred thousand U.S., the same day Lu Hao went missing."

Knox whistled. "Four hundred grand. Which is why they didn't want you getting hold of their books. It took you only a matter of hours to connect it."

"There are a hundred ways to hide such things. They are either arrogant or ignorant. Both are crimes when it comes to accounting."

"So they made a couple balloon payments, probably to the Mongolian. Thanks to Sarge, we know the Mongolian has connections to Beijing. So the payments went north. But that doesn't get us any closer to extraction? To finding them. I mean, this is all well and good—and fascinating," he mocked, "but we've already established the Mongolian is as interested in finding Lu Hao as we are. So he's a . . . distraction."

"Selena claimed that Marquardt and Preston Song would never travel together unless for due diligence on a future project." Grace lowered her voice. "Connect that to Beijing, where the government decides all the biggest construction projects. Lu Hao wasn't paying off the Mongolian to aid the Xuan Tower. He was paying for information on a new government project. Such projects can be worth billions."

"Speculation."

"A logical deduction based on research and information. We must act!"

"So, Lu Hao makes the second payoff. Why does the Mongolian give a damn about him after that?"

"Protect the Beijing superior," Grace said. "If Lu Hao talks, heads roll."

Executions of corrupt officials were not uncommon in China. It had been a while since the last.

"Interesting," Knox said. "But again: it doesn't get us any closer to extraction."

"Listen," she said, "Marquardt hired us to get Lu Hao out. But he could be as panicked as the Beijing contact. If The Berthold Group is seen to be involved in influencing a government official, they, he could be imprisoned. The Australians were given twelve years." She was referring to a recent trial that had made international headlines. "Maybe they could negotiate their way out of criminal charges on the Xuan payments. But not something of this size tied directly to Beijing."

Knox wasn't going to repeat himself.

"Perhaps Lu Hao's records confirm this."

"Not to be rude, but who cares?" Knox said. "Honestly, I don't care who's paying whom at this point. I want an address. I want extraction."

She was silent for some time. "Lu Hao's records are our only source of possible information."

Knox closed his eyes and tried to work it out. The money trail was apparently fascinating to an accountant, but he'd grown tired of it. The big payments to the Mongolians and on to Beijing were clearly significant. "Yang Cheng could be behind the kidnappings," he said. "It was his men in the alley behind Quintet. He knew about your hire at Berthold, so he obviously has an insider there. He wanted you to abandon Marquardt. Make things more difficult for Marquardt. Maybe we can trade for the hostages."

"If Yang had Lu Hao he would have Lu Hao's information. Yang is not the kidnapper."

"You know what? Who gives a shit? What's important to us is that with Sarge down, there's no ransom money."

"Yes."

"We won't want to trade the accounts until we know what we're giving away."

"Again, I do not follow."

"Lu's accounts may reveal who has the most to fear, who has the most to lose. Therefore, who will pay the most."

"John, are you talking to me?"

"The accounts are the prize—it explains all the attention on Lu's apartment. The attack on us."

"You and I want the same thing, if for different reasons," she said. "Lu Hao's books."

"You sound like a marriage counselor."

"Do not get your hopes up."

"Ha! Regardless," he said, "once we have Lu's books we can start dealing. Yang Cheng, the Mongolians, maybe Marquardt as well."

"You want to sell the information for cash. To raise money needed to pay the ransom," she said.

"I thought you said you weren't following." He paused. "Amy knows this guy—I've met him a couple of times. Sells counterfeit video games. A computer brainiac. He can help us."

"So call this person," she said reluctantly. "Selena owes me a copy of Marquardt's redacted credit card statement. I will ask her again. This may help as well."

"You don't have to sound so excited about Amy helping us," Knox said.

"This has nothing to do with you. It is Chinese. You would not understand."

"Face? I understand face."

"Westerners intellectualize face. Chinese live it. It is very different."

5:40 P.M.

Knox did not like the idea of putting them all in the same room together—pigs for the slaughter—but saw little choice. Carrying a black backpack containing Lu Hao's digital photo frame, he checked the street for surveillants at every opportunity. Changed his look every few blocks with baseball caps and sunglasses.

He arrived early at the rendezvous, a dismal-looking beauty salon with a white, pink and blue barber pole outside. Walked past and continued for another block. Crossed through traffic. Cut back at the next light and approached the salon for a second time.

He paused by a curbside dice game being played on an inverted cardboard box in the shade of a plane tree. Cigarettes dangled from wet lips. Spitting tobacco bits, and sipping cold tea, rheumy-eyed men competed fiercely.

Amy arrived at the salon first, taking no security precautions whatsoever. Grace followed, also performing a walk-by before entering. Selena had e-mailed Marquardt's electronic AMEX statement; Knox had left her studying it, unsure if she'd pry herself away for this meeting; glad she had.

He awaited a city bus to screen himself from the opposing sidewalk and, as the bus passed, slipped into the salon.

Amy occupied the third of three chairs to the right, her hair foaming, her attendant shooting a stream of water from a squirt bottle onto her head while working up the suds. Despite the wet application, it was referred to as a "dry" shampoo. Grace, in the middle chair, was being prepared.

Knox greeted the owner, a fit man in his early forties with a cataract film covering his left eye. The man checked with Amy in the mirror. Amy nodded.

"You wait, few minutes, please," the man said in passable English. He pointed. "Waiting area in back, past curtain."

Knox and Grace exchanged a meaningful look. He wondered if she, too, had spotted the Mongolian following Amy.

Knox wondered how the Mongolian had possibly made the connection to Amy—the cocktail party? Quintet?

The curtain was a Simpsons bedsheet thumbtacked into the doorjamb beyond which was a tiny sink and stool. Knox was forced to turn sideways to slip past the sink and into a narrow hallway that led to a back door. He inspected the door, checking the lock. The door opened on to a sublane where laundry was in bloom. Clear both directions. He turned. Homer and Marge laughed at him in faded glory.

The tiny storage room's shelves were crowded with hand towels, hair product, a rice cooker, a cutting board and a plastic pail of green vegetables. Near the far wall, half a wooden door on rusting file cabinets served as a desk. At the desk, his back to Knox, sat a twenty-something Chinese boy with a lousy haircut. If he stabbed the laptop's keys any harder he was going to break it.

He spun to face Knox. A poor attempt at facial hair. He was chewing purple gum. He spoke English. "Ready when you are, professor."

"Tom," Knox said, introducing himself.

"Randy."

As if.

Amy came through wearing a towel on her shoulders and her hair spiked punk rock by shampoo.

"You two make introductions?" she said.

"Yes," Knox said.

Grace entered next, crowding the space. Her eyes tightened, dancing between Amy and Knox.

"Let's have a look," Randy said. It sounded rehearsed. The kind of guy to practice lines in front of a mirror.

Knox provided him the digital frame. Amy had made all the arrangements; she carried the anxious concern of a worried hostess.

Grace seemed more interested in Amy than the laptop. "It is crowded here. We will give you room."

Knox stayed. He wasn't leaving a stranger in possession of the frame and its possible contents. Randy connected the frame to the laptop by wire, and began typing. Ten minutes passed, feeling like thirty.

"Memory is partitioned," he said. "One side encrypted. You care about frame?"

"Only its contents," Knox said.

Randy pried the frame open with a screwdriver, startling Knox.

He spoke as he continued disassembling the device. "Common mistake is try to break encryption." He exposed a small circuit board. Using a magnifying loupe, he studied the board as his hand blindly searched the desktop for the screwdriver.

"But that's what we want," Knox said. "We want the data from the encrypted partition."

"I understand," Randy said. "Breaking such code can take days. Weeks."

"We don't have days or weeks."

"No. But we have this," he said, holding up the screwdriver, his attention still trained onto the loupe and the circuit board.

"The CMOS battery is soldered," he said.

He sat up and addressed Knox.

"Just like laptop, the board uses small watch battery to hold password. Dead battery, no password. Sometimes battery is soldered to keep it from separating. That is case here. Screwdriver too big. Need paperclip."

"How about a bobby pin?"

The man looked at him, confused. "Bobby?"

"Hair clip? We're in the right place for hair clips."

"Excellent!"

Minutes later, Randy had used a metal bobby pin to short the board and drain the small battery's charge. The full directory of the partitioned side of the frame's memory now appeared on his connected laptop.

The women rejoined Knox.

"Contents?" Knox asked.

"A dot-xls file. Microsoft Excel. Also some small audio files. Photos. I will download for you." He handed Knox a thumb drive.

"Give us a minute please," Knox said, eyeing Amy and indicating for Randy to leave the room.

"The upper back massage is most pleasant," Amy said, escorting Randy out of the small room. "Only takes ten minutes. You will try now."

Grace opened the spreadsheet. Five minutes passed, Knox standing behind her, impatient. Anxious. The spreadsheet notes were all in Chinese characters. He could read some, but not all of them.

When she spoke, she spoke English.

"It is everything," she said. "Lu Hao used full names. Phone numbers. He recorded all payments. Very much money, John. More than is accounted for by The Berthold Group of course. Over past six months, nine million *yuan*. Over a million, U.S.

"With this kind of inside information," she continued, "any construction company would be ensured of success. On the other hand, if the government got hold of this list, they would jail every one of them. The inherent value of this is astronomical."

"How many contacts? How many getting payments?"

"The same. No new locations."

"The Mongolians?"

"No sign of the most recent payments."

Knox mulled this over. "Seriously?"

She nodded. "The four hundred thousand is unaccounted for."

"Why so much detail? How stupid could he be?"

"Lu Hao is not stupid. Ambitious? Overconfident? Yes. But not stupid. It is doubtful keeping records was his idea," she said. "Someone must have required it."

"But then why's it incomplete?"

She shrugged.

Knox attempted to clarify. "You're saying Berthold wanted this accounting."

"It is far too much money to entrust without some form of accountability. A person could embezzle a small fortune."

"Do you think that's what happened? Lu Hao put his finger in the pie?" That would explain kidnapping and holding the man.

"Not Lu Hao," she said.

"Who would he have reported to? Marquardt?"

"Certainly not! This would put him at a direct risk of prosecution. Someone Marquardt trusts. Preston Song, I think, maybe. My immediate boss, Gail Bunchkin, is also possible. But I think Song. His being Chinese helps the company if it is investigated—keeps the charges off a foreign executive, which would look very bad. It is most likely Marquardt would have received only a verbal report on anything to do with Lu Hao's activities."

"Okay," he said, compartmentalizing. "So as soon as we turn this over, the bribes will likely begin again."

"Without a doubt. This will allow the Xuan Tower project to get back on schedule."

Sensing a change in her, he said, "What is it, Grace?"

"As we have discussed: if The Berthold Group is working against us, then the moment they have Lu Hao's accounts they no longer need Lu Hao. With all the attention being paid to him, it might be more convenient if he disappeared. The police will want to speak to Lu Hao. Maybe others in the government."

"Yes," Knox said. "I've been thinking the same thing. And now, with Sarge out of the equation, maybe there's no ransom money anyway."

"I remind you of Marquardt's trip to Chongming Island. Again, I suggest this trip had nothing to do with the Xuan Tower, yet possibly everything to do with Lu Hao's disappearance."

"Explain."

"My mother claims Lu Hao was on Chongming Island on the sixteenth for a four-day fete. The seventeenth he left me the voice mail."

"You're beating yourself up over that call."

"He was on Chongming Island on the seventeenth! The bribes," she said, pointing to the laptop, "are for favors. Inspectors. Suppliers. There is a banker on here."

Knox nodded. He knew the participants—up close and personal—from his earlier visits.

"I suggest," she said, "the two payments of two hundred thousand U.S. had something to do with Chongming Island. My home. Lu Hao's home. I believe the payments were made through an intermediary—the Mongolians. Lu Hao's phone call to me . . . he was frantic. Maybe he got stupid and pushed too hard. Got himself into trouble. My point is that he had seen something. My mother confirmed he was on Chongming Island the day he phoned me, only days behind Mr. Marquardt's trip."

Knox liked this as a possible motive for the man's kidnapping, and said so. "That has teeth."

"I have the name of the driver Marquardt hired on Chongming Island," she said. "Marquardt's credit card statement," she supplied. "We can follow his trail. We need to determine the purpose of this trip of his. Perhaps it leads to Lu Hao and Mr. Danner."

"It's beyond our purview," he cautioned.

"You talk about the power this accounting holds," she said. "And of course, you are right." This was her first such concession—that possession of the information, more than even the information itself, gave them leverage with which to negotiate. "But knowledge of whatever secret exists, whatever secret they wanted hidden, would give us far more understanding and possible leverage."

"Marquardt is not the enemy. He's who hired us. Did he play it close to the vest? Of course! But we can use this trip of his without knowing the exact details. It's called 'finesse.'"

"Once I deliver the accounts," she said, "there may be no Lu Hao. No Danner. Finesse that! What if Marquardt's—Berthold Group's—only interest in working through Rutherford Risk is to find out how much, if any, of this malfeasance can be discovered by third-party investigators?"

Knox had already considered this same idea—that he and Grace were being used as proxy investigators. *Expendable* investigators.

"Sarge wouldn't do that to me," he said. "Marquardt wouldn't do that to Rutherford Risk. It doesn't make sense."

"Please, John. We must find out how Marquardt's visit to Chongming Island fits into this. I believe this is the key to the kidnapping."

"No time," he said. "The accounts give us all the leverage we need. A bird in the hand. We go with what we have. We're going to dangle the accounts. I promise that neither Lu Hao nor Danner will suffer for it."

"To suffer, one must be alive," she reminded.

"We need Randy to make two copies," he said. "Encrypted copies on thumb drives. You will see to that. When he's finished, Amy and Randy will leave separately, Randy by the back, Amy out front. We must make it abundantly clear to them that they need to leave the city immediately. No returning to work or their apartments. They must go, now."

"The Mongolian," she said. She, too, had spotted the surveillance.

"Yes. I'll handle him. But that's why they must leave now."

"Understood."

Five minutes later, with everyone in place and briefed, Knox left by the back door, taking the sublane behind the shop to a dead end where he climbed a wall and up into a tangle of bamboo scaffolding. He moved through a work crew repairing a tile roof to where he had a view of the street, including the Mongolian, who hadn't moved from his post. Knox searched the street carefully for others, eventually spotting a second Mongolian at some distance.

The closest Mongolian carried a policeman's arrogance, almost daring his mark *not* to spot him. The intimidation factor. Had the Mongolian relocated over the course of the past hour, Knox might have missed him. So why make Knox's job so easy? What could the man hope to win?

Knox texted Amy, and a minute later she left the salon's front door, walking confidently. Neither Mongolian moved.

Knox sent a second text and Grace left, screening herself with an umbrella. Surprising him, she stood at the curb attempting to hail a taxi, scarce because of the light rain. They had agreed to avoid taxis following the Dulwich setup. But, as it turned out, the ruse was simply to give the Mongolian a good long look at her, as she turned and hurried toward a bus stop. The Mongolian slipped onto his motorcycle.

Knox sent a third and final text, this time to Randy's mobile:

go

. . .

6:45 P.M.

For Melschoi, staying with a bus was child's play. The simplicity of the exercise lulled him into complacency—it was like trying to spot an aircraft carrier amid the barges on the Yangtze River.

The flow of bikes and scooters maintained its usual controlled chaos. Melschoi's attention remained divided between the bus and his rearview mirror.

When a helmeted rider closed from behind him, Melschoi slowed, testing. Had this man been watching the hair salon as well?

The bus gained, pulling away in the flow of vehicles to his left. The helmet behind him kept coming—it did not slow with him as a surveillant would. Melschoi jockeyed for position in order to stay with the bus, knowing the move would also give him a better view of the approaching helmet. He checked his outside mirror: *nothing*. The rider must have turned or pulled over.

He happened to glance over to his inside mirror. Too late. The helmeted rider had jumped the sidewalk to pass the slow mass of bikes. The rider reentered the bike lane now only feet from Melschoi, who instinctively swerved right toward the curb, knocking some bikes out of his way. The resulting crash worked against him—he gave the scooter a virtually empty space to navigate. Impressively, the scooter rider leaned heavily to his right and came alongside of Melschoi, avoiding any collision. But Melschoi had the advantage: a slight nudge from him and the scooter would be thrown into the traffic.

Only then did he catch sight of the construction barricade blocking the bike lane. The rider had distracted him, and had boxed him in. The bike lane was narrowing and being forced into the traffic.

That split-second of realization cost him. The rider raised his leg like a dog pissing on a hydrant and kicked out.

Melschoi attempted to block the effort, but lost control as his front wheel tangled with a bike. He went down hard, wheels forward. His front rim caught the curb, catapulting him and the bike airborne. The last thing he saw was a plywood barricade.

7:35 P.M.
HONGQIAO DISTRICT
SHANGHAI

Amy Xue climbed the concrete back stairs of the International Pearl City market, navigating past the litter abandoned by lunchtime employees. Knox be damned! There was no way she could leave the city without some money. She cursed the trouble Knox brought her, though did not dismiss his warning entirely: she'd entered through the back of the mall. Her jewelry store was one of only two that had stair access.

She surprised Li-Shu and Mih-Ho, two of her best stringers, at work knotting custom-designed necklaces. Unaccustomed to their boss using the back stairway, they sat up. Amy greeted them and headed directly to the safe.

Her back to them, Amy said, "Has anyone asked after me?"

Mih-Ho answered, "Some regular customers, of course."

"Strangers?"

"No."

"If they should, you have not seen me. Understand?" The safe opened. She slipped off a necklace and used the two keys hanging from it to open an inner door.

"Yes," both girls answered.

"You will text me immediately if you see anyone suspicious or asking after me. Is that clear?"

"Yes. Certainly," Mih-Ho answered for them both. "Is everything okay?"

"Does it look like everything is okay? I am not kidding around."

"So sorry."

Neither girl had ever seen their boss in such a fit. Li-Shu caught a glimpse of the stacks of *yuan* Amy transferred into her purse—forty thousand or more. A fortune!

"Store hours as normal," Amy instructed, relocking the safe, and then closing and securing its outer door. "If anyone asks, I am with a client appraising an estate collection. You do not know the location. You will offer to call me, only if necessary, and then report that you were unable to reach me. I am gone for the National Day holiday."

"Very well."

"Tell the others exactly as I've told you."

"Of course."

"And no wagging tongues." She directed this at Li-Shu. "This is not a game, Second-cousin's Daughter. Lips sealed. Pure mind, pure heart. Your rumor-mongering could do me great harm."

Li-Shu blushed, embarrassed to be so easily read. "Yes, Auntie. I promise."

"Lock this door behind me. Why was it not locked? What kind of fools leave this door unlocked? Lock it and leave it locked!"

According to the sign, it was never to be locked. Neither woman said a thing.

Amy slipped out the back of the shop and into the stairway. Hearing the lock turn behind her, she began her descent, her senses on immediate alert. An offensive cologne she hadn't noticed before now permeated the air. Superstitious by nature, and on edge because of Knox, she hurried down.

Damn the maintenance men for allowing so many lights to be burned out. *Had it been so dark a moment ago?* she wondered.

Rapid footfalls came from behind her. She arrived at the next stairway landing and encountered a man standing there. She gasped involuntarily.

The man grabbed her wrist, spun her and slapped his hand over her mouth.

She tried to call out, but only groaned. *The shop door is shut and locked*, she thought. *No one will hear me.*

She reared back to hit him, but was no match. He lifted her off her feet like a rag doll and carried her down the stairs.

Paralyzed with fright, she fought to keep from passing out. It felt like swimming for the surface when deeply underwater.

Her feet bounced down the steps. Another man caught her legs.

They arrived at the ground level to a set of doors. She kicked free, caught the door as it came open and smacked it into the forehead of the man at her feet. He dropped her. The one behind her let go of her right arm. She elbowed this man in the throat, and fell to the stairs as he dropped her completely. The door to the outside thumped shut. She scrambled to her feet and ran into the building, a grid of aisles and shop stalls.

Amy knocked shoppers aside, trying to distance herself from her pursuers. She had the advantage of familiarity. She knew these shops and their keepers.

The two coming behind her split up, taking parallel aisles. They were attempting to box her in. She hurried, dropped to her hands and knees, and crawled into a clothing stall to her left.

"Cousin!" she called out, moving for the back wall. "Muggers! Thieves! You must help me! The door! The door!"

The woman shopkeeper did not hesitate. She raced to the back wall, slid some dresses aside and popped open the hidden door to the storage room. Most shops had such hidden doors.

"Not a word!" Amy said, still crawling. The door clicked shut behind her.

7:40 P.M.

At the intersection of aisles the two men met with a silent exchange— they'd lost her. The leader waved his partner forward and together they began a search, stall by stall.

They tipped over racks, pulled down shelves and cursed at the top of their lungs.

7:41 P.M.

Amy heard the shopkeeper cry out, followed by the sound of destruction. A *smack* silenced the woman. Then a rake of hangers.

The door to the hidden room broke open.

Amy struck the first man with the tine of a metal hanger, punching a hole in his chest. He screamed and jumped for her, but she ducked and avoided him, smacking the second man. She ran her nails down his neck and let go.

Squeezing past and out into the shop, she ran. Just as she reached the first intersection of aisles, she was tackled from behind. Her arm was twisted behind her and she found herself being carried out the back.

At the moment she was struck by the fresh air, there came a sound like a melon hitting the kitchen floor. Warmth speckled her face.

Blood.

The men dropped her. One lay on the concrete, out cold and bleeding.

A monster with half his face scraped off—a Mongolian, or northerner—brutalized the second man.

Before she fully came to her feet, someone grabbed her from behind and dragged her into a van. She was thrown inside and her abductor followed in behind her. The door slid shut. The tires squealed.

A flurry of Shanghainese cursing. The driver said something to the man hovering over her about "going back for him." More cursing. A rag was stuffed down her throat, followed by duct tape across her face.

She blacked out.

7:53 P.M.

Melschoi dragged the man deeper down the alley, already softening him up by kneeing him repeatedly in the chest. The man bounced away from him like a puppet.

"Who do you work for?" Melschoi asked in passable Mandarin.

"Feng Qi."

"Yang Cheng's man?" Melschoi said, holding him tightly.

"*Dui.*"

Melschoi contemplated the angles like a mathematician.

"Where have they taken her, these men?" The road rash on his face had not had time to scab, leaving him looking like he'd made out with a cheese grater.

The man's eyes rolled back in his head. Melschoi was losing him. Melschoi lifted him off the ground and kneed him in the groin, jolting him awake.

"Where?" Melschoi said, his hand now clenching the man's throat.

The man volunteered an address on Moganshan Road, a former warehouse district that had been partially gentrified into art galleries.

Melschoi knew the area. He leaned in close to the man. "You work for me now. We always have eye on you. You try to run or double-cross me and I will cut off your manhood."

Melschoi took the man's mobile phone one-handed and dialed in his own number in order to save it into the man's phone.

"Whatever you hear, you will pass along to me *immediately*," Melschoi said. "If I do not hear from you *regularly*, you will hear from me." He held up the man's wallet so he'd be sure to remember Melschoi possessed it.

He let him fall. "If you try to warn your associates, I come back for you."

8:40 P.M.

Amy Xue vaguely recalled swallowing something bitter. Her limbs were numb. She tried to speak, but her words were slurred. She took a moment to place herself in her surroundings. Two men: one bruised and beaten. Her shirt hung open, exposing her breasts and belly. She could see she wasn't wearing pants, but couldn't feel anything. Her wrists were held to a bamboo pole with plastic ties, the pole tied between pipes.

A man's low voice spoke Mandarin close to her ear. "The American and the Chinese woman. Names. Mobile numbers. And where to find them."

She perceived a need to lie, but surprised herself.

"John Knox," she answered. "The woman is called Grace."

"We have your phone. Which are their numbers?"

He held her mobile phone up in front of her, but she couldn't focus. The room was swirling and fuzzy. She felt physically numb and mentally empty—as if all resistance had been bled out of her. Her tongue had a mind of its own.

"The top number," she said, finally seeing the screen, though dimly, "is his."

She considered herself such an expert liar—perhaps the best bargainer in all the pearl market. She didn't know this woman she heard speaking.

The lighting changed as if a door had come open. A gray hue spread along the ceiling. Whatever it was, it caused the man in front of her to turn around, for which she was extremely grateful.

Do something, she willed her body. But it was gone. All sensation, gone.

Melschoi recognized the minivan from the abduction at the pearl market. *Amateurs.* It was parked in a muddy lot on the back side of a storage building that, according to the sign, was leased to Yang Construction. *Idiots.*

Melschoi climbed atop the van and had a look inside. No guns. Three men without so much as a knife between them, he guessed. They'd stripped the woman naked, which offended Melschoi. He thought back to the rape of his dead brother's wife. He gained a newfound energy.

He kicked in the door, shouted, "Police!" and headed straight for the one whom he'd seen was in charge. The announcement bought him enough time to cross the space without being attacked. Their expressions changed as Melschoi's torn face caught the lights. Two of them had just met him an hour earlier.

He grabbed an electric drill off the wall and swung it by its cord like a chain mace.

One of the men made for the door. The drill clubbed him at the base of the neck and he fell.

"Next," he said in Mandarin, moving inexorably toward a man who hoisted an office chair. Melschoi used the flying drill to break his ribs and then club the side of his head.

The third produced a knife.

Melschoi stepped onto the fallen man's back, using him like a doormat. He swung the drill in a figure eight in front of him.

"Be certain she is worth it," he said.

His opponent circled to his right.

"Tell your employer he should leave this to others. It is a cemetery for those who stay." He motioned an invitation toward the open door.

The man backed out of the warehouse slowly. Moments later, the van started and raced away.

Melschoi tied up the fallen pair with electric cords. He faced her, having noted the spilled pills and Gatorade on the desk.

Mandarin did not come naturally when his adrenaline flowed.

"I can leave you here," he said. "Maybe they return. Maybe someone else comes along. We both know what they will do with you." He ran his eyes over her. She stared into space, unblinking. "I know you can hear me. It must be agony, not to be able to move. So, where do I find the foreigner?"

He started the drill swinging again.

"I do not know," she said.

He trusted her answers, knowing the effects of Rohypnol.

"The hair salon," he said.

"Computer files."

"What kind of files?" he asked.

"Spreadsheet."

"The foreigner has the spreadsheet?" he said.

She stared off into space; he was losing her.

"His name?" He stepped closer, knowing she could hear. He raised his voice. *"His name?"* The words reverberated in the space.

"John Not."

"'John Not'?"

He could see the light go out. He closed her eyelids for her. Touched her carotid artery and felt a weak pulse. He picked up her discarded pants and purse from which a pile of money spilled. He took the purse. Cut her down and carried her like a sack over his shoulder to his bike.

He drove her up the road to a bus stop and sat her down on a bench, covering her lap with her pants and buttoning her shirt. He patted her on the cheek, half-tempted to thank her.

16

"This had better be good!" Allan Marquardt declared, glaring at Grace as she stood at his front door.

Elegant Gardens, a gated expatriate compound in the Hongqiao District, was home to several dozen three-story McMansions on small, manicured lawns.

Grace had announced herself at the compound's main gate, forced to wait to see if Marquardt would admit her. Now, his eyes irreverently inspected her.

"My apologies, Mr. Marquardt," she said. "It is urgent."

Reluctantly, he showed her inside. A television played somewhere within. A thin and beautiful middle-aged woman in white linen pants and an aquamarine silk top approached. Marquardt introduced his wife, Lois. He introduced Grace as an employee.

"Tea, please, darling," Marquardt said.

He led Grace into a sitting room filled with crowded bookshelves and Asian art. The yin-yang love seat he offered was more than two hundred years old. He sat in a leather chair, facing her from across an Indian elephant-saddle coffee table.

Grace said, "May I talk freely?"

"Yes. The house is secure."

"My associate and I," she said, avoiding naming Knox, "have located and obtained Lu Hao's accounting of the incentives."

Marquardt seemed to float for a moment. "Excellent!"

She opened her hand, revealing a USB thumb drive. Then closed her hand, trapping it inside.

"I will turn it over to you along with the encryption code necessary to read the files, as soon as you explain the reason for your trip to Chongming Island." This had not been part of Knox's plan.

Marquardt's composure flagged. "I beg your pardon?"

"Chongming Island."

"I . . . know the place."

"You went there with Preston Song. I need to know why. It has become critical to our saving the hostages."

"I remind you that you are, indirectly, my employee. If you'd like me to call Brian, I'd be happy to. Extortion is not your best option."

"I looked into the reasons for the two hundred thousand dollar payments at our lunch. I was stonewalled. You and Mr. Song visited Chongming Island after the first payment, a payment Mr. Lu never accounted for in the Xuan Tower incentives. Why not? A second such payment preceded Mr. Lu's kidnapping by a matter of hours, according to your own records. That also needs explaining."

Lois Marquardt arrived with the tea. She fixed two cups and turned to leave.

"My associate and I have been followed," Grace said, appealing to the man's wife, who turned to listen. "My apartment is under video surveillance. I cannot return there. I have been followed repeatedly from work. I can no longer risk going there. *Anywhere*, for that matter. One of my associates has been hospitalized in serious condition. Presumably, much of this relates to the files on this thumb drive and, I believe, your trip to Chongming Island with Preston Song."

"Allan?"

Marquardt eyed his wife, clearly wanting her gone.

"I've got it, dear. Thank you for the tea."

"If you need anything," she said to Grace, "give a holler." She left.

"I don't see how our trip could possibly be connected to the kid-napping."

"Then you admit it."

"How did you find out?"

"It is not important."

"It is to me. More important than you can possibly imagine."

"You need not know the details. Part of my job is to protect you," she said.

"I can't tell you a thing about it. You've wasted a trip over here, I'm afraid."

"That's unacceptable."

"Ms. Chu, we are on the same side. What you're asking is impossible. If I could, I would. But I cannot." He paused. "The thumb drive, please."

"We have lost the ransom due to a complication—our associate being hospitalized. Your trip to Chongming Island—whatever took you there is relevant to the kidnapping, I assure you."

"Not possible. And, yes, Brian updated me on the ransom. It's a bum deal."

"First, you will explain Chongming Island," Grace said levelly. "Then you will raise as much U.S. cash as possible before tomorrow morning at nine A.M. The rest we will raise from other parties interested in the drive's contents."

Marquardt coughed. "The content of that drive is *my* property. You will most certainly not be auctioning it off. I will detain you here, if nec-essary. You've overstepped your bounds, young lady."

Marquardt produced a BlackBerry from a waist clip and worked it one-handed.

"I would not do that, sir," Grace said. "Your phone is being monitored by the Chinese. Count on it. You do not want them knowing we have located Lu's accounts." Grace paused. "They will descend upon us like locusts."

"Then turn it over," Marquardt said, his thumb hovering over the green key.

"I cannot do this."

"You're out of your depth, Ms. Chu. You don't want to threaten me. I'll have you detained."

"Unlikely," she said.

"I've spoken to Brian and we're trying to raise as much cash as possible. The proof-of-life comes at the storefront on Nanjing Road. You will be there with the money, but it looks as if it'll fall short of fifty thousand. Threatening me does not help your cause."

"Less than fifty thousand? Unacceptable. They are expecting five times that."

"Brian believes they might accept one hundred. We won't know until you deliver it."

"Too risky."

"This is a game of risks, I'm told. The thumb drive, please."

Grace caught a glimpse of the phone. The BlackBerry was already connected.

"More tea?" he asked.

She'd barely touched her cup. He wanted her to stay. The call had been to security. The compound's team? His own? Did it matter?

Grace stood. "Highest bidder wins the drive and its contents."

"Do not do this," Marquardt said calmly. "You will be crushed."

Security would post men at the front and back doors, providing there were at least two men, which she doubted. More like a single bodyguard with contact to the compound's team.

If indeed a single bodyguard, he would pull back to a position with a view of both doors. That, or he'd enter the house.

"Save your career while you still can." He opened his palm to her.

She hurried from the room and nearly plowed over Lois Marquardt, who'd been in the hall within eavesdropping range. Lois and Grace's eyes met. Lois glanced at the front door and she shook her head. Grace scanned the stairs.

Lois nodded and said softly, "Fire ropes in the window seats."

Grace bounded upstairs.

There was a child asleep in the first room she tried. She moved on to the end of the hallway—the master suite. Spotted the window seat and, pulling off its cushion, opened it. A chain ladder was bolted to the wall. The window faced the access lane and the drive. Men watching the front and back doors would not see her here. She fed the ladder through the window and followed it outside. It danced unpredictably; it took all her strength and balance to descend without whipping it against the house and revealing her position.

She dropped into the landscaping and ducked, keeping low. Plotting her escape. The support team would arrive momentarily; if she weren't out of the compound by then, they would have her. The compound was essentially a twenty-acre cul-de-sac with a gated single entrance, surrounded by a twelve-foot rock wall topped with broken glass set in concrete. Designed to keep people out, it also kept them in.

She crept through shadow in the direction away from the gated entrance, reaching the end of Marquardt's house. No security man in sight. It was a one-man show until support arrived, and the bodyguard had chosen the front door—and the compound's entrance side—to guard.

Grace took off at a run, house-to-house, keeping in shadow whenever possible. She had taken the bus to come here. Now she was on foot.

There was no way she would make it past the gate without close-quarter combat. The gate guards were untrained in anything but raising their hands and checking documents. If there were just two, she could take them. But if they'd summoned their patrols—another two or three keeping watch within the compound—she'd be outnumbered.

She spotted a bicycle dumped in a driveway. Carried it to the access road and climbed on. She circled around the western side of the compound—the booth guards would be expecting her from the east. It might buy her an extra few seconds.

Porch lights from houses lighted the lane only in patches. She held the bike to the far curb beneath towering bamboo, and therefore mostly in shadow. Street noise intensified as she approached the gate and the only break in the high wall. Lights blazed around the small guardhouse where she now spotted *two* uniformed men.

They spotted her.

One stepped in front of the red-and-white striped pole arm blocking the vehicle entrance. He raised his hand for her to stop.

The other man kept to just outside the guardhouse, a gap in the entrance for pedestrians—nannies and *ayis*—blocking this as well.

Grace slowed, wishing to appear cooperative. She swung a leg off, but remained balanced on the left pedal, the bike coasting. A matter of yards from the guard at the pole, she hopped off and launched the bike into him, running for the surprised booth guard. He, too, comically raised his hand for her to stop. She broke his left knee; drove her own knee into his nose as he wrenched forward. He went down hard.

The guard who'd gone down with the bike was up and running. He caught sight of his buddy reeling, and when Grace turned to face him, stopped stiffly, unsure how to proceed.

She juked a hard step toward him and he flinched backward. She knew she had him.

"I am not worth it," she said, speaking Shanghainese. "Jilted mistress. Nothing more. I will put your nut sack in your intestines if you come after me."

She turned, but did not run. The guard took several steps toward her, but as she shot him a look, he stopped again. His friend groaned. He turned to help him.

Grace lowered her head and fought to contain her adrenaline, wanting so badly to run, but knowing it would only give her away. A dark blue van slowed to turn into the compound—two Chinese in the front, the right age and look for corporate security.

She waited for the van to turn into the gate area and then took off at a run.

In the distance, a bus approached the bus stop.

11:50 P.M.
HUANGPU DISTRICT
SHANGHAI

In the glow of dimmed ceiling lights, Yang Cheng paced past an oil paint-
ing by Eddie Lim, a violent eruption of red, white and black. Behind him
was the panoramic view of the Huangpu River, and the colorful neon
from the tourist ferries plying its waters. Rain pelted the window.

"I am most disappointed in you," Yang Cheng, brimming with anger,
said to Feng.

"I understand."

"Do you know where I was just now? A dinner with two investors
from Brussels. They have agreed in principle to supply me up to one billion euros in capital for the New City construction. One small problem.
I have not yet won the bid. Reason I have not yet won the bid? I have
not submitted bid. Reason I have not submitted bid? Tragic Lu remains
in captivity of kidnappers in possession of Magic Number. Pearl Lady was
connection we needed, and now . . . where is Pearl Lady?"

"I am to blame," said Feng, still suffering from the pain of the bruises
inflicted by the Mongolian. "Inexcusable. I offer my resignation."

"I will not let you off so easily." Yang Cheng continued pacing.
"One man?"

"A northerner. Mongolian, perhaps."

"Scum. Inbreds."

"Of course."

"Pearl Lady?"

Feng said nothing at first. "We must assume the Mongol has her. In
our favor: she will be of no help to him for another twelve hours. Perhaps
longer."

"Not an entire failure then."

Feng awaited more admonishment. When it wasn't forthcoming he
dared to say, "If I may suggest—?"

"No, you may not." Yang spun his wedding ring. "Go ahead," he said.

Feng considered his words carefully. "If the ransom exchange takes place, if Tragic Lu is recovered alive, then likely the New City bid number—the Magic Number—if in fact Lu Hao has it, as we suspect, is in Marquardt's possession."

"This is nothing I do not know."

"But should the ransom delivery fail, we are given additional time to find Lu Hao before the others."

"A man's ears are never shut," Yang said, looking at Feng for the first time in the past twenty minutes.

"We have the video and audio recordings of Chu Youya in her apartment. She clearly received corporate books of a suspect nature from a woman professing to be Marquardt's assistant. This alone could get her fired. Perhaps even investigated by banking authorities."

Yang nodded, beginning to follow. A smile struggled onto his otherwise anguished face. "Yes."

"The videos could be delivered, anonymously, of course," Feng said. "I also have photographs of Chu Youya taking lunch with the *waiguoren*. Papers exchanged here as well, and we have waitress as witness. The *waiguoren* might find himself sought for questioning as well, making the ransom exchange impossible."

Yang nodded. "You are shit for brains, but your shit smells sweet at this moment. I mentioned such tactics earlier," Yang said, always needing to claim authorship.

"Of course you did. I am only reminding you of your worthy recommendation. It was stupid of me not to recognize its brilliance at the time."

"The authorities will not take kindly to such third-party surveillance. The recordings must not be traceable back to us. Not ever."

"It will be handled like eggshells. All measure of secrecy and security."

"You will handle this yourself."

A career death sentence for Feng should it fail. He'd be a department store rent-a-cop if he failed.

"I am honored to be valued with your trust," he lied.

Yang's mobile phone rang where he'd left it on his desk. He checked the caller ID.

It was his secretary, Katherine. Late for her to be calling. Perhaps she'd reconsidered his most recent advances. He waved Feng out of his office dismissively.

In the distance, the flashing lights of a jet descended into the Pudong airport—another plane full of *waiguoren*, no doubt. The poison continued.

They spoke in Shanghainese.

"Yes?"

"I have had a call from the woman, Chu Youya. She wishes to meet with you."

Yang thought it had to be some kind of disturbing joke, he and Feng having just spoken of her.

"Sir?"

"You've spoken to her directly?"

"Yes. Tonight, if possible. I informed her I thought you available."

He found his voice. "My office. Fifteen minutes." He checked the clock. "Can you arrange it?"

"Yes, of course."

"I will want you here at your desk."

Face.

"My pleasure," she said.

"Make it thirty minutes," he said, giving Katherine added time to reach the office building. "Bring her up the private elevator." He tossed a crumb her way: no one used the private elevator but him.

She said brightly, "Thirty minutes."

"You've done well." Another crumb. If he played his cards right, he might even win her services by the end of the night as well.

He called Feng back into his office. "You will have video or audio set up in this office in the next thirty minutes."

"But it's—" Feng caught himself glancing at his watch, his mind reeling. "Right away," he said.

FRIDAY
October 1

The exchange

17

"An unexpected pleasure," Yang Cheng said, addressing Grace in Shang-hainese.

She reached into her purse and came out with the thumb drive. "Lu Hao's accounts," she said in Mandarin, finding Shanghainese too coarse and rapid for business negotiations.

Yang's eyes flared slightly. Otherwise, he was a picture of executive comportment: interested, but not overly excited. "Am I supposed to know what you're talking about?"

"Perhaps not," she said, returning the drive to her purse. "And since you do not, and might be considering other means to explore the topic, let me just say the drive's contents are encrypted—highly encrypted—the key to which requires me to make a certain call from a specific phone at a specific time. And not before lunchtime today, at any rate."

He nodded glumly. "Let us assume I can imagine what you mean by 'Mr. Lu's accounts.'"

Grace eased her purse shut, its magnet snapping sharply.

"I require a bid in excess of one hundred thousand USD by nine A.M. Delivery before noon."

Yang smiled, cat-like. "Is that so? I warned you about working for Mr. Marquardt. You should have accepted my job offer."

"Perhaps it is not too late."

"It is very much too late. Selling corporate secrets is a punishable offense, Ms. Chu."

"So is buying them, I imagine," she said. She looked around the office. "And for the sake of whatever recording devices you have in place," she said, "let me just say you are the one calling these files corporate secrets, not me. To my knowledge, these files are not from a corporation but an individual, one Lu Hao, and I believe you will find he grants me access to these files insomuch as he is presently captive and in dire need of funds to secure his safe release."

Yang felt his forehead perspiring. If the camera hadn't been running he might choke the life out of this pest. She'd been nothing but trouble for him.

"What you ask . . . it is a great deal of foreign currency to raise on such short notice," he said. "Perhaps *yuan* would suffice?"

"USD," she said. "Highest bid wins. Nine A.M."

"One hundred thousand? A week or two at the earliest. The banks, you see? Noon today? Never."

"Noon," she said, standing. "Katherine has my phone number."

"She will show you out."

"I look forward to hearing from you."

"Tread lightly. This is a great risk for you, Chu Youya."

She quoted a proverb that translated: *How can you catch tiger cubs without entering the tiger's lair?*

"How many others?" he inquired.

"Enough," she said.

"Same conditions?"

"I will accept bids up until nine A.M. The cash, by noon." She nodded. "If I'm followed from here—and believe me, I'll know it—you are off the list."

2:10 A.M.
CHANGNING DISTRICT
SHANGHAI

Grace microwaved some frozen Bi Feng Tang barbecue pork buns. She and Knox ate on the half balcony of the safe house apartment overlooking other people's laundry. They drank beer.

"You are dressed in all black," she said. "You have been sweating and your eyes are dilated from adrenaline."

"As are yours," he said.

"Did you confront him?" she asked. "The Mongolian? Was he there?"

"Tell me about Marquardt. Yang Cheng?"

They both sipped their beer.

She said, "I am waiting."

"As am I?"

"This is childish," she said.

"I paid a visit to the Mongolian's room as we discussed. And, yes: I made sure he wasn't there," Knox said. "I had a look around."

"And?"

"If you crossed a monk with a Marine you'd have this guy nailed. Neat and tidy, and very few possessions, if you discount the false wall behind the prayer rug," he said.

"Please explain," she said.

"Four screws in a false panel. The man's a pack rat." Knox's wound made him wince. "There was a video camera hidden in there. A professional camera. Pretty beat up. Two handguns—both Russian. And a considerable amount of *yuan*. Maybe eighty or a hundred thousand."

"The missing cameraman," she said. "The one the Iron Hand seeks."

"Yes. And if he's as damaged as his camera, we can cross him off the list of the living."

"Any footage on the camera?"

He passed her his iPhone. "Excuse the quality. I videotaped the little monitor on the side of the thing." He upended his beer and drank loudly.

"Asphalt crew?" she said. "I do not understand."

"Neither did I. But keep watching."

Her eyes flared. "Who are they?"

"Too small to see. We need a much bigger monitor and a better copy. But the guy on the left is big enough to be our Mongolian. And the other guy is fat enough and well dressed enough to be rich."

"You brought the tape." She made it a statement.

"It's a disk. But no. I left it in the camera."

She glanced at him, frustrated. "But why?"

"We know where to find it. And if it goes missing, we've played our hand. You need to keep watching."

She returned her eyes to the phone's video.

"An asphalt crew at night," he said, "in what looks like a light industrial area." He rolled up his sleeve, revealing Chinese characters written in pen on his forearm. "This character is seen on a sign on the building in the background."

"*Chong,*" she said. "This means 'honor, esteem.' Chongming Island . . ."

"Yeah. That occurred to me. Keep watching. It's coming up any second."

"Why film asphalt being laid?" she asked.

"Why hold on to a camera if this guy is dead? And if he's missing a hand, he's likely dead," he said. "If the Mongolian's working for the police, for this inspector, then I can see it. Cops retain evidence in order to convict or to—"

"Extort."

"Yes," he said. "Or as insurance. Agreed."

"And if that fat guy with the Mongolian is a Beijing party member . . ."

She gasped loudly.

"You've got good eyes," Knox said. "I didn't see him until the second time I watched."

She rewound the video and paused when a man's head appeared on the far left of the frame—a man hanging on to the wall and peering over into the compound. The frame then moved to encompass the spy and the lens zoomed to capture his face in close-up.

"I recognized him from the pictures in the digital frame," Knox said.

A pixilated Lu Hao stared into the camera lens looking like a deer caught in headlights.

She'd gone a pasty color. "Oh, Lu Hao."

"Whoever laid that asphalt did not want it being seen."

"In China," she said, angry with him, "we work all hours. This is nothing."

"They're hiding something," he said. "Count on it."

"And Lu Hao saw it."

"And the fat dude," Knox said. "He saw the fat dude. And whoever that other guy was."

"This is why he called me." She went suddenly very quiet.

"You can't beat yourself up over it."

She had tears in her eyes when she looked up at him.

Knox felt fatigue drag him down over the next several minutes of her brooding silence. For his part, Knox was celebrating that the video he'd shot was clear enough to make out some detail. He thought that on a bigger and better screen he might be able to make out faces.

He touched her arm. "Seriously. There's nothing you can do about it now except fix it. We're going to fix it."

She filled him in on her meeting with Yang Cheng and Marquardt.

"One of them will come through," he said. "If not, we'll drop a duffel of newsprint and improvise."

"They will kill them."

"They won't get the chance. You'll see."

"There is only the two of us. Marquardt should not have made that call. By now the Chinese know we have Lu's records. We are marked."

"We knew there'd be speed bumps. You do what you have to do."

She eyed him curiously.

"An American proverb," he said.

"What now, John?"

He wanted another beer. Maybe five.

"I need to call Randy," he said.

"For the encryption code? I thought he gave it to you." She sounded defeated.

"He did. Yes. Not the encryption code. The new proof of life," he said. "Primer will demand a final proof of life before making the drop. That's our chance."

18

The Friday start of National Celebration Day coincided with the Mid-Autumn Festival, resulting in a migration involving over three hundred million Chinese. Nearly a hundred million round-trip train tickets would be purchased, accounting for one hundred eighty million passengers in less than three days. Two hundred million others would travel to their family homes by bus, car, bike, motorcycle, boat or by foot. Flights would be added to every route, and every plane was overbooked. Ferries would be jammed, their passenger count well exceeding the posted limits. Chinese citizens were duty bound to return to their ancestral homes. Expats seized the week-long celebrations as opportunities for vacation travel in and out of the country. China would effectively shut down. First was the celebration in honor of the founding of the People's Republic; then, the autumnal equinox—a holiday dating back three thousand years. The human exodus would empty the streets and sidewalks of Shanghai, and the city's population of twenty million would be drained to less than half that.

Among those not going anywhere were Knox and Grace.

With Knox having contacted Primer, they slept in shifts awaiting a return call, waiting for bids for the Lu Hao accounts from Marquardt or Yang Cheng.

At seven, they showered, ate *baozi* from a street vendor and drank Starbucks coffee. The sun shone brilliantly though Knox had read the forecast—the receding edge of typhoon Duan, a storm that had devastated the Philippines three days earlier, was on track to sweep onto the mainland by afternoon and stall, dumping rain amid hurricane-force winds.

For construction projects like the Xuan Tower, the timing of the storm couldn't have been worse. With no manpower due to the holiday exodus, there was no labor force to secure the hundreds of sites, to batten down equipment or secure scaffolding. The government put out a call over the radio and television for all workers to return to the city. It would go largely ignored.

Grace's iPhone rang. She and Knox stared at it briefly before she answered.

"Hello? Wait please . . . I will put it on speakerphone."

". . . you out of your mind?" Primer's voice was tight. "Extorting a client? Pitting him against his competition?"

Knox heard the man's venting, but thought only of Dulwich holding out an identical phone and showing him the tracking location of the Mongolian.

Without introduction or apology, Knox said, "You got my text about demanding a final proof of life?"

"Who the hell do you think you're talking to?"

"Any progress with push-back?" Knox asked calmly.

A long pause on Primer's end. "I don't deal with rogues."

"If we'd gone rogue, we wouldn't have recommended you require a final proof of life and we wouldn't have answered your call. Ask Marquardt about Chongming Island. He's been withholding on us. We're fucked here. We could use someone with some spine. We need the deets of the drop."

A long pause. Then, "Time is clearly their bugaboo. They're in a hurry. We negotiated it down to a hundred K. It's to be Grace only. She arrives fifteen-thirty with the money and no one following. People's Square Metro station. It's a Dirty Harry. A run and drop. The proof of life will be a storefront video with real-time tags. Hostages to be released within twenty-four to forty-eight hours following a successful drop. It works for us."

Knox scribbled out the details. The storefront proof-of-life intrigued him.

"What the hell were you two thinking?" Primer asked.

Knox answered. "Without Guangzhou, we're a little light on funds, and it occurred to us with the hostage's accounts turned over, the value of the hostages diminishes. Substantially."

"We're contracted to make the drop."

"*You* are, yes," Knox said. "We're committed to extraction and we're a little short-handed here. Sarge's situation, our own situation . . . we're improvising."

"Marquardt can raise forty."

"It's not nearly enough," Knox said.

"You will *not* auction off the accounts."

"I'm afraid we will honor whichever bid comes in higher. But more importantly, we can now eliminate Yang Cheng from our suspect list for the kidnapping. If he had Lu Hao, he wouldn't need to pay for the accounts. He'd have beaten it out of him."

Primer's breathing could be heard. "I can see that."

For a moment, no one spoke.

"Grace," Primer said. "Turn the accounts over to Allan. You know the drill."

She looked into Knox's eyes. "I am afraid I . . . that is, we, must accept the highest bid."

Knox relaxed noticeably, and smiled at her.

"Shit." Primer had tried to keep it from being heard.

Knox said, "The plan is for extraction. By the time the drop is made, I should have them back."

"Don't be a fool. You'll get them killed. Wait! You know their location?"

Knox reached over and ended the call.

Grace suppressed a smile. "I should have taken Yang's offer of employment."

At 8:45, Grace's personal phone rang and she clapped it up, answering immediately.

"Ms. Wu," she said, so that Knox understood it was Yang's assistant, Katherine Wu. She listened. "Yes. Thank you. I will call you right back."

She disconnected the call.

"Two hundred thousand, U.S."

"Impressive on such short notice," Knox allowed.

"But I am afraid we must not accept it," she said.

"Because?"

"Mr. Primer. The Berthold Group is the client. We do not know the repercussions of turning that information over to Yang. He could use it so many ways. No matter what, he is certain to use it to destroy The Berthold Group. This is our client. Much face would be lost. An American firm accused of bribing officials? This is not good for anyone."

"First, the kidnapper is our client. We serve the kidnapper. Second, they are expecting a hundred thousand. Do you want to deliver Marquardt's forty? We take forty from Marquardt and sixty from Yang. We're up front about it: we let them both know the other guy is getting Lu's accounts. We give Marquardt an unencrypted version. It'll take Yang days or weeks to decrypt. That gives Marquardt time to be ready for whatever Yang throws at him. It's the best we can do."

"We promised it to the highest bidder."

He shrugged.

"It is an interesting compromise," she said.

"I'll take that as a compliment."

Knox had been unable to raise Amy; his concern for her compounded with each passing hour. But he'd hired Randy to consult on the proof-of-life's delivery to a storefront.

"We're good? You and me?" he asked Grace.

She nodded. "We are good."

11:00 A.M.
ZHABEI DISTRICT

A blue Buick minivan pulled to the curb, cutting through a thick column of bikes and scooters and motorcycles, all burdened with extra passengers and belongings. Knox threw open the side door. A duffel bag was strapped by seatbelt into the captain's chair.

Knox unclipped it and swung the door shut. The van sped off.

He and Grace met three blocks to the east. She arrived carrying a similar duffel. They sat side by side on a park bench, the hundred thousand U.S. on their laps.

Knox kept a constant watch, his eyes shielded by a pair of knock-off Ray-Bans.

Grace said nervously, "The Metro station. I am expected there for the drop."

"It's a runaround," Knox said.

"I heard Mr. Primer refer to this. I do not understand, exactly."

"It's Dirty Harry." He could see her disconnect. "A movie—a character in a movie—a cop. Inspector Harry Callahan. He had to make a drop. He's forced to run pay phone to pay phone to separate him from his backup."

She inhaled sharply, as if she'd been punched.

"What?" he asked.

"Nothing."

"Scared?"

"Maybe a little." But her eyes said differently. He saw concentration, heated thought. Anything but fear.

"Are you going to tell me?"

"Tell you what?" she said.

He nodded. Whatever had shook her up, she'd quickly recovered and did not want to discuss it.

But the question remained.

elschoi rubbed the stubs of his two fingers lost to frostbite over eighteen months earlier, warding off the shooting pain that foretold an impending storm. He praised the gods for his good fortune, grateful to be moving on his motorcycle instead of caught in traffic. As he headed toward the intersection, he'd received a call from Feng Qi's man, his Yang Cheng insider. It was the fourth such call he'd received from the man.

"Authorities intercepted communication from a Berthold Group executive," the man reported. "A woman, Chu, is handling the ransom drop. She is to go to a store along Nanjing Road to receive proof the hostages live."

"What store?"

"Is unknown."

"Your team will be watching?"

"Nanjing Road is long. Many stores."

"Here is how it will work: if your team spots her, you will call me immediately. If I should call you, you will report seeing the woman where I tell you."

The line remained open.

"I have your wallet. Your address. The address of your family," Melschoi said, reminding the man, not appreciating his hesitancy. "Do not think. Just do."

"Feng has given police a video of the woman."

"Why?"

"Figure it out."

The man disconnected the call.

The ransom drop was set. Feng wanted the Chu woman arrested before the ransom could be paid.

Melschoi felt poised on the verge of a great success. The bee would not be far from the honey. He could nearly taste the air of the steppes. Could see his children's smiles.

1:00 P.M.
LUWAN DISTRICT
U.S. CONSULATE

The massive blob of forest green and blood red jerked rhythmically across Steve Kozlowski's computer screen, indicating the steady advance of the approaching typhoon. Kozlowski's eyes narrowed. His daughter, Tucker, enjoying a holiday from the Shanghai Community International School, was at a play date with a friend. He was considering calling their driver, Peng, and having Tucker picked up before the storm hit. At that moment, his phone rang.

"Kozlowski," he answered.

"I'm close to making a deal on the bike," the voice on the other end said.

He heard a series of soft clicks and a change in the voice quality as Knox said, "You still there?"

Kozlowski slid open his desk drawer and glanced at the white iPhone taken from the hospitalized imposter. He'd placed a call on the phone to test it. He recognized the sound of the service-shifting sound quality that made the call impossible to trace or eavesdrop. That Knox possessed such a phone surprised him.

"I warned you there might come a time I couldn't help you. That time has arrived." He eased the drawer shut.

"Don't hang up! Please. Is this line secure?"

"What do you think? How about on your end?" he said knowingly.

Knox didn't answer.

"I was shown some video of a Westerner putting the hurt on some locals. Not once, but twice. I don't take kindly to being called to task by the city police."

Knox wasn't going to lie to him, so he said nothing.

"Word to the wise: the Chinese have the most advanced face recognition system out there. On your way out of the country, stay away from the airports and train stations and keep your head down when out on the streets. You're a marked man, Knox. I would get the hell out of Dodge while the getting's good."

"The guys were Mongolians, not Chinese," Knox said, wondering if the face recognition explained his being tracked to the wet market. "Hired muscle working for a Beijing big with unusual financial ties to The Berthold Group. One of these goons has a commercial quality hi-def video camera hidden in his wall. Ring any bells?"

Kozlowski held the phone away while attempting to calm himself. He returned the phone to his ear. Knox was still talking.

"—interest you."

"Say again."

"A video camera. Expensive, though banged up and still able to play its contents. I thought maybe that might interest you. It's engraved—'property of Road Worthy Film and Video Supply in Glendale, California.'"

"I am aware of the stolen property. Yes."

"This being China, I thought we might negotiate."

"I'm listening."

"I need safe passage for four."

A long hesitation. "The U.S. government is not in the practice of—"

"You're either interested or not. It'll be later today. Evening. Maybe into the night. You can, or can't?"

Kozlowski had worked hard through a career that currently involved paperwork and e-mails where once it had meant working the backstreets of Nairobi or Delhi. God, how he'd loved the work as an operative. That marriage and a child had made him more cautious, more career-motivated, was a personal tragedy of sorts. He envied Knox his predicament, understood the importance of his own role, yet had no desire to annul all the tedious hours that had led to this moment: four years from retirement at the age of forty-nine. A lifetime ahead. But the video camera and what

it represented was a gold ring. Solving the disappearance of the cameraman was paramount.

"I'll evaluate the video camera," Kozlowski said.

"*After* my friends and I are safely out of here."

A pause. "If you get yourself arrested, I'm left with nothing. No deal.
The camera. Then I'll do what I can."

The subtle shifting of tone punctuated the line.

"Can it be done?" Knox asked.

"A contact could be arranged. How it works out . . . well, no promises.
This is China."

"What kind of contact?"

"I give you a company number to dial. It's a real estate front. I can
walk you through it."

Company number. *CIA*, Knox realized. "So start walking," he said.

"First the location of the camera. I'll sit on it until I hear from you,
or I hear you've been taken into custody. But I must have it in advance.
Those are the terms."

Knox described the narrow lane in the Muslim quarter. He told
Kozlowski it would be easier to lead him there in person.

"This is my city, Knox." He took several minutes to walk Knox
through making contact with the company.

"You still owe me a motorcycle," Kozlowski said, ending the call.

2:30 P.M.

"I e-mailed product inquiry to store," Randy said over the phone in his
chopped English. "The store e-mailed me back. This gives IP address and
routing in the source code."

"Which means?" Knox said, his patience taxed.

"It was your idea to track possible video transmission to source."

"What's that got to do with e-mail?"

"Technical matter only. This helps me. You. No problem for you.

Tracing video back to source will take time. Maybe quarter hour. Maybe half."

"That's too long," Knox said. He could picture himself arriving to find Danner and Lu Hao ten minutes dead. "The minute they send that video—providing they do at all—I'll have less than thirty minutes to arrive at the location."

"It is possible . . ."

"Go on," Knox encouraged when Randy failed to say more.

"You see, if I am this person I would test bandwidth ahead of time. Maybe one hour. Maybe thirty minutes ahead. Be certain transmission goes successful."

"Which gives me the time I need."

"Yes. It is true."

It was a hell of a risk to take.

"And if they e-mail a video instead of a live transmission?" Knox asked.

"File size very large. But e-mail moves in packets. This piece here. That piece there. All pieces join and arrive to your computer. Make problem for us."

Knox had surveyed the electronics store to be used for POL. In the front window was a television and camera setup that showed the window shopper standing on the sidewalk looking in. The moment he'd spotted the arrangement, he'd pictured the hostages being shown on that same television. The kidnappers could have a second camera, or a team watching the streets making sure Grace was alone. It struck him as a quick and efficient way to deliver the proof-of-life. They'd used video twice before. People stuck to what they were comfortable with.

"Maybe I make suggestion?"

"Go ahead," Knox said.

"I could crash the store's e-mail server. This would then force them to use live video."

Knox worried the effort might tip their hand and told Randy so. Better to leave them believing it was business as usual.

19

Grace had never seen the streets so crowded. With the Friday holiday rush fully underway, the sidewalks and streets remained in their "crush hour" state, as they had all day. Carrying the duffel bag of money, she approached the electronics store named by the kidnappers and fought to remain stationary, flattening herself against the window.

Knox had advised her to keep alert. The proof-of-life might come in the television screen currently reflecting her image, or an image in one of the many digital frames, or in the LCD on the back of one of the many cameras. It might be something presented or shown to her by a clerk beyond the cluttered window display. Perhaps even Lu Hao or Danner himself briefly making an appearance.

She waited there at the window, time moving more slowly, weighed down by her performance over the next hour. She was responsible for a human life. It was no longer drills, or practice, or textbooks, or lecture. She pushed away the credit she might gain with Lu Jian if successful. Until Knox had verbalized it earlier, she hadn't fully seen her ulterior motives, hadn't fully acknowledged them. Perhaps there had been hidden motivations for her taking the assignment. So what? Perhaps others— even relative strangers—could see her more clearly than she could see herself.

She took in every camera, every display, her eyes ticking one to the next. She watched for movement or a signal from the clerks inside, all the while jostled and bumped and her feet trodden upon by inconsiderate passers-by. Twice, she was knocked away from her post and had to fight the human stream to reposition herself.

Amid the noise of traffic and pedestrians, no one heard her gasp as the screen of a portable DVD player flickered to life.

"Lu Hao," she gasped as he and a *waiguoren* appeared side by side. They sat on scuffed, three-legged wooden stools, their arms at their sides—their hands no doubt bound behind their backs—against a backdrop of a bedsheet. They each had several days' growth of beard, the *waiguoren*'s eyes pinched in fatigue. The bedsheet wavered with a breeze—someone entering or leaving the room?—and briefly stuck to the wall behind them, a jagged shape appearing in shadow. A phone was shoved into the frame, covering Lu Hao's face, the small screen clearly showing the date and time—a website. The phone stayed there long enough to be read and then disappeared. The screen went blank.

Grace breathed again. For a second time, a sickening nausea spread through her—the first having occurred following Knox's reference to the Dirty Harry ransom delivery. A film reference. The letters scratched into the hostage chair at the empty warehouse were not "44" but initials. She had not shared her suspicion with Knox. Even now, she could not fully admit it to herself, unable to define and articulate what felt like a poison running through her.

She was brought out of it by the sound of a phone ringing nearby. It took her another two rings to realize it came from the duffel bag. She reached down into a side pocket and came out with a mobile phone—not her phone. In the jostling of the crowded sidewalk, someone had planted the phone on her.

She answered. *"Dui?"*

"Go to Robert De Niro clothing store, three doors down. Enter changing room number one. Pull the curtain and wait for instructions."

The call disconnected.

She moved forward robotically. Knox was somewhere out there, watching her. With little choice but to follow orders, she made her way to the boutique and entered changing room 1, pulling the curtain closed. She expected the drop would take place here, before she ever reached the People's Square Metro station. A ruse.

The new phone rang again. "We are watching you." She glanced overhead and saw the crude hole carved in the ceiling tile—big enough for a small camera. "Strip. Everything off, now. Naked. Dress in the clothes you will find there."

She set down the phone and hurried out of her clothes, offering her back to the overhead camera. She heard the voice in the phone and picked up.

"Keep the phone to your ear until I tell you. Now, turn around. I must see you fully naked. *Kuai! Kuai!"* Fast! Fast!

She showed herself, spreading her arms and turning, feeling violated. Then she quickly donned the loose-fitting clothes that had been left for her.

The male voice directed her to transfer the ransom money into a Nike duffel left under the bench.

They wanted to see the money move between the two bags while also removing any chance the original duffel contained a tracking device. Their final check before the drop. A stationary drop—leaving the money here in the shop—would be considered too great a risk. They wanted her moving. They wanted the confusion and chaos of the Metro station—the multiple exits and trains.

As she dressed—no underwear, no bra—she found a travel card in the pocket of the workout pants. They had her in an orange tank top. She juggled to get into it while keeping the phone in place. The bright color

would make her easy to track in the suffocating crowds she was certain
to encounter in the Metro. A pair of ill-fitting rubber sandals would make
it difficult for her to run.

"Keep the phone close. Now you go to the Metro."

She left the boutique, weakened somewhat by the embarrassment of
disrobing, but regained her strength quickly. She was more determined
than ever to defeat these people and yet fully aware she would need
Knox for that.

3:15 P.M.

Melschoi's man, whose Mongolian nickname was Rabbit for the six children he'd sired, spotted the electronics store on Nanjing Road and immediately recognized its significance.

"An electronics store," he told Melschoi over their phones.

"What of it?"

"What better place to send proof of the hostages' condition? There
are dozens of computer and television screens in the window. You see?"

Melschoi didn't enjoy being beaten to the punch. "Yes. It does seem
a strong candidate. Okay. You stay with that."

"And if I see her?"

"Follow her. What else, you fool? But whatever you do, watch out for
the *eBpon*. He's nothing but trouble."

3:20 P.M.

From the window of a second-floor Cantonese restaurant, Knox watched
Grace through a pair of ten-dollar binoculars as she emerged from the
Robert De Niro boutique. She raised her arm and scratched her head—
their signal that she still had the money, a surprise given the switch of
duffel bags. She now carried a black duffel, a knock-off, given that the
Nike Swoosh was absurdly oversized and its tail smudged, making it look

like a plucked eyebrow. He hurried downstairs and battled the tsunami of human flesh cramming the sidewalks in order to stay ahead of her, putting himself between her and the Metro station entrance. Knox wore blue jeans, wrap-around sunglasses and running shoes—looking like any other *waiguoren*.

They were a few minutes into the play and he and Grace had already been outsmarted—an end-around that had her in new clothes and carrying a new duffel. Her iPhone would be turned off. Her private phone didn't answer. If he lost sight of her, he lost her; and yet his back was to her.

Aware that the kidnappers, the Mongolians and possibly the Chinese police might have her under surveillance, Knox maintained his lead, a fifty-yard bumper, and entered the station first.

He traveled through a crowded corridor, loud and smelling of human sweat. He held his phone in his right hand, watching its reception bars reduce the deeper he penetrated. He needed the message from Randy— needed to know if the kid had managed to trap and trace any data flow involving the electronics shop at the time of Grace's standing at its window.

Knox had no intention of disrupting the drop, but he intended to protect Grace through the process or for as long as possible, and to make any observations he could.

He queued up in the rapidly moving security line. All purses, totes and bags were placed onto an X-ray conveyor. The process involved nearly everyone, given it was the start of the National holiday, and the security was lax. The magnetometer sounded its warning beep with each person, yet no one was stopped. The X-ray conveyor ran constantly—its operator giving only a passing attempt to pretend he was studying the monitor.

Knox funneled into a single file with the others and, with nothing to X-ray, slipped through the magnetometer, causing it to sound. He carried three phones and a Mongolian switchblade in Dulwich's gray jacket. If they patted him down it was going to get ugly. No one blinked.

He continued toward the turnstiles, waited in line and swiped his travel card. He was in. He checked his phone which now read in Chinese: NO SERVICE. No Randy. He couldn't stay down in the bowels of Shanghai for long.

He waited and watched the security check.

Finally, an orange tank top appeared.

Grace arrived at the longer security line, awaiting the conveyor, a hundred thousand dollars strapped over her shoulder.

3:40 P.M.

Rabbit followed the woman to the Metro station entrance, allowing her to descend the stairs a good distance before following. He would try to time it so that he passed through the turnstiles *ahead* of her. People rarely looked in front of them for tails—they were always craning their heads to look back.

20

The KFC franchise on Huaihai Middle Road was well over its legal seating limit by the time Steve Kozlowski pushed his way inside.

Inspector Shen stood at a counter along the wall, eschewing the window area. He had shoulders as wide as a vending machine.

Kozlowski abandoned the idea of waiting in any of the lines, all thirty people long, simply for the sake of appearances. He cut through the crowd, making directly for the man. He was not easily intimidated. He'd spent his career in remote outposts of the world managing others and learning to put the fear of God into them. But the presence of Inspector Shen raised his hackles. The People's Armed Police was a department unto itself, reporting to no one. Its officers wielded too much power, often worked unsupervised and were known to hide their deeds. The closer he got to the man, the more he felt his intensity.

They acknowledged each other with a nod. The din in the place covered their low voices.

Kozlowski said, "The video camera's been found."

Shen looked him in the eye. Kozlowski saw nothing in there, like squinting into an empty steel pipe.

"I have an address, but am not free to turn it over for at least a few more hours. I wanted to give you time to pull your men together."

"No men," Inspector Shen said. "Only me."

Kozlowski had never heard of People's Armed Police officers working solo. It caused him to wonder if he weren't speaking to an MSS agent—Ministry of State Security, the Chinese equivalent of the CIA.

"First the hand, now the camera—found in bad condition, by the way," Kozlowski said. "It does not bode well for the camera's operator. We would like to find him as much as you would."

"For different reasons," Shen said. "I will expect your cooperation in this matter."

Both men knew that was unlikely. Volunteering the camera was as close as Kozlowski would go. Pursuing such evidence in the name of the U.S. government was impossible without serious repercussions. As much as he might have wanted to, his hands were tied by embassy protocol.

"I will pass along location the moment I can. If he's found dead, I request a thorough investigation that includes my people."

"As agreed previously. Yes."

It had long since occurred to Kozlowski that Shen had killed the man himself and was in the process of unofficially cleaning up his own evidence. Such a scenario prevented Kozlowski from getting too knowledgeable about the case without the risk of his scooter being hit by an army truck.

"How certain are you the camera is his?"

"I have not seen it," Kozlowski clarified. "However, from what I've been told, it could be no other."

Shen shot the man a look. "He has violated the terms of his visa," the man said. His use of present tense made it sound as if a man with no hand and no camera might still be alive. If the cameraman was already in custody and the Chinese were seeking evidence to bring charges, then Kozlowski was playing directly into their hands. The smell of the deep-fat fryers was getting to his stomach. He coughed up some bile. His fucking stomach had been a wreck since a bout with dysentery four months earlier. Jokes about bowel movements were more common in the consulate than blonde jokes.

"Only lies put us in this situation," Shen said.

"Lies and secrets," Kozlowski said. They could agree on something.

"You will write down the location for me," he said. "Please."

"When I have confirmation," Kozlowski vamped.

"Now, please. I will not act until I receive your call. My word to you on this."

Kozlowski understood the fragility of the moment. This man's word was as reliable as the FBI warning on a bootleg DVD. But cooperation between governments and departments of those governments transcended individual need. It was the same whether in Somalia or Athens. Or Shanghai: he could get more from creating long-term good relations with the PAP than he ever could from saving the hide of John Knox. He was gaining *guanxi*, the most elusive and important aspect of any Chinese business relationship.

Kozlowski hesitated only briefly as he took out his pen and wrote down the address on a KFC napkin. He hoped he had not just signed Knox's death warrant.

21

Amid the sweltering crush of thousands of people hell-bent on cramming their way onto an arriving Metro car, Knox kept his back planted against a cylindrical post, like clutching a fallen tree in a spring flood. Any of these people could be kidnappers. The choice of this particular day and time was brilliant. Millions of people released from work and determined to leave the city as quickly as possible. With the slightest spark, the chaos would turn into pandemonium. He checked his watch for the tenth time.

He had to get back into cell phone range—awaiting a second call from Randy—if he were to have any chance of extraction. Randy had picked up a test video signal and had been data-mining it, hoping to give Knox a location fix. But if Grace were abducted, all was lost. Danner would be executed and Grace along with him. The ransom would be gone. Knox would be found and imprisoned. He wanted to keep an eye on Grace at least through the drop.

Very much aware of the ceiling-mounted security cameras, he kept the bill of his hat low, heeding Kozlowski's warning of the sophistication of China's face recognition capability. The last thing he could afford was the police bearing down on him.

He maintained his position, flashes of Grace's orange shirt jumping from the horde, while keeping an eye on the man who'd entered ahead of Grace. Of average height but sturdily built, the man had stopped at a support post, using it to separate him from the crowd, while taking a look back. Then he'd made a brief call. Too brief. The kind of call reporting one's position. Right or wrong, Knox tagged him as one of the Mongolian's men and added him to his list of complications.

Grace moved through the turnstiles, instantly swallowed up by the crowd. Wary of the Mongolian, Knox cut against the flow, following the occasional flash of orange. When a khaki security cap appeared behind him at the same post where Knox had just been standing, Knox took note. They were onto him incredibly quickly.

A wink of orange. Grace headed for a stairwell down to the Line 2 platform. Knox kept the Mongolian between him and Grace.

His cell phone vibrated—he'd been in and out of coverage. He viewed the small screen:

```
Hongkou
```

Randy had narrowed the origin of the proof-of-life video signal down to a neighborhood north of Suzhou Creek that included the new cruise-ship port as well as the former Jewish ghetto—an area home to more than a quarter million people.

Knox returned a text:

```
more specific
```

Moments later his phone buzzed a second time:

```
need more time
```

Knox:

```
no more time
```

Then, nothing.

Knox faced the choice of abandoning Grace in favor of the hostages. It would take ten or fifteen minutes to reach the Hongkou District by taxi—more, given the congestion. His feet told him it was a race for Danner's life; his head, that he couldn't abandon one partner in favor of another, that he couldn't leave her with the Mongolian tailing her.

Consumed by the phone, he'd lost sight of her. Searching frantically, he spun around and came eye-to-eye with the security guard standing where Knox had been only a minute before. There was no mistaking the flash of recognition on the guard's face as he saw Knox.

A wall of human impatience separated them. Again Knox lowered his shoulders to blend in. He joined the flow, overhearing the guard shouting for people to move aside. Knox knew it wouldn't happen; on a Chinese holiday break it was every man for himself.

Another speck of orange up ahead.

Grace spotted him too, her face wormed with anxiety. Knox pushed people aside and gained on her. He endured elbowing and cursing, but drew close enough as the subway car arrived at the platform. A thick wall of people, the Mongolian among them, separated them.

"Xintiandi is next! Ice cream parlor!" she called out to him in English, caught in the flow of bodies.

Knox shook his head, trying to stop her from saying any more.

The Mongolian spun his head around and spotted Knox, and the two locked eyes.

"On the video . . . a bedsheet behind them. Broken glass! Broken glass behind the sheet. Both alive!"

Knox shoved ahead to reach the Mongolian, but the crowd was practiced at stopping line jumpers. The collective would not allow him forward progress.

The train pulled in and stopped. A river of passengers disgorged, coming directly at Knox. Grace and her tail were carried onto the train car by the crush. Grace held to the duffel tightly, tugging its strap higher onto her shoulder. The bag briefly jumped into view.

The Nike Swoosh was the correct size, and unsmudged.

Knox stood frozen on the platform, trying to process this change as the doors closed.

The Mongolian looked back at Knox, cocky with his achievement.

Knox had lost sight of Grace. He grabbed his phone but there was no signal.

He looked to his right: the security guard pushed closer to him, a walkie-talkie held to his mouth.

His memory replayed like film: her leaving the boutique carrying a knock-off duffel; beating her through the turnstiles and watching her go through security; following her to the platform . . .

He rewound the film: the boutique, the knock-off duffel, the platform, a different knock-off duffel.

It hit him: *Security.*

His mind replayed that part of his visual memory: his attention had been on Grace and her orange shirt. She'd deposited the duffel onto the X-ray machine's black rubber conveyor belt.

She'd picked up the duffel on the other side amid a dozen people grabbing and fighting for their handbags.

A different duffel had come out the other side.

The switch had been made inside the X-ray machine—the original duffel trapped, a second duffel released and allowed to pass through the machine.

Knox turned and fought the tide of bodies, heading straight for the guard, who wore his surprise openly on his face. Knox grabbed him, kneed him and slammed him into a concrete pillar. He stole the man's walkie-talkie and released him, leaving him to slump to the platform.

He lowered his head like a running back and parted the sea. Once that money was delivered, Danny was a dead man.

3:48 P.M.

Melschoi's phone intercom beeped.

"The woman boarded a train, Line Two," Rabbit said. "I am in the next car back."

"Excellent. And the *eBpon*?"

"Unable to board. I left him on the platform."

"Line Two," Melschoi confirmed.

"Yes."

"Watch for him," Melschoi warned in an ominous tone.

"I left him behind, I'm telling you!"

"Watch for him, Rabbit. I'm telling you: chances are, you did not."

22

Xintiandi, a high-end commercial development set in a renovated Shanghainese lane neighborhood of the 1920s, occupied eight city blocks, its buildings and now wide concourses home to luxury retail stores and four-star restaurants. An important tourist destination, it was also a home for the Platinum Card set. On the start of the National Day holiday it looked like a mosh pit at a rock concert.

Into this chaos arrived Grace, claustrophobia already wearing on her. The shoves; the cigarettes; the body odor; the perfume all served as catalysts for her anxiety.

She bullied her way forward, the heavy duffel slowing her down as it collided with others in the crowd. A light rain began falling. She pushed for the Cold Stone Creamery around the corner, fighting the dense crowds.

She arrived at the ice cream parlor, gripping her phone tightly in her hand, waiting for the next call.

And waited.

And waited.

The phone's screen remained blank. She mentally urged it to ring.

Silence.

The rain fell harder.

Had she been too late?

She glanced around, immediately spotting two uniformed police moving methodically through the throng.

Had the kidnappers spotted the police? Canceled the drop?

The isolation from Knox was killing her. She wondered when she had allowed herself to become dependent upon John Knox.

She dropped the heavy duffel to the concrete, clinging to its strap tightly.

No call.

No contact.

She looked down at the duffel. The two zipper tabs met dead center in the bag; this was not right! She had pulled them both to one side, having had experience of heavy bags coming open when the zippers were centered like this.

She distinctly recalled pulling the zippers to one side.

She knelt, the rain beginning to pour down. She hardly felt it.

There, in the middle of the crowds flowing around her, in the middle of an all-out downpour, soaked to her bones, Grace nervously grabbed hold of the zippers and separated them. Hesitated only briefly before tugging the two sides apart.

She saw a bag filled with stacks of newspaper bundled together with twine. Unable to breathe, she looked up into the rain as if expecting answers. *When? Where? How?* She had put the money into this duffel herself—her reaction went far beyond bewilderment to outright denial. *This was impossible!*

Impossible or not, it was. She dug through the newspapers just to make sure.

The two cops were closing in on her. The Mongolian was back there somewhere. She had but a matter of seconds. The orange shirt gave her away.

She abandoned the bag.

She had no money, only a travel card with twenty *yuan* left on it—about three dollars. She hurried away from the police, approaching a T-shirt kiosk.

She stole a shirt, not by lifting the hanger off the peg, but by bending over and pulling the shirt down, off the hanger. Ten yards later, down on one knee, she delighted a pair of high school-aged boys by peeling off the orange top and donning the stolen T-shirt.

She returned to the Metro entrance, passing within a few yards of the police, who seemed to be looking for her.

Behind her, lying wet atop the plaza's concrete pavers, they would soon come across the orange tank top, trod upon, dirty and already torn.

23

Knox prodded the taxi driver to stay with the blue Volvo sedan sandwiched in traffic up ahead.

He'd returned to the Metro security station in time to catch the four P.M. shift change, had watched as one of the uniformed security men had left carrying a heavy black duffel with the oversized, smudged Nike logo on its side.

The guard cut through People's Square indifferent to the steady rain and the gloom it produced. Knox skillfully avoided being seen, reveling that the shoe was on the other foot. The guard continued two blocks on foot until meeting the blue Volvo.

The first decent break of the past week came as a woman and her daughter disembarked from a taxi heading the same direction on Dagu Road as the Volvo. *In the rain. In Friday rush hour.*

Knox took it as an omen.

Now his taxi driver ran a light as its timer expired. The man used the right lane to pass two vans, nearly paving two cyclists in the process.

"Hen hao!" Very good! Knox called out from alongside the driver. They'd caught back up—less than a block separating them from the Volvo.

The driver smiled widely, his few remaining teeth cigarette-stained and crooked.

24

A defeated Grace descended into the Metro station. Her legs burned; her throat was dry; the soaking wet green T-shirt stuck to her like unwanted skin. Acutely aware of the probing electronic eyes and the possibility of a Mongolian still following, she hung her head and attempted to blend in with the hundreds—thousands!—of Chinese swarming the underground station.

The operation was blown. Her face was known to police. She'd lost Knox. She'd lost the cobbled-together ransom money. One of the Mongolians was following her.

Lu Hao would be killed. Danner, along with him. She'd come to believe the switch had been made in the X-ray machine back in People's Square. It was the only place she'd been removed from the bag. It was a devious, clever deceit.

She knew there was only one person to blame for it coming off so flawlessly.

25

4:20 P.M.

North of the confluence of Suzhou Creek and the Huangpu River, Knox's taxi sped through the area northeast of the Garden Bridge that in the past 160 years had been home to American traders, Russian refugees, Japanese merchants (and then military occupiers) and the European Jews whom the Chinese required to live in squalor during the war. An uninspiring and neglected part of the city for decades, it had recently undergone gentrification, and was now home to hotels, coffee shops and office buildings.

He tapped the driver's forearm. "Slowly, cousin," he said, speaking Shanghainese. "Straight on."

"Excuse me. The car—"

"Straight," Knox repeated. "Turn around and pull to the curb."

"But—"

"*Kuai, kuai, kuai!*" Fast.

The Volvo had slowed and taken two successive rights. Evasive action to check for tails. Knox was betting it would take two more, returning to its former route. The pause to look for tails was a good sign: they were getting close.

He'd had the taxi turn around so he could see through the Volvo's windshield in order to confirm its passenger had not left the vehicle. The sleight-of-hand trick with the duffel weighed heavily upon him.

Knox checked his watch, forgetting it had stopped hours ago. The moment that money was delivered, Danner and Lu Hao would be killed. Close wasn't going to cut it. The stopped watch suddenly seemed prescient.

The driver, his face animated, waited for him to say something. Knox could hardly think.

Too long! The Volvo hadn't been trying to lose surveillance; the two consecutive rights had been the result of a missed turn or one-way streets. It was nearing its destination.

He texted Randy.

```
need location
```

A moment later a text returned:

```
soon
```

Knox directed the driver in the direction they'd last seen the Volvo. Recalling Grace's mention of broken glass in the background of the video, he realized they were in the wrong neighborhood.

"Abandoned building or old *lilong* near here?" he asked the driver. "Broken windows?"

The driver's face contorted. "Power station by river, many years," he said. "Made new most recently."

"New does not work," Knox said. He pointed for the taxi to take another right, the Volvo nowhere to be seen.

His phone buzzed:

```
south of Kunming Rd, east of Dalian
```

Knox defined the area for the driver.

"We are close!" the driver said, accelerating and crossing Dalian Road two blocks later. "Is large area."

"Yes," Knox said, peering through the smeared windshield.

The driver offered a thumbs-up, then pointed out his side window.

It wasn't the Volvo he'd spotted, but a brick fortress set back from the curb.

With hundreds of broken windows.

HUANGPU DISTRICT

Rabbit had lost the woman in Xintiandi, leaving Melschoi wanting to break something, starting with Rabbit's head.

He called his source inside Feng Qi's group.

"What can you tell me?"

The line went dead. The man couldn't talk.

Minutes later the man called back.

"We are monitoring police radio. The foreigner has been spotted in People's Square Metro station."

"Tell me something I don't know!"

"Our people are headed there."

"You're too late! He's gone."

The *eBpon* would suffer for this—if he ever found him again.

HONGKOU DISTRICT

Knox faced a pair of crumbling four-story brick blocks. The roof and windows were riddled with holes. Given the location provided by Randy, and the description, by Grace, it was a strong candidate.

Danner's time clock was quickly expiring. Knox had to test the waters.

The compound was set back from the street across a patch of bare

dirt and weeds and surrounded by high brick walls that met at an elaborate archway where a wrought-iron gate hung open. Inside the archway
were aluminum lawn chairs occupied by a handful of overweight women,
smoking and cackling in Shanghainese.

Electric wires had been strung through several of the second- and
third-floor windows in the building on the left. The structure on the right
appeared fully abandoned.

A nail-house by all appearances—a residence condemned to demoli-
tion where a few determined squatters had "nailed" themselves down,
refusing to be relocated.

He had no great desire to confront a group of Shanghainese matrons;
they were considerably more frightening to him than the Mongolians,
but they would know everything going on in those buildings.

He crossed the street and approached them. Soaking wet now.

The woman closest to the street wore an armband symbolizing her
affiliation with the government as a neighborhood observer. Only in
China, he thought, could a squatter hold a community position.

On the dry concrete protected by the archway, he saw fresh wet
tracks leading into the compound. *The security guard*, he thought. Or a
courier who had met the Volvo and taken possession of the duffel.

He was tempted to follow the tracks and ignore these women. But he
knew they could be paid sentries. No time to shorten Danner's time clock.

"Heavy rain!" he said in English.

The youngest of the five women—mildly attractive—nodded faintly,
though the one in charge shot her a penetrating look, apparently not
wanting a language bridge between this *waiguoren* and their group.

"Rain," Knox said, in intentionally poor Mandarin.

The head matron cocked her head. He tried again, improving only
slightly.

She nodded, and then rattled off in Shanghainese that *waiguoren*
spoke with rocks in their mouths. The other women chuckled—all but
the youngest. Knox had an ally in her.

"You live here?" Knox asked, sticking with intentionally poor Mandarin. "These building?"

The lead woman stared at him through suspicious eyes. In Shanghainese she let him know it was none of his damn business, her language so foul that one of her friends looked to the brick walkway demurely.

In Shanghainese the younger woman said, "Be polite, you old witch. He is guest in our country. He and his kind bring commerce and prosperity."

"They bring the avian flu and KFC. To hell with them all," the older said, carrying on the national rhetoric that had pinned the avian flu's origin on the United States.

"Indeed, we live here," the younger woman said to Knox, in slow, halting Mandarin spoken so that he might understand.

"Any young men, men my age or younger, recently join you?" he asked her.

In rapid-fire Shanghainese the lead woman said, "Shut your mouth, pretty flower, or I will report you and your tribe as running a brothel and have you imprisoned for generations. Do not test me."

Her admonishment sobered the others, while telling Knox all he needed to know. He caught the eye of the young woman, who was blushing.

"What floor?" he asked in English, knowing the matrons could not understand him. "Show me with your fingers. I will not betray you."

"What does he say? What does he say?" snapped the old bitch. *"You will not speak! You will not answer him!"*

But Knox had already turned away from them having seen the young woman's left hand, resting on her knee, touch thumb to pinky—the Chinese hand signal for "three."

He took two steps, stopped and turned, now back in the rain. Addressing the lead woman, speaking perfect Shanghainese, he said, "You are a bitter old cow with the brains of a potato. I had five hundred *yuan* I was prepared to offer you to help me with the magazine article I am writing. Now it remains in my pocket, and you remain in the chair, poorer for your rudeness."

He tromped off through the standing puddles. Immediately, the women were on their leader with vicious crude remarks and admonishments. Knox knew the arguing would continue for a good fifteen minutes. With luck, time enough for him to get in and out without detection. Ironically, the only one of them he worried about was the youngest, fearing she might see through to his intentions.

At the end of the compound was a wall shared with a five-story apartment building. Wet to the core, Knox turned at the apartment building and went up and over the wall. He slurped through mud to the far edge of the brick tenement, finding an opening where a door should have been.

He entered a dark hallway, rainwater coursing down the interior wall. The warped floor was littered with trash and broken beams and pieces of brick, all covered in layers of filth. Faded printer's proofs of posters were held to the wall by rusted thumbtacks. Improvised wiring snaked in tangles up the banister. Knox fingered the tangle. The cleanest of the wires was a phone line—new. The residents of such places weren't the kind to install phone service. But a gang of kidnappers might pirate the service from a nearby pole in order to have Internet. Knox's confidence built as he crept silently up the staircase, pausing every few feet to listen. The pounding of the rain covered all sound.

If the money had been delivered, then Danner's time was up.

At the first-floor hallway, he checked two nearby rooms, their doors missing or open; both were unoccupied and cluttered with construction debris.

The second floor was darker, the result of cardboard blocking a hallway window. The wires separated here and ran like grape tendrils to various rooms. Two, one thick—electricity—the other thin—the phone line—were tied in a pair leading still higher.

Adrenaline charged through his system as he anticipated the action at the end of the wires. The moment he'd come for: Danner. He climbed, following the wires, moving more cautiously now. He was led to a door, third down on the left. A set of wet shoe prints had soaked into the wood floor—a recent arrival.

His eye fixed onto a shiny new brass key lock—an amateur move.

Ever so gently, he turned the doorknob and applied the slightest amount of pressure to the door.

Locked.

4:30 P.M.
HONGKOU DISTRICT

Knox heard muted voices in a heated discussion from the other side of the locked door. He leaned his good ear against the wood: muted Shanghainese from at least two, possibly three. Mandarin spoken by at least one. He stared at the footprints saturating the worn wooden floorboards.

As he listened, his fingers involuntarily counted out the number of voices: *four.* Difficult odds, given that he was armed with only the Mongolian's switchblade.

He considered using the window at the end of the hall and working from outside the building, increasing his element of surprise. But the building face was sheer, and the old witches at the gate might see him.

He dropped to his knees and peered through the space at the bottom of the door, covering his right eye. Four pairs of feet by table legs; two pairs—scuffed dress shoes so typical of Shanghainese men, standing; one, a pair of Nikes; the sitting man's feet tapped nervously, his legs dancing— not bound to the chair, Knox noted. The fourth pair of shoes by the table was black and rubber-soled above a cuffed pair of pants. A fifth pair of shoes could be seen to the right, against an exterior wall. What held them closely together, Knox couldn't see, but they were large, size thirteen or fourteen. *Danny!* That made five.

Knox sat back against the wall and exhaled. He fought the impulse to kick the door and let adrenaline rule. *Think!*

But he'd not come here to think. He'd come here for Danny.

He stood and kicked the door alongside the lock, shattering the jamb. The second kick flung the door open.

Three men standing—two to the left of a central table, one at the back. One man sitting, to the right. Danny was blindfolded and duct-taped to a chair to Knox's right. He looked haggard, *but alive.*

Knox's elation at seeing Danner nearly cost him. The man on the far side of the table pulled a knife.

The duffel was open, a stack of bound bills alongside it. One of the three men on the left had his hands in the duffel. Knox took him out first, while hip-checking the table and slamming its edge into the man with the knife. He flopped over.

Knox chopped at this man's hand, dislodging the knife, while fighting through the next man—a wiry guy who took a punch poorly. But the man possessed sharp, exact movements, and was fast. He landed a blow in Knox's side—his wound—and Knox's knees went out from under him.

The one who'd had the knife stood up, now weaponless—it was two-to-one against Knox. Three-to-one, as the man in the chair leaped to his feet.

Knox returned to standing using his back to overturn the table onto the one coming out of the chair. The duffel fell. The cash spilled. He throat-punched the wiry man, causing the man to blanch and grab for his own throat. Knox defended a blow coming from the knife man, countered, and then blocked again.

This man was the most practiced fighter. Knox defended well and managed to make the man take a step back, establishing Knox as the dominant. His opponent kicked for Knox's right knee and might have broken it had the table not moved, putting a table leg between them. The table leg broke, not Knox's.

The remaining blows came fast. Knox drove the man back one final step and took him down with a left to the kidney and a right to the heart.

A man jumped onto his back. Knox caught the flash of the fallen knife. He blocked the attempted blow, elbowed the man off of him and turned to finish him.

The man lying on the floor, cowering—the man who'd been sitting in the chair watching the money being counted—was Lu Hao.

26

Knox towered over Lu Hao, his foot raised and ready to break the man's rib cage, sternum and all. The mix of surprise and anger was toxic. Lu Hao, hostage and kidnapper, all in one.

Lu Hao dropped the knife, threw it to the side like a person waking from a dream. A bad dream at that.

"You?" Knox said. "You piece of shit."

"I must explain!" Lu Hao said, his voice quavering as he pushed away from Knox.

"Damned right. And you will."

Knox surveyed the damage he'd done. Took in Danner.

"You okay over there?"

The gagged Danner nodded slightly.

Knox took up the knife. Kept it where Lu Hao could see its tip twisting toward his eyes. Used shoelaces to tie hands behind the backs of the three men who were on the floor. Stuck banded bunches of hundred-dollar bills in their mouths as gags. Instructed Lu Hao onto his stomach and patted the man down.

Found two mobile phones on the man and pocketed them. Worked his way carefully over to Danner and cut him loose, never taking his eyes off Lu Hao. Handed Danner the knife and then took out his own so they were both armed.

Danner tried to stand and fell over.

Knox reached an ice cooler where some chips and cold pizza had to be moved to open it. He handed Danner bottled water and a red Powerade.

"Seriously," Knox said. "You okay?"

"Go easy on him," Danner said, meaning Lu. "He's an asshole, but he treated me good. Wait until you hear his story. The guy's fucked six ways to Sunday."

Knox noticed the bloody bandage on Danner's hand.

"Seven," he said, not taking his eyes off the man.

"It's complicated," Danner said.

"I've been getting a lot of that. You sound like a Stockholm Syndrome victim to me, Danny. You're free now. We're out of here."

"The three of us," Danner said.

"Yeah, I suppose. But only because I owe someone . . ."

"They fed me. They kept me bound but moved me. It could have been a lot worse. I'm telling you: it's better than it looks."

"They cut your finger off. He would have killed you."

"No . . . no!" cried Lu Hao. "Never!"

"Shut it!" Knox said, lunging for the man. Lu Hao scooted backward, eyes wide in terror.

Knox felt like those first few moments in a fun house when the lights are dim and mirrors distort your own image. Danny defending Lu; Lu Hao not a hostage; all the money spread around the floor. "Shit," he said, lit by adrenaline and wanting to destroy Lu Hao. He kicked the overturned table. It skidded across the floor and slammed into one of the downed men, who groaned.

Danner had cut the duct tape and was peeling it from his wrists.

"Just do me a favor," Danner said, "and wait to kill him. It's not like I forgive him or anything."

Knox breathed loudly. "That's better." He looked back at Danner and allowed the shadow of a smile.

"If you want to kill him after you've heard his story," Danner said, "I'm first in line. This is not coming down on you. Not after all you've done."

"I think you'd better shut up, too," Knox said, dismissing Danner suddenly with a heated glance. It hadn't been 44 that Danner had scratched into the arm of the first chair he'd occupied; it had been initials: LH.

His brain was set to a high boil. He couldn't make sense of things. The fatigue. The wound. The risks. Lu Hao had kidnapped himself. Knox still wanted to pulverize him, punish him. He thought of Grace. He wondered what came next, knowing the answer: Dulwich. He couldn't leave Dulwich behind.

"Repack that bag," Knox said. "The money comes with us."

27

To the right of the number 3 entrance of the Nanjing Road East Metro station was an unmarked, oversized black metal door pasted with stickers for music albums, American guitar and amplifier manufacturers, and posters for local rock bands, a door easily overlooked.

Grace knocked and the door was opened by a bald, middle-aged man with a crooked but flat nose and clear eyes. From behind him came the muted but grating strains of heavy-metal rock and roll being played grossly out of tune. The man recognized her from earlier when she and Knox had rented the underground practice room. He swung open the heavy door, admitting her to a landing and a set of dimly lit metal stairs.

She was sixty feet underground by the time she reached a long concrete corridor, passing through a pair of blast doors hung on heavy hinges. An overhead tube light flickered with each pulse of the music, not one band, but two or three.

This was but one of the dozens of such bomb shelters built under Mao to house city residents and his army in fear of a Soviet missile strike. The memory of the Japanese occupation and slaughter had never left the Chinese consciousness and never would. Some of the bunkers were now open as mini-museums around the city. Others, like this, had been taken over by squatters and were open for commerce—rehearsal space for wannabe rock stars.

She reached bunker number 4 and opened another heavy metal door—appropriate to the music thumping down the hallway. She moved inside and shut it behind herself.

The room smelled foully of sweat, cigarettes and stale *hefan*. Eggshell foam rubber was glued to the gray concrete walls. Carpet samples covered the floor. Electric conduit and outlets had been crudely retrofitted. Two dim compact fluorescent lightbulbs hung from the ceiling.

It had come to this, she thought: hiding out in a hole dug underground like some kind of animal. Reduced to lie and bribe one's way into a small, dismal room, all because of another's lying and bribing. *Evil begets evil.* She felt a shudder of release swell within her—grief, sorrow, the aftershock of the adrenaline that had built up during the ransom run; her failure of having moved around the city with nothing but newspaper inside the duffel. How would that affect Knox and his efforts at extraction?

Wet and shivering, she glanced over at the closed door, wondering when Knox might arrive, or if, by losing track of the money, she'd compromised their mission.

5:26 P.M.

Knox delivered Lu Hao and Danner to the subterranean music rooms, arranging for Grace to care for Danner and keep a close eye on the turncoat, Lu Hao.

Few words passed between him and Grace. The contrition with which she'd met him at the bunker door told him she knew Lu Hao's story—a realization that sucked Knox's lungs dry. He couldn't make sense of her expression, couldn't reason his way to how she might possibly know; but she didn't so much as flinch at the sight of Lu's hands bound, and she treated him like a wet dog as she dragged him inside.

"Later," Knox said, patting the duffel bag containing one hundred thousand dollars.

"Where are you going?" she called out.

"Possession is nine-tenths of the law," he returned.

Knox arrived at the Muslim quarter dressed in the pale blue jumpsuit worn by city sweepers and trash collectors. He carried a Nike duffel bag. His face was covered with the ubiquitous surgical mask worn against smog. Along with the brim of a ball cap pulled down low, he hid his race as best as possible.

The duffel was somewhat out of place on a street sweeper. But with the start of the National Day holiday, no one paid attention to anyone else: it was every man for himself.

He splashed through the rain-flooded lane, the full force of the approaching typhoon yet to arrive, moving toward the Mongolian's small apartment.

He was less concerned with the Mongolian, and far more with the police or whoever Kozlowski had likely already sold him out to, for he knew he'd been thrown under the bus. He'd traded Kozlowski the Mongolian's address for a chance to leave the country—and had filled Danner in on the details of the contact in case he didn't make it back to the bomb shelter. But the final piece of the frame was worth the risk. If the kidnapping and ransom collection fell onto the Mongolian, neither he nor Grace—nor Lu Hao!—would be accused of involvement. Furthermore, Kozlowski seemed the only one powerful enough to get Dulwich out of the country in one piece.

He moved down the narrow lane quickly now, feeling eyes boring into his back.

Knox broke off the tip of the switchblade, jimmying the Mongolian's lock and getting the door open, but was inside without too much telltale damage to the jamb. He relocked it behind himself, and made quick work of opening the wall panel that hid the video camera and Chinese currency he'd seen here before. He removed the disk from the video camera—evidence that might come in handy—and pocketed four 10,000-*yuan* packs of currency, enough cash to buy favor. The space was too small to accept the full duffel, leaving Knox no choice but to take the time to unpack the dollars and stack them into the available space in an orderly fashion. When completed, it looked as if the wall was insulated with hundred-dollar bills. He folded and stuffed the empty duffel into the remaining space inside. Neat and tidy.

He was tightening the panel's last screw when he heard the splash of footfalls in the alley. They came to a stop by the door to the room.

Knox grabbed a pair of socks and rubbed out his wet tracks that led to the wall panel. No matter what, the Mongolian must not discover the cash ahead of the police. The lock rattled. Knox slid open a dresser drawer and messed up the contents to give the impression he'd been rummaging.

The door swung open. Rain blew in from behind the Mongolian. The man withdrew a blade.

Knox wrapped his left hand in a T-shirt from the drawer.

"Do you know why I'm here?" Knox asked in Mandarin.

"I think you wish to negotiate. But you have nothing I want. Except your life, of course. I want to end that. Badly," the Mongolian answered.

"I have Lu Hao *and* his accounts," Knox said, dropping it like a bombshell.

"I think otherwise."

"I can make a call."

"Why buy what I can take?" the man said.

"Because you don't know where he is," Knox answered.

"Oh, but I will in a matter of minutes. That, or you will be dead. Either way it is satisfactory to me. You have been a pain in the ass, *eBpon*. I will be glad to be rid of you, if that is your choice."

"You will kill him," Knox said.

The Mongolian laughed a legitimate laugh. He shrugged.

"But not until you have his accounts."

"You are less stupid than you look, Round Eyes."

Knox did not speak as the Mongolian shut and locked the door behind himself, his manner relaxed, his demeanor calm. The man understood strategy—he made no move toward Knox. Instead, he blocked the only way out. Knox would have to come to him, giving the Mongolian a formidable advantage.

Knox backed up a step; a man that size would have a hell of a reach. The room felt impossibly small.

"We have interests in common," Knox said. "You want Lu Hao gone. I want Lu Hao out of the country. Tonight, if possible."

"You have caused me much trouble," the Mongolian said.

"You exaggerate. I am but one man up against many."

The Mongolian huffed. "Your math amuses me. I counted four at the hair salon. And then there is the one you put in the hospital by making that stupid switch."

"You put him in the hospital," Knox said. "I owe you for that."

"I am standing right here," the Mongolian said.

Knox charged, his left hand outstretched to take the blade that winked as the big man wielded it. Knox struck him with his shoulder and drove him into the door. The knife flashed, nicking Knox's cheek. He blocked the second swipe, but was cut on the arm.

A flurry of knife thrusts, blocks and counterpunches. They were well matched—Knox's speed and agility against the Mongolian's power.

Knox had fought such men. He appreciated the challenge at hand; he wasn't often the underdog. He understood the punch he had to land had to be effective. The Mongolian would expect the jaw. All fighters expected the blow to the jaw, and worked to defend against it. But Knox would break his fingers and hand on a jaw like that, all for winning a few loose teeth. The routine required of him was like a physical chess game; he had to work the abdomen and the groin, trying to pull the man's arms down in defense, trying to open the jaw and make the man focus on its defense as well, all of it a ruse to gain an opening to the heart punch. You didn't stop a truck by smashing its windshield or even popping its tires—you killed the engine.

Like his colleagues, the Mongolian had been trained as a wrestler. Knox had the advantage of that knowledge. A big man, he was also likely accustomed to throwing people around at will. By blocking the doorway, he trapped himself in the corner of the ring—up against the ropes. Knox used this against him, throwing punches, dancing back and trying to tease the man out into the more open space of the room. He dodged well-delivered knife thrusts, wincing with two more cuts, both on his wrists.

Knox landed a good blow just inside the man's hip joint. It had to hurt. The Mongolian's face went scarlet and he craned forward, unable to stand straight. He'd pee blood for that one. He swung out with the knife a little clumsily, still trying to catch his breath.

Knox took advantage of the opening and punished his lower ribs, feeling one crack.

The Mongolian roared, and Knox knew he'd scored. He'd ticked him off as well; lost composure was a lost fight. Knox landed a third straight blow, low on the man's abdomen, just above the lower pelvic bone. The Mongolian, understanding his vulnerability bent over as he was, overreacted and stood up too quickly.

Knox finally had his opening. He stepped forward, risking the close quarters, and delivered the heart punch as if trying to put his fist out the man's back.

The Mongolian's eyes rolled back in their sockets as his heart skipped a beat. He went down like the air had been let out of him.

Knox stole the man's phone but left his ID for the police to find. He pulled the door shut behind him. He tried to run, but he was spent. He crossed his arms to hide the blood and walked briskly.

He texted Kozlowski, believing it an act of futility. But a promise was a promise, and he needed Kozlowski's connections to get Dulwich free.

the camera is yours

―――――

5:30 P.M.

Shen Deshi spotted the *waiguoren*, still wearing the same street sweeper's blue coveralls that he'd worn on the way in. He came out of the lane and joined the horde.

He'd spotted him on the way in, not because of the sanitation worker coveralls, but because of his height and the spring to his step.

Shen understood the importance of criminal informers, knew this man was significant to Kozlowski. The police and secret police thrived off information gleaned from such sources. The *waiguoren* matched the description of a man they were looking for. To collar him would be a credit to all other Iron Hands and would put Shen in good favor with his superiors. But ultimately, his department's relationship with the Americans superseded any one arrest. He had given his word he would not move until contacted. He did not move.

When, only minutes later, he received the highly anticipated call from Kozlowski, Shen referenced the police captain's business card and phoned him. He reported to the captain that he'd seen the wanted *waiguoren* only minutes earlier. He provided cross streets.

"Once he is arrested, I would appreciate the sharing of any information the suspect may *volunteer*."

"Yes, of course, sir. Any such information will be immediately forthcoming." The captain sounded like a man given a second chance at life.

A favorite credo of Inspector Shen's: why do the dirty work when others will do it for you? He'd let the worried captain beat the shit out of the foreigner and keep the blood off his own hands.

Now he moved with deliberate haste down the crumbling lane to the Mongolian's door. He never considered knocking; he threw the sole of his shoe into the door and it exploded inward.

The Mongolian sat on the edge of the floor mat that served as his bed. He raised his head defensively, hands out in front, but the fight had been beaten out of him. Shen could see it in his eyes.

"Special Police," he said slowly in Mandarin. "You understand?" He displayed his ID. "If you strike me—"

The Mongolian swung his right leg deceptively fast. Shen blocked it and undercut the effort by hooking the man's leg. He threw the Mongolian over backward. Shen placed his foot into the man's crotch and kneeled, pinning the arm holding the knife. With his free hand, he seized the man by the throat. "If you strike me," he began again, "you will face charges and serious jail time, you yak-fucking Mongol piece of shit. You understand?"

The Mongolian glared.

Shen could feel his opponent's strength returning.

He rolled the man over and cuffed him, facedown.

"You so much as twitch," Shen said, "and I'll use your own knife to castrate you."

He searched the small room methodically and quickly, coming across the panel in no time. He used the Mongol's knife as a screwdriver and loosened the screws. U.S. currency fell out as the panel gave way.

"What the fuck?" the Mongol moaned.

Shen complimented the *waiguoren*. He'd underestimated the man's resourcefulness. An excellent strategy! He'd have to compliment the man once the police captain had had the snot beaten out of him.

His day was looking up.

There, behind all the money, he located his prize: the video camera. He smiled privately. Nearly a week of gumshoe work and worry, and now this. He took a photograph of it in the secreted hole with his phone's camera. Several more as he emptied the cash into a duffel lying there. The Mongol was screwed: the duffel would no doubt show up on one or more surveillance tapes involving the ransom drop. The *waiguoren* had framed this guy well.

"This is not mine!" the Mongolian shouted.

"Shut your hole!" Shen hollered. "Fuck but it's a lot of money."

Shen considered the amount. It had to be fifty, sixty, seventy thousand U.S. dollars. A fortune. Retirement passing through his hands. He had carefully navigated a career prone to bribery, had turned it down, waiting his turn. Instead, he'd worked the system using *guanxi* and favor. But this amount . . . his throat went dry at the thought. He regarded the piece of shit on the floor. Temptation plagued him.

Even more currency in *yuan*: perhaps two hundred thousand.

He discovered a plastic bag containing a Mongolian passport, some family photographs and a small amount of Mongolian currency. Alongside the passport was a policeman's ID wallet.

The sight of it stopped him briefly.

"Ah ha!" he said. "I see we are brothers." He sat down on the mat, surrounded by money—drugged by it—the Mongol's head at his feet. "So let me ask you this, *brother*: put yourself in my position. All this cash. You are alone with a suspect who is a spineless kidnapper, an illegal foreigner, and, by the existence of this camera, more than likely a murderer. Huh? Do you wait for the long arm of justice, or take matters into you own hands?"

The Mongol shook his head and squirmed.

"For the sake of conversation," Shen said. "Humor me. What's your next move?" He eyed the money. *Five years salary? Ten? Twenty?* He'd avoided the penny-ante stuff all these years, but now the jackpot. Was he supposed to turn it over to someone only to have *them* make it disappear, and maybe him along with it, just to tidy things up? He could strike a compromise: share it with a superior and ensure no one questioned his sudden retirement.

"Actionable intelligence," Shen said. "You tell me all you know and then we take a drive, you and me. Okay, *brother*? A small ferry on the Huangpu. A man I know. If I am happy with your cooperation, I deliver you to the police over in Pudong. If I am not happy . . . then no one can save you."

"I have someone I have to call," the Mongolian said. "One call and we are both rich, and you promoted. This, I promise."

"A call?"

"To Beijing."

Shen Deshi's blood flowed hot. What had he walked into? Beijing?

He eyed the money, and then regarded his hostage, wondering what to believe.

28

Danner was asleep on the floor by the time Grace finally overcame her anger. She sat down next to Lu Hao, his hands and ankles bound by plastic ties.

Concealing her true emotions, something every Chinese child learns at a young age, she said calmly, "What have you done, Lu Hao?"

"A thousand pardons, Chu Youya. I beg your forgiveness. I have made a mess of everything, my family's honor most of all. I deserve whatever punishment you wish to bring upon me." He kept his head down, staring at the stained carpet squares.

"Explain yourself before I turn you over to the American and allow him to do to you what I, too, feel you deserve."

"It was a matter of bad luck, nothing more. Happenstance. I saw a face—a man I knew from my deliveries for Mr. Song, for The Berthold Group. The employment you offered me. I should have left it at that."

"You paid out large sums to the Mongolian."

Lu's eyes went wide, impressed with her. He nodded. "Yes. All for the envelope that is now in my back pocket. Four hundred thousand U.S. All for a number."

"A number?"

"I swear. All that money for a single envelope. A number, nothing more."

Grace fished the red envelope from the man's pocket, refusing to believe the events of the past week could have their origin in nothing more than a number. She examined the envelope.

"You opened it," she said.

"Fourteen billion, seven hundred million. What does it mean? What was I to do? Once inside the building, he beat a man. Beat him until he fell. Killed him, I assure you. While the other one watched—the government man."

"What government man?"

"He arrived in a government car. I saw the plate—the number six. Nothing more. A high-ranking government official. I was scared! Terrified! I trusted no one. I called you, Chu Youya. Who else? You got me this work. You of all people must know. Did you not get my call?"

She remained silent.

His eyes pleaded with her for an explanation.

She had none.

"The second delivery—two hundred thousand—I was told to accept an envelope. But this man . . . the look he gave me during the exchange. I must have betrayed myself. I swear he knew I'd witnessed him and the other man and the killing. Don't ask me how."

The video, she was thinking. Just as she and Knox had identified Lu.

Lu Hao sounded on the verge of crying. Little Lu Hao. Always depending on his brother or father to pull him along. "I envisioned a story. I would be kidnapped. The envelope's contents would give me great value to my employer, certainly in excess of four hundred thousand U.S. I would demand a ransom and my father would be returned the money

I owe him. Then, of course tragedy would strike. I would be believed killed, my body never found." He paused. "My parents regain their future and our family, face. I vanish. Australia. America, perhaps. It was a plan not without sacrifice." He looked over at the sleeping Danner. "Then . . . him."

Grace looked over as well. "Slow down!" she said. "A number?" Staring at the envelope.

"I'm telling you. Four hundred thousand U.S. for that."

She looked at Lu Hao, puzzled, while thinking back to Selena Ming's explanation of Marquardt and Song traveling together: due diligence on future projects. The Mongolian's reported connection to Beijing, where all important decisions were made. "Dear God," she mumbled, taking in the size of the number. Too big to be a bribe. But a bid on a government construction project? It was large, extremely large, but not out of the question.

"Lu Hao . . ."

"The American. If we'd only left the American. But all such plans are doomed. Tell me it isn't so," he said.

"Lu Hao."

"They will kill me, Youya. What is to become of my family? I have failed them all. I had no choice."

Grace tried to process all that she'd learned: the size of the number The Berthold Group had paid for indicated what? No bribe could be in the billions of RMB. What *could* such a number represent?

"The *waiguoren* took the ransom money. Get it back, cousin. Get it to my father."

"It is too late for that, Lu Hao. It has gone to buy you your freedom."

"I should have realized the depths they would go to, these people."

"Who are they?" Grace asked. "Who are these Mongolians?"

Lu Hao shrugged. "I am but the messenger. The delivery boy. How should I know? But I tell you: the man is cruel, his eyes dead."

"This factory," she said. "The one in the video—"

"You've *seen* the video?" Lu Hao rose to his knees.

"Where is it? Tell me its location." This place seemed the center of the storm, wherever, whatever it was.

She was splattered with something warm. Lu Hao slumped forward, his head thumping onto the foul carpet.

Clete Danner stood over Lu Hao holding a mike stand. He recoiled, reloading his strength to strike a second time.

Grace sprang off the floor and caught his wrist in her hands, preventing the second blow. The man's eyes were glazed.

"Stop it! Stop it!" she shouted.

He possessed the size and strength to knock her aside. Grace used leverage to prevent the next blow, but could be easily overpowered.

"Enough! Enough!"

Danner was dazed—half sleeping, half waking. His eyes weren't tracking. He didn't speak. Didn't seem to hear. Sleepwalking? A trauma-induced narcosis? He tried again to lower the bloodied stand onto Lu's head, but the effort was half-assed, the adrenaline retreating. She managed to wrestle the stand from him. Danner stumbled back into the wall and sank down, burying his face in his hands.

"It's going to be all right," she said calmly.

But Lu Hao remained unconscious on the floor, bleeding badly. In fact, he looked half-dead.

5:45 P.M.

Knox arrived to the bunker with two bags of athletic clothes and a pair of umbrellas. He knocked on the bunker door. Grace answered, despair on her face.

"I wasn't paying attention," she said, as Knox saw the unconscious Lu Hao, his head bloody and sporting a bloodied stack of paper towels from the bathroom.

"Your friend came awake in a rage," she said.

Knox took it all in: Danner slumped against the wall. Sleeping? Lu

Hao on his back with his head propped up. A bloody mike stand lying on the carpet.

"Jesus Christ! An hour ago, he was *defending* him."

"Shock? Who knows? He wanted to kill him."

"Fuck!"

"Lu Hao's out. He is hurt badly."

"No, no, no . . ." Knox muttered, running his free hand through his hair.

"Lu Hao . . . it was all Lu Hao's idea. It wasn't forty-four scratched into the chair, it was LH—Lu Hao. Lu Hao, all along."

They talked for several minutes, Grace relating her brief discussion with Lu. She had more questions than answers.

"We're getting him out of here," Knox said. He patted his coat. "I have the disk—the video. That should buy Dulwich's freedom. I need to call Kozlowski. If anyone can arrange it . . . I brought everyone dry clothes. We leave in five for the rendezvous."

Inside, he, Danner and Grace stripped and donned the fresh clothes and ball caps. They got a ball cap over Lu's wound to hide it. The man's eyes were open, but his brain was on hold; he had yet to utter a word. It was imperative he get medical attention as soon as possible.

Danner remained in a stupor, his eyes glazed over. Knox's attempts to communicate won little but distant stares.

"We'll travel in pairs. Heads down. I'm going to need help with Lu. You understand?"

Danner nodded.

"You try to fuck him up anymore and you answer to me," Knox said.

Danner spoke for the first time in several minutes. "I'm sorry, boss."

Knox placed an understanding hand on the man's shoulder. "No sweat. Nearly there. Hang in."

Danner nodded again.

Grace flashed Knox a look of concern. One man barely conscious. Another traumatized. Yet another in a hospital room.

"We're good," he said reassuringly. Even he didn't believe it.

They climbed the stairs to the street, Knox waiting for a decent cell signal. Halfway up, he had it and he focused on the instructions Kozlowski had provided.

Knox dialed.

"White Star Realty?" A Chinese woman speaking good English.

"I'm calling for Frances."

"Frances is not in."

"I should have called last night."

Knox hung up.

A moment later his phone rang, and he answered.

"White Star Realty," the same voice said.

"I'm looking for a two-bedroom condominium in Shanghai with a river view," he said. A Shanghai extraction; water travel preferred over rail, air or surface.

"One moment please."

He waited. The iPhone shifted, the faint sounds of lines being switched, carriers changed.

"I can help you." A different woman's voice. "Any restrictions?" she said.

"No higher than the twenty-fourth floor." No later than midnight.

"How many beds?" How many traveling?

"Three beds."

"Let me check our listings please."

"Four. You mean four!" Grace said.

Knox indicated for her to sit down and be quiet. He had given the correct count.

More clicks and pops on the phone line.

The woman's voice returned to the line. "We have a nice flat with a lovely view that may fit your needs. It's 1800 Zhongshan South. One of my representatives could meet you to view the property." There was no 1800 Zhongshan South Road. But 18:00 hours equaled six P.M., which meant it was 600 Zhongshan South. The Dongmen Lu Ferry Terminal was at that address, and the Hotel Indigo next door.

"What floor?" he inquired. What time?

"The twenty-first floor. Eight P.M." 21:00 hours. He ignored the time, an intentional miscue to mislead any eavesdroppers.

"Thank you." Knox had no idea how they would make the connection once to the terminal, but that was for later.

"We appreciate your inquiry and the chance to serve you."

The line went dead. Knox pocketed the phone.

"Three beds?" she repeated.

"First of all, it wasn't beds, it was people. Three people."

"Same question."

"I'm not leaving Sarge behind," he told her. "We get you three out now. He and I will follow shortly."

"Mr. Dulwich can handle himself," she said. "Mr. Primer will not allow anything to happen to him."

"Just like nothing has happened to us," Knox said sarcastically. "Sarge is expendable. We all are. We went over this. You're leaving. You and Danner and Lu. They both need medical attention. Sarge and I will follow. No arguments."

She looked poised to object, but they'd reached the street and the chaos of the crowds and the downpour of rain.

6:15 P.M.

Knox flagged down two pedicabs—safer than taxis or public transportation.

Grace and Danner climbed onto wet plastic benches beneath a wind-torn canopy. Knox helped Lu Hao into the front cab. The drivers kept the three-wheeled motorized carts to the bike lanes.

Twenty minutes later, they approached the ferry terminal and the hotel just beyond. Thousands of Chinese were queued out into the street awaiting ferries. Darkness had fallen quickly, and the crowd seemed anxious, bordering on turning into an angry mob.

The four entered the Hotel Indigo, wet all over again. Knox informed the desk attendant White Star Realty had sent him. They were shown to two second-floor rooms—never above the fifth floor—across the hall from one another. The decor was Euro-chic, lots of stainless steel and frosted glass.

Knox and Grace inspected Lu's wound. Grace tried speaking to him in Mandarin, but Lu Hao was hiding somewhere behind the blinking, bloodshot eyes.

"He is bad off," she said.

"Yeah. Not long until we get him some help," Knox said.

Grace excused herself to the toilet and returned with her hair combed. Danner was asleep on a bed in seconds. They propped up Lu Hao and put ice on his wound.

Knox ordered room service, including black tea, as it promised to be a long night.

"We must talk," Grace said. "Across the hall."

"We can't leave these two," he said.

"Five?" she said.

"I have a bargaining chip," he said, touching his coat. "The tape from the video camera. I should be able to buy Sarge a ticket home, but I'm running out of time here. Can we put a pin in it, and I'll get back to you?"

She shook her head but did not counter.

"I promise we'll talk."

He headed out the door and into the room across the hall.

Knox placed the call to Dulwich's iPhone. After four rings, Kozlowski answered. "Go ahead," Kozlowski said.

"It's me," Knox said. "These phones are safe," he reminded.

"You've been busy. You have moved yourself right to the top of the city police's most wanted list."

"I gave you the place and the people responsible!"

"And I called it in for you. But with no hostages and no ransom money, it looks more like another assault. One of a string attributed to you."

"I can't worry about that."

"Just beware of it. I would lay real low if I were you."

"I want the person you took that phone off. Tonight. With me. Here."

"First: I don't want to know where you are," Kozlowski said. "Second: it's not going to happen. They caught one of the drivers. They know it was a conspiracy and they've posted a cop outside your friend's room. He's not going anywhere."

"You have to change that," Knox said.

"Do you happen to remember a conversation we had? One in which I warned you about how far you could take this?"

"I have the video your missing cameraman shot before he went missing."

A long pause on the other end.

"Come again?"

"You heard right. It shows Lu Hao as an eyewitness to a possible crime—a murder, Lu Hao claims. It shows an individual—the Mongolian—rushing the camera. And after that night, your cameraman is never seen again. Am I right?"

Another long silence.

"Wouldn't you like to close that disappearance?" Knox asked. "In the video, the Mongolian's clearly doing business with some kind of fat cat. Rich. Portly. Chinese. This whole mess has something to do with Marquardt and The Berthold Group paying out huge sums on the sly to obtain a number. The Mongolian's the middleman. The fat cat's got to be the source."

"What kind of number?"

"A big number," Knox said. "A very big number."

"I don't get it."

"Neither do I," Knox admitted. "But my best guess is the Mongolian's job was to see the number reach the people who paid for it—The Berthold Group—and he understood Lu's importance to that end. Who knows what might have happened once it reached the buyer, but the kidnapping came along, so we'll never know." He withheld Lu's culpability in his own kidnapping. "The disk for my friend. He has to be delivered tonight."

"Circumstantial evidence isn't going to convince anyone of anything. I wish I could help you. I really do. But I know these people. It's not going to happen."

Knox had been so profoundly convinced he'd bought Dulwich his freedom that he felt the wind knocked out of him. "I have the video," he repeated.

"And I, for one, can get mileage out of it. Yes. You're right about me wanting to close this disappearance. But as we both know, I'm forbidden from investigating. I can't even ask probing questions. So I'd have to play the video right, and even then it will maybe help start a dialogue, but that dialogue is not going to lead to the release of your friend. He was the target of a commissioned crime. The authorities are going to want answers from him."

"You've got to get him out of there." Knox knew Dulwich wouldn't cooperate, and that if he didn't, he'd serve jail time.

"I know what you're thinking: you're thinking you'll bust him out of Huashan Hospital. But guess what? You won't. He's well-guarded and he's in bad shape, pal. He's going home on a stretcher right now. It takes two to carry a stretcher, last time I checked."

"You and me," Knox said.

"Right."

Knox searched for some kind of solution. Every time he advanced an idea, it ran into a wall.

"This fat cat you described," Kozlowski said. "A businessman?"

"Not according to Lu. Government pool car. Shanghai."

"Do you have *that* on film? That's exactly what we need."

"Negative," Knox said. But what he heard was: "we."

"Any way to make that ID?"

"My guy is comatose at present, even if he knew, which he doesn't. I've got wheels-up at eight P.M."

"Never going to happen." Kozlowski added, "Some storm, huh? Been here six years, haven't seen one like this."

"And if I brought you this guy's name?" Knox tested, his mind reeling. Kozlowski, prevented by law from investigating, wanted Knox to do his dirty work for him. Knox didn't need it in neon lights. It made him wonder how inaccessible Dulwich really was.

"It would change things," Kozlowski said.

"Change things, how?"

"Listen, if he really *is* government . . . a minister, let's say . . . or someone prominent in the party . . . and he's involved or even partially responsible for a pair of killings? That shit sells, Knox. That right there buys your buddy a free pass, no question."

"You'll guarantee that."

"TIC. No guarantees."

"Passage out, if I stick around to do this? For two—one on a stretcher?"

"Same answer. But will I try? Of course I will."

"You're using me."

"No, no, pal. We're using each other."

"You gain enormous cred," Knox said.

"No. Whatever you dig up, it can't come from me. That suggests I investigated it myself. But there are ways around everything. Bring me that name—a corrupt official. Match that to your eyewitness—a Chinese eyewitness at that. Are you kidding me? In this country, in the current environment, that's currency. Serious currency. Trust me."

"I don't," Knox said.

"You know for a while there, I had you figured for a fool," Kozlowski said. "Are we done here?"

"Keep that phone charged," Knox said. "I'm going to be calling you back on it."

"Remember, pal: I don't know you."

"Love you, too," Knox said, ending the call.

29

The rain hit the hotel room windows like water from a fire hose. The river view was supposed to look across to Pudong, but all Knox saw was the swarm of people on the docks below.

"So?" she said, inquiring about a phone call Knox had placed to Rutherford Risk's Brian Primer.

"He wants us out," Knox confided.

"See?"

"But he has nothing in place for Sarge's extraction. He was unaware of his detention. It clearly put him back on his heels. I pushed for some kind of plan, and said 'first things first,' wanting us out."

"And I agree."

"And I don't," Knox said. "He doesn't have a plan, nor will a plan do any good if Sarge is moved to a Chinese jail. Kozlowski knows the ins and outs better than anyone, and he said it's going to take leverage, and I believe him. I'm staying. You're leaving."

"I doubt it. With these winds, the river like that, they will close the ferries, if they have not already," Grace said. "We should be making alternative plans."

She sat on the corner of the bed, slurping down a bowl of wonton soup.

"This is the alternative plan. Besides, they won't have us on a ferry," Knox said. "They're just using these docks for the rendezvous."

"You cannot identify this Party man without me," she said, repeating an argument she'd championed for the past hour.

"Watch me," Knox said.

"How can I watch you from Hong Kong?"

"Touché."

"You have to understand—"

"We discussed this. You wanted Lu Hao out. I wanted Danny out. We've got them both and now you need to see them out. I made sure the blame for the kidnapping wouldn't fall onto Lu Hao. By now the Mongolian is likely under arrest. If we could get to him, maybe he'd give up the name, but we won't see him again. End of story."

"We," she said, quoting him.

"This is non-negotiable," he said. "What if Danny wakes up in a rage again? Someone has to be there."

"They can keep them separate on the boat," she said.

"You know that, do you?"

"I know you need me."

He knew it too, but wasn't about to admit it. "I need you to be there when Lu Hao can finally talk to us. I need the location where that video was shot. I need some leads."

"Lu Jian, his brother can help. If Lu Hao was on the island on the seventeenth, then it was because he was there with his family. Lu Jian can help us fill in the blanks. But they will not help you. Not without me."

He hadn't considered the family angle. "When Lu Hao wakes, you can get at least the location of the factory out of him. You need to be there to listen."

"Someone needs to be there," she said. "It does not have to be me. Not necessarily. It could be Danner."

She was right about that as well. Danner had expressed remorse over his assaulting Lu; he wasn't going to do that again. And Danner spoke the language fluently.

"He's weak. Malnourished. Exhausted. Traumatized."

"Do you question his abilities for even a moment?" she asked. "You do not, do you? Neither do I. He can do this for us."

"We're going down to those docks, and the three of you are getting on that boat."

"We do not know if a boat is there."

"I'm done arguing."

"Do not be ridiculous," she said. "You enjoy the arguing."

9:00 P.M.
DONGMEN LU FERRY TERMINAL

The ferry terminal teemed with several thousand soaking wet and terribly unhappy Chinese with nowhere to go. Debris, rain and the spray of filthy river water were carried by a ferocious wind that gusted at eighty kilometers an hour. Ferry service had been suspended. From the milling crowd, pressed belly-to-back, arose the sense of an impending riot.

Knox, Grace, Danner and the rag doll that was Lu Hao entered the melee. Knox worried that given the crowd, they would not be spotted by their contact, but he said nothing to the others. At least they were among the only Caucasians.

"We'll try the ticket booth first!" he shouted to Grace.

Both Danner and Lu Hao had regressed rather than recuperated during their brief stay in the hotel room. Lu Hao could walk, though barely, the concussion serious. Danner was drained and tapping all his reserves to keep up.

The four found themselves moved against their wills with each shifting wave of the crowd.

"If this comes apart on us," Knox shouted to be heard, "*when* it comes apart—we don't fight it. We go with the flow and try for the edge as quickly as possible."

Maybe the others hadn't heard him; no one said a thing.

"No matter what," he said, "don't fall. We lock arms and we stay standing. It's the stampede that kills."

Knox locked elbows with Danner on his left and Lu Hao on his right. Grace had Lu's other arm holding him upright. It was cumbersome and difficult to move.

The situation deteriorated quickly from crowd to mob as resentment, anger and claustrophobia created its own personality.

Knox, a head taller than most, could see the crew of a ferryboat trying to hold back the leading edge of the mob, all of whom were determined to board the boat and escape the crush. A crew member swung a fender, banging heads, and a fight broke out. It spread quickly, fed like flames. Stranger turned on stranger.

Only minutes later, the peal of police sirens announced the arrival of a riot squad. The mass surged from the street and away from the police. Lu Hao raked forward and nearly went down. Knox and Grace righted him and allowed themselves to be carried by the flow.

A line of police appeared on the upper plaza. Blue helmets and Plexiglas shields.

A second line of police appeared from around the Hotel Indigo and sealed off the possibility of escape to the south.

"Here we go," Knox said, mostly to himself.

With elbows locked, Knox leaned into the effort as the crowd shifted away from the police to the south. His team worked against the pressure, aiming for the ticket terminal.

The police strategy proved to be flawed: as the lines squeezed the crowd, the only release of pressure was to the docks and the river, forcing more people to leap for the empty ferries, whipping up the fighting.

Knox wiped rain from his eyes. As they worked toward the ticket terminal, he spotted a tourist sign held by a slender arm: WHITE STAR ADVENTURES.

"There!" he shouted.

The woman was Chinese, petite, overdressed and soaking wet. She shook Knox's hand and welcomed him to the "tour." If she were playing a role, it was to a T. She never broke from her smile, never referenced the weather.

"Our boat is tied up other side of third ferry—ferry to the south," she said. "Terminal is crowded today. Four traveling?"

Knox had referenced three passengers over the phone.

He hollered to be heard. "Three will be traveling!"

"John!" Grace called out sharply.

Knox silenced her with a look. The guide caught it all.

"We together then?" the guide said.

"Yes!"

"Very well. You follow me, if you please," she said, still hoisting her sign.

Knox gently lowered her arm and the sign. "I think it's best if we don't advertise."

Rain coursing down her cheeks, she nodded and grinned. "Very well. This way, please."

The south line of riot police stretched shoulder to shoulder from the hotel to the river. The crowd moved away from them, leaving a gap between themselves and the brewing mob. Knox steered their tour guide toward that gap, knowing the police would not rough up Westerners. He and the others slipped down the gap nearly unimpeded.

The scuffle now approached a brawl, leading to increased pressure from the line of police nearest the road. With the river as the only release point, the result was catastrophic. Those positioned at the river's edge of the docks were pushed off. People reached for boat railings and missed. Ferry crews slapped them off. They fell into the water in droves, some caught and crushed between the concrete wharf and the bouncing ferryboat. Bubbling screams cried out, driving an already terrified mob into a frenzy.

The woman led Knox's group to the southern edge of the wharf, where it wasn't much better. She calmly placed them on the lee side of a steel containment railing. Chinese rammed into the dock's final railing and tried to clamber over as they were crushed. More people slipped through the boarding gates in the railing and fell into the water, crying out for help.

The huge ferries, buffeted by gusting winds, banged against their bumpers, crushing more of the fallen.

Among those in the front line, Knox spotted two small kids, terrified and helpless against the power of the crowd. He lunged and snagged the first just before the boy went into the river. He passed him to Grace and grabbed the other—a girl, who clung to him in a vise grip. He and Grace held the children, using the railing to shield them from the crowd.

Raising her voice, their tour guide called out, "We cross deck of last ferry to reach boat! Ferry crew know me—we have arrangement—this could make difficult situation."

Difficult? Knox was thinking. *Try impossible.*

"We must act quickly and rely upon crew. Do not pause, please. Must go directly to boat!"

The black water now foamed with the efforts of the fallen and drowning. The sickening sounds of people drowning filled the air, mixed with wind and the drumming of torrential rain on boat decks.

Panic infected the crowd. Violence spread down the quay. Scores more were heaved into the water.

"We go together as group!" the guide cried out, the first sound of frailty in her voice.

Knox, the child holding fast to him, glanced over into Grace's dark eyes, the rain running down her face like tears. She implored him.

"Two of us are staying!" Knox cried out. "We'll get these children to safety."

Happiness flowed from Grace. For a moment it was only the two of them on the dock.

"This was not arrangement!" the guide shouted to be heard.

"It's the new arrangement. Go! Take these two, and go!" Knox cried. "Get them medical attention as soon as possible."

The guide looked at Knox and Grace, then out into the sea of violence and chaos. Her look said it all.

"Come with me, please!" she shouted, taking Danner by the arm. Danner, in turn, held the unresponsive Lu Hao.

Danner glanced back over his shoulder at Knox. If he spoke, Knox did not hear it.

With great difficulty, the ferry crew held back the throng with billy clubs while admitting the guide, Danner and Lu Hao to the deck. It was a horrific moment as Chinese were beaten back onto the wharf. Grace looked away. The three scrambled across the deck and were gone.

Knox edged along the rail, and Grace followed. He steered them toward the police line and, reaching it, cried out in Shanghainese to be allowed through. To his surprise, two of the policemen parted. He and Grace and the children pushed through, Knox knowing his skin color had saved them.

They placed the children into the care of the hotel staff and then headed for the upstairs room.

G race was toweling off her hair.

"You're a fool to have stayed," Knox said.

"You are welcome," she said, continuing with the towel.

"We'll stay here for the night," he said. "I'll take first watch. I'll wake you in three hours."

Grace said, "A Chinese woman traveling during National Day holiday is no problem. But with a *waiguoren*? And one wanted by police!"

"Thank you," he said, turning his back, allowing her to change out of her wet clothing.

30

Just beyond the Dongmen Lu Ferry Terminal, barges plowed through the white-capped Huangpu River despite the storm. Passing between them was a four-car flatbed ferry with only one car on deck. It was tossed like a toy as it crossed from the western banks of the Bund toward the eastern banks of Pudong.

Inspector Shen Deshi had remained behind the wheel of the vehicle, but only briefly. He hadn't wanted to be separated from the duffel bag, presently hidden beneath the back seat. But the strain of the chains binding the car to the deck as the small ferry was tossed proved too terrifying for him. He'd paid the pilot a small fortune for the ten-minute crossing, but had no desire to show him the Mongolian's face. He led his hostage out onto the stern amid the downpour. It felt far safer out here.

For twelve years, Inspector Shen had served the Ministry of State Security while carrying a People's Armed Police ID as cover. Twelve years of a pathetic salary, of skillfully sidestepping trouble—the protection rackets, the small-time scams and back-room payoffs that complicated a career. Twelve years of watching his fellow agents prosper around him. For the past four years, he'd been one of a very few officers trusted to pursue corruption at all levels. During that time, he had uncovered *tens of millions* of *yuan*—some of which had been offered to him as hush money. He'd never taken a *fen*.

Now, the decision of his career. Of a lifetime. One he made without hesitation. A hundred thousand U.S. dollars. Another hundred and forty thousand *yuan* the Mongol had carefully stacked into plastic bags and hidden in his wall. All counted, more than twenty years of salary. Finally, an amount that could not be passed up. He would be rich for the rest of his life, provided he came up with an exit strategy that would not arouse suspicion. He thought he knew just the man to approach about this.

But at present, he had some tidying up to do. He accepted the complications that came with such a decision. Some lives would be lost by his hand, starting with the Mongolian and the ferry pilot; evidence would be destroyed. Lies would need to be carefully crafted. Throughout his career he'd been required to beat suspects. Nothing new there. No doubt some of them had died. This wasn't so very different.

By now the *waiguoren* should be in jail, or beaten at the hands of the precinct captain. He would have to follow through with that. The *waiguoren* would need silencing, along with his companion. Simple enough.

If other obstacles surfaced, they would be handled. Opportunity knocked. He intended to answer.

"I need for you to pay attention," he said to the Mongolian over the roar of the rain and the steady grind of the boat engine. He unhooked a linchpin and opened the boat's railing.

"This ferry is going to Pudong. It is up to you whether one or two of us get off."

Melschoi glowered, searching for a way out of this. He tested his wrists and ankles; bound so tightly they were never coming off.

His only possible advantage in this impossible situation was that the cop was clearly uncomfortable on a boat. He looked about to puke.

"Where was the video shot?" Inspector Shen hollered.

"Chongming Island," Melschoi hollered back. As a cop himself, he knew this was no time to play coy.

"Who hired you?"

"I met the man only once. No names. A pig civil servant was threatening blackmail. I took care of him."

"A *waiguoren*?"

"No. Chinese. A surveyor. I killed the man. A *waiguoren* was spotted. He was making a video. He did not belong. Killed him, too."

"You severed his hand?"

"I severed it all. Fucking journalists," Melschoi said.

"Excellent!"

"I dumped him like fish chum into the river."

Inspector Shen delighted in what he was hearing. "You are winning much favor with me. *Neh?* And as to what he was filming?"

"I believe you must know."

"Then humor me," Inspector Shen said. "What was the purpose of this laying of the asphalt?"

"A man does what he is paid to do."

"Why kill a man over something so mundane?" Inspector Shen asked.

"I do as I am told."

"But who orders such a thing?"

"My payments were left in the back of taxicabs, or placed into sacks with take-away food orders. It was never the same. And don't think I haven't tried to find out! I met the man and still do not know his name. The fruit falls not far from the tree. He is located in Beijing. This, I know. He is someone very powerful, obviously. His car carried Shanghai plates, but the car was loaned to him for certain."

Shen Deshi licked his chops. If he could only identify the man, he could use him to leverage his own situation.

"The phone number, then."

"The fucking *eBpon*—the foreigner—took my phone."

The *waiguoren* would most definitely have to be found and dealt with. Shen owed the police captain another call.

"Certainly you must have memorized it."

"My wrists and ankles. Then, once ashore, we will talk. At a distance."

Inspector Shen grinned. "I should know better than to try to question a former policeman." He crossed his arms to make his point. But by doing so, he lost his balance and staggered forward.

Melschoi rocked and head-butted the man's knees.

Inspector Shen went over backward. Melschoi aimed for another head butt; he took a shoe in the face, his nose bent and bleeding.

Shen Deshi seized him by his hair and dragged him to the opening in the rail.

"No!" Melschoi screamed, kicking out.

"The phone number!" Shen Deshi thundered.

"Yours, if you free me!"

"I'll free you forever, if you're not forthcoming."

Shen Deshi repeatedly kicked him in the chest and belly. Behind him, the car groaned and cried on its chains. The boat lurched side to side.

"The fucking number!" Shen Deshi roared.

Melschoi opened his mouth to answer, but the ship rocked heavily and Shen Deshi's next kick caught Melschoi in the throat, crushing his trachea and collapsing his larynx. Melschoi sucked for wind.

The boat rose and shifted again. Shen Deshi lunged to stop him, but Melschoi slid off the wet deck and out through the open rail, swallowed by the black waters of the Huangpu.

SATURDAY

October 2

31

By midnight, the brunt of the storm had passed. Riot police had contained, arrested and dispersed pieces of the mob. Knox monitored it all from the window while Grace snored gently from the bed. As the rain subsided, the streets quickly drained and recovered from the flooding. And then—only in Shanghai—the city sprang back to life as if nothing had happened. Detritus was cleared. Traffic began moving again. People appeared on the streets from all directions. Taxis were running. It was like kicking an anthill, only to see the ants swarm back to work minutes later and begin rebuilding the hill.

He never woke Grace for her shift. He let her sleep. When morning finally came, and they'd eaten and Knox had drunk multiple cups of black tea, they spoke.

"So, here we are."

"Indeed," she said. "I take it you have a plan."

"The island," he said.

She nodded.

"Your friend."

She eyed him furtively. "I know that I suggested this, but I would rather not. My preference is to start with Marquardt's hired driver or the hotel where he and Song stayed."

"You still love him," he said.

"Westerners think in terms of love beginning and ending. It is not so for the Chinese."

"The shortest distance between two points is a straight line. Whatever the driver can tell us is good. You'll call him and arrange a time to meet. But the brother will know more than anyone. I know about brothers. Time is critical. Sarge will be jailed, if he hasn't been already."

"I do not believe Mr. Primer will allow him to be in such trouble," she said.

"Even his reach only extends so far."

She shook her head in disbelief.

"A single day in a Chinese jail is one too many," he said.

"You will have no disagreement from me."

"The brother, then. But call the driver first and arrange for him to drive us."

Again, that put-upon look of hers.

"Please," he said.

"I believe that is the first time I have heard you use this word," she said.

"There's a first time for everything."

Knox hot-wired a Toyota in the Indigo's parking garage. He wore a pair of sunglasses to hide his eyes and a headband that covered his ears, and makeup applied by Grace that widened his cheekbones and narrowed his chin—all in hopes of avoiding the prying eyes of computerized face recognition.

Grace drove, Knox in the back seat, so only a Chinese face could be seen through the windshield.

The city had already emptied out by half. Traffic was lighter than usual. They drove the tunnel to Pudong, headed for the ring road and eventually the Hushan Expressway toward Chongming Island.

The wind had died down. The rain continued at a drizzle; dark clouds threatened. The farm roads of Chongming Island were debris-strewn and partially flooded. Residents milled about, looking dazed.

They reached the town of Chongming, for which the island was named, thirty minutes later. Grace pulled the Toyota into a semicircular driveway of a five-story apartment building and parked.

She reached for the door handle.

"Be careful."

She paused to look back at him. He saw sadness bordering on grief. She said, "Do not leave the car, John. You will stand out in this city. This is not Shanghai."

"So Marquardt would have stood out here as well," he said, knowing she exaggerated. Hotels and private car companies didn't exist for the pleasure of the locals. Much of the island was soon to be urbanized. "I can be less memorable than you might think."

"There are closed-circuit cameras here as well," she reminded.

She left the car. Knox looked around at the plain buildings that were a holdover of the Mao era.

The gray skies. The litter.

He wanted outside.

The apartment building wasn't much to look at, its location nothing special. Chongming was a backwater island that, no matter what amount of funds the government injected into its economy, would never be much more than an outpost of rice paddies and pig farms.

Grace knew all this, had considered it important once, but what she would have given, what she would have changed, in order to possess a key to the door she now faced.

Her heart beating wildly, she raised her hand to knock, only to lower her arm to her side. This was no ordinary door. It opened to her past. She wanted it to open to her future. She'd imagined and dreamed of this moment for six years. Now, it suddenly felt too soon.

The door's fisheye security lens winked. He'd heard her—or *sensed* her. Her heart fluttered. She forced a smile for appearance's sake, and then knocked lightly, wondering what was taking him so long. Hoping the lump in his throat was as big as hers.

The door opened slowly and there he stood before her. Imperiously. Formally. Capable of English or Shanghainese, they would speak their Chongming dialect.

"Jian," she said. He'd aged hardly at all, though he had always looked older than he was. He wore his hair shorter now, more in keeping with his job as a civil servant. His hands appeared smoother, his nails immaculate. The same quiet confidence showed in his eyes. She felt slightly faint.

"Youya."

"It warms my heart to see you."

"You are as lovely as ever." He sounded more formal than sincere. She read meaning into his every gesture, his every look. He paused and said, "You will please come in?"

She entered, removing her shoes and placing her purse alongside them.

He showed her into a modest living room. "Tea?"

"It would be my pleasure to prepare it," she said sincerely.

"I will be but a minute."

His rebuff hit her hard. He wanted no such intimacy. Five minutes passed as he worked in the kitchen, out of sight. She took in the flat-panel television and DVD player; the elliptical workout machine; a rack of free weights. The rain-stained windows looked out on a sea-gray sky.

"That was some storm," she called out loudly.

"We lost power for most of the night. It has only come back on in the past hour."

She noted the apartment showed no sign of a woman's touch. Perhaps the woman she'd seen him with in Lu Hao's digital frame had been but a fling. On the other hand, if he had married, her mother never would have told her, fearing she might do something drastic. She spotted photographs of his family. Her breath caught, spotting her own image among them. She remembered the exact day at the market together, remembered his smile. She saw no other woman among the photos and took this as a very good sign.

"This is oolong," he said, placing the tea tray down before her.

"This is uncomfortable," she said.

He laughed.

"For you as well?" she inquired.

He tried to suppress his smile, and she wondered why. "Yes, I suppose."

"You never answered my letters," she blurted out. She had a million things to say, but hated herself for breaking the formality.

"What could I say?" he asked.

"It was my fath—"

"I do not need to hear it again," he said, cutting her off. "Your father is an honorable man. I respect his wishes."

Liar! she wanted to shout. *You did not respect them at the time, and had you come after me I would have eloped with you.*

"Have you seen them?" he asked. "Your parents?"

"No. I came here first." She paused. "To you."

He clearly didn't know what to say. He made himself busy with the tea, pouring it too soon.

"Lu Hao is free," she said. "He is, by now, out of the country and safe."

Lu Jian set the teapot down and bent over, throwing his head into his hands, sobbing.

She reached out and tentatively placed a hand on his shoulder, wanting so much more.

Sitting up, wiping tears away, he said, "How could you possibly know this?" Distrustful.

She wondered how much to reveal. "It was I who arranged the job, as you will remember."

"I have heard nothing. My parents have not been contacted."

"No. It is not official."

"But you are certain?"

"Yes, of course."

"Will you excuse me, please? I will call my parents now and end their grief."

"No, Jian. Please . . . there are complications. I need your help."

With tears brimming in his eyes, he said, "You bring me great joy, Chu Youya! Great joy, indeed."

"I need . . . a favor."

"Anything!" He bordered on euphoric.

"You are an important civil servant—if my mother does not spread foul rumor."

"She exaggerates, as always. I am of little consequence, I am afraid." His ambition, or lack thereof, had been a sticking point for her father.

"I hear you have risen quickly." She had heard more, much more, but wasn't sure how to play her cards.

"I have the benefit of unusual motivation," he said, his eyes boring into her. His ambition was now to show her father wrong.

"Lu Hao was over here in September."

"Yes."

"Visiting the family?"

"My mother's birthday."

"You must congratulate her for me."

"What of this visit?"

"Lu Hao saw a man. He followed him to a remote location."

"Did he?"

"He spoke nothing of this with you?"

Lu Jian shook his head.

"This man he followed met with a prominent official. Did Lu Hao mention such a man to you?"

"I am sorry, Youya."

"This place—it is a large blue building. Old. Like a factory. Chong-ming is in its title."

"As in so many companies," he said. "I do not know of such a place."

"This official," she said. "I believe it is possible that he may be connected to the construction industry. That he may oversee or be connected to, in some way, such projects. Projects in the billions of *yuan*."

"Indeed, with the selection of Chongming as the seventh city, it is entirely possible. I do not doubt it. Such powerful men visit our city often these days."

Fifteen years before, the Party authorities had identified seven cities, all suburbs of Shanghai, to be incorporated into the city by rail, highway and commerce, thereby expanding Shanghai's territory. Chongming was the final area to be developed in the master plan.

"It is important I identify the man Lu Hao observed at this meeting."

"You have asked Lu Hao, of course."

"Just a face to him. Nothing more." She hesitated. "A life depends upon this information. The life of a man who helped win Lu Hao's freedom. My immediate superior."

He sucked in air sharply. His eyes lingered on her and she felt like a flower in the sun. But then he looked off, concentrating.

"Construction?" he echoed. "So much of it now in planning."

"This is large. Very large. Something worthy of deception and betrayal. Of fierce competition among the heavyweights."

"A hotel? An office building? What?"

"Bigger. My sense is land development. Something in the tens of billions of *yuan*."

His eyes flared. *"Tens of billions?"*

"If you could ask around. I need a lead to follow. Quickly. I need to know what project might attract the attention of foreign construction companies."

"Foreign?"

"I have evidence that supports this."

"You saved my brother. I will do anything."

"I do not wish you to take any risks. These people . . . we suspect them of serious crimes."

"We?"

"A co-worker."

"Are you still betrothed?" he said, as if the words simply escaped. His eyes told her he wanted to take the question back.

She hung her head. "Yes."

"Six years this man waits for you."

"Yes. And sixty more."

"You shame your parents."

"It is true."

"Why?"

"Must you ask?" she said.

He looked away. "I will make inquiries. My brother's life is a debt I cannot ever repay."

"There is no debt between us," she said. "Only the past."

He recoiled. She'd overstepped her bounds.

"How do I reach you?"

She wrote down the number for Knox's iPhone. "You should not call from your phone. Buy a new SIM card before you call. For safety's sake."

He nodded. "You are in trouble."

"I take precautions. So should you."

"You have come here at personal risk."

"It is now a risk for both of us, I am afraid. Your efforts must be quiet, Jian. You must take great care. Trust no one."

"The police?"

"Not them either."

"You can stay here. With me."

Her heart nearly burst. "This is very kind of you. But sadly, I cannot. Many know our history—yours and mine. If inquiries were made, authorities would look here first."

"Is it that bad?"

"I am afraid so. If questioned, you must take great care, Jian. Do not deny my visit. Tell them you sent me away. Tell them I came out of love, not business. That you sent me away."

"Never."

"You must not incite their interest in you."

"I have much *guanxi* here. I have made many friends."

"I would never believe otherwise." Tears threatened. "I must leave," she said.

"You have not touched your tea."

She reached out her hand and placed it onto his. "I have not touched you."

He allowed their touch to linger. Then he withdrew his hand and eased back his chair.

"If such a project exists, there will only be one that size. I will look into it."

"Carefully."

He stood from the chair.

She walked to the door, waiting for him to stop her.

Instead, she found herself awkwardly fumbling with her shoes. She located her purse and stepped into the hall. He closed the door behind her without a goodbye.

32

Knox knew it wasn't easy stealing something in China—there were too many eyes everywhere, both human and electronic. Ignoring Grace's plea to stay in the car, he hunted down side lanes where closed-circuit cameras were unlikely to be. From there he stole two sets of license plates and slipped them up the back of his shirt.

Speed-trap cameras routinely captured license plates. If the Toyota had been reported as stolen, a data trail might already exist. What Brian Primer said was true: it wasn't worth having two or three people wind up in Chinese jails in an effort to save one. He had no intention of giving Primer the satisfaction of being right.

Because of this, even after switching plates, the Toyota would have to be abandoned. Accommodations would need to be found. With each challenge, the probability of mistake escalated. The longer they remained on the island—by definition, a place with limited egress—they increased their chances of capture.

Grace approached the car looking like she'd been mugged. Knox kept quiet, eyeing her from the back seat as she drove.

"He will call if he uncovers anything," she finally said.

"Providing he tries to uncover anything."

"Of course he will try. Face demands this of him. We have rescued his brother. He cannot repay this debt."

"If he passed on you, he's an idiot," Knox said.

Her eyes flicked to the mirror.

"Marquardt's driver?" Knox asked. He wasn't as convinced as she that Marquardt's secret trip to the island connected to the Party member seen in the video, the one whose name they needed. But Marquardt was connected to the Mongolian through Lu Hao's deliveries, and the Mongolian was connected to the heavyset government man, so it wasn't impossible that Marquardt's trip here was related. And they had nowhere else to turn.

"He is to meet us in front of a men's club," she said. "It is known to be frequented by the influential. It is therefore one of very few places we can be sure has no cameras."

"Clever of you."

"One of the advantages of island life. Very few secrets."

"What about you, Grace? What are your secrets? And you're not allowed to say that, if you told me, they wouldn't be secrets anymore." He'd hoped he might win a smile from her; he got nothing.

"I will park the car. We will leave separately and meet inside the club." She turned a corner and slowed. "Keep your head down. You go first."

The establishment's waiting area smelled of sandalwood incense. There was an electric fountain plugged into the wall, spilling water over a miniature landscape carved out of jade. There was a curtained window above the back of a couch, and two lovely young women in maroon *qipao*s behind an elegant counter. A red dragon inlaid into black lacquer was coiled on the wall. Knox was greeted and welcomed, both women's smiles slipping into girlish giggles. A *waiguoren*! In poor, choppy English,

Knox was asked if he would like a cocktail. It was not yet lunchtime. He ordered a beer.

The women in charge sat down across from him and explained the cost of club membership, which was discounted if visits were purchased as part of a package. He was told the cost of entertainment would be discussed once he was upstairs and his membership had been approved.

The beer was fantastically cold and easy to drink, and if the hostesses looked anything like these two, there was no questioning the popularity of the place.

Grace entered and she sat next to Knox. The senior woman in the *qipao*, clearly accustomed to female clients, began pitching the membership to her as well.

"Vodka rocks," Grace ordered. She rattled something in the Chongming dialect at the hostess so fast that Knox only caught a piece of it— something about Knox being her man and that after a drink she'd be taking him home. She laid a hundred-*yuan* note on the coffee table and sat back comfortably.

Her vodka arrived. Grace hit it hard and easily. *We all have our secrets,* he thought.

Knox pulled out a fifty-*yuan* note and asked the hostess to sign him up and show him upstairs.

Grace grabbed him by the wrist. "What are you doing?"

"The driver isn't here. We can't just *sit*! We'll attract attention." What the hell was she thinking?

He drank half the beer in a few neat swallows. "I've been looking for a place like this. My kind of relationship: intense, but quick." Then he added, "Not too quick. Don't get the wrong idea. Short-lived is more what I meant."

"*Sweetheart,*" she said, playing her part.

"Why don't you join me?" he offered. "Us."

She released his arm. "I will not be here when you come down."

The vodka was gone, the ice barely melted.

"If you change your mind," he said, "you know where to find me."

Knox headed upstairs with the hostess. Below, he heard Grace calling for another vodka.

The second-floor lounge housed seven women—girls, some of them—some prettier than others. Some shopworn while trying hard not to look vacant. He sat between two of them and ordered another beer.

He was nearly through the beer when Grace arrived at the top of the stairs, looking slightly drunk. She said something caustic in Shanghainese to the pretty girl next to him and took her place, moving the girl over.

"What's taking you so long?" she said. "Pick one."

"To be honest, the oldest profession has never interested me. Call me a contemporary."

"Then why come up here? To punish me?"

"You? It has nothing to do with you."

"Then why?"

"I pinched a good deal of money off the Mongolian. If we're caught . . . more likely, *when* we're caught, that money will be confiscated and end up in some cop's home entertainment system. Here, maybe it buys one of these fine specimens," he said, running his finger into the cleavage of the girl sitting next to him, who grinned and placed her hand on his inner thigh, "a second career."

Grace put her own hand into Knox's crotch and moved the girl's hand.

Things were getting interesting.

"Acting noble doesn't make one noble," she said, working the vodka.

"Thanks for that clarification." He swilled more beer, and drew an abstract pattern on its sweating glass.

"So pick one," he said. "Someone deserving."

"Me?"

"Why not? I'm an equal opportunity employer." The joke was lost on her. He felt sorry for her, and then wondered how many of her jokes he missed, only to realize she didn't make jokes. At which point he felt sorry for her again.

"Do you honestly believe we are not going to get through this?"

He thought that was the vodka talking, so he let the beer answer. "I'm hedging my bets. You turn over rocks, bad things crawl out. And no, that's not an American proverb, just an observation."

He placed the beer down, promising himself no more.

She drained the second vodka. "Mmm," she said.

"I'm still waiting for you to pick one," he answered when her look turned cloudy.

"She will just send the money home. She will be on her back once again tomorrow."

"That's her choice."

"How much?"

"Ten thousand."

"You would not! How much did you take?"

"More than that."

She stared at him for what felt like several minutes. He met her gaze, looked away from it, and met it again.

"This one," she said pointing across the narrow room. The girl—and she was just a girl—misunderstood and rose, her face beaming.

"Because she's the youngest?" Knox said.

"It's not like that," Grace said. "It's not her age."

The young girl stood in front of Knox, lightly swaying her hips and smiling devilishly.

"You realize I'm missing out on the mileage points here," he said.

"Whatever you do, do not give it to her in front of the others," Grace said.

"I trust you're talking about the money."

The vodka apparently caused immunity to his humor.

The girl clearly delighted in winning the favor of the *waiguoren*. Knox allowed her to lead him down the hall and into a comfortable though spare room. He was studying the sad bed, considering sleep and nothing more. When he turned around, she was naked, having slipped out of the dress. It lay at her feet. Small, high breasts. A flat, hungry stomach. More like nineteen or twenty. Comfortable with her nudity. Confident in her smile. Knox kneeled in front of her and she misunderstood, widening her stance. He lifted the dress up, slowly covering her. He turned her around, securing the frog and loop at the top.

He passed her the bundle of *yuan* from behind. Speaking proper Mandarin, he said, "This is to be spent on the future, not the present. *Neh?* Do not tell the others. There are many jobs. It is a bountiful time in all of China." He kissed her at the base of the neck and drank in her intoxicating scent.

A knock advanced the opening of the door.

"He's here," Grace said.

12:00 NOON
CHONGMING

Grace negotiated with the clean-shaven young man who had driven Allan Marquardt for one weekend in mid-September. She and Knox occupied the center bench of the blue Buick van. The driver must have sensed the assumed value of the information he possessed, yet Grace bought his cooperation for seventy-five U.S. dollars, with another seventy-five promised on top of his hundred-a-day rate.

The driver remembered three men, two foreigners. From his description Grace identified Preston Song and Allan Marquardt, but was stumped by the third. Song had done most of the talking. Marquardt had had his head in his BlackBerry most of the time.

"You will take us there, now," Grace said.

"We have an agreement, lady," the driver said.

"Something is not right," Grace told Knox, speaking in English.

"Because?" Knox said.

"Why is he reminding me of the agreement?"

Knox leaned forward and spoke Mandarin. "Your mother will not recognize her son if you fail to hold up your end of agreement." He leaned back in the seat.

"But there is nothing to see!" the man replied, craning back to look at Grace. "I swear you will be disappointed. Farmland. Nothing more."

"But you recall which farm roads," she stated.

"Yes. Of course. I grew up here."

"So did I," she said. "So do not try to play with me."

"Farm roads, cousin, I swear. Nothing more!"

"Show us," Knox said.

Grace looked at Knox excitedly. "Farm roads. Land development." He heard her pride, the sense of victory. Maybe the vodka.

Grace leaned her head back, sighed, and fell quickly to sleep, a smile faintly on her lips.

A few minutes out of town, they time-traveled back two or three hundred years. Half-acre rice farms, manicured to precise detail, formed an uninterrupted patchwork. Decaying dwellings lined the roads. Young children led beasts of burden by nose rings, or carried live chickens hanging by their feet.

"Where are we?" she asked the driver, opening her eyes.

"River road on way to Chong'an Cun," the driver said.

"This is Chong'an Cun?"

"Precisely, cousin! You are indeed an islander!" He pulled the van to the side of the road. "This was our first stop."

"How was it identified?" Knox asked. "How did they direct you here?"

"Village name," the driver said.

"Only that?" Knox asked. "Nothing more specific?"

"Village was name enough," the driver replied.

"Only this one village?" Grace inquired.

"No. Next we went to Wan Beicun."

Knox took pictures with the iPhone. "Take us there, please," Knox said.

The going was rough and slow on narrow mud roads meant for *tuo la ji* and water buffalo. They traveled through a half-dozen poor villages and arrived twenty minutes later at a crossroads. Again, the van stopped.

"This is it?" Grace asked.

"This was last stop before return to Chongming."

"Your GPS," Knox said. "Pass it to me, please." Knox accepted it and wrote down the current lat/long location. He asked the driver to point out their position on a map he carried.

Knox spoke English to Grace, softly so the driver could not hear. "There was a second car service. They took a second car."

Grace faintly nodded. "Damn," she said. It was the first time he'd heard her swear.

"That way no one driver had the full picture of the land parcel," he said.

She nodded. "Yes. But not a single parcel. Too big for that. It must be a project involving the expansion of several small towns. Something like that. We will never know. They have defeated us," she said.

While she considered their failure, Knox was wondering how long it would take, once they left the car, for the driver to contact Preston Song and sell him the information that two people were trying to retrace his steps. How long after that for Song to notify the police?

"We need more than this," she said.

"Marquardt and Song weren't taking a Sunday drive. Your instincts were right."

"We have nothing but a pair of small villages."

The forty-minute drive back to Chongming was interminable, both of them exhausted. Knox fought to stay awake while she slept off the vodka.

They were dropped off and walked two blocks to the Toyota. Knox was switching out the plates as his phone rang.

She listened, spoke softly and hung up, cradling the phone to her chest.

"So?" Knox asked.

"Lu Jian has found nothing involving a land deal, big or small. Nothing beyond the seventh city projects already announced and underway. None involve Chong'an Cun or Wan Beicun."

"That's depressing."

"But in the process of his asking around, he turned up a news story worthy of our interest."

"Because?"

"A hit-and-run fatality, last month. A surveyor by the name of Yao Xuolong. A civil servant. This man was struck and killed along the roadside near Yuan Liu Qidui. The driver was never found."

"And it means . . . ?"

"Yuan Liu Qidui is a small village also surrounded by nothing but farms." She snatched the map from Knox and took a moment to find it. "Here. You see?"

When combined with the two locations they had just visited, three quarters of a perfect rectangle were formed—that, or a right-angled triangle. It was impossible to miss the symmetry.

"It's massive," Knox said.

"He provided me the man's family's home."

Knox said, "I'm game."

"It may be nothing. A twenty-minute drive, a waste of time."

"We need to get out of here," Knox reminded. "I trust that driver about as far as I can throw him."

"You switched the Toyota's registration."

"Yeah," Knox said. "But believe me, they're not that stupid."

33

In a small office cubicle, one of a hundred identical cubicles in a warehouse-like facility in a northwestern district of Shanghai, a woman was alerted to a priority status license plate match.

She called up the source video, recorded less than six hours earlier: the plate belonged to a stolen Toyota crossing over the bridge/tunnel to Chongming Island. In one video, the face of a *waiguoren* was spotted looking out a rear-seat side window. Her chest pounding, she called her manager, who assigned her additional eyes to help inspect plate capture video in an ever-widening grid.

Within twenty minutes, the information was texted to the phones of all law enforcement officers, including that of Inspector Shen, who had traveled to Chongming Island because of the Mongolian's remark. With

the text, Shen now had reason to visit the local precinct and solicit manpower and information.

If, during the arrest or incarceration or questioning of the *waiguoren*,
the man was killed accidentally, it would be viewed as official business.
Perhaps even attributed to the local police, instead of him.

34

Off a narrow hard-packed dirt road, marked by a crumbling pair of stacked stone columns, a rutted lane led into a compound of five timber-built houses, the exteriors scabbing paint. Smoke rose from chimneys and hung in the air, tasting of cooking oil. Knox and Grace approached on foot.

A withered woman greeted them. She wore a loose-fitting white cloak under which could be seen the wide legs of simple three-quarter-length pants of coarse cloth and ancient black cloth shoes that might once have been embroidered with colorful birds and peonies.

"The grandmother," Grace said. "She is getting her daughter. The white she wears is for mourning."

A woman in her forties wore her grief as fatigue in what had once been spirited eyes. Knox and Grace were shown into a dim room and offered low stools around an open fire pit where a carbon-encrusted teapot boiled and steamed.

Knox kept up with introductions despite the woman's difficult accent: the grandfather was a clay potter, this woman's husband, his apprentice; the couple's son, Yao Xuolong, had attended the local school and had gone on to be a surveyor.

Grace explained that she and her foreigner friend had heard that the son had been involved with a project of enormous significance bringing great honor to the family and that his importance in the project could not be easily measured. That they were interested in documenting the son's achievements.

The mother showed them a photograph of her son and then proudly carried on for fifteen minutes while Knox and Grace sipped green tea. Grace did not interrupt, displaying an unusual patience, a quality Knox did not share with her.

"Now this charade," the mother said angrily, her eyes brimming with tears.

"Please explain," Grace said.

"They know nothing of my son! I explain to police many times, and yet they sweep me out the door like dust."

"What do they not know of your son?"

"His clothes, lady! He dies in his finest clothes, those saved only for evening. For town. For courtship. Business. He is found by the side of road in finest clothes, but with the equipment for work. Not his own equipment either! How is this possible? I tell you, it is *not*. I do not know why these lies are told about my son, but a lie is a lie!" The tears arrived. She wiped them away.

"How recent is this photo?" Knox asked her.

"Not so very," the woman said.

"Did he wear his hair like this?"

"Shorter," the woman answered. "You know the young people nowadays."

Knox tried imagining this same man with shorter hair, working to match him with the man in the video seen entering the factory. It wasn't an impossible match.

"How tall was your son?" Knox asked.

"One hundred sixty centimeters," she said. "A little more."

Knox did the conversion in his head. Five-foot-four or five, a decent match with the victim. He sat up taller, his blood pumping.

"Tell us about this problem with the equipment," Knox said softly. "You said it was not his own. What do you mean?"

"Indeed! Not his!" The woman motioned to her husband, who'd been standing in shadow. He immediately headed upstairs.

She then explained that her father had given the son the latest surveyor's equipment upon his acceptance into civil service. The equipment was expensive, representing years of savings on the grandfather's part. The dead man had taken great care of the equipment. But he'd been found on the side of the road in possession of state-owned equipment, a contradiction that hadn't been explained.

The husband came downstairs holding a common plastic tote in one hand and a large plastic case in his other. The tote contained the clothes the son had died in. The shoes—dress shoes, Knox noted—had adhered to the tote's plastic. Knox pulled the shoes free and studied the clothing, passing each piece to Grace.

The mother, sobbing, spoke of her son's watch and shoes, how he would never—ever!—have worn either in his fieldwork.

Knox had a tar-like substance on his hands from handling the shoes. The father offered him a soiled rag and he cleaned up. He opened the large case, revealing a clean neon-orange tripod and a high-tech sextant.

Knox studied the equipment.

"It's a sextant," Knox told Grace. "With *GPS*," he emphasized. "Sophisticated stuff. Must have cost a fortune."

Knox asked the mother and father if he might inspect the sextant more closely. He was granted permission.

Knox switched it on. A small green screen lit up, revealing menus with Chinese characters. He moved through the menu as the others watched.

"It records and saves the ten most recent locations," he said, speaking English.

"Something wrong?" the mother asked.

"It's all good," Knox said in English. Then, Mandarin. "This information helps us greatly." He ran his finger along the second lat/long, wondering if Grace recognized how close it was to the number Knox had taken from the driver's navigation device. Only a few seconds off.

Grace wrote down all ten coordinates.

"Do you have your son's cell phone?" Knox asked.

The father returned upstairs and came down minutes later wearing a look of bewilderment. He and his wife exchanged some heated questioning.

"It is lost," the mother told them.

"I'll bet," said Knox.

Knox wanted to leave them money, but Grace stopped him from offering. It was agreed they would buy several pieces of the grandfather's pottery, which they did. Each piece was carefully wrapped in newspaper, a time-consuming process that left Knox anxious.

As they reached the Toyota, Knox already had the iPhone out. He input the first of the sextant's coordinates—the most recently recorded waypoint. A blue pin dropped onto the phone's map. A second. A third. The line pointed back toward Wan Beicun.

"He's a shrimp—the right height for the guy in the video," Knox said.

"Yes."

"The guy in the video was also wearing decent clothes."

"Yes," Grace said.

"So maybe it's him and they dumped him away from the factory."

"It is possible," she said, climbing behind the wheel.

Knox worked the finger of his right hand. "Shit!" he said.

"What is it?" Grace asked, looking over.

"My fingers are on fire." He spit onto them. "Crap! Pull over!"

She gasped at the sight of the raw flesh.

"Chemical burn," he said, having seen similar things during his time in Kuwait.

She pulled the car to a stop and Knox jumped out, washing his hands in a puddle. He returned five minutes later.

"Better?"

"Barely," he said. "Caustic stuff."

"The shoes!" she said.

"Yes. Our boy was someplace nasty before he died."

"Like a factory," she said. "We plot all the coordinates."

"Whoever did this—providing we're right—wanted his death to look like an accident. A hit and run while he was surveying. Otherwise, he just disappears."

"So his disappearance would raise unwanted questions," she said. "Questions we must now answer."

For the next several hours, they passed through tiny farming villages as they tracked the surveying equipment's GPS coordinates across a large area. Two of the ten lat/longs closely matched locations they'd visited with Marquardt's driver: Chong'an Cun and Wan Beicun. They stopped there.

Grace studied the map, upon which Knox had drawn connecting lines.

"Are you still thinking it's a group of small towns?" he asked.

He'd sketched three sides of a perfect rectangle.

"It is so large. So much land."

"Measured in square miles, not acres," Knox said. He watched her studying it. "Any ideas?"

Grace looked up and outside at the flat expanse of rice paddies stretching to the horizon. "It is a New City," she said. "A resettlement city."

The Chinese government occasionally created a new technology center or manufacturing district in a remote area and relocated millions of people to live and work there.

"Doesn't that fly in the face of Chongming being the seventh city?" he asked.

"Not actually. It supports it. It is to be a resettlement city," she said, her voice more confident. "Similar to one I once saw outside Chengdu."

It was a new term Knox had not heard, and he said so.

"China is no longer able to feed her people. We import even basic food like rice. The problem is farming efficiency. We have over seven hundred million farmers, yet the average farm is less than half a hectare.

Our government has calculated we need a minimum of one-point-five hectare per farmer to be self-sufficient. It means we must find new work for one out of every three farmers. We are in the middle of the largest migration of humanity in the history of world," she said, sounding somewhat proud.

"Resettlement," he said.

"Yes. Resettlement cities are built on empty tracts of land, just like this." She indicated the open fields. "High-rise housing. Typically, four to five million people."

"Million," Knox said, trying to wrap his mind around it.

"Such a construction project would be worth—"

"Billions of *yuan*," he said. "Fourteen billion, seven hundred million, to be exact. The number. The prize."

They sat in the idling car, neither of them speaking. For both it was an epiphany, the weaving together of frayed ends. For both, their fatigue suddenly weighed even heavier.

"I owe you an apology," Knox said. "Marquardt's trip meant something."

"Accepted."

"Lu's red envelope," Knox said.

"Passed along by a Beijing official. The first two hundred thousand was likely for the coordinates, so Marquardt could visit the proposed property. The process would be closed bids. By seeing the property beforehand—"

"He'd know the approximate cost of developing it, refining his bid."

"The second two hundred thousand was perhaps to buy the bid amount acceptable to the Resettlement Committee. The fourteen billion, seven hundred million. This would allow Marquardt to undercut all other bidders."

"Yao Xuolong understood what he was looking at," Knox said. "It's a small island. He figures it out just as we have. Maybe he offers to sell the coordinates to Yang Cheng or another Berthold Group competitor, or maybe he wants money to keep his mouth shut. Whatever his move, it gets him killed."

"But he knew who to contact," she said. "He knew who to call. How would he know the Mongolian?"

"Maybe he didn't," Knox said.

"The government official," she proposed.

"It's possible. And if he figured out who it was, so can we."

The only flaw in the trapezoidal shape formed by the coordinates was at the southeast corner, where an irregular box connected the parcel to the shores of the Yangtze River. Both of them spotted it.

"I am familiar with that area of the island," she said. "A long time ago, it served as a ferry dock. Now it is warehouses and light industrial."

"So they annex a piece of ground onto this New City, ground that's already zoned for light industrial. It offers a manufacturing area and river access. Makes sense to me."

She took Knox by the hand. "Your fingers burning. Light industrial."

"Chemicals," he said.

"Chemicals," she echoed.

35

"Goddamn Chinese," Kozlowski blurted out to his wife as he hung up the phone.

"Honey!" She motioned to their daughter, Tucker, who was playing on a DSi.

"It's Saturday," he said, "of a national holiday weekend, and of all the days, the lab chooses today to return a forensics report."

"So they're working. But you're not."

"If only."

"Please."

"I have to. There's a heavyweight cop involved with this. And Knox. You know Knox."

"He's in trouble?"

"He is. Up to his keister. I should have never answered the phone."

The call had explained that the severed hand retrieved from the

Yangtze was cut from a dead man, not a living one. The DNA IDed him as a Caucasian with O-negative blood. Flesh burns on the wrist were consistent with chemical burns. Soil samples taken from beneath two of the fingernails returned high traces of heavy metals: mercury, lead, cadmium, chromium and arsenic.

"Which means?" Kozlowski had asked the lab technician.

The man replied: "These metals are in densities twenty-three percent higher than Shanghai garden soil."

Shanghai garden soil? Who the fuck asked about Shanghai garden soil?

"This is soil from Chongming Island."

"Say again," Kozlowski said.

"Soil on Chongming Island is the only location for a radius of several hundred kilometers with this same approximate concentration of heavy metals."

Kozlowski swallowed hard. He'd had two men following Inspector Shen Deshi since their meeting at the KFC. His men had lost him to a river crossing in the storm but had reconnected and followed him onto Chongming Island.

"What kind of chemicals, exactly?" Kozlowski had asked, continuing the conversation.

"In combination with the chemical agents discovered on his wrist: sodium hydrosulphide, soda ash and sodium metabisulphite. I might suggest a livestock tannery."

"A tannery on Chongming Island," Kozlowski had mumbled.

"Correct," the lab man said.

Kozlowski had hung up fearing Shen Deshi was about to beat him to the physical evidence of an American videographer's murder. Evidence the man would destroy as quickly as possible. Any chance at justice lost.

Kozlowski made contact with his two agents.

"He's in a police precinct in Chongming."

"Stay with him," Kozlowski ordered. "If he so much as farts, I want to hear about it."

36

Inspector Shen Deshi sat imperiously, legs crossed, in the corner of the brightly lit assembly room of Chongming's PSB, fifth precinct. He wore dark glasses. He studied the group, amazed at the youth of the precinct's few patrol officers, trying to remember if he'd ever been that young.

His decision to keep the money had put him in a reflective mood. The surprise on the Mongolian's face as he'd slid off the ferry would not leave him. Perhaps he'd been too hasty. If well-connected, the Mongolian's employer could make hell for him. So could Kozlowski, if any evidence surfaced that the Mongolian had chopped the American cameraman to pieces. He needed to pull a blanket over all of this and let it go to sleep. A deep sleep. And quickly, before it got out of hand.

The police captain called his group to order. Their uniforms were loose and ill-fitting; three were women, two old dogs not yet thirty and one quite the stunner, who managed to fill out her uniform nicely. He thought this woman might accompany him on his rounds.

He listened to the captain detail the situation: a fugitive foreigner, considered dangerous, in league with a Chinese woman, both wanted for questioning on multiple assaults, possible kidnapping, extortion and a homicide. A big case on Chongming Island was a stolen water buffalo; the patrol officers were collectively drooling at the thought of pursuing a real-life fugitive, not because they would enjoy the pursuit, which they would, but because the only way out of a hellhole like Chongming Island was to gain the attention of one's superiors and request reassignment. For the nine officers gathered, their captain was waving a lottery ticket in their faces.

Shen considered the stop a necessary diversion. He wanted to establish himself with the local police in the event things went as badly as he expected they might; and he hoped to wave the scent of the fox in the face of the hounds and send them scampering in the wrong direction, leaving him to pursue the prize alone. Or almost alone. The young female officer seemed worth taking along.

Fifteen minutes later, they were seated side by side in his car; she hung on his every word, knowing better than to ask where they were going.

"I have contacts in the private sector," he told her, knowing he impressed her. "In this case, it's a crime lab used by the Europeans and Americans. I was offered information an hour before the Americans were to receive it. I am looking for a tannery on the island. One in operation in the recent past."

"Chongming Tanning," she said immediately.

"What of it?"

"My late uncle on my mother's side worked there until it was closed by authorities. The closing brought his family much hardship."

"A blue building?" he said. "Near water?" He'd seen the Mongolian's video. He was guessing it was near water because the cameraman's hand had been found in the river.

"The same."

"Please, direct me to this place."

"Take a right at the next street," she said.

Shen steered the car sharply right. She reached out to brace herself, and leaned against him, exactly as he'd wanted.

"How long?" he said.

"Ten, fifteen minutes, at the outside," she said.

"I like your mouth," he said. "The shape of your mouth."

She blushed and looked away. "Thank you."

He took her by the hair and turned her head to face him. "I would like it better in my lap."

She flushed. Her lips went white.

"You do not wish to displease me, *neh?*"

He enjoyed seeing terror on her face, the sense of power it instilled. Officers took sexual favors all the time, but not Shen Deshi. He intended to make up for lost time. He slid his seat back and pulled her face into his lap. "You are about to earn yourself a promotion," he said.

He nearly drove off the road as she finished him off, his right hand down her shirt, his left choking the steering wheel.

She collected herself and then it was as if it had never happened.

"You will direct me to within a quarter mile of the tannery," he said. "I will park someplace out of the way. You will stand watch and notify me of anything out of the ordinary."

"It is a deserted area," she said. "After the tannery closed, other companies moved out as well."

Land, any land, was too precious to abandon. "Why would they do this?"

"Local committee declared the area a future park."

"What was the real reason?" he asked. There was no point in building a park on a sparsely populated island.

"This was the only reason I ever heard."

"Tell me, how did your uncle meet his end?"

She said nothing for a moment. "Illness. Cancer of the blood."

"Was he alone in this?" Shen Deshi said.

"You'll turn left soon," she said, pointing.

He swung the car left.

"This road leads to River Road. Then right on River Road."

"I see I picked the right partner," he said. "You have done well."

She flushed with anger and embarrassment.

"I am glad for the chance to work with you," he said. "Cooperation between departments is to be rewarded."

"Take the next right."

He traced her jawline. "We work well together, is it not true?" he said.

She shivered. Looked as though she might be sick.

"Pull over please!" she called out softly.

Shen Deshi yanked the car to the side of the road.

The woman threw open the door and vomited.

37

Through the haze, the air over Shanghai bulged as a pink smudge on the horizon. Nearing the confluence of the Yangtze River and the China Sea, the shipping traffic spread out; low-slung barges lumbered alongside towering container ships. Jets floated on final approach into Pudong International.

Grace drove the Toyota, now sporting a third set of license plates. She turned the car off the River Road onto a rutted mud drive, entering an area of dirt and weeds and abandoned warehouses. A gravel yard's towering equipment was silhouetted by the last vestiges of the sunset.

"It's a ghost town," he said, climbing out. Grace joined him.

"National Day holiday." Cinder-block walls separated the abandoned buildings. Grace kept close to one as she led them away from the gravel yard.

"I suggest you take up position there, on the sand pile," said the former army officer, pointing to the gravel yard. "From there you will be able to see all the buildings. It is good cover."

"Agreed," Knox said. "But you'll be the one standing guard, not me."

"A Chinese woman wandering around these places will be treated much more gently than a *waiguoren*." She stopped, too small to scale the wall.

"But I can climb the walls without someone's help," he said, smugly.

Knox helped her over the wall, then followed. They cut across a mucky, foul-smelling stretch of saw grass and mud and scaled a second wall into the gravel yard. The sun sank into the layer of smog. Night fell quickly, dusk lasting all of five minutes.

Together they crawled up the sand pile, winning an elevated view of the industrial buildings to their left.

"Third building over," Knox said. "That's not dirt."

"Asphalt. I cannot read the sign from here."

"If you could, it would be the same sign as in the Mongolian's video."

"Speculation."

"If you climb that conveyor, you'll have an even better view."

"You have an extra phone or two."

"So what?"

"Give one to me and call me from up there if you see anything."

Knox smiled at her. "Nice try."

"As a woman," she said, "and a native of this island, I have much better chance of talking my way out, if caught."

"As a man, I don't talk my way out," Knox said.

"My point, exactly. Should talking fail, neither will I. If I need help, I have you."

"And how do you intend to get over the walls?"

"There is only the one wall," she said, pointing. "You see? The second wall is crumbling. Not a problem."

"Then we go together," he said.

"You are a *waiguoren*."

"I noticed."

"It would be asking for trouble. Be reasonable."

"Don't ask the impossible."

"Help me over that first wall. If I am not approached, we will investigate together."

It was a compromise he could live with—though reluctantly. Knox handed her the phone. Minutes later, he helped her over the wall and then watched as she climbed the conveyor that rose on a steep angle into the sky.

Reaching the freshly paved compound, Grace stayed in shadow, close to the wall. Her chosen route screened her from Knox but was preferable to crossing the yard out in the open.

As she worked around the interior perimeter, the building's faded blue sign became not only legible but also recognizable: CHONGMING TANNING. Only the first word had been captured in the video.

She bided her time in a dark corner and watched. Five minutes stretched to ten. In the background she heard the rumble of passing ships, the slap of river water, the steady roar of frogs and night insects. Finally, she positioned herself to match the angle of the video, wondering about the late-night paving.She crossed the asphalt, trying to do so casually, not sneaking up on the place, but just out for a walk, in case she was spotted.

She felt Knox's eyes on her back.

A pair of huge sliding doors formed the center of the structure. They were padlocked with a new lock. A second door for people was to the right. It, too, was padlocked, all the windows barricaded with a grid of welded rebar.

She returned to the center doors and found a few centimeters of play in the assembly. She improvised a pry bar out of a section of discarded pipe. With upward pressure, the door on the right pulled off its track, revealing a gap at the bottom. She rested and then pried a second time. When she leaned hard on the pipe, the door swung out a foot at the bottom. If she could block it there, she thought there might be enough room to crawl through. A two-person job. No doubt Knox was watching her, thinking the same thing.

She resented needing him. To ask for his help was to invite him to join her, and she did not want that.

The phone he'd given her vibrated in her pants pocket. She made no effort to retrieve it. She didn't need his cynicism and sarcasm.

She spotted a pile of discarded cinder blocks. *Ingenuity*, she thought. *Focus. Commitment.* Her army training returned effortlessly.

Minutes later, she heaved once again on her pry bar and simultaneously shoved a cinder block into the gap with her foot.

She lay flat and crawled through the narrow space, elated that Knox would never have made it.

She was inside.

P erched on the exoskeleton of the conveyor's steeply angled arm, Knox willed Grace to answer the damn phone. He'd lost a pair of headlights coming up River Road from the direction of Chongming. Of the many explanations he considered, the most likely was that the vehicle had pulled off the road and switched off its lights—a pair of teenagers seeking back-seat romance; a cop settling into a speed trap; or something much worse.

As if to confirm her independence, she wouldn't answer her goddamned phone. Never mind that he'd been impressed by the ingenuity of her entering the building, he'd have gone after her if he'd thought he might squeeze under those doors as she had. But there was no way.

Instead, he concentrated on locating the vehicle belonging to the missing headlights. A minute passed. Two. Three. Nothing.

Maybe it had been lovers after all.

U sing the phone's screen as a flashlight, Grace followed the bluish glow deeper into the tannery. She passed steel carts fixed to tracks laid in the concrete floor. Giant metal vats lined the aisle on either side of her. A tangle of plumbing. The stench of bleach and chemicals over which hung the unmistakable fetid odor of decay.

Her eyes adjusted, allowing her to navigate by the phone's glow more easily. She passed beneath an elaborate network of catwalks, tracks and winches. A pair of forklifts sat like tusked animals alongside a central doublewide trailer. An array of dozens of stacked fifty-five-gallon steel drums.

Only as the buzzing of bluebottle flies rose like a chorus and the decomposition choked her did she sense what had happened. Rounding the corner of the doublewide, she faced a line of steel-framed, butcher-block dressing tables beneath a set of fluorescent tube lights. The dressing tables had their own sets of knives and cutting tools. Drains and PVC tubing ran to grates set into the floor. She turned and retched. The table nearest her had been cleaned too hastily. Flies clustered around bits of bone and flesh. Blood coagulated along the edges and the drains.

But it was the shredded pieces of bloodstained clothing that caught her eye. Frayed cotton and bits of denim. A human slaughter, not cattle for tanning.

Yao Xuolong's death had appeared to be a hit-and-run, not a butchering.

Instinctively, she backed away from the crime scene. Her shoes caught and she tripped, reaching out for purchase. She grabbed at a hanging chain, but let go immediately, the chain sticky with what she was certain was blood.

She brought the phone's screen close. Not red, or black, but a leather-colored brown goo. Whatever it was came from overhead as a steady drip to the floor, where it collected in a syrupy puddle by a drain.

She wiped her hand on a butcher's apron hanging within reach. Her fingers began to warm. Then, sting. Then feel as if they were rotting off her.

She hurried through the maze of floor machinery, left, right, down a narrow aisle in search of a sink. She reached an emergency chemical wash station, placed her hands under the sunflower showerhead and bumped the lever with her knee. Nothing.

She hurried along the wall, half-blind, knocking tools and cans to the floor. She found a wall sink, turned the faucet and plunged both hands beneath the spit of water just as her phone rang.

The pain was too great to remove her hands. She would call him back as soon as she got the chemical off her skin.

She grabbed a worn bar of soap and worked up lather. Slowly—too slowly—the pain subsided. Her palms were raw and close to bleeding.

She connected her burns with Knox's. *From handling the surveyor's shoes.* She wanted to tell Knox what she'd found, but as she withdrew her hands from the water, they hurt so badly she doused them again.

Her phone buzzed for a third time. She braved the pain and reached for it, stuffing it into the crook of her shoulder and thrusting her free hand back into the water.

She awkwardly worked the phone, shoulder to ear. The device slipped and squirted out, landing with a clunk and the sound of shattered plastic. Its screen went black.

38

An imposing figure took long strides toward the tannery and made no attempt to conceal himself. A cop. He was large-headed but not wide-shouldered enough to be the Mongolian. Not tall enough for Kozlowski.

Knox called Grace for a second and third time. The phone jumped to Chinese voice mail—the building's superstructure defeating the reception, he thought.

He kept track of the cop as he backed down the conveyor arm, fearful he was silhouetted against the sky.

The cop turned once he made it through the yard's front gate, carrying something at his side. A gun? A tire iron?

Chinese police were not permitted to carry handguns, although People's Armed Police officers were. Could this possibly be Kozlowski's guy?

Knox paused as the man angled toward him, then continued down the rock conveyor as the intruder turned toward the tannery's doors.

A moment later, a pair of loud metallic pops pierced the air.

Knox vaulted one wall, then the next. He pulled himself up and held his head over the wall of the compound.

The man had pried the lock off the doors.

He was headed inside.

With the loud sounds at the doors, Grace shut off the water and ran for cover. Only as the pulleys whined did she realize it had been the doors coming open. She cowered within the equipment as footfalls—Knox?—moved deeper into the building.

Not Knox. The man trained a small flashlight on the floor. She caught punctuated glimpses of his dark silhouette walking past the vats. Not as tall as Knox, but thick-necked with a head like a caveman.

The Mongolian? she wondered. *Police? Security?*

She slowed her breathing in an attempt to squelch her adrenaline rush. She used the shifting light to plot her own course out of the building.

Staying low, she inched her way down the aisle, dodging the boxes and tools she'd spilled. Halfway to her freedom, her curiosity got the better of her.

She turned and followed him. Like her, he seemed to be taking inventory of the place—hardly the actions of a man returning to a crime scene or a security man who knew his beat. She knew better than to stay, but was drawn to him. He reached the dressing tables and, like her, studied them long and hard.

A cop, judging by his confidence and his methodical nature.

His flashlight swept the tables and the cutting tools, the drain in the floor. It found the chain and followed the dripping goo to the puddle, then up to the drums.

He removed his leather coat and hung it carefully over a valve, stepping incredibly close to where she hid. She could see a well-worn leather shoulder holster beneath his left arm.

If he was a cop, then maybe he was an officer of the People's Armed Police. Kozlowski's Iron Hand?

The man ran a faucet and got a stream of water going from a hose she hadn't seen. He washed down the soiled dressing table.

She choked back her surprise: he was destroying the very evidence that Kozlowski had told Knox both men wanted. Why not preserve evidence that might work against the Mongolian?

The answer seemed obvious: because there was no Mongolian.

His mobile phone pealed Metallica. He returned to his coat and answered the call, speaking curtly.

K nox hung from the compound wall, peering inside. He didn't want to jeopardize Grace if she'd managed to hide or escape. He didn't want to leave her if she'd been discovered and abducted.

He schooled himself to have patience, to let the situation develop. He had just climbed to the top of the wall as a pair of headlights swept the asphalt. He lay down flat.

A Range Rover swung onto the fresh asphalt, aimed at the open doors. The driver climbed out.

Steve Kozlowski.

Knox nearly called out, but stopped himself as he realized Kozlowski was meeting up with some Chinese cop—a bad-ass cop, according to Kozlowski himself—and on a Saturday night on a holiday weekend at a remote location.

Kozlowski, bent?

The consulate man left the Range Rover running and the headlights filling the doors. He entered the tannery with a commanding authority, a take-no-prisoners stride.

Knox rolled and dropped off the wall. He ducked low and ran for the Range Rover.

H eadlights lit the tannery's interior walls as Grace moved to the far aisle and climbed a ladder to an overhead catwalk. She lay down on her belly and watched the man hosing down the dressing table. He worked quickly now in an almost maniacal effort.

A second man appeared in silhouette at the doors. He walked like he owned the place. Turning, she caught him in profile and nearly gasped. He fit Knox's description of the consulate security chief, Kozlowski.

Interesting bedfellows.

Kozlowski broke his stride to grab a length of pipe as he continued deeper into the facility led by the spray of water.

Maybe not bedfellows.

He arrived to within several meters of the Chinese man. The water ran red into the drain.

"Don't do that," Kozlowski said in English. "Step away, now!"

Shen continued his work. "Go away, Mr. Kozlowski. It is no concern of yours."

"You are destroying physical evidence of a possible homicide of a U.S. citizen. Step away and desist."

Shen Deshi said coolly, "I advise you to go away now. You are trespassing. You have no authority to be here."

"I will not have you destroying evidence. You will stop . . . or I will make you stop." Kozlowski raised the pipe.

"If you remain here in this place you do not belong, I will bring the charge of industrial espionage. A government spy. Do you really want such trouble?"

"Destroying the blood evidence will not make the case go away. I assume you intercepted the forensic evidence intended for me?"

"I know nothing of what you speak." Shen Deshi turned around, the hose splashing water onto the concrete floor. "Do not be naïve, Mr. Kozlowski. You have a hand found in the river. No body. You are prohibited from investigating in this country—an act you are currently engaged in. You are inside a facility of a private company, which constitutes industrial espionage. How much trouble do you want for yourself?"

Kozlowski said, "Chemicals and soil samples from the hand link directly to this facility. The hand is Caucasian. The DNA will come back for the missing videographer, an American. I am within my rights to protect evidence."

The scientific link caused Grace's heart to flutter. A murder had taken place here. Possibly more than one. Lu Hao would never be safe. His plan to kidnap himself seemed suddenly much more understandable.

"When do you expect the results of a DNA test? Six weeks? Eight weeks? Do you want to spend eight weeks in a Chinese prison? Be my guest. Even if you prove such a connection, this cameraman was far from his assignment. This, too, smells of U.S. spying. You will be tied to him, and him to you. Is this what you want for U.S. Consulate? This is violation of agreements made between our sovereign nations. Very bad for everyone."

"Step away."

Shen trained the hose back onto the dressing table. "You must leave now," he said. "Last chance. I do not wish such trouble on you. Of all blessings, charity is the highest."

"A U.S. citizen has been murdered—most likely by a Chinese. We both know this," Kozlowski said. He lowered the pipe, raised his phone and took a photo. "Destroying evidence is also a crime."

With the flash of the camera phone, Shen Deshi dropped the hose and marched toward Kozlowski, withdrawing his handgun.

"Stupid fool. Drop the pipe. Keep both hands in view."

"You can't be serious."

"Your CIA uses a cameraman, a member of the Xuan Tower documentary crew, to attempt to embarrass Chinese government, or to challenge the WTO environmental agreement. Who knows what might be the reason? More American tricks."

"That's nonsense!"

"Lower the pipe."

Kozlowski lay down the pipe. It clattered against the concrete.

"Hands behind your back." He waved the gun. "Onto your knees."

"You arrest me, it will be a national incident. Think how that will affect your career?"

"It is already a national incident. Espionage is no game. Do not worry about my career, Mr. Kozlowski. Worry about your health in Chinese prison. How your family will cope."

"I have diplomatic status."

Shen Deshi stepped forward with astonishing speed for such a big man. He pistol-whipped Kozlowski, stunning him. He cuffed the man's hands behind his back. Removed Kozlowski's cell phone and disassembled it one-handed. He smashed all the parts with an angry foot.

"Up!" Shen said, ordering Kozlowski to move.

Grace used the commotion to cover the sounds of her climbing down from her perch. She hurried toward the open doors, staying low and moving fast. A second car arrived, trapping her. She settled into a tight spot alongside one of the large vats.

The driver of the second car was a young woman wearing a police uniform. She entered and helped Inspector Shen move Kozlowski toward the yard. Shen directed her to drive "the prisoner" into Shanghai and drop him at an address he recited.

"I will call ahead," he said to her. "Much will be made of your cooperation."

Kozlowski said to the inspector, "You are bringing a shit storm onto yourself."

"This foul-mouthed *waiguoren* will tell you a dozen lies," Shen told the young woman. "All foreigners have golden tongues. Pay him no mind."

"Yes, sir."

"Commendation and promotion must certainly follow on the heels of such loyalty and the *expert conduct* of one's duties." It sounded like a rehearsed speech.

She slipped behind the wheel of the Range Rover.

Shen put Kozlowski into the back seat, tying the seatbelt's shoulder strap tightly around the man's neck. The recoil mechanism held Kozlowski upright. If he leaned forward, he choked.

"Beat the damn spy with your flashlight if you have to," he told her. "He deserves every blow."

"Gladly," she answered.

Shen shut the car door, banged on the side of the vehicle and it drove off.

He returned inside, holstering his weapon and then lengthening his stride.

As the second car arrived, Knox slid beneath Kozlowski's Range Rover and hid. He overheard much of what went on inside, and moved to the second car in hope of stealing its keys or rendering it useless.

If he could get Kozlowski and Grace into the Range Rover . . .

He quietly opened the sedan's door. He punched the jamb's interior switch, preventing the inside light from turning on. The keys were in the ignition.

He banged his head into the rearview mirror, dislodging it. Reached up to try to leave it close to where it had been.

It was aimed into the back seat.

Knox froze as he saw a black strap protruding alongside the center seatbelt clasp: a Nike Swoosh.

From the back seat of the Range Rover, Kozlowski realized his diplomatic plates would work against him. No traffic cop would dare ticket the car or pull it over. She drove around the tannery and aimed for the front gate.

One of his daughter's puzzle books stuck up from the seat pocket, the sight of which caused a knot in his throat. He'd run out without so much as a goodbye. For all the fairy-tale endings, as a man in service to his country, he knew how the final acts to most such lives played out: a blindfolded and handcuffed body found slumped and collecting flies in a city dump or along a shoreline.

Pleading his case with his driver wasn't going to cut it. Once he was in Chinese custody, his life was all but over.

The Range Rover slowed to clear the posts defining the compound's front gate. Kozlowski leaned. The seatbelt tightened around his neck.

The driver-side window exploded. A man's hand appeared and the cadet's head rebounded off the steering wheel. The hand tripped the door locks and the driver's door came open, the car still rolling. The slumped cadet was pulled from the seat and John Knox took her place. Knox must have tried for the clutch, but he hit the brake and the car stalled. Knox reached for the ignition.

A shot rang out, exploding the rear window. Shen Deshi screamed in Mandarin, "Stop or I will shoot!" He was close. He had a good shot at the back of Kozlowski's head. With his neck held by the seatbelt, Kozlowski wasn't moving.

"I will shoot him!" Shen called out again, this time in English. "Maybe you make it. Maybe not."

Knox gripped the ignition key more firmly. He slipped the gearshift into Reverse.

"Now! Out of the car! You! The driver!"

"You shoot him, I'll run you over," Knox called through the blown-out window. "So, you'd better make the first shot count."

"Knox?" Kozlowski hissed from the back seat.

"You'd better make damn sure you kill me, too, because I'm only going to cripple you with the car. I'll save the good stuff for last."

"You talk too much!" Shen called out. "Get out of the car. Now!"

Knox swung his legs out.

"Are you out of your mind?" Kozlowski said.

G race swung the pipe, intending to strike the man's right arm and break it while simultaneously crushing his ribcage. She'd come up from behind the man while Knox bought her time by keeping the conversation going. She wasn't going to kill a Chinese cop—but if she had her way, he might wish she had.

She drove the pipe with the power of a tennis serve. She felt things disintegrate with the contact.

The cop folded in onto the blow, dropped the gun and then sagged left, tumbling over. Grace kicked the gun away and raised the pipe where he could see her, prepared to take a head shot if necessary.

S hen Deshi had no intention of going down at the hands of a woman. His broken and dislocated arm clutched to his fractured ribs, he sprang from the asphalt and knocked her back. The pipe clattered. He reached for it instinctively, but screamed behind the pain, his right arm useless.

G race rolled over the fallen pipe. The cop kicked out but only grazed her. The next kick landed, however. Just below her ribs. And the next in her hip.

Knox connected with the cop in a football tackle. Knocked him five yards into the backfield, and hammered three consecutive rights into the man's dislocated shoulder. The cop let out a cry.

The cop then backhanded Knox across the cheek, wheeled around, pivoting on the ball of his left foot, and connected his heel into Knox's face. Knox hit the asphalt hard—too hard—and saw stars.

S hen blocked the pipe as Grace swung it. He took hold of it, and twisted it from her, catching her off guard. He owned it. He took a swing, but she jumped back.

The *waiguoren* was up on his feet, but dazed. The man's nose was bleeding, his eyes unfocused. He lowered his head and charged like a bull. Shen couldn't believe it—the *waiguoren* was a dead man. He hoisted the pipe high overhead bearing down with all his power. The pipe stuck behind him. Wouldn't pull forward.

He spun around: it was the cock-sucking cadet, both hands on the pipe, a defiant look in her eyes. She held to the pipe. The *waiguoren* hit him so hard he lifted up off the asphalt, and landed with two hundred pounds atop him.

He cried out as his opponent took him by the shoulders—the shoulders!—and smashed him to the pavement. Once, twice.

Darkness.

G race held the cop's gun trained on the cadet, who stood there with the bloody pipe in her hand, breathing heavily, her eyes locked onto the fallen man.

For a moment, the three of them looked back and forth at one another. Exhausted. Paralyzed.

"There will be no killing here," Knox told the cadet in Mandarin.

Enough killing, Grace was thinking. Surprised by Knox. Again.

"He will not dare to report this," Grace said to the girl. "Too much he cannot explain. Drop the pipe and walk away."

"Drop the gun," the young woman said.

Grace ejected the magazine and placed it down onto the asphalt by her feet. She retained the handgun and the one bullet remaining in its chamber.

"Together?" she offered.

The cadet nodded.

Grace and the woman moved in concert, placing the pipe and the gun down nearly simultaneously.

"We can drop you somewhere," Knox offered in Mandarin.

The woman spat onto Shen Deshi. She backed up, facing them until reaching the Range Rover. She finally turned and walked off into the headlights and down the River Road, in no particular hurry.

"What if he can give us the name?" Grace asked Knox, looking at the fallen policeman.

"This guy? It would take a lot of good drugs and a couple weeks to get his own name out of him."

"We just . . . leave him?"

"I'm open to suggestions," Knox said, rubbing his head to make sure it was still attached to his body.

"We have nothing! For all this, we gain nothing."

"We have Kozlowski. We have the tannery and whatever's beneath the asphalt. The waypoints of one massive chunk of land."

"The Chinese have this place," she corrected. "Any evidence will be long gone by morning. Americans can't investigate, anyway."

Grace walked closer to the fallen Iron Hand and kicked him hard enough in the shoulder to make sure he wasn't play-acting.

"I'll do it," Knox said.

Grace reloaded the magazine into the handgun and held it on the man as Knox searched him. He found his phone and smashed it. He found a wallet and a passport belonging to a Mongolian. He passed these to Grace.

"That answers that," Knox said.

"Every bone in my body says not to leave him here . . . not alive," she said. "Not like this."

"Hey, the girl's prints are on the pipe. You want to cap him, be my guest. We can put this on her."

"But you said . . ."

"Listen, that was for her sake. I'm trying to be supportive here."

She allowed a small laugh to bubble up from inside her. For the second time, she disassembled the handgun, this time throwing the pieces into the field.

"That's the first time I've seen you laugh," Knox said.

"His car?" she asked.

Knox reached into a pocket and dangled the keys.

"Always a step ahead, John Knox."

"Not always," he said. "Sometimes."

"Sometimes is good," she said. "Very good."

Knox slammed the Range Rover's hatchback into place. He'd taken a moment to put the section of pipe into the back—the pipe containing the cadet's fingerprints—as evidence, in the event the inspector did not survive his injuries. He wanted all the bases covered.

"What the hell are you doing here?" Kozlowski said, immediately after being untied from his noose. Knox occupied the front passenger seat.

Grace pulled the driver's seat forward and adjusted the rearview mirror. She drove.

"You're welcome," Knox said.

"I'm serious," Kozlowski said.

"I saw you pull up, I thought you were bent. Imagine my surprise."

"What the fuck were you doing here, Knox?"

"Your work for you. The work you asked me to do."

"Don't mess with me."

"A surveyor, here on the island," Knox said, "was killed and his death made to look like an accident. Chances are he was attempting to blackmail the Beijing higher-up you and I discussed. This, because he'd figured out what he was surveying—a New City development that will eventually hold four million people. My guess: he wanted money to keep his yap shut. So the Mongolian shut it for him."

"What Mongolian?"

"And Lu Hao saw the whole thing. So did your one-handed cameraman. Only, the one-hand part came later."

Kozlowski leaned back and rubbed his neck. "You're an asshole."

Knox and Grace spent the next hour filling Kozlowski in on what they knew, and still had yet to find out.

"You demanded I find the name of the government type in the video," Knox said. "You put Dulwich's life in hock for that. How do you think I feel about that?"

"And I care because . . . ?" Kozlowski said.

"More to the point, how would the Consul General feel about that?"

"This is not the road you want to go down," Kozlowski said. He wasn't talking MapQuest.

"We give you everything we've got. You let the intelligence community run with it. But you get Sarge out of Huashan Hospital, and the three of us out of the country by noon tomorrow. We've put in our time."

"He saved your life," Grace said.

The car engine hummed. The highway was alive with a million cars again. It was as if the storm had never happened. They sat in traffic for twenty minutes trying to get over the Lupu Bridge.

"I love this city," Knox said.

"I hate this place," Kozlowski complained. After a moment he spoke again. "You said The Berthold Group was attempting to buy the acceptable bid price on this New City project? And that that's where the government official comes in."

"I said that's how it looks." Grace tossed the Mongolian's credentials into Kozlowski's lap.

"My guess," Knox said, "is your best witness is going to report late for work."

"You're right about our guys. If there's a connection between the tannery and a committee member in Beijing, they'll find it."

"It's there," Knox said.

"But it's not like we can out him, regardless of who it is."

"Because?"

"Because we're Americans. We don't investigate," Kozlowski reminded.

"And there is the matter of face," Grace said. Knox sighed. "It would be great dishonor and shame for the Chinese government's internal corruption to be exposed by a bunch of foreigners. It would never be admitted, no matter how obvious."

"So we did all this, and we have to sit on it?" Knox asked irritably.

"Allan Marquardt started all this," Kozlowski said. "He'll pay."

"Allan Marquardt played the hand he was dealt. Give me a break! Like he's the only American company paying out incentives?"

"He's the only one we've caught," Kozlowski said. "This week."

"By the time Marquardt's books are audited," Knox said, glancing over at the driver, "they'll be clean as a whistle."

"That's not right," Kozlowski said.

"TIC," Knox answered.

"I know a way," Grace said, winning the attention of both men. "A way to keep this Chinese."

"Believe me," Kozlowski said, "it's already *very* Chinese."

"You have my attention," Knox told Grace.

"If Mr. Kozlowski can determine the identity of the corrupt official, there is someone who will gladly turn over this official to authorities without revealing his sources."

Several minutes passed. Traffic picked up some.

Kozlowski said, "You're telling me Lu Hao ended up at that tannery the same night as the videographer."

"Go figure," Knox said. "You make your own luck. Lu Hao's turned bad."

"Very bad," Grace said.

"It's a toxic site," Knox said, rubbing his burned fingers together. "It's not much of a stretch to see them paving it over to hide the contamination."

"This has a much greater significance," Grace said, again winning their attention. "Chinese law is very specific as to clean-up of such sites. It falls upon the *developer* of any land parcel."

"Not the owner?" Knox said. "How could that be?"

"She's right," Kozlowski said. "It's only been on the books a couple years. A U.S. firm tested this law, and lost, I might add. The original owner of the property is held responsible to protect the public from contamination. And that's all. In any subsequent development of the property, the developer is responsible for the clean-up. The idea being, as warped as it is to us, that the original owner may lack the funds for full clean-up."

"So, had Marquardt won the bid, he would be stuck with the bill?" Knox asked. "That's not right."

"Shit," Kozlowski said.

"Waiguoren," Grace said. "You see?"

"Apparently not," Knox said.

"Mr. Marquardt's own greed is used against him. Mr. Marquardt wants to win the New City bid so badly, and the tract of land is so enormous, he cannot do the proper due diligence. Time is of the essence. It's entrapment. In fact, there are millions of U.S. dollars' worth of hidden costs in the clean-up of the tannery. Marquardt wins the bid, but loses money when his costs run over. Loses face. This works out well for Chinese who wish to see *waiguoren* like Marquardt fail."

"And it's damn convenient for the original owner of the tannery," Knox said.

"So that's where we start," Kozlowski said.

"'We'?" Knox said.

"Fuck you," Kozlowski said.

Knox leaned his head back against the headrest, grinning. And immediately fell asleep.

39

The Ministry of State Security Superintendent occupied a red leather chair behind a plain and unattractive desk in a small gray office with no view. Overweight and jowly, he had wet lips, an auditor's scowl and an impatient disposition.

Shen Deshi, wearing a sling, a piece of his head shaved and stitches showing, tried to look confident in the uncomfortable chair facing the man.

"What a cock-up," the superintendent said, speaking Shanghainese. "I would ask you to repeat all that, but I don't wish to hear it. If the Americans push to bring charges against you—"

"Yes. I understand."

"You took him at gunpoint?"

Shen kept his mouth shut. His forehead and upper lip were perspiring, telltale signs of weakness. The superintendent could cut his balls off if he wanted.

"You were to secure any evidence of environmental contamination. To tidy up any loose ends before this hand recovered from the river spread trouble like a disease."

Shen Deshi shrank in the chair.

"Instead, we face a possible inquiry from the Americans? If I'd wanted this kind of attention, I'd have hired a public relations firm."

Shen looked to buy his way out. He collected himself and spoke with courage. "I have some physical evidence outside," he said, "that implicates the American cameraman. His video camera."

"Destroy it, you fool."

"Of course. As you wish."

"The last thing we need," the superintendent said.

"There is another matter," Shen said, leading up to his moment of truth.

"Explain."

"One hundred thousand U.S.," he said. "Also one hundred forty thousand *yuan*."

The superintendent lit up like a dragon boat festival parade. He squinted at his major and rubbed the back of his pudgy right hand across his lips.

"What is it you propose?" He pulled open a drawer and lit a cigarette. Located a chocolate bar and broke off a chunk and stuffed it into his pink hole. Smoke escaped as he spoke and chewed. "Please, Major."

"I retired last week. Should an inquiry arise, I was acting on my own."

"I was thinking the same thing," the superintendent said. "I will have the paperwork prepared. Lay low for a day or two. I will call off the search for you within forty-eight to seventy-two hours. Just long enough to look like we gave it an effort."

Shen Deshi nodded. "As you wish."

"This is good for us," the superintendent said.

Us, was all Shen heard. "Indeed."

"Your integrity has never been questioned."

Shen swallowed dryly. "I thank you, Superintendent."

"And the evidence?"

"The contents of the duffel remain unreported. I came to you directly, as you advised. Therefore, not filed. Not recorded."

"We do not want such evidence filed! It's a fucking mess!" Smoke surrounded him now.

"Precisely so, sir."

"So it must be decided what to do with this . . . evidence . . . no doubt."

"No doubt."

The man wanted Shen to propose the alliance. He would not do so himself.

"I could turn the funds over to PAP."

"One possibility."

"Or attempt to return it to those who paid it out."

"Kidnapping ransom? A Western insurance company, no doubt. They will hardly miss it."

"This had occurred to me also," Shen said, his heart quickening. "Yes."

"There must be *another solution*," the superintendent said. The moistness of his lips had spread to the butt end of his cigarette, which was now smeared with chocolate. "Hmm?" he said, encouraging his major.

"It had occurred to me how much good such funds could do for schools, for earthquake and flood victims. But of course it could never be seen to come directly from the Ministry."

"Heaven forbid!"

"But individuals. That's another matter."

"Entirely," the superintendent said.

"If we were to, say . . . divide the sums . . . in a percentage that takes into consideration your seniority, of course, Superintendent. My ten years with the Ministry. Your fifteen. Say, sixty, forty."

"Seventy, thirty."

"Sixty-five, thirty-five."

"Agreed."

"We could oversee the distribution of the sums far more responsibly than any bureaucracy like the Ministry."

"Your point is well taken. Well said, Major. Yes. I see the clarity of your thought on this matter." He hesitated. "When can we see to this resolution?"

"At your convenience. Of course."

"Not here. The park. This evening's tai chi. A bench in the park."

"Of course," Shen Deshi said.

"Do not disappoint me. No second thoughts. Hmm?"

"No, sir." Shen Deshi could only imagine the hell that would befall a man who crossed Ho Pot.

"Dismissed," the man said.

Shen Deshi stood, painfully and slowly. The Ministry of State Security was commissioned to combat corruption and corporate environmental abuse. He marveled at the irony.

"Let's get one thing straight," the superintendent said. "Technically, this is not blood money." He was asking, not telling. He didn't want to hang for the offense.

Shen Deshi thought of the Mongolian's face as he slipped off the boat. He thought of the butcher-block table inside the tannery where the Mongolian had filleted the cameraman. The buzzing of the flies.

"No, of course not," he said. "Just lost and found."

"Lost and found."

"Yes."

"Well, then. Let's get on with it."

Shen dragged himself to his car with great difficulty. He unlocked it and, deciding to check on his future, opened the back door and leaned inside.

Opening the back seat could be a hassle. The mechanism jammed even when a duffel bag was not packed beneath it. And so it did again. Given his cracked ribs and bad arm, Shen could hardly move, much less heave the hinged seat forward, but he finally gave it one strong pull and the seat came open.

It was said that when one died, his life passed before him, from childhood to the present, that the gates to heaven were more a mirror than a door. Shen's life flashed before him, and yet, except for some broken bones, he lived.

The back seat was empty.

It took him a moment to process not only the reality of his situation, but its enormity. He moved the seat back and forth, as if a heavy duffel might have slipped out onto the car floor when the seat came open.

He'd hidden the money there himself. Had been in the car with it all but the few minutes . . .

The whore!

He'd left her in the car while he'd gone to inspect the tannery. She'd pulled the car around following the American's arrival.

He brooded over what the hell to do about it, while from the back of his mind raised the Greek chorus: *Run!*

SUNDAY
October 3

40

Shortly after breakfast the following morning, Grace received a call from Lu Jian. She'd told neither Knox nor Kozlowski about soliciting her former lover's help. As a civil servant, Lu Jian had access to information it would take even U.S. Intelligence days or weeks to collect and analyze.

"*Wei?*" she asked.

"It is not a single owner," Lu Jian began, as if mid-conversation. "The tannery. It was owned and managed by a company with a ten-person board of directors. The company ceased doing business, and the tannery was closed, two years ago."

"When the environmental laws went into effect," she said.

"The timing would be right. Are you going to tell me what this is about?"

"Are you able to identify the members of the board of directors?"

"I have done so already."

"I really do love you. You know that."

It was the wrong thing to say, and she regretted it immediately. She'd been on a high since arriving safely at the consulate. For a moment she thought he'd hung up on her.

"I can give you the names. Do you have a pen?" he asked. All business.

She wrote down the Chinese characters, slowly and carefully, and read them back to Lu Jian and he listened and did not correct her.

"Is that it, then?" he asked.

Was it? she wondered. "I hope not," she said.

"I received word from Lu Hao. He is indeed safely out of the country. As his older brother . . . his family . . . our debt to you—"

"Please! There is no debt."

"I wish to express our sincere appreciation," he said, very formally.

"For a starter, you could visit me in Hong Kong," she said. Chinese women were expected to be much more guarded than this. She hoped it wouldn't push him even farther away.

"Yes, of course."

"That is, if you want to," she said.

"What one wants and what one accepts are very different."

"You have my address," she said. "It has not changed."

"You are leaving the country then?" he asked somewhat anxiously.

She reveled in hearing that tone from him. She said nothing, allowing it to replay in her head, over and over.

"As soon as possible. Today, tomorrow?"

"I see."

"It's a short flight. An easy flight."

"But for me, a journey."

"I'll be expecting you."

He hung up. Grace placed the phone down and stared at it, again reliving the conversation. Looking for nuance. Re-creating it in ways that revealed hidden meaning.

A knock on her door brought her back.

It was Knox.

12:30 P.M.

Grace passed the board member names on to Kozlowski and rode the next several hours on a roller coaster of emotions. Knox napped for twenty minutes, then worked down two more cups of tea. She spent her time alone by a window of the consulate guesthouse living room, looking out into sunlit gardens. Steam rose from the soil. It was going to be a hot day.

A while later—it seemed liked hours, but it was not—a Marine led them across to the mansion house. They were shown into Kozlowski's office. It felt to Knox like the last time he'd visited had been six months earlier. It had been a matter of days.

"First," Kozlowski said. He'd showered and shaved and changed clothes, though had not yet been home to his family. "The U.S. government has no knowledge of the members of the PRC's Resettlement Committee."

"Understood," Knox said. He was telling them he had full knowledge of that very information.

"Second. I'm continuing to explore the possibility of using back channel diplomacy to expose this official, but I'm told that will likely not happen."

"I have a way around that," Grace said. "Please continue."

Kozlowski passed a hand-written note across his desk to Grace. "We have a match. One of the tannery board members serves as chairman of the Resettlement Committee. His name is Zhimin Li. Chairman Zhimin Li."

Grace broke into tears. *Tears of relief,* Knox thought.

"Grace has a plan," Knox said.

"Which is?" Kozlowski asked.

"Do you really want to know?"

Kozlowski shook his head. "I suppose not."

"You're going to have to smuggle us out of here," Knox said, "in case Shen Deshi and his boys are watching the place."

Grace explained to a perplexed Kozlowski, "This cannot be done over the phone. And the contact I have in mind would never allow himself to be seen entering the U.S. Consulate."

4:05 P.M.

With Knox wanted for questioning on multiple assaults, and Grace having been identified as an accomplice, the idea of leaving the protection afforded by the consulate's diplomatic immunity was gut-wrenching.

Any number of ideas had been put forward: from Grace acting alone—her idea; to the use of consulate vehicles—Kozlowski's; to a simple ruse—Knox.

In the end, it was the Consul General, a woman of outstanding character whose husband ran a B&B in northern Idaho, and who had come to the job in a time of turmoil because of the world financial meltdown, who stepped up.

At four P.M., with dusk approaching, the Consulate General's Marine-driven black Suburban pulled out of the consulate gates, as it often did at this hour. She jumped out of the car and began railing in Mandarin at the Chinese National Guard up the street about the lax security.

At this same time, the day laborers left the compound on foot as they always did: gardeners, mechanics, maintenance men, waitstaff, housecleaning.

Among them were Knox and Grace. He slouched and wore makeup to darken his face, and a tam to cover his head. Twelve workers walked the length of the street and rounded the corner to a bus stop. Two of them kept on walking.

41

On the deserted seventh-floor terrace of M on the Bund, Knox looked down through binoculars at the congested swarm of people populating the Bund's riverside promenade. The sunlit afternoon had brought twenty thousand tourists, mostly Chinese, crammed in to get a piece of the famous view across the Huangpu River. Among the steel and glass towers rising into the sky was the Xuan Tower, its scaffolding torn and dangling, shredded tarpaulins flapping. In the aftermath of the typhoon, there was no manpower to clean it up. Every construction project in the city had suffered staggering losses due to the storm.

His iPhone in hand, Knox kept watch on the promenade for a red umbrella carried as a parasol, despite the setting sun. Eventually he spotted it coming from the proper direction, knowing Grace hid beneath it as she climbed the promenade steps to join the masses on the river walk.

It joined other umbrellas and parasols, along with baby strollers, balloons and stick kites. The umbrella stopped in the center of the choke. And waited.

A black Bentley arrived at the curb. A man wearing a dark suit was let out the back by a busy chauffeur. Though the passenger appeared to be alone, Knox and Grace knew better. Yang Cheng was never alone.

"I've got you. He's on his way up," Knox said, speaking into the iPhone.

"It is so crowded," came her reply. "Police?"

"I've got two by the subway entrance on your side of the street. Two more up by the Peace Hotel."

"This is normal."

"Yes. All right. Stand by." She left the call open, as planned, allowing Knox to overhear. She would dangle the ear bud/microphone around her neck, like an iPod on pause.

G race hid below the red umbrella, finally angling it to make eye contact with Yang Cheng as he stood next to her. The claustrophobic press of Chinese tourists disturbed her. She tried to blot them out, to make it only her and this man, as she'd been trained. But it wasn't so easy.

They spoke English because the majority of those around them did not.

"I can deliver the name of a minister, with accompanying evidence, to the anticorruption authorities. There will be no choice but to void The Berthold Group's contract on the Xuan Tower and reassign it."

He drew in sharply, as if she'd hit him. If there hadn't been so many people around, she might have heard his heart beating from three feet away.

"While interesting, it is not this I seek," he said calmly.

"What you seek is fool's gold. The strike price for the New City bid," she said. His eyes widened, despite his attempt to keep them from doing so. "It is a trap meant for the *waiguoren*."

"Is that so?"

"The parcel was annexed to include what will turn out to be a contaminated site."

He whistled unintentionally as he drew a breath in through his teeth.

"I save you much face and a great deal of money."

"You would say anything to improve your situation. You and the foreigner are wanted by police."

"Fourteen billion, seven hundred million *yuan*," she said.

He was focused on her, unmoving, as people teemed around them.

"But if you act upon it, you will rue the day, believe me. The plan was to have the expense fall upon Marquardt. What I have for you is far better: the name of the person who leaked the number. You may not be praised publicly but we both know you will be richly rewarded for bringing such a man to ground."

"And in return?"

"An insignificance."

He huffed. "That, I doubt."

"An American in hospital. A trifle. It's a standing request of the consulate's."

"This American?"

"His release. Yes."

"From the hospital."

"There may be the intent to question him, to trouble him. But he is not well."

"An insignificance? Hardly."

"By comparison," she said.

Yang Cheng debated all this internally.

"The choice is yours, but the offer will be made elsewhere if you pass."

"What else?" Yang Cheng asked, sensing it in her.

"The four of us will not appear on any watch lists or wanted lists. My citizenship and visa status, and that of Lu Hao, remain unblemished. Clean slate."

"Face."

"Yes."

"A man cannot promise such things. These take time and expend much *guanxi*."

"Precisely why I have come to you, honorable Yang. You have twenty-two hours to free the man hospitalized," she said.

"Absurd! Two weeks or more! A single week if I'm lucky!"

"You will explore possibilities. When the man called David Dulwich—the American in hospital—arrives to the consulate, you shall have the name of the corrupt official. And all evidence. By this time tomorrow I will seek another to do business with."

"This is not business, it is extortion."

"Business makes for strange bedfellows," she said.

"We will always have a place at Yang Construction for one as cunning as you, Ms. Chu. You have my number."

Grace collapsed the umbrella—her signal to Knox—and moved into the throng.

Yang's man joined him at his side and shot a look back at her. She recognized him as one of the two from the alley attack.

She pushed north through the crowd, trusting that Knox was watching her. She returned an ear bud.

"Do you have me?" she asked.

"Wave," he said.

She lifted her arm.

"I have you. You're clean." He paused. "What was all that visa nonsense?"

"This is my family home. Lu Hao's family home. We cannot return here if we are fugitives."

"You attached it to Sarge. That wasn't our agreement."

"We did not have an agreement, John. We had an understanding."

Ten minutes later, a black Range Rover pulled to the curb in front of the Peace Hotel. The car's rear door swung open. A tall man and a petite woman climbed inside and the door closed.

The Range Rover pulled back into traffic.

MONDAY
October 4

42

The rain had begun falling heavily again an hour earlier. Knox, Grace and Kozlowski stood on the mansion steps, under the cover of an awning.

Just beyond the consulate gates, still in Chinese territory, an ambulance waited, a single red light spinning above the windshield.

The gates opened and the security blocks lowered. The ambulance did not move.

"Come on . . ." Knox said, willing it to cross onto American soil.

Grace held Knox's iPhone to her ear. "Katherine, please," she said. "The ambulance is at the gate." She rolled her eyes at Knox. They had been waiting for Yang Cheng to pick up.

She covered the phone with her palm and whispered, "He is not going to do this over the phone. He is too careful."

"Then, what? Here?" Knox said. "Where?"

"I believe it is more a question of how," Grace said. "Yang will not risk being seen or overheard taking a name of a Chinese official from an American, and then later turning this same man over to authorities. He obviously understands we could be playing him, that it all could be an elaborate trick of U.S. Intelligence."

"And of course he'd be right," Kozlowski allowed. "Given that U.S. Intelligence was smart enough to dream up such a ploy. To remove a top official by rumor and innuendo would be a coup."

Grace cradled the phone to her cheek. "Katherine? Please inform Mr. Yang the offer is good for forty minutes. I will be waiting at the front gate at the U.S. Consulate on Wulumuqi. I will turn over the information to either you or Mr. Yang. No one else." She ended the call.

The red light pulsed across their faces.

"Why?" Knox said, imploring her.

She answered. "If they send someone from the Ministry, for instance, there is no guarantee the deal for Mr. Dulwich will be honored."

"But Yang will honor it?" Knox asked sarcastically.

"Of course."

"Because?"

"Face," she answered absolutely. "He will not go back on his word. This, I promise."

Knox carried an umbrella for Grace as he escorted her to the front entrance security check and then stood at the gate to get a better look at the ambulance. The music of U2 escaped from a Humvee, manned by a lone Marine who guarded the gate. The wipers of the Humvee were out of sync with the music; the engine was not running.

It was one of the longer walks of Knox's life. Careful to remain on the consulate side, he craned to peer through the ambulance windshield, its wipers thumping. The ambulance driver, believing Knox was looking at him, pointed to a cutout of Kobe Bryant hanging from a mirror and, pointing to it, offered his index finger to signify "Number 1." Knox was looking past the spinning Kobe at the man on a side bench in the back. A paramedic, a woman, sat next to him while the knees of a dark blue uniform could be seen, sitting across. Police. Dulwich held his arm in a sling and was wearing gauze on his head like a yarmulke. He looked like shit. Knox nodded faintly at him and Dulwich squinted back, either not seeing him or choosing not to acknowledge him.

Behind and alongside the ambulance were two police cars, each with four officers inside. Knox considered an extraction, but eight-against-one, nine, counting the cop inside, were not the best odds. Still, if the ambulance backed up—if the brokered deal fell through, he didn't rule it out.

He looked both ways down the unusually quiet street, searching for Yang's black Bentley he'd seen at the Bund. A few cars and taxis moved in both directions, along with a few dozen bikes, but no Bentley.

He cursed the Chinese for erecting walls within walls of honor and shame, defenses to rival an Umbrian hill town. Rules within rules. Codes within codes. They seemed to shift according to need; despite his claims, he did not understand it.

Ten minutes passed more like forty and he was still standing in the same spot, rain drumming on the umbrella. He was still looking when a taxi pulled to the curb. A woman climbed out, shielding her hair. From a distance she could easily have been Katherine, if memory served. But his memory was crippled by fatigue and he couldn't be sure. The woman went through to security.

Knox waited. The taxi idled.

She couldn't have been inside more than thirty seconds before she reappeared on the sidewalk and climbed back into the waiting taxi, which then drove off. Knox looked to the ambulance, expecting it to move. It did not.

Grace came out of security and hurried across the carefully manicured pebble walk and atop the close-cut grass—like a putting green—and joined Knox under the umbrella.

"It is done," she said.

"So?"

"Now it is up to Yang Cheng to judge and value the information, perhaps verify, even partially, that Zhimin could be culpable. To determine if he is important enough for Yang to risk his reputation and the expenditure of *guanxi*."

"Perfect."

"You are considering a move on the ambulance," she said.

Knox stewed. He didn't appreciate being read like that.

"It is all well and good. That is the expression, is it not?"

"It is the expression. It's not the case."

"If the ambulance leaves, then we know we have failed." Said so calmly.

"If the ambulance backs up, it won't make it ten feet."

"John."

"Grace."

She placed her hand on his upper arm and stood close to him, out of the rain. "There has not been a minister to fall in many years. The government will gain great value from it. The Party, no. But the number one grievance of the Chinese people is corruption. The government cannot possibly resist such a trophy as Chairman Zhimin."

"But bringing down a politician . . ." Knox said.

"You will see."

But the ambulance did not move, forward or back. The driver toyed with Kobe Bryant, while Dulwich hung his head, looking defeated.

Another five minutes passed.

"Yang is not going to do it," Knox said.

"Give it time," Grace said.

Through beating wipers, Knox saw one of the policemen respond to a dashboard radio call, and watched as a heated discussion ensued between him and the driver, who pointed back, clearly explaining they were boxed in.

The cop who'd taken the radio call climbed out of the police car and headed for the second cop car, the one blocking the ambulance. This man shot a smug look in Knox's direction. In that look was confidence and spiteful victory. Knox saw it in slow motion—malicious superiority.

Knox looked back through the gray toward the mansion, where Kozlowski stood keeping his distance. Back at the ambulance. Then to the Marine behind the wheel of the Humvee. And finally, to the winch mounted on the front of the Humvee.

Knox jogged to the winch, slammed down the release lever and spooled off fifteen feet of steel cable. He walked the hook on the end of the cable toward the gate.

"Knox . . ." Grace called out anxiously.

The Marine was out of the vehicle. "Hey!"

Knox slid through a puddle across the threshold into Chinese territory, where he was a wanted criminal, and partially under the ambulance, as beneath the vehicle he saw the police car to the rear backing up. He hooked the ambulance's tow bar, and scrambled back out as the sound of car doors signaled the police coming for him. He crawled and dove back across the gate line, a border defining the consulate property, and rushed to the winch, opening a plastic box and throwing a switch. The Chinese police had missed him by inches.

"You can't do that!" the Marine said to Knox. But the man was clearly more engaged with the two Chinese policemen whose toes were nearly touching the consulate boundary. The Marine marched toward them and stood nose to nose.

The winch cable tightened.

The Marine held himself rigid, the spit from his words mixing with the rain on the face of the policeman directly across from him; but his message was for Knox.

"Cease and desist, sir!" he shouted. "That is United States property!"

The slack out of the winch, Knox hurried to the open door of the vehicle and set the brake. As the cable tightened, the ambulance groaned and jumped. The Humvee buckled and skidded forward. A tug of war.

Knox dislodged a large stone that defined the pebble walkway and used it to block the vehicle's front tire. Now it was all Humvee: the ambulance crept forward, skidding on the wet surface, slowly drawn toward the gate.

The two policemen understood the physics and the mechanics. They grabbed hold of the steel cable, but to no avail.

Kozlowski arrived at a run, out of breath. He headed straight for the door to the Humvee, where Knox blocked him.

One of the Chinese policemen ran to the police car. He pounded on the trunk and the driver released it and the trunk popped open. The policeman came away with a pair of bolt cutters.

The ambulance's front bumper was only inches from the gate.

"That's a U.S. service veteran in that ambulance, Marine," Knox hollered. "He's headed to Chinese jail if we don't get him across that line."

The message was meant for Kozlowski as well, who stood eye to eye with Knox as the Humvee's electric winch ground steadily away, and the ambulance slid forward.

It was clear to Knox that the distance between the ambulance and the Humvee wouldn't allow the ambulance to make it all the way inside the compound. He waved Dulwich forward and watched as a man with a head compress and an arm in a sling took out a police guard sitting across from him on the opposing bench.

Dulwich ducked and moved to the front of the ambulance as the cop with the bolt cutter aimed the tiny jaws at the steel cable. The Marine kicked out across the line, knocking the bolt cutter off its mark. The ambulance bumper crossed into U.S. territory.

The policeman stepped across the line in an effort to cut the cable, and the Marine pulled his weapon. The cop backed off, resigned now to watching.

"Corporal!" Kozlowski shouted, leaving Knox. But not before whispering, "You motherfucker," under his breath at him.

Knox smiled at a worried Grace.

The ambulance windshield was in the compound.

The rear door of the ambulance flew open and three cops piled inside and rushed the front of the vehicle, after Dulwich. Dulwich threw himself up onto the dash of the ambulance while the driver recoiled.

Kozlowski was shouting for the Marine to holster his weapon.

"Sir! This is my duty, sir!" the Marine called back as he raised the weapon and trained it on the first of the cops in the ambulance.

"*Hey!*" the Marine hollered, winning the cop's attention. The man blanched. "Remove yourself from U.S. soil!" the Marine shouted.

The ambulance skidded forward at an angle, snagging the wrought-iron gate and collapsing it inward in a metallic cry. The Marine held his weapon on the policeman, who did not move. It took two more minutes for the ambulance's passenger door to cross the threshold. Knox stopped the winch.

Dulwich climbed out of the vehicle, met there by Kozlowski and Grace, who helped him deeper into the compound. Knox released the cable.

The Marine kicked at the cable. Knox reached under and cleared it.

The Marine shouted at the ambulance driver, looking down the barrel of his pistol at him. "Sir! Your vehicle is improperly on U.S. soil. I ask that you remove it at once!"

It was doubtful the driver understood English, but the ambulance jumped back so quickly that the cop in front lost his balance and fell over, and the ambulance then rammed the police car behind it, knocking the cop fully to the ground.

Six Marines raced from the mansion carrying M16s and joined the corporal, including the staff sergeant, who took charge.

Knox and Kozlowski supported Dulwich between them. A Marine approached Knox and offered to take his place.

"No, thank you," Knox said, tightening his grip around the wounded man.

TUESDAY
October 5

43

Shen Deshi sat behind the wheel of his car across from Chongming Police Precinct 5, awaiting the shift change. He'd been parked there nearly nine hours, going over and over it in his head. This woman cadet had double-crossed him. She would return his money; Shen Deshi would divide it as agreed with his superintendent, and he would officially retire. There was still hope.

She emerged a few minutes later, unlocked and climbed onto a bicycle and rode off. Shen Deshi followed, giving her a good lead.

She lived in a rundown four-story building of a kind he was well familiar with. There would be five or six families in all, each occupying what was essentially one large room. He climbed out of the car and followed her. No one was better at foot surveillance. When she entered the third-floor flat, she did so blissfully unaware of him.

Shen Deshi did not want to give her time to get settled. He marched to the door and kicked it in with a single blow. The door bounced against the wall and came back at him, and Shen Deshi danced to the left, allowing it to try to close on its broken jamb.

He held a rock in his right hand.

She held a baby.

Sight of the child stopped him. The woman was so young; he'd pictured her sharing the apartment with four or five other women just like her. Instead, he faced a second policeman to his right, a man—a large man, his uniform shirt unbuttoned. An unhappy man. A man holding a switchblade.

"It's him," the cadet said. "The blow job."

Shen marveled at his own stupidity. Allowing haste and emotion to dictate his actions. Since when? *Since this bitch stole my future from the back seat,* his brain answered.

"All I want is my money," Shen said.

"What money?" the woman said in a compelling tone.

The husband said nothing. He took a step toward Shen, the knife casually at his side.

"You are certain?" the husband finally said.

"Do you doubt me?" the cadet answered. "You don't forget such a thing." She spat onto the floor. "I can still taste him."

The determination in the husband's eyes was troublesome. Shen nearly abandoned his quest for his money, but he would not allow himself to be intimidated by a pair of common country thieves.

"The money," he said, "and I'm gone." But he'd gravely miscalculated the husband, who came not at him, but moved to block the door. The exit.

The wife had put the toddler in a portable crib. She too now brandished a knife.

"We can negotiate!" Shen said, the rock feeling useless in his hand. It wasn't that he couldn't imagine defeating a man and a woman, both with knives. He might be cut and stabbed, but he could survive the outcome. It was the look in the husband's eyes that stopped his blood from pumping.

"Not here," the husband said calmly to his wife.

"I know the place. Remote. Abandoned. Just the place," the cadet said.

In his mind's eye Shen Deshi saw the bloodstained water running from the butcher-block table and coiling down the drain.

"Let's be reasonable," he said.

44

Two employees of Rutherford Risk met Knox, Grace and David Dulwich at Signature Flight Support's private terminal at Hong Kong's Chek Lap Kok airport. They were quickly processed through immigration and then herded into a black Mercedes. Dulwich and Knox were dropped at the nearby Princess Margaret Hospital. Knox's Super-Glued wound was examined; he received an antibiotic injection and was given a prescription. He waited there for word on Dulwich.

Grace went home to unpack and clean up. The chauffeur popped the trunk and walked behind the car.

"It is okay," Grace said. "I have no luggage."

"The gentleman said to give you this, miss," the driver called over to her.

He pulled a Nike duffel from the trunk and delivered it to the curb at Grace's feet.

"And this," he said, reaching into his jacket and withdrawing a red envelope.

"Thank you," she said, dumbfounded. She had nothing to offer as a gratuity. The driver shut the trunk, unfazed, smiled and returned behind the wheel and drove off.

Grace found her throat dry, her limbs tingling. She opened the envelope and pulled out his note to her.

For Lu Hao.

Face.

No signature. She bent to take the duffel by the strap and remembered the weight of it as she hoisted it onto her shoulder. Had forgotten all about it. Had no idea—none whatsoever, how Knox could have possibly come up with it. But the note left little doubt. It had to be him.

She lugged it into the elevator and up to her apartment, placed it on the floor and sat on the couch and stared at it. The sobs rose up from her chest and through her clenched throat, and out her eyes to where she hung her head into her palms. All the events of the past week came up like oil from a well, a release that left her exhausted and elated and hungry.

She never unzipped the duffel, never confirmed its contents. She called Lu Hao at his hotel and asked to pay him a visit. He invited her over.

WEDNESDAY

October 6

45

The following morning, Grace and Knox met in Brian Primer's office. They sat across from each other. Knox avoided her eyes.

Dulwich had been discharged from the hospital and was supposed to be under private care at his residence. He showed up at the meeting ten minutes behind the others.

"Events are happening quickly over there," Primer said, wearing a gorgeous silk suit and a dark tan from a golf outing in Vietnam. They were seated in the same area where Grace had first received her instructions.

He tossed a newspaper to Knox. Below the fold was an article about the arrest of Chairman Zhimin on charges of bribery and corruption.

Grace and Knox finally met eyes and she gave him an I-told-you-so look.

"Allan Marquardt got out of the country," Primer said, "but faces charges. The Berthold Group has been caught with their pants down. It won't go well for them. But the Chinese wasted no time. Yang Construction appears first in line to be awarded the completion of Xuan Tower. If you believe the blogs. That could have—*should* have—taken months. It happened in one day."

"So, we're done?" Knox said.

Dulwich said, "Not hardly."

"You two did outstanding work," Primer said.

"Thank you," Grace said.

"We intend to *compensate* you well. In your case, Mr. Knox, that includes the use of the company jet to get to wherever you need to go next."

"I'd like to speak with Danny," he said.

"Mr. Danner is stateside with his family."

"No, he's not. He's checked in at the Four Seasons in a suite on sixteen with an elevator lockout. I could go to the trouble of breaking in, but your blessing would make things easier."

Primer shrugged. "This is a . . . fluid business, John. May I call you John?"

Knox shrugged. Dulwich's eyes bore into Knox. He sensed where Primer was going but Knox had no desire to field an offer. The only thing holding him in the chair was Grace, and after a moment he thought that foolish as well. What was he waiting for? Done was done.

"So?" Knox said. "I'm free to go?"

Grace looked over. She smiled warmly, and he back at her.

"See you," he said to her, standing.

"Talk to my secretary about scheduling the jet," Primer said, proudly offering his toy again. "Ninety minutes is all the lead time they need." He added, "She has your check."

"Thank you," Grace said, her hand extended to Knox. "For *everything*."

They shook hands. It felt impossibly formal after what they'd been through. Impossibly Chinese.

Primer said, "The point is . . . you two, there are opportunities like this that arise."

"All the time," Dulwich added.

Knox let go of her hand and headed for the door. "Tommy awaits."

"Speaking of your brother," she called out to him, "I finally got a look at your company books, John."

Recalling the failed payment to Amy Xue, he stopped.

"You are going to need my help," Grace said.

"Is that right?"

"That is right," she said.

"All right then."

He left the room, not looking back. Stopped at the secretary's desk and couldn't help but sneak a peek inside the envelope. The check was written for an eye-popping amount. He folded the envelope and slipped it into the rear pocket of his jeans.

"I'd like to book that plane, please."

1:00 P.M.
FOUR SEASONS HOTEL
HONG KONG

Knox rapped lightly on the hotel room door. Waited. Tried again. At last the jamb and lock made a noise and the door cracked, then opened more fully. Knox went in. The two men embraced, Danner holding his bandaged hand away from contact.

"Primer told me you'd found me."

"I nearly bought into your having headed home," Knox said.

The room was a business suite: a king bedroom with a couple chairs around a larger-than-usual table. Fresh flowers in a glass vase.

"I wish," Danner said. "I entered without a passport. The Chinese wanted to lock me up. We agreed on here as my purgatory. The usual red tape trying to leave. It'll sort out tomorrow or the next day. Consulate staff's on it."

"Peggy?"

"Out of her mind about this whole thing. And expecting any day."

"Yeah, I heard. You know if it's a boy or girl?"

"No. But I know what we're going to call it, either way."

"You can't call a girl John; it'll scar her for her life."

"Ha ha. Grace is a nice name."

"It is."

"She's a nice lady."

"She is."

"Tough."

"No doubt," Knox said.

Danner offered him a beer from the minibar. They both drank.

"So . . . why'd you do it?" Danner asked.

"You'd have done it for me."

"No, I wouldn't have," Danner said, stone-faced.

"Selfish reasons," Knox said.

"The money?"

"I could lie. It was definitely in the mix."

"Tommy. The money, I mean."

"Tough sledding right now. His medical costs are through the roof. Selling nose flutes isn't exactly covering it."

"How is he?"

"Stable."

"Good."

"Yes."

"And you? How are you dealing with it?"

Knox considered this carefully. "I try to make enough income to cover my guilt over being away."

"One doesn't work without the other," Danner said.

"Yeah . . . right," Knox said.

"I wouldn't beat myself up over it."

"Yeah, you would."

"Yeah," Danner said, "I probably would."

"You're the next in line. Godfather. Keeper. Caregiver. Whatever. That's why," he said, answering the earlier question.

"I hope you're kidding," Danner said.

Knox answered by leveling a look across the table.

"You can't run an engine on guilt, Fort." It was a nickname that Knox hadn't heard in years. It took him back to a different life. "You've got to get beyond that shit. It'll destroy you." He added, "You don't owe me anything simply because I'm willing to help out if you go MIA."

Knox said nothing.

"I will figure out a way to pay for Tommy's stuff."

"No," Knox said. "You won't. Not unless you plan on robbing banks."

"I'd be good at it."

"You probably would be."

"Bank on it." Danner grinned. He noticed Knox staring at his bandage. "This is not your fault. Don't go there."

"The initials in the chair," Knox said. "We thought it was forty-four. We lost a lot of time reading that wrong."

"I'm telling you: don't go there."

"The GPS paid off."

"My bike?"

Knox nodded.

"You found my bike?"

"Grace's idea."

"She's a keeper."

"No doubt."

"Small price to pay," Danner said. "At least I won't be flipping any-one off."

"You're going to joke about it?"

"Any other ideas?"

Knox coughed.

"I owe you, man."

"Bullshit."

"Big time."

"Not true."

"You say jump," Danner said, "I'll ask how high."

"No one's going to do any jumping."

"I'm staying with Berthold. Just so you know. Peggy will give me shit, but I love the life, and the money's incredible."

"The baby will change your mind," Knox said.

"The baby will change everything," Danner said. "They always do."

Knox lifted the beer can. "Here's to its health."

They were both thinking of Tommy.

The cans clunked dully.

"I wouldn't have done the same," Danner confessed. "But I will now."

"Understood," Knox said. "Let's hope I never need it."

"Yeah, let's hope."

3:03 P.M.
HONG KONG

The Signature terminal at Chek Lap Kok airport was obscenely plush and comfortable. Gorgeous flight attendants offered Knox drinks and finger food while CNN International played on a flat screen. He'd asked to file a flight plan back to Cambodia. He had business there to tidy up. But the thought of it troubled him. The lure of selling bronze statuettes wasn't exactly calling out to him.

The skyline was. The distant shimmer of a few million people competing for the same few square miles of land, the same few tons of rice and fish and tea. There was something narcissistic and primitive about the drive for survival that appealed to him. More to the point, he wasn't thrilled to be alone. He barely recognized himself.

His phone rang, and he hoped it would be her, but he recognized his brother's voice immediately.

"Johnny? She . . . I screwed up."

"Tommy. Easy!"

"Evelyn. That bitch!"

Their accountant, Evelyn Ritter.

"Tommy?"

"She jacked all the accounts."

"Tommy? Chill! Breathe! Start from the . . . whaddaya mean *all* the accounts?"

"She didn't show up this morning. I thought she was sick. What the fuck do I know?"

"She doesn't have access to all the accounts," Knox said, feeling relief. His brother could be mistaken about so much. "Only the checking, and there's never much in it. You're saying she drained the checking? Have you called the police? Who the hell do you call? FBI?" he was thinking aloud.

The resulting silence grew intense. Knox thought briefly about the Nike duffel bag and closed his eyes, deciding he would never think about it again.

"Tommy?"

"She said she had to move a bunch of stuff around. Said you usually did that but that you weren't around."

"You did *not* give her those passwords." He made it a statement. The company did their banking online.

"It can't just vanish, right? I mean, that kind of thing . . . there's ways to follow it, right? That's a *shitload* of money we're talking about, bro."

"You gave her the passwords."

"She said it had to be done, that you usually did it. I screwed up, didn't I? I screwed it all up! Don't get mad at me, Johnny. Please don't get mad at me!"

Knox held the phone away from his ringing ear and shut his eyes. Took several deep breaths.

"You are going to need my help."

Knox returned the phone to his ear. "I'm not mad at you, Tommy. Okay? It's going to be okay."

"We're broke, man. Cleaned out. It's *not* going to be okay. We, like, owe a shitload to a lot of people. But we can find it, right? Get it back? There're people who do that, right?"

Knox felt the check in his back pocket. It had seemed like so much money a few hours ago. The pilot came through the door looking for him.

"Ready when you are, sir."

"Hang on, Tommy." Knox cupped the phone. He asked the pilot,

"Mr. Primer said anywhere . . . anywhere I wanted to go. Does that offer still hold?"

"You want to file another flight plan?"

"Can that plane reach the U.S.?"

"With a refuel in Hawaii, yes, sir."

Knox returned to the phone. Tommy was running at the mouth, working himself into a frenzy. Stumbling over apology after apology. He sounded about ready to cry. Knox didn't want him going down this road. He worked for five minutes to talk him down.

Tommy said, "The Pearl Lady sent an e-mail."

"Amy?"

"She said all business with us is over. She sounded really pissed off at you."

"We'll see."

"Said bad things came out of her friendship with you. What does that mean?"

"It's been a busy week here, Tommy. I'll sort it out." *It's what I do*, he thought.

"I like the Pearl Lady."

"So do I."

A silence formed between them. Then Tommy spoke.

"There're people who do that," he said, repeating it like a mantra. ". . . people who do that."

"It's okay, Tommy. We'll find the money." But if they didn't? Tommy's monthly health care costs alone would sink them. "There are people who do that." To bring his brother back, one had to snap the tape loops in the kid's head. He repeated what he'd just said. Tommy's breathing calmed.

"I know someone," Knox said. "She does this kind of thing."

"Seriously?" Knox heard a ray of hope in his brother's voice. "Do I know her?"

"No. But you'll like her," Knox said.

EPILOGUE

On a cold November day, wet with rain and sharp with wind, Steve Kozlowski rose from the couch and his DVR'ed Eagles game to answer a knock on the front door. The events of a month before were all but forgotten, swept aside by more urgent matters—an impending state visit by the vice president, chief among them.

Liz came out from the kitchen, not realizing her husband could be broken from the spell of football. She was driven in equal parts by a sense of responsibility, and a curiosity what neighbor might be calling on them. If the knock was an outside visitor, the compound's gate guards would have notified them by telephone.

As she saw her husband approach the door, she stopped. But she didn't turn back. She wanted to see who this was, anticipating that her husband would want nothing to do with any of their neighbors.

Kozlowski opened the door and just stood there.

"Sweetheart?" Liz called out. "Who is it?"

Her husband did not move, silhouetted by the pale gray air and the pale gray security wall in the distance that surrounded the compound.

She tried for a second time. "Steve?"

"A friend," he answered.

Determined to see whatever was going on, she approached.

"Get a scarf," he said.

"It's raining!" she complained.

"That's why you'll need a scarf," he said, still not turning toward her. "And grab a ball cap for me."

"I'm not going out there."

"Yes. We both are. We're going to get wet, and we're going to enjoy it."

"What the hell are you talking about?" Her patience with him was sapped.

Kozlowski stepped through the door and out into the drizzle, and as he did, Liz could finally see beyond him to the object in the front yard. It was a spit-shined, black motorcycle and sidecar, an antique, with polished chrome and new leather. Steve circled, admiring it from every angle.

She gathered the scarf and ball cap. Called upstairs to Tucker that she and Daddy were going out for a few minutes and would be right back. She walked out into the rain, envious of the bike for the smile it brought to her husband's face.

She closed the door behind her.